Praise for *Strong Enough to Die*

"The book is a page-turner, the pace blistering, the characters well-drawn, and the action hot. The plot is timely, exploiting fears of border smuggling, torture, high-tech snooping into private lives, and out-of-control private security companies." —Associated Press

"From the opening salvo to the wrenching conclusion, *Strong Enough to Die* is a novel that can only be read in one sitting. Blisteringly paced, complex in character, and terrifying in scope, this book will make you think twice about turning on your computer or your television ever again. Not to be missed!" —James Rollins, *New York Times* bestselling author of *The Doomsday Key*

"Like a skilled painter, Land mixes a contemporary conspiracy thriller with the Wild West legends of the Texas Rangers. . . . Land is one of the best thriller writers out there, and his latest deserves a wide audience. Don't miss this one!" —*Library Journal*

"Land introduces a tough original heroine, Caitlin Strong, a fifth-generation Texas Ranger, in the first of what hopefully will be a long crime series. . . . The revelations are constant, the characters compelling, and the action fast and furious." —*Publishers Weekly*

OTHER BOOKS BY JON LAND

*Published by Tom Doherty Associates

STRONG ENOUGH TO DIE

◆

JON LAND

A TOM DOHERTY ASSOCIATES BOOK
NEW YORK

This is a work of fiction. All of the characters, organizations, and events portrayed in this novel are either products of the author's imagination or are used fictitiously.

STRONG ENOUGH TO DIE

Copyright © 2009 by Jon Land

All rights reserved.

A Forge Book
Published by Tom Doherty Associates, LLC
175 Fifth Avenue
New York, NY 10010

www.tor-forge.com

Forge® is a registered trademark of Tom Doherty Associates, LLC.

ISBN 978-0-7653-5115-9

First Edition: May 2009
First Mass Market Edition: April 2010

Printed in the United States of America

0 9 8 7 6 5 4 3 2 1

For America's booksellers, big and small.
Thanks for being there.

ACKNOWLEDGMENTS

We meet again, and much quicker this time than the last. A good thing because I've got a great story to tell you.

But first there are people to thank for helping me to tell it better and for giving me the chance to tell it at all. That list starts with the Forge Books family headed by Tom Doherty and Linda Quinton. The kind of support they've given me on this one and all the others is what publishing should be all about. Paul Stevens and Patty Garcia are always there for me as well, along with Natalia Aponte, who has now proven herself to be as great an agent as she is an editor.

An answer to any question, meanwhile, remains only a phone call away thanks to Emery Pineo, my former junior high science teacher and still the smartest man I know. Additional technical assistance on this one in the realm of computers came courtesy of Gabriel Porras (He's also my website designer. You can check out his work firsthand at www.jonland.net.) and Micah Stevens. And if you're wondering how I know so much about the various psychological conditions referenced in this book, it's thanks to Dr. Ralph Montella.

A final acknowledgment to the terrific books that encompassed the bulk of my research into the legendary Texas Rangers. As much as I'd heard about their story, the books noted below told it even better. And for those whose interest is captured by the Rangers' mystique as much as mine was, I recommend visiting the Texas Ranger Hall of Fame and Museum either in person or online at www.texasranger.org.

Speaking of stories, I've got one to tell myself, so let's turn the page and begin.

Texas Ranger Tales by Mike Cox, Republic of Texas Press, 1997.

One Ranger by H. Joaquin Jackson and David Marion Wilkinson, University of Texas Press, 2005.

One Ranger Returns by H. Joaquin Jackson and James L. Haley, University of Texas Press, 2008.

Ranger's Law: A Lone Star Saga by Elmer Kelton, Forge Books, 2006.

The Texas Rangers: A Century of Frontier Defense by Walter Prescott Webb, University of Texas Press, 1965.

Lone Star Justice: The First Century of the Texas Rangers by Robert M. Utley, Berkley Books, 2003.

The past is never dead. It's not even past.

—WILLIAM FAULKNER

PROLOGUE

No man in the wrong can stand up against a fellow that's in the right and keeps on a-comin'.

—Texas Ranger Captain Bill McDonald to
Albert Bigelow Paine

EL PASO, TEXAS, NEAR THE MEXICAN
BORDER, 2004

"It's bad, Caitlin," Charlie Weeks said, head resting against the boulder they'd taken cover behind. He squeezed a hand against the spreading patch of red staining his khaki shirt, looking shiny in the night. His other hand held fast to his SIG P226R, standard-issue Texas Ranger pistol.

Caitlin Strong ejected the spent magazine from her Ruger Mini-14 semiautomatic rifle and snapped a fresh one home. "You die on me, Charlie, and I'll kill you myself, I swear," she said, as a fresh barrage of gunfire chipped rock splinters out of the boulder. Sharp flecks showered over them, feeling like drizzle drops at the onset of a spring storm.

"This one's on me," Charlie said. "This ends bad, everyone should know that."

"It ends when the last of those mules is down."

"Senior man," Charlie resumed, paying her no heed. "I shoulda known better." Charlie ran his tongue over his parched lips, his mouth crackling dryly. "Your dad be proud of you, your granddad too, first woman Ranger and a damn fine one to boot. I tell you that lately?"

"Can't hear it often enough."

Heat lightning lit up the sky, briefly illuminating the remaining gunmen firing from the other side of the arroyo. Then the night went black again, the mules visible only from their muzzle flashes taking brief bites out of the air in rhythm with the staccato clacking of their assault rifles. The stiff breeze carried the musky smell of chaparral and the sweet scent of mesquite, mixing uneasily with gun smoke.

"Shit, what a mess," Charlie Weeks said, trying to steady his SIG in a now trembling hand. His breaths were coming faster now and sounded soggy. At sixty, he was a dozen years younger to the day than Caitlin's father would've been if he were alive, the two of them having shared a birthday and much more.

Caitlin sighted on the muzzle flashes and fired off some rounds from the Ruger. Across the dry, water-carved gulley separating them from the drug mules, a yelp sounded, more animal than man. Even with two down now, that still left five more to contend with. Caitlin ran an ammo count in her head: fifteen shots left in her Ruger and eighteen, a magazine and a half, for her holstered SIG. Charlie's 12 gauge had all eight shells primed and ready, but he was down to the last bullets for his sidearm.

Caitlin tried to dab the sweat from her forehead with a shirtsleeve, but found it too soaked already. The blast-furnace heat of the day had given way to a windswept cool night that could do nothing to relieve the layers of perspiration gluing her shirt to her back and turning her jeans heavy with dampness.

The Texas Rangers had been called in after border patrolmen had unearthed a massive tunnel beneath the Chihuahuan Desert running back to the Mexican border, big enough to drive a vehicle through. The kind of energy and organization required for such an effort strongly suggested drug as opposed to people smuggling, later confirmed when Caitlin's own forensic check of the tunnel revealed clear traces of marijuana and a powder later identified as black tar heroin. The border patrol had discovered another three comparable tunnels along the Texas-Mexican border, and Rangers were dispatched to stake out each one.

Every night for the past eight, Charlie Weeks and Caitlin had parked their SUV behind the cover of a rock bed and hunkered low in the natural cover of the arroyo. They had positioned themselves a hundred feet across from each other in order to catch any emerging vehicle in their crossfire, if it came to that. As senior man, that had been Charlie's call, although the positioning left their rear flanks exposed, making them prime for an ambush. Not shy, Caitlin had pointed this out to Charlie, only to be rebuked.

She was eyeballing the culvert dug out of the desert floor from her position opposite Charlie's when chips of stone suddenly burst into the air around them. Caitlin recognized the gunfire an instant before there was a heavy *whump* followed by a sound like air being let out of a balloon, as Charlie Weeks hit the rock face hard and slumped, clutching his side.

Caitlin returned the fire blindly with her SIG, not on mark but enough to buy her the time she needed to reach Charlie and drag him back behind the trio of boulders beyond the arroyo. He collapsed just as they got there, Caitlin with gun in one hand and radio in the other.

"Officer down!" she told the nearest highway patrol dispatch, following with her call number and location. Except there wasn't a responding vehicle anywhere within hours of them, so unless the Rangers or highway patrol could get a chopper scrambled fast, she and Charlie Weeks would be fighting this battle alone.

The heat lightning and cool breeze meant storms would be dotting the air all the way across southwest Texas, playing hell with any chopper pilot crazy enough to fly into a gunfight to begin with. The gunfire from across the arroyo ratcheted up again, and Caitlin knew it was only a matter of time before the mules used their superior numbers of men and bullets to circle around to her exposed rear flank. That meant if she and Charlie were going to get the most out of their remaining ammo, it had to be now.

"Ready to get a move on, Charlie?" she asked the Texas Ranger who had fought battles like this a dozen times alongside her father.

"I think I just dreamed you saying that."

He took a deep breath that shook his chest when he let it back out. Caitlin propped him up higher against the boulder, the smell of his blood heavier now, its coating leaving a thick sheen across his midsection.

"We're gonna make a run for the vehicle, old man."

"Old man? Anyone calls me 'old man' better be able to take me in a bar fight and that includes you, Caitlin Strong."

"I'm buying soon as we get home."

Charlie Weeks gazed down past his waist. "I can't walk. My legs went dull a pint ago."

"I'll carry you."

"Good plan, if you had an extra pair of hands."

"I do," Caitlin told him.

"That's nuts."

"Alternative's worse."

"We use our ammo. Wait 'em out."

"They'll circle round and take us in a crossfire, soon as they realize we're down to our last shells. Better we take it to them, than wait for 'em to come."

"Who taught you that, your dad or your grandpa?"

"You, Charlie."

Charlie Weeks smiled through his own pain. "They ever tell you about the time we went after those moonshiners?

Christ on a crutch, I don't think I was much older than you then, a damn rookie riding into trouble alongside two Ranger legends. Know what I remember thinking?"

"No."

"We was all wearing the same badge, theirs being a bit more scuffed and dulled than mine the only difference."

"Stop changing the subject, Charlie."

Caitlin took the 12 gauge in one hand, the Ruger in the other, testing their heft. Then she handed her SIG to Charlie Weeks.

"Ready, Ranger?"

"As I'll ever be," Charlie sighed, grimacing in pain as he pulled his knees into his chest.

Caitlin slid in against him so her shoulders were square with his chest. Charlie Weeks wrapped both his arms around her neck, a SIG clutched in either hand as Caitlin reached to take the 12 gauge in her left and Ruger in her right. Charlie's weight bent her spine inward when she tried to rise up. Their SUV was two hundred yards away, an interminable distance considering the pace at which it'd be covered.

Still, no choice.

Caitlin felt the warmth of Charlie's blood soaking through her damp shirt and hoisted the 12 gauge and Ruger into position.

"It's time, old man."

"I warned you not to call me that."

Caitlin visualized Charlie's smile dissolving into a pained grimace and lit out from behind the boulders. The drug mules' fire roared at them, answered immediately by the twin pistols in Charlie's grasp. The reports deafened Caitlin even before she started firing alternately with the 12 gauge and Ruger. The shotgun was semiauto with a cut-down barrel, but it was also little more than a gaudy noisemaker at this distance. Her shots from the

Ruger stayed on line, though still serving more as distraction than anything else.

Bullets whizzed past her, the sensation curiously like mosquitoes buzzing near on a hot summer night. Caitlin felt something like a kick to her side just over her hip and knew she'd been hit, at least grazed, but kept going with the SUV just a hundred yards away now, fifty beyond the west bank of the arroyo.

One of Charlie Weeks's pistols clicked empty, the other on its last shells with the SUV still barely in sight and Caitlin's left leg beginning to stiffen.

"Put me down, for God's sake," he rasped at her.

"The hell you say," Caitlin shot back, still firing through the dark blanket of night.

A thin ribbon of moonlight opened up between the clouds, allowing her to spot the mules who'd emerged from their cover.

"Kill the fuckers!" one of them screamed in perfect English.

An American giving the orders to Mexican drug mules. . . . What the hell was this?

Caitlin saw motion flash against the dark landscape, the mules opting for an all-out charge. She fired off rounds from the 12 gauge and Ruger to chase them back, slowing their attack. The same shaft of moonlight revealed the SUV to be closer than she thought. She was angling for it when something sharp bit into her back and sent the hard ground up to meet her.

BAHRAIN, 2008

The man stood before the plate-glass window in a place the signs, in both English and Arabic, called City Gardens. Squinting through the painful glare of light, he studied the reflection looking back at him, trying to place it. It had been so long since he'd seen a reflection of anything; the room he had known as home from the beginning of his memory had no windows or mirrors. There was a bowl of water to both wash and brush his teeth with twice a day. It would be there and then it would be gone, the man left trying to reconstruct the time in between.

He shuddered with fear, the sensation nearly paralyzing him even though he could not remember what it was that scared him. There had been another life before the new memories and the man wondered if it belonged to the face looking back at him in the window glass. Often the men who came to him in his room addressed him by name. But it wasn't his name. It may have been once, but it wasn't anymore.

He had no name. He told them that, but they never believed him.

The man noticed the reflection in the glass was shuddering too. He started to twist away, felt a bolt of searing pain rack his spine, and saw the reflection wince.

He started on again. His aching feet felt heavier, dragging across the road, the man too weak to lift them. His eyes hurt from the sunlight, telling him it was daytime. Night and day had ceased to have meaning long before, the distinctions between them as blurred as his very existence. More signs told him he was in a place called Bab Al Bahrain, surrounded by strangers in an outdoor market where handicrafts and brass coffeepots were on display amid elegantly woven carpets. Sharp-smelling spices roasted beneath the blazing sun.

His legs throbbed terribly, hot jabs rising through them with each step. His arms hung limp by his side, the slightest movement causing his shoulder joints to feel disconnected from the muscles around them.

The man was aware of puzzled stares being cast upon

him and swung round painfully, half expecting to find
the reflection in the window glass staring back again.
Words were being thrust his way in languages he did not
understand until he passed under the shade of an overhang
that turned the ache in his skin to a dull throb.

"Would you like some?"

The man turned to see a robe-clad merchant extending
a glass that smelled like mint toward him.

"Yes," the man said, not recognizing his own voice.
"Thank you."

He took the glass, sipped, and then drank the sweet brown
tea. He could not remember drinking anything other than
water, often tasting like soap or something worse.

The man handed his glass to the merchant who refilled
it with a smile and handed it back.

"You have money?" the merchant asked him.

"Money?"

"Cash? Credit cards?"

The man touched his pockets, sank his hands in. "No."

The merchant winked, playing the game. "You like the
tea?"

"Very much."

"You wish to see my wares. I have beautiful Bahrain
pearls, wonderful pieces of jewelry for your woman. Is
she with you?"

"Who?"

"Your woman."

"I don't have a woman."

"A man, boy perhaps?"

"No, no man. No boy."

"Just you then, eh?"

"Who?"

"You."

"No, not me. There is no me."

The glass felt suddenly too heavy to hold, so he returned it to the merchant with a trembling hand and moved on, aware that the hand ached badly now as well. He held it up to his face as if to look for the source of the pain, coming away only with the realization that the fingers looked gnarled and swollen.

He walked, as if trying to find a place where the pain would go away. If he closed his eyes and tried very hard to detach himself from his body, sometimes he could. But he couldn't close his eyes now, couldn't stop, spurred by the vague awareness of something out there worse than the pain that would catch up to him if he let it.

He approached the luscious smells of food roasting on spits and outdoor grates. The food sizzled and hissed amid the pungent scents of garlic and lemon. Merchants served heaping plates of it up to waiting customers who carried them away in search of a seat at the chairs and tables set in the shade of a crowded veranda.

The smells turned the man's shrunken stomach. He tried to remember eating, could not recall a single bite or swallow. He came to an empty spot at a table in the shade, abandoned with a half-full plate left behind. The man touched his hand to the thick sauce pooling on one side, swiped his tongue across his fingers.

Coughed, gagged, retched. Sank to his knees.

Soon he was surrounded by a circle of people looking down, seeming to see him. But that, of course, was impossible.

Because there was nothing to see. After all, he didn't exist.

WASHINGTON, D.C., 2008

Harmon Delladonne saw Clayton coming and snapped up from the bench overlooking the Mall. His suit trousers flapped in the stiff breeze, and he ran his hands through his slicked-back dark hair before setting off down the street to let Clayton catch him in stride.

"Fifteen minutes late, Clayton," Delladonne greeted, feeling a slight drizzle dampening his shoulders. "Fifteen minutes."

"I came as soon as I could, sir."

"That's time I'll never get back, valuable time lost for good."

"We could have spoken by phone," Clayton suggested weakly. Like Delladonne, he stood just over six feet, though much broader in the shoulders with narrow high-pitched cheekbones and a wide forehead that had an almost Neanderthal quality about it. "My line's secure."

"Never trust machines, Clayton," Delladonne told him. "Don't even use a cell phone. Too easy to track a man's movements with it. I know because my company does it. All the time. Anybody in the country. Anytime, anywhere. One of MacArthur-Rain's many government contracts."

Delladonne understood the technology he had helped create well enough to know how easy it was to become a victim of it. Even the outdoors weren't totally safe, not with surveillance cameras on every street corner and long-range listening devices that could hone in on a conversation from a quarter mile away. But stay on the move, keep your lips angled low when you speak, and you could feel relatively insulated. So whenever in Washington, Delladonne never took meetings in his satellite office, never took meetings at lunch, hardly ever took meetings at all. The one exception was the Senate hearing he had been called here to testify before, only to have an ally remove his name, temporarily anyway, from the witness list at the last moment. A good day indeed, until he heard about Bahrain.

"I assume you wanted to discuss another of those contracts with me," Clayton was saying.

"Your initial report about Bahrain has been confirmed. Now tell me how this happened."

Delladonne's route kept the Mall, Capitol Building and White House in view at all times. He liked it that way, liked the sense of ownership it implied, even if right now that ownership was going to hell. The day was gray and dismal with the promise of rain. Back in Houston it had been hot and sultry, the air holding signs of a blistering summer. But all that had been chased back by the dreariness of Washington, a city he had come to loathe.

"Our Bahrain operatives panicked," Clayton reported. "Heard a U.S. government oversight inspection team was coming in."

"Government oversight," Delladonne repeated. "What a joke." But he didn't sound at all amused.

"The Bahrain facility wasn't supposed to be on the list released to the new administration. It was private, after all."

"They were all private, Clayton."

"But the CIA worked the site originally. Extra funds spent on soundproof padding the walls. You know the drill."

"MacArthur-Rain didn't retain your services to tell me what I already know."

Clayton remained silent, feeling Delladonne's stare boring into him. Clayton knew how to intimidate even those to whom he was subservient. But Delladonne was different. Delladonne might be thin enough to break over his knee but he was the first man, enemies and associates alike, who actually scared Clayton.

"May I speak plainly, sir?"

"Be careful, Clayton."

"My people in Bahrain went at this man for six months to get out what he was hiding in his head. They failed."

"You mean, you failed."

"Yes, sir."

"Then say it. Say you failed."

"I failed," Clayton conceded.

"Accepting responsibility—that's a good start. What comes next?"

"We find him."

Delladonne stopped and turned to face Clayton, his eyes like black daggers of ice. "What makes 9/11 such a great tragedy, Clayton? What's the first thing that comes to your mind?"

"This country attacked. All those deaths."

"This country being attacked, yes. But the real tragedy lay in not *enough* deaths."

Clayton just looked at him.

"We knew an attack was coming eventually," Delladonne continued. "We had the level of response the country would accept down to a cost-benefit analysis of the number of lives lost. The first reports putting the death toll over 20,000 would have been the best thing that ever happened to this country because people would've embraced everything MacArthur-Rain wanted to do overnight. But when it turned out to be barely 3,000 we had to scale back. The world did change that day, just not as much as it should have."

Clayton bristled. "I lost friends, sir, and, frankly, I don't understand what you're getting at."

"We all lost friends, and I'll tell you what I'm getting at. We're close to that point again. The gains we've made are incremental, but they're there. And what this man you lost has locked up in his brain can give us the power to accomplish everything we've always wanted. The key to securing the future, Clayton, and I am not exaggerating."

"If it's still in his brain, you mean, sir," Clayton cautioned.

"What I mean is that if we can't get it, you've got to make sure no one else does either."

HOUSTON, 2008

"Want a sandwich, Davis?"

His wife's voice drew him from his trance, and Davis S. Bonn looked up from his computer, flexing his fingers. His middle name was actually Lewis, but Bonn had adopted the *S* because it looked better on his byline. "Sure," he said, "I'd love one."

His wife Tayanna tried to see what he was writing but he shifted in his chair to block her view of the monitor. They had met a decade before while Davis Bonn had been researching a story about the Khmer Rouge's alleged intrusion into Thailand. The story had gone nowhere but Davis had fallen in love with his interpreter and managed to wrangle a visa for her to return with him to the States.

"Come on," she whined, "just a peek."

"Not until I'm finished. You know the rules."

"I just thought that this time . . ."

"This time especially," Davis told her, holding his ground.

Tayanna relented and started for the door, looking back at him before she closed it. "Just so long as you're sure about this."

"Why wouldn't I be?"

"Because these are dangerous people."

"All the more reason to bring them down."

"Always the crusader."

"Just a jounalist, Anna." Davis cracked a smile, as he always did when he called her that. "A journalist in search of a book deal."

"So long as you live to see it published."

"And the check cashed."

Tayanna smiled and, this time, closed the door behind her. She'd already mixed up the chicken salad and made sure the toast was just the way he liked it, the lettuce cut thin, before laying the sandwich on a plate surrounded by potato chips. Taking it in hand, she returned to Davis's office and entered without knocking.

"One sandwich made to—"

Tayanna stopped. The plate fell from her grasp and shattered on the floor, the twin halves of the sandwich leaping in opposite directions.

Davis Bonn lay slumped on the floor convulsing, bulging eyes fixed on the ceiling where a faint wisp of smoke had risen.

"Dtaay!" Tayanna screamed.

She rushed to her husband and dropped down, trying to still the spasmodic tremors in his arms and legs.

"Davis!" she screamed, noticing only then a thin trail of blood dribbling from his right ear. "Davis!"

His eyes failed to acknowledge her and then locked open altogether, his extremities settling stiffly. Tayanna bent over him and began administering CPR, continuing until exhaustion and hopelessness finally overcame her.

By the time she dialed 911, twenty minutes had slipped away into some mournful netherworld, and the stench of burnt wires she'd already forgotten was gone.

PART ONE

By 1823, there were serious problems with raids by the Comanche, Tonkawa and Karankawa Indians. Under Mexican law, [Colonel Stephen] Austin was authorized to form a militia to ward off Indian raids, capture criminals and patrol against intruders. In May, while Austin was in Mexico City, his lieutenant, Moses Morrison, used this authority to assemble a company of men to protect the Texas coast from the Tonkawa and Karankawa Indians.

After returning to Texas in August of 1823, Austin asked for [an] additional ten men to supplement Morrison's company. He called for "ten men . . . to act as rangers for the common defense. . . . The wages I will give said ten men is fifteen dollars a month payable in property." These two companies are regarded as the first ancestors of the modern Texas Rangers.

—Mike Cox, with updates from the Texas Ranger Hall of Fame and Museum staff, "A Brief History of the Texas Rangers"

I

"But you made it," Rita Navarro, director of the Survivor Center for Victims of Torture, said from behind her desk, after Caitlin had left her story off with being felled by the second bullet.

"Barely," Caitlin told her.

"And the other Ranger, Charlie Weeks?"

"He didn't make it."

Navarro slid back slightly from the edge of her desk chair, checking the résumé before her again as if in search of new information. The light in her cramped office, once a treatment room in the clinic that had formerly occupied this building, came from ceiling-mounted, overly bright fluorescents. But natural light wasn't an option since the room's windows had been frosted over by a thick layer of dust and grime. Sometime during the transition from clinic to treatment center, the building had been allowed to fall into a state of disrepair requiring more funds to remedy than were available.

"I'm glad to have had the opportunity to meet you, Ranger Strong—"

"I'm not a Ranger anymore."

"—but what exactly are you doing here? We never advertised for a security specialist."

"No, you advertised for a counselor and therapist. That's what I'm applying for."

"Oh," Navarro said dismissively, and flipped to the second page of the résumé. She was younger than Caitlin had expected. Her name suggested a Hispanic heritage, but Caitlin thought she detected some Native American, Comanche probably, in her peaked cheekbones, narrow jaw and straight dark hair that dropped to the midpoint of her back. She had an engaging smile that Caitlin had so far glimpsed only upon exchanging a quick handshake, finding Navarro's firm and slightly callused, evidence of a woman who liked to garden in her free time.

Caitlin crossed her legs, then uncrossed them. The stiffness of the wood chair forced her to hunch forward, leaving her shoulders tense. And she was beginning to regret her decision to swap her jeans for pressed light cotton slacks. The jeans did a better job of accentuating her curves and making her long legs stand out less. At five foot nine she had her father's height and grandfather's short torso, a model's body she'd often been told before adding substantial muscle to her frame with regular weight lifting workouts. Her wavy auburn hair was the longest it had ever been, tumbling just past her shoulders. Besides the hair, Caitlin looked no different than she had five years before. Maybe she was trying to freeze time going back to that night in the West Texas desert near the Mexican border. Do that and maybe she could figure out how to make it run backward too.

She still got out in the sun a lot, leaving her skin drier and tighter than she'd prefer. But her complexion was smooth and dark, the rosy cheeks she'd been teased about as a child staying with her to this day.

"After leaving the Rangers, I went back to college and got a master's in psychiatric social services," Caitlin explained. "Got myself certified in crisis management and intervention. Nice complement to my undergraduate degree in sociology."

Navarro went back to the first page. "You were, let's see, seven years with the highway patrol before you joined the Rangers."

"You need at least that much service with the Texas Department of Public Safety before the Rangers will even consider you."

"I understand only one of every hundred applicants actually makes it."

"Something like that. Since I was the one I didn't give it much thought."

"Family tradition, it seems."

"Yes, ma'am. My granddad was the last of the real gunslingers. Took down a gang that had robbed four banks in the street outside number five."

"By himself?"

"He happened to be having a cup of coffee in the diner across the way. My dad could hit the bull's-eye with his pistol from a hundred yards nine times out of ten. And my great-granddad and great, great-granddad took part in some of the most famous Ranger campaigns in history."

"The Mexican War being one of them."

"That'd be my great, great-granddad. He was there all right, fighting skirmishes on both sides of the Rio Grande. What makes you ask?"

Navarro tapped her desk with her index fingers, flashing a look that suggested she was leaving something unsaid. "I looked you up on the Internet. Seems like you were in the process of making your own legend with the Rangers."

"Not really."

"But you took down the man they called the most dangerous in all of Texas. McMasters or something."

"Masters. Cort Wesley Masters."

"You didn't list that on your résumé."

"It was just an arrest. I made dozens of those."

"Only female Ranger ever, is that right?"

"There've been a few others, but it never quite worked out, ma'am."

"I imagine it could be a tough job for a woman."

"Well, truth be told, it's a tough job for anyone, but it's a lot to ask of a woman, especially, to ride into some Texas town been doing things a certain way for a long while and tell the elected sheriff that you're the resident Ranger on a case he thought he was in charge of."

"Didn't seem to bother you much with this Masters."

"I had some luck, ma'am."

Navarro let it go at that, passing Caitlin a faint smile that said she knew there was plenty more to the story. Caitlin was grateful, in no particular mood to rehash her near gunfight with the most feared man in the state. Today was about moving forward, not back.

Navarro studied the pages again, less cursorily this time, no longer feigning interest. "You received a commendation for what happened at the border, saving your partner and all."

"I didn't save him for long."

"Special Medal for Valor, it says here."

"I didn't deserve it."

"Why?"

"Because we got ambushed. Seems all wrong getting rewarded for being ambushed."

"You left the Rangers on your own?"

"I did, ma'am."

"Not on disability, it says here."

"I wasn't disabled."

"Six months after the gunfight in which you were wounded."

"There was the hospital stay."

"Two months," Navarro said, after consulting the pages before her, "to treat two primary bullet wounds."

"Something like that."

"Rehab cost you another two," Navarro read. "Then you rejoined the Rangers for two months, before leaving for good."

"You want to know what happened."

"I am curious as to the circumstances."

"How much you wanna hear, ma'am?"

"How much you want to tell me?"

2

EL PASO, TEXAS, NEAR THE MEXICAN BORDER, 2004

Caitlin had never been shot before, knew in those moments she was lying on the ground intertwined with Charlie Weeks that all the stories she'd heard about the feeling didn't do it justice. It wasn't the pain that scared her; it was the heat and the awful stench of her own burnt-smelling blood.

But she had the good fortune of dropping into a slight depression in the dirt that offered the measure of cover she needed to right herself and the Ruger.

"Where are they? Can you see them?"

The words were shouted in English again, the speaker closer than he'd been before.

She sighted on a drug mule rushing in toward them wildly with a nonstop staccato burst pouring from his assault rifle's barrel. But it was Charlie who downed him with rounds fired from the SIG he still had a hold of. Charlie Weeks, who had gunned down bank robbers and prison escapees, managing an impossible shot while lying on his back bleeding from a gunshot wound to the gut.

Caitlin saw another mule coming at them and let loose with the Ruger. Wild shots, breaking every rule of the range her father had taught her. No one had ever explained how to shoot from the ground with at least one bullet dug deep inside her. All that experience, instinct was supposed to take over, but in the end it was panic and having enough bullets left to get the job done.

Caitlin saw the mule go down as if someone had yanked his legs out from under him, heard him crying out in Spanish and screaming. She propped herself up to find him writhing in a fissure of radiant moonlight. Strangely, he stopped moving in the very instant the clouds released the darkness once more, his own light extinguished at the same time.

She'd lost count of how many there were, how many were left. She heard shouts from voices sounding more distant, moving farther away from her and Charlie instead of closer. Caitlin counted out the seconds.

"Come on! Come on!"

An engine flared, followed by the sound of tires spitting gravel and pebbles in their wake before headlights blazed into the tunnel and then disappeared.

"I think they're gone, Charlie," she said, her breathing steady again. "I think we're good now. Charlie?"

She twisted round to find Charlie Weeks's eyes closed and his head drooped toward his chest.

"Don't you die on me, Charlie Weeks! You hear? Don't you fucking die on me!"

Caitlin didn't know where she found the strength to stand back up and lift him into her arms. Didn't remember the final stretch to their SUV that ended with her laying Charlie across the length of the backseat. Her next clear memory was the sight of flashing lights miles and miles down the same gulch-ridden desert road that had nearly delivered Caitlin and Charlie Weeks to their deaths.

The night played tricks with the distance, the lights much farther away than they had originally seemed. But an EMT wagon was among the vehicles responding. Turned out she'd driven eighty miles, the memories of which must have seeped out of her with the blood.

EMTs laid Caitlin and Charlie Weeks side by side on gurneys inside the wagon and she was sure he was alive when her mind finally gave up its last tenuous hold on consciousness. She felt her eyes closing and dreamed she was sitting with her father, the great Jim Strong, under a cottonwood tree near their favorite swimming hole. They were eating peanut butter and banana sandwiches and drinking root beer from bottles cold with frost from the cooler, while Jim Strong told stories of the exploits of Texas' infamous hanging judge Katherine Hansen.

When she woke up at the hospital, Charlie Weeks was dead.

3

SAN ANTONIO, THE PRESENT

Caitlin ended the story there, studying Rita Navarro's expression that had paled to the point of looking as if someone had borrowed the blood from it. She regarded Caitlin differently; tentatively, Caitlin thought, with a slight bit of unease, maybe fear, making her regret that she had held nothing back.

Finally Navarro leaned forward and rested her elbows

on her desk. "I'm skeptical—skeptical that a person of your background is best suited to work with those who've been victimized by violence."

"Because I practiced it."

"Quite well, apparently."

"Torture's a different kind of violence. It's more like rape. The strong dominating the weak."

"You know a lot about rape, Miss Strong?"

"I know a lot about strength and weakness, Miss Navarro."

"Missus."

"Sorry."

"So am I sometimes."

Caitlin felt the tension in the room ease a bit. Something had softened Rita Navarro's stare. She wasn't sure what.

"I dealt with a number of rape victims with the Rangers," Caitlin told her. "It doesn't say that in those pages, but I did. Ended up holding a lot of hands waiting for the sheriff's department or highway patrol to show up. I once had to do a rape kit in a service station bathroom."

"You want this job."

"I do."

"You feel yourself qualified."

"Yes, ma'am."

Navarro glanced down at the pages before her again. "Your application lists you as married to a Peter Goodwin, but you're not wearing a ring."

Caitlin smiled faintly. "Another old habit, I'm afraid. My dad was the best shot I ever saw and he never wore any jewelry, not even a watch. Only metal he wanted near his hand was his Colt 1911 model .45. Everything else just got in the way. As for my husband Peter, he passed away."

"I'm sorry. How?

"Iraq."

"A soldier?"

"Nope. Worked in computer software for one of those private contractors. He was working on a cable television system for Baghdad when an IED blew him up."

"You never took his name," Rita Navarro noted.

"Guess I felt it'd be doing my dad a disservice. My mom passed 'fore he got the son he wanted, so responsibility for the family name fell on me."

Navarro tucked the pages of Caitlin's résumé back into the file folder with her name stenciled on the tab. "Why victims of torture, Miss Strong?"

Caitlin had thought long and hard about that question, knowing it would be coming sooner or later. She'd even rehearsed answers—nice, neat and pat—except none of them stuck or sounded even halfway genuine.

"How much you wanna hear, Mrs. Navarro?"

"You asked me that before."

"As much as I want to tell you, you said. So lemme say I've been on both sides of some pretty bad things. You do 'em and you live with 'em, 'cause it's what you are and what you figure you'll be left with when everything's said and done. But sometimes said and done comes quicker than it's supposed to, and you don't like what you're left with at all."

Rita Navarro rose stiffly from her desk chair, Caitlin figuring the handshake and polite good-bye were coming.

"Let me show you the facility, Miss Strong," she said. "See if it might be what you're looking for."

4

HUNTSVILLE STATE PRISON, THE PRESENT

Cort Wesley Masters followed Warden T. Edward Jardine down the long caged walk toward his freedom.

"Wanted to see you off personally, Mr. Masters," Jardine told him.

"Seems a bit of a hollow gesture at this point, don't it?" Cort Wesley shot back. "Considering I never should've been here in the first place, I mean."

The pungent stench of disinfectant, laid over stale urine and feces that wafted out of the cell block, dissipated the closer they got to the other end. Cort Wesley never thought he'd welcome a sound as much as the sound of his boots clacking atop the worn linoleum floor. Those boots were the one thing he'd taken into Huntsville he was taking out. He shifted his feet about inside them, thinking about how many livers, kidneys and ribs had perished to their steel-toe boxes.

"Being bitter is no way to start your first day of freedom."

"I been bitter a lot longer than that, Warden. You wanna stand there and try telling me I don't got call to be, then go ahead."

Jardine didn't. "May I make a suggestion?"

"Free country, last time I checked. For most, anyway."

"I'll expect you to take full advantage of the next phase of your rehabilitation."

"Rehabilitation . . . that what you call it? I never should've been jailed in the first place, so there's not really anything I gotta be rehabilitated from. Right or wrong?"

"Technically, right."

"Glad we got that straight, Warden. DNA test fully exonerated me. No parole or probation. You and me, we're on the same terms. That's why we look so much alike now. Equal ground. Man to man. How's the view from where you're standing?"

Jardine's upper lip quivered ever so slightly. Cort Wesley watched him glance over his shoulder to check where the nearest bull was. Cort Wesley grinned, teeth even whiter than they were when he came in thanks to an almost religious ritual of brushing twice daily. One of the things he held onto that helped him get by.

"Don't worry, Warden. I'm not gonna hurt you," he said from inside a shirt stretched at the seams by the hard layers of muscle stitched along his torso. The stiff prison-issue khakis he'd been given sagged some in the waist and the belt didn't have enough holes to hold them up. Cort Wesley didn't like the way they felt, reminding him too much of the way Latino gang members wore theirs to suggest toughness by having their boxers showing.

"You managed to keep yourself out of trouble for almost five years, Mr. Masters. In a place like The Walls, given your reputation, that's a heck of an accomplishment and I'd hate to see it squandered."

"Not my intention, I assure you."

"Temptation's a powerful thing."

"I gave up drinking my first day in."

"I wasn't talking about alcohol, Mr. Masters."

"What then?"

Warden T. Edward Jardine looked at Cort Wesley's shirt, as if seeing through it to the tattoo beneath. "Your tattoo, 'Vengeance Is Mine.' "

"Yeah?"

"See that it remains a slogan and not a prophecy. People who are falsely imprisoned have to fight the urge to lash out, to get back at those who put them away."

"Got that ink before I came in, Warden."

"I think you're missing my point."

"What's that?"

Jardine's eyes narrowed, as if he were about to share a secret. "If I were you, I'd use the legal system to your benefit. Sue the Texas Rangers, the forensic lab that originally IDed that blood sample, and everybody else involved. That's between us. Anybody asks, I never said it."

"Prefer dealing with such things my own way, Warden. Anybody asks, I never said that."

They reached the first of three gates Cort Wesley would have to pass through before he was truly free. Beyond those gates, the sunlight shed a different glow than it did over the prison yard he'd been lucky to see for maybe an hour a day over the past five years. Cort Wesley couldn't wait to feel it against his face.

"You'd be better served to take advantage of this opportunity," said Jardine. "Move on and put the past behind you."

Cort Wesley stopped and flexed his fists. Slowly, liking the feel of wrapping his fingers tight into his palms. "You ever lose something mattered to you, Warden?"

Jardine wasn't going to answer, but the look in Cort Wesley Masters's eyes left him afraid of what would happen if he didn't. "My wife died of cancer three years ago."

"Meaning you won't be getting her back. Bet that chews at you, leaves you up at night staring at the ceiling angry 'cause there's nothing you can do to change it. Kind of like the five years of my life I lost, Warden. I'm never getting them back neither."

"If you're talking about your wife and sons—"

"She's not my wife."

"I . . ." Jardine stopped there, the rest of the sentence gulped down his throat.

"That's none of your affair," Cort Wesley continued, the blacks of his eyes seeming to swallow the whites. "Just leave it be."

"Nothing I can do about my wife," Jardine said, finding his voice. "Nothing you can do about those five years."

"We'll see about that."

Jardine handed him an envelope containing his release papers and a state of Texas check in the amount of fifty dollars, extending his free hand.

Cort Wesley didn't take it.

"You really kill as many men as they say, Mr. Masters?"

"Don't know, Warden. Why don't you ask them?"

5

HUNTSVILLE, THE PRESENT

From The Walls, Cort Wesley walked two blocks through the sleepy town of Huntsville in the scalding sun to the Greyhound bus station. The sweat soaked through his shirt and made him long for a cold shower in a stall by himself without his back pressed against the wall to ward off a shank attack.

He could have gone anywhere but opted to buy a ticket for San Antonio, as close to a home as he had, using some of the change from the fifty dollar check he'd cashed at the local bank to buy a pack of Marlboro Lights. He smoked three outside, trying to just relax and watch the world go by around him, but failing badly. The tension and anxiety clung to him like a stench he couldn't wash off. Cort Wesley figured it was the fresh air. Make yourself accustomed to living in rancid squalor with quarters the size of a closet long enough and smells like flowers and charcoal-broiled meat spewed by restaurant exhaust fans were all but unrecognizable and scary in their unfamiliarity.

Cort Wesley knew the town of Huntsville was actually home to nine state prisons with The Walls the most dangerous of any here, perhaps in the whole country as well. The mixture of Latin, Asian and African-American gangs inside mixing with the Nazis, bikers, and an all-around miserable assortment of violent criminals who had committed horribly heinous acts which they wore inside as badges of honor. It was the mad ones, the crazies, Cort Wesley knew to avoid most of all. Unaffiliated whack jobs with no allegiance or collective identity to rein in their actions or lend a balance to them.

At first the Latinos sent a few massive pump monkeys and cherries after him, a few of them having come up on the short end of run-ins with Cort Wesley in East San Antonio. The Latin gangs there didn't understand territory, figured it consisted of whatever they could steal from everybody else and that their advantage in guns would overcome all else. Cort Wesley represented the interests of the Branca crime family that had migrated to Texas after being chased out of Louisiana and Florida by a conflagration of brutal storms and an unforgiving judiciary. They played by the rules and expected their competitors to do the same. When those competitors didn't, they called Cort Wesley.

His reputation spread quickly among the Latinos, most of it well earned except for the crazed tales of him wiping out entire families and households—that legend adding to their fear of him. They weren't hard to scare really, their bravado based on sheer numbers and believing that the side with more guns won. The Latinos stockpiled men, kids mostly, whose hard edge was more defined by their tattoos. Covered themselves in ink, then hoped it passed for courage and toughness. And mostly it did, until they ran up against Cort Wesley Masters who painted a much more impressive mosaic in blood than in ink. When he went after someone, he always took down whoever was running with him at the time, further intimidating the Latinos and helping to turn them against each other.

The guards known as bulls in hard-edged prisons like The Walls didn't so much as control things as preside over the deadly sense of order imposed by the prisoners on themselves. The cons were the ones who really ran things and dispensed justice to those who broke whatever code was in place at the time.

Cort Wesley tried keeping to himself and was mostly left alone save for the occasional young crazy out to make his reputation by taking out a Texas legend. Cort Wesley had killed four of them, including a kid with such rage and self-hatred in his eyes that he thought he was an instrument of suicide more than anything else.

He continued smoking outside the bus station, recognizing a couple of Mexican kids from the inside who must've gotten their parole papers. The Mexican kids never looked back at him. He made sure his gaze was enough to keep them away. They probably came in for some drug-related offense and came out battle-hardened, world-weary punks whose spirits and souls had been sodomized as much as their bodies.

I might have been the one innocent man in there.

Cort Wesley was not a man easily touched by irony but even he was struck by the absurdity of that. To get away with all the things he'd done over the years only to be jailed for something he hadn't.

He flicked his cigarette into the gutter and watched the rest of it burn away, his lungs left burning enough to make him fight off a cough.

It was the Texas Rangers who'd put him away. The fucking Texas Rangers, used to be out there riding the badlands on horseback. Cort Wesley thought they directed traffic these days until a woman Ranger drew on him in an El Paso bar where he was making a cash pickup for the Brancas. He remembered it all so vividly, right down to a roadside portable sign still advertising a band called The Rats that had played the week before. It would have been funny if the look in her eye hadn't told him she had him beat six ways to Sunday, apparently not much impressed by the reputation everyone else was.

A woman of all things!

Cort Wesley was glad that much hadn't reached the inside. Otherwise more would've come after him, perhaps too many to fend off. Everything came down to odds; sooner or later somebody gets you. Simple as that.

But that doesn't mean you can't get them back.

6

SAN ANTONIO, THE PRESENT

"Almost all our patients are refugees," Navarro said to Caitlin, closing her office door behind them, "foreigners lucky enough to have found asylum and safety in the United States. I use the term 'lucky enough' ironically, because many of them left their families behind or worse. Left pieces of themselves wherever it was they came from, both figuratively and literally. You see the scars, the missing limbs, the burn marks, the agony in their eyes, and you think of the physical pain they've endured and often are still enduring. But it's the mental pain, the emotional anguish, we treat here."

Caitlin nodded, studying Navarro in the corridor's murky light. She could see through the glass squares built into the ceiling that several of the bulbs behind them had burned out. Remembered that many of the older buildings in San Antonio were plagued by wood and framework swollen by humidity to the point that slide-out pane panels didn't slide anymore. They mostly just shattered from the slightest jarring.

"These kinds of victims are living in a nightmare they can't wake up from," Navarro continued. "Almost all are suffering from some form or degree of PTSD, Post-Traumatic Stress Disorder. That means no matter how much they want to break from the past, they can't. Many, if not most, have lost relatives, parents or children our treatments are never going to bring back."

"What about medication?"

"There are differing theories. We tend to proceed with antidepressants and antianxiety drugs on a case-by-case basis. Antipsychotics are prescribed, as a last resort, when a patient is deemed to be a danger to him- or herself."

They kept walking, seeming to head in no particular direction, as if Navarro wanted Caitlin to take in what she saw, perhaps become alienated by it enough to leave. Navarro might have been advertising for a counselor-slash-therapist, but that didn't mean she expected someone like Caitlin Strong to show up with those specifications tucked in her pocket.

The Survivor Center for Victims of Torture was housed in a former halfway house on a street well back from San Antonio's famed Riverwalk but still in view of the Alamo from the right angle. From a halfway house it became a walk-in clinic before the Survivor Center moved in with substantial grant money behind it. Caitlin knew a lot of those funds were internationally based, coming in through such outlets as UNICEF, Catholic and Jewish charities such as the Anti-Defamation League, smaller humanitarian efforts and various alliances that were likely hastily hidden fronts for nations trying to absolve themselves of guilt.

Rita Navarro stopped at the end of the dingy hall before the stairs and elevator, past the closed doors of the treatment rooms where sessions were currently in progress. "We have a staff comprised of eighty providers, both paid and volunteer, consisting of psychiatrists, social workers, attorneys, physicians and interpreters. The interpreters are especially important, given that many of our patients speak English poorly, if at all. The good thing is that a number of those interpreters are actually former patients."

"Successful graduates," Caitlin said, immediately wishing she hadn't.

"There's no such thing really," Navarro explained. "Recovery from torture is similar to recovery from alcoholism. The fact that you were a victim never goes away; if you're lucky, you learn how to live with it—live being the operative word."

"I understand."

"You do?"

"Been volunteering up at the recovery center for Iraqi war veterans," Caitlin told her.

Something changed in Rita Navarro's expression. At first it looked to Caitlin that she'd winced, until the gaze froze into a scowl. "And you think that qualifies you to work here?"

"I was hoping so."

"You're wrong. Nothing can qualify you for what you're about to see and hear, if you stick it out."

"I'm no quitter, ma'am."

"Then why aren't you with the Texas Rangers anymore?"

"Simple question with a complicated answer."

"I'd like to hear more."

"I've said as much as I can on the subject."

"Then maybe you should just keep volunteering with wounded war veterans." Rita Navarro's eyes continued to blaze into her, reminding Caitlin of a hard-core criminal in the last instant before he goes for his gun. "How's it feel?" she asked suddenly, stepping close enough to Caitlin to make her feel uneasy.

Caitlin stepped back. "What?"

"Being helpless. Having someone else hold all the power."

"Ma'am?"

"I don't expect you've experienced that much, Ranger. But now you know what it feels like, a microcosm of what our patients will live with for the rest of their lives. What's been done to them physically, as reprehensible as that may be, is nothing compared to how their spirits have been broken. They've got scar tissue layered over their souls, and if you think holding their hands and reading them bedtime stories amounts to successful treatment, then you've come to the wrong place."

Caitlin straightened her shoulders, the way she did while staring into the mirror as a little girl, making sure she looked tough. "If I thought that, I wouldn't be here, Mrs. Navarro."

Rita Navarro's expression didn't change much. "There are only thirty-five centers like ours in the entire United States and only a hundred and fourteen worldwide, Ms. Strong. If you want to Google that, you do it under 'torture treatment center' but we prefer the term 'recovery,' or 'survivor,' for obvious reasons."

Navarro pushed the button on the elevator even though they were only going to the second floor. "Like to hear more?"

"I would."

Caitlin couldn't tell if Navarro was pleased or surprised. "This is where I lose some applicants."

"I'm still here, ma'am," she said, certain Navarro was pleased now.

Navarro nodded, satisfied. "Our center is unique in that we offer in- as well as outpatient services. Puts more demands on our staff and keeps us open twenty-four hours a day, but we're one of the few centers that can treat those victims who otherwise would end up in the cesspool of state psychiatric hospital wards or on the street. Also means we see some of the most challenging cases."

The elevator door opened and Caitlin followed Rita Navarro inside.

"We have eight treatment rooms, lab facilities and physical exam rooms on the first floor," she said when the doors had closed again. "The second floor has a dozen inpatient rooms and the third houses our administrative offices. There've been times, though, where we converted those offices into sleeping quarters. You do what you have to when you don't want to turn anyone away."

The elevator stopped. The door slid open. Rita Navarro led the way out, Caitlin wondering if this woman truly understood the kind of evil capable of putting men and women in a survivor center. Such monsters were a species unto themselves who feasted and thrived on the inability of normal human beings to conceive of their capacity for violence.

These days the problem has become identifying them. Caitlin's dad and granddad had been Rangers when the bad guys pretty much announced themselves and their intentions. These days, though, the monsters have moved into the kinds of neighborhoods people go to to escape them. John Wayne Gacy played a clown and civic humanitarian while burying the bodies of thirty-eight molested boys in his subbasement. The BTK killer was a Boy Scout troop leader.

That made Caitlin wonder what she was doing here, applying to help the victims instead of going after those who had victimized them. Navarro led her down a hallway that had six matching rooms on either side of the hall. The doors were all open, revealing simple dormitory-style furnishings within. A few of the rooms had been spruced up with personal items.

The first held a legless black man seated in a wheelchair. His skin was ebony colored, Caitlin guessing he was a native of Nigeria, Kenya or some other African country mired in perpetual civil war. His pupils were barely distinguishable amid the whites of his eyes and the lids didn't seem to be working properly.

The next room down was occupied by a woman with an eye patch and her right arm missing below the elbow. Her face was peppered with light spots set against her otherwise olive skin, making her nationality difficult to determine. She turned toward the doorway and caught Caitlin looking at her. Her one eye registered nothing, before shifting back toward a television, the glow of which framed her face in a deep shadow she seemed ready to vanish into.

The next patients lay in their beds, only their faces exposed. A woman peeked out fearfully from beneath the covers, weeping and whimpering. Considering what might be revealed with those covers pulled back sent a dread chill coursing up Caitlin's spine. But all the expressions left their mark, a mix of fear and resignation thanks to memories so painful and powerful that the past would never let them go.

"You don't really have the qualifications to work here," Navarro told her along the way. "I'd be doing you a favor by telling you no. But something tells me otherwise. Something tells me the things you've seen and done might help you reach some patients traditional therapists can't. Like our latest one," Navarro finished, stopping just before the last door on the right. "Been here two weeks and none of us have managed any progress with him whatsoever."

Inside the room, a figure in a faded cotton bathrobe sat in a faux-leather chair, his back to them facing the window.

"We don't know his name, what exactly was done to him, or why," Navarro resumed. "We only know that he suffered some of the most prolonged physical and mental torture we've ever encountered. John Doe."

She stepped into the doorway, beckoning Caitlin to join her, and knocked. "John? There's someone here I'd like you to meet."

The man in the chair turned slowly, mechanically. A simple response to stimulus from someone battered on the inside and out. Caitlin met his blank stare and felt her insides turn to grating glass. Her whole body went numb and her breath bottlenecked in her throat, making her feel light-headed.

Because the man in the chair was her dead husband, Peter Goodwin.

7

EAST SAN ANTONIO, THE PRESENT

Pablo Asuna's head was ducked under the hood of a souped-up Chevy Cavalier when Cort Wesley Masters's boots clacked across the slick floor of his two-bay garage. Asuna wiped the sweat from his brow with a greasy rag and looked up at him, then down at the boots.

"Hey, I gave those to you."

"Told me you took them off a dead man."

"A lie, amigo."

"What a shock."

Asuna had always been a key contact who knew where to find the Latino gang members Cort Wesley was gunning for. An overflowing fountain of information as good with sources as Cort Wesley was with bullets.

Asuna came out from under the Cavalier's hood, accepted Cort Wesley's hand and wrapped his other arm around his back. "It's good to see you, amigo. I heard you were getting out."

"How?"

Asuna backed off and wiped the rest of the grime from his face with the lower half of his white T-shirt, exposing his substantial, beer-fed gut. Cort Wesley remembered it being about half that size when he went in.

"Don't know," Asuna shrugged. "I hear things, that's all. Didn't think I'd be seeing you, though."

"I need something."

"Name it."

"Where to find the bitch Texas Ranger who framed me."

Cort Wesley's thirty-day housing allowance came in the form of an efficiency room in the Alamo Motel, featuring a badly chipped coonskin cap on the marquee. He stopped long enough to drop off the stuff he'd kept in storage for five years. Then decided to try on some of his old, musty-smelling clothes just to see what the years had done to him. Yanked on a pair of jeans that sagged on his thinner waist and could feel the tightness in an old chamois shirt's shoulders thanks to hours of pumping iron on the inside, part of a ritual that included five hundred push-ups a day to pass the time as much as anything. He studied himself in the mirror, barely recognizing the face that looked back. Not because he'd changed, since other than the milk-pale features from lack of sunlight, he looked pretty much the same; he just hadn't looked at himself much in prison. Add some length to the prison-cropped haircut to discourage lice and he could have been the same man who went inside nearly five years back. But the old clothes felt wrong on him, so he redressed in the khakis and work shirt issued by Huntsville before heading over to Pablo Asuna's.

"I don't know, man," Asuna said, moving to a small, grease-stained refrigerator. He came out with three beers, tossing one to Cort Wesley.

"What don't you know?"

Asuna laid one can down on a workbench and popped the tab off the other, swigging some down. "Giving you the 411 on this Ranger bitch sounds like a recipe for disaster."

Cort Wesley held his beer, but didn't open it. "I seem to be getting that a lot today."

Asuna guzzled the rest of his can, tossed it aside, and swiped a sleeve across his mouth. "Hey, amigo, things are a lot different now than when you went in. Time's passed you by. It's a new world out there, man, a new world. Your old bosses, they pulled up stakes and went back to New Orleans. The city rebuilds after Katrina, business comes with it, so the Brancas stepped in to fill the void, *comprende?*"

"What's your point?" Cort Wesley asked him, tightening his grip on the unopened beer can.

"Your old friends in the Latin gangs learn you got no cover, they'll be bringing the heavy artillery." Asuna started to reach for the second beer, then stopped. "My advice: shack up for a while away from the game."

"That Ranger framed me, Pablo. Think about it, me working the border with a bunch of Mexican drug mules under Emiliato Valdez Garza. Now there's a pretty picture. What's wrong?" Cort Wesley asked, seeing Asuna go tense.

"Garza, man."

"You ever meet him?"

"Nobody ever meets him. Man's a fucking ghost. They say, you see him, you're already dead."

"You think he's the one wants me dead?"

"Hey, take your pick, amigo. Once his Mexican Mafia, or the Juárez Boys, or MS-13 find out you're walking the streets, you're gonna have lots bigger problems than this bitch Ranger who planted your blood in the desert. That's all."

Cort Wesley felt the beer can compress in his grasp. The aluminum finally burst at the seams, sending a quake of liquid and foam spewing in all directions.

"All the more reason why I need a gun, Pablo," he said, giving no quarter for Asuna to escape his stare. "Now."

PART TWO

Certainly one of the most famous early-day Texas Rangers was John Coffee "Jack" Hays. He came to San Antonio in 1837 and within three years was named a Ranger captain. Hays built a reputation fighting marauding Indians and Mexican bandits. An Indian who switched sides and rode with Hays and his men called the young Ranger captain "brave too much." Hays's bravado was too much for many a hostile Indian or outlaw. In dealing with persons deemed a threat to Texas, Hays helped establish another Ranger tradition— toughness mixed with a reliance on the latest in technology.

—Mike Cox, with updates from the Texas Ranger
Hall of Fame and Museum staff,
"A Brief History of the Texas Rangers"

8

HOUSTON, THE PRESENT

"You may be seated, Mr. Delladonne," the chairwoman of the Government Oversight Subcommittee said into the microphone, her voice echoing through the chamber.

Harmon Delladonne lowered his right hand as he eased himself into his chair. "Thank you, Senator Winstrom."

"It is the chair's duty to remind you that you have the right to have counsel present, sir."

"I've waived that right, Senator. In writing."

"In that case, Mr. Delladonne, let the record show that this committee thanks you for honoring its request to appear without subpoena."

"And I thank you for being so understanding about the postponements of the testimony I'm here to give today. Let me begin by making a request that these proceedings be held off the record," Delladonne said coolly.

The windowless, wood-paneled chamber looked cramped and claustrophobic when packed from front to rear but absurdly large in a closed hearing like this. The ventilation was always poor and the summer months inevitably birthed a stale, musty odor like warmed-over standing water no amount of disinfectant could relieve.

"I'm afraid that's impossible. If you wish to retain counsel, this committee will gladly entertain a re—"

"Ma'am, I have no need of counsel. It's the members of

this subcommittee I'm more concerned about," Delladonne said, rotating his unblinking stare among the five
senators seated on the dais before him.

Senator Letroy Raskins leaned in toward his microphone. "I'm sure we members of this committee can take
care of ourselves, Mr. Delladonne."

"Oh, I'm sure you can, Senator."

"Then let's proceed, shall we?"

"Please do, sir. I have nothing to hide."

Senator Franklin Bayliss, seated next to Raskins on
the far left of the dais, cleared his throat. "This committee has convened in closed session to review the actions
of your company, MacArthur-Rain, Mr. Delladonne, not
yourself."

"I am my company, sir. When you look into it, you
look into me."

"Then let me say," started Senator William Gottlieb
from the far right, loud enough to cause a screech of feed-
back through the chamber's speakers, "that we have serious questions about the actions undertaken by both of
you."

"By which, you mean . . . ?"

Gottlieb donned a pair of glasses and consulted a page
in front of him before responding. "Specifically, the development of so-called passive surveillance techniques
and systems under contracts previously approved by the
full standing Oversight Committee and the Senate as a
whole."

"What I believe the senator is saying," picked up
Chairwoman Winstrom, "is that we have yet to see any
reports on the contracts dispensed at a cost of roughly
$500 million."

"You question their effectiveness."

"Right now, sir, we are questioning their very existence,
since we have not seen one single shred of demonstrative

evidence that taxpayer money has bought us anything worthwhile or, in fact, anything at all."

"Security issues," said Delladonne. "Any report as to function would reveal technological specifications I am not about to share publicly."

"This is a closed hearing, Mr. Delladonne."

"With all due respect, Madam Chairwoman, the only things closed here are your minds."

"Sir," followed Winstrom, her voice cracking slightly as the pitch picked up, "I'd like to remind you who signs your checks. And that ink will dry up just as soon as we give the word. I hope I'm making myself clear."

Delladonne nodded, apparently in concession until his dark eyes fixed forward. "And me thinking it was the American *people* who signed my checks. For doing my job. For doing everything I can to keep them safe."

"We are those people's duly elected representatives, Mr. Delladonne. And, as such, you will answer to us."

"Whatever you say, Senator."

"And I'd like to add," bellowed Senator Angelo Cataldi, his voice booming through the chamber even though he was seated too far back for his microphone to pick it up, "that right now the five of us *are* the American people."

"What a pity."

"Could you repeat that, please?"

"You heard me, Senator. You hauled me in here because you don't believe project Fire Arrow works. I'm telling you it does and, for your own good, to leave it at that."

This time Cataldi spoke into his mike. "What exactly is that supposed to mean?"

"You'd like me to demonstrate the efficacy of Fire Arrow."

"I believe we've already made that point quite clear," said Chairwoman Winstrom.

Now it was Delladonne who leaned forward, close enough to his microphone to smell the metal and dried sweat. "Then, ma'am, how do you suppose your constituents would feel if they found out one of the Senate's foremost pro-life advocates underwent an abortion last year?" Delladonne paused to hold the senator's shocked stare. "Or your husband?"

Winstrom drew the mike toward her but said nothing through her trembling lips.

"You're out of order, Mr. Delladonne!" Angelo Cataldi shot out through the silence.

"As you are on the nights you visit your twelve-year-old stepson's bedroom."

Cataldi seemed to lose his breath for a moment before his features flushed with a darkening hue of red. "You are heading toward a contempt citation, sir, along with slander." He looked toward the other senators in search of support, but none met his gaze. "You think you can come into this chamber and intimidate us with your baseless allegations? This is the United States Senate, sir, not a corporate boardroom."

"Baseless? Perhaps, Senator, you'd like me to quote, for the record, the dates and times of your visits, starting with last Thursday at 1:25 A.M." This time, Delladonne held Cataldi's stare until the senator looked down, pretending to consult the pages before him. "Do you need to hear more, Senator?"

"That won't be necessary, Mr. Delladonne," Senator Winstrom said, recovering her voice. "None of this display on your part is necessary. I remind you where you are."

"I know where I am, and I'll tell you what is necessary, Madam Chairwoman," Delladonne resumed, turning his gaze on Letroy Raskins. "Inspecting the financial records of the Third Baptist Church located in the honorable

Mr. Raskins's district. I wonder how the parishioners would feel if they learned a quarter million in unreported dollars from collection plates helped finance his last campaign."

"That's a bold-faced lie!" yelled Raskins, rising from his chair so fast that he spilled over his water glass, soaking the papers before him. He seemed not to notice.

"I can produce the passive surveillance that proves quite the opposite." Not giving Raskins the opportunity to answer, Delladonne jerked his gaze toward Franklin Bayliss. "Or how about I produce the computer logs that reveal you, Senator, have a penchant for visiting pornographic sites specializing in bondage and sadomasochism?" Then, to William Gottlieb, "Or that you, Senator, struck your wife on four occasions last month and three the month before. I can provide the precise dates and times, if you wish," Delladonne continued before Gottlieb could protest, "just as I did for Senator Cataldi. How about I do that for you, Senator?"

Gottlieb breathed heavily into his microphone, the sound carrying over the room's hidden speakers.

Delladonne let the committee see him smile slightly. "Since you have all been so vociferous in your criticism of Fire Arrow, I thought it best to give you a demonstration of its effectiveness firsthand. Now I probably committed upward of a dozen violations of the current statutes in the process, but I don't think we want the record to reflect that, do we? Nor did I think it wise to bring the visual evidence of your indiscretions here with me today. I thought it best to store them elsewhere, for safekeeping."

Cataldi, Raskins and Bayliss all began to speak at once until Winstrom flipped a hidden switch to shut off their microphones.

Delladonne rose from his chair casually. "If there are

no further questions, Senators, I'll be on my way," he said, stepping back from the table. "If you need the documentation I spoke of, you have my phone number." He started to turn away, then swung back toward the dais. "Just like I have yours."

Harmon Delladonne picked up the receiver as soon as the door to the limousine was closed behind him. No calls could either be received or placed from the phone; for security reasons it served only as a message board with encryption software that changed the number a dozen times per hour. Delladonne hit a single button and heard the recording of a familiar voice greet him.

"It's Clayton, sir. I've found Peter Goodwin."

9

SURVIVOR CENTER, THE PRESENT

Caitlin sat on a chair at the side of her husband's bed. A husband who recognized neither her nor himself. She made sure her back was to the wall-mounted camera so as not to betray the conflicted agony twisted across her features in stark contrast to the tense stare etched onto Peter's.

She could not say why she hadn't told Rita Navarro the truth immediately. And with each passing second, then minute, then hour, her lie of omission became so firmly rooted in her psyche that she couldn't turn back.

Why?

Because she would've been removed from the case, if

not from the center entirely. Because, knowing Peter as she did, Caitlin felt herself better equipped than anyone else to help him become the warm, sensitive and brilliant man he'd once been. Because at the heart of all this was a mystery the Texas Ranger in her needed to solve. And, down deeper, Caitlin wanted to find who had done this because, because . . .

That was what she did, what she was.

Except she wasn't anymore, thought she was past it all until she saw her husband utterly helpless, his expression as pained as his once fertile mind was empty and his body broken in more ways than she could imagine.

Peter Goodwin, government contractor pronounced dead in Iraq last year. Someone was behind the subterfuge. Someone had scrambled her husband's brain and left him for dead.

Someone Caitlin was going to make pay.

"Ms. Strong?" Rita Navarro had prodded when Caitlin's eyes remained fixed on Peter in disbelief.

Caitlin quickly brushed the shock from her face. "What's wrong with him?" she managed to ask.

Navarro led the way out of Peter's room and spoke when they were back in the hallway. "It's called Cotard's syndrome."

"An identity disorder, right?" Caitlin managed.

"I'm surprised you've heard of it. Not many have. A French psychiatrist named Jules Cotard treated several patients who suffered from a syndrome he referred to as délire de négation, *characterized by the delusions that one is dead or the world no longer exists," Navarro explained. "Some patients feel they have literally dissolved, that their brains have rotted away or their insides are gone."*

Caitlin's neck muscles had locked to the point where as much as she wanted to turn her head to look back at Peter inside the room, she couldn't.

Navarro unhooked a clipboard from a wall-mounted hook next to the doorway and consulted it before resuming. "In New York, the patient was treated with a regimen of haloperidol, followed by a combination of valproic acid and fluoxetine. When this regimen failed to produce any discernible results, the patient was treated with electroconvulsive therapy."

Caitlin shuddered, the heat in her throat turning cold in an instant.

"That treatment resulted in further withdrawal and a transfer to the survivor center in Tampa. Once there, his dosages of haloperidol and valproic acid were tapered. Fluoxetine was increased to forty milligrams per day, and risperidone was initiated and titrated to three milligrams a day."

Rita Navarro hung the clipboard back on the hook and took off her glasses. "The Tampa center felt they were too short staffed to fully care for the patient's needs and requested a transfer here. We have continued the recommended drug protocols while initiating a course of traditional psychiatric therapy, during which," Navarro finished, "the patient has remained mostly unresponsive thus far."

Caitlin felt the need to say something, lest Navarro's suspicions began to flare anew. "What happens if that continues?"

Navarro frowned, regarding Caitlin's question with a grimness that seemed to turn her expression sallow. "Then we'd have no choice but to conclude that a convalescent or nursing home might be better suited to take care of his needs. That's where too many torture victims end up. And once there, they almost never leave."

Caitlin held up a picture in front of Peter of him happy and smiling, her hand trembling slightly. The picture had been taken just before he left for Iraq, and she'd peeled it out of its frame at her apartment that morning. If Rita Navarro noticed, she'd likely assume the picture had been part of his file.

"Do you know this man?" Caitlin asked Peter, feeling the hot clog forming anew in her throat and forcing her to push her breath past it.

Peter regarded the picture vaguely. "No."

Now, instead of pushing her breath, she pushed herself to remain professional. "Does he look familiar?"

"No."

"A little maybe?"

"Maybe."

"Does he look like you?"

"There is no me."

"Tell me something you remember."

Peter's eyes flickered back to the picture. "Looking at that."

"What about before?"

"There is no before."

"We met yesterday. Do you remember that?"

"There is no yesterday."

Physically, Peter had aged a decade in the eighteen months since he left. His once long glossy brown hair had been cut short and had thinned noticeably, whitening at the temples. His skin had a sickly gray tone to it, and all the life and color had been bled out of his eyes.

"Physically, the patient has suffered multiple hairline fractures of the hands and feet, clearly inflicted to induce

pain," Rita Navarro told her. "Both his rotator cuffs have been torn from being placed in a stress position for long periods of twenty-four to forty-eight hours at a time, and he suffers from a heart condition consistent with hypothermic distress from similarly prolonged exposure to freezing water, also known as ice baths. Lung scarring and diminished function indicates repeated so-called waterboarding techniques meant to simulate drowning—"

"In your experience," Caitlin interrupted, "who would use those kinds of techniques?"

"As in?"

"As in countries, nations, governments."

"Well, we've only had experience with two Americans prior to this one and both of those were soldiers who'd been prisoners of war, one in Iraq and one in Afghanistan."

"And?"

Rita Navarro looked as if she didn't want to answer Caitlin's question. "Ranger Strong—"

"It's 'miss,' ma'am."

"Is it? Because right now you sound more like an investigator than a therapist. The source of our patients' suffering is germane only when it pertains directly to their treatment. If you want to find out who did this to him, I suggest you rejoin the Rangers."

Caitlin thought about pressing things but didn't, afraid that would result only in her being removed from Peter's case. Better to let the string play itself out and find the truth from the best source of all: Peter himself.

IO

Cort Wesley sat in the car across from the neat Mexican-style ranch house in a cul-de-sac in Shavano Park. Twenty miles from San Antonio was close enough for him to keep an eye on the two sons he'd never actually met and far enough to keep his enemies away. He had parked in the shade of some elm trees, not planning to stay long since trespassers in such suburbs were inevitably noticed and reported. Especially if they were driving a beat-up Ford with bad plates lent to them by Pablo Asuna.

Asuna had also gotten Cort Wesley a Smith & Wesson 9 millimeter. Not his favorite gun, but a reliable firearm generally with a fifteen-shot magazine and polymer frame normally reserved for law enforcement. The gun was tucked under the passenger seat now, well out of view of any dutiful cop who might happen to approach.

Cort Wesley never sent his boys cards or gifts for birthdays or Christmas, sent his ex-girlfriend Maura extra cash around that time of year so she could buy them something nice instead. Maura's father was Mexican and his sons had gotten most of their dark, brooding looks from her, although he felt certain, even at this distance, that the oldest boy had his eyes.

Dylan, almost fourteen now, was so middle class it almost made Cort Wesley smile. He and his younger brother Luke used their mother's last name Torres, which suited Cort Wesley just fine. Arranging money for them while in prison had grown increasingly difficult, Pablo Asuna shedding light on a situation that had his former employers gone from the area. Out of sight, out of mind, as far as they were concerned regarding him. Since Cort Wesley's services were no longer required, they had no need to honor their commitment to keep funneling money through Asuna to his sons. That thought left him gripping the faded, steamy dashboard covering just over the console hard enough to leave fingertip impressions in the vinyl.

Maura had let the boys build a skateboarding half-pipe, sharply sloped twin sides fashioned out of plywood already showing marks and wear from the wheels, in the front yard. Cort Wesley found himself transfixed as he watched Dylan ride it. Doing air-grabbing tricks that left him soaring toward the sky only to land back on his board, his long black hair flying in all directions. Inside The Walls, Cort Wesley had known a number of Latino gang members with hair like that, often tied back into ponytails. He remembered this now because he'd used a plastic knife to cut off the ponytail of an especially irksome one in the middle of the cafeteria for all the maximum security cons to see. Not one of the punk's fellow gang members came to his aid or so much as moved a muscle, not about to risk a substantially worse fate at Cort Wesley's hands.

Cort Wesley pushed his fingers deeper into the console, while one of Dylan's friends took a turn on the half-pipe, wondering what he was feeling here. It felt like pride that his son was the leader of the boys assembled, the biggest and best of the group. He could tell how the others deferred to him, thirsting for his attention and approval the way cons inside would do anything to win a glance or a nod from Cort Wesley. He also noticed a klatch of neighborhood girls gathered nearby, doing everything possible to get Dylan's attention without appearing to.

The half-pipe had been built to take as much advantage of the yard's shade as possible. But the angle of the late-afternoon sun sliced through the branches, splaying a combination of light and shadow across his son's face. The effect was to make him seem like two people in one and Cort Wesley couldn't help but wonder if there was some crazy reason why he thought of that.

He wanted to be the same man he was before he went inside. Longed for the simplicity and clarity his old life had provided. But something had changed in him inside The Walls, something he didn't totally grasp yet.

Cort Wesley hated his efficiency room at the Alamo Motel because it was too big, not too small. After making forty square feet home for the better part of five years, five or six times that seemed massive. Made him feel like he was going to get swallowed up by all that space he couldn't fill. First night in, he had to shove the bed up against the wall, like his bunk in Huntsville, in order to sleep. Ended up turning the light on because it was never really dark in the corridors of The Walls.

He knew the esteem that his well-earned reputation had earned him. Knew cops would never risk pulling him over after running his plate. Knew gang-bangers would switch to the other side of the street or duck down an alley if they saw him coming.

But his kids didn't know him at all. And it was too dangerous to start now, especially with the umbrella of protection provided by his former employers gone with them to New Orleans. The same gang-banging assholes that used to cross the street might think differently now. He'd like to move Maura and the kids somewhere safe, like a Caribbean island or a bank vault. Maura had never married, and the thought of another man in his sons' lives left Cort Wesley gnashing his teeth and tightening his grip on the rim of the dashboard. Before he knew it, his fingers had dug into the vinyl covering and began peeling it back like flesh off a bone.

Cort Wesley wondered if things would be any different if he hadn't been inside for so long, which made him think of Texas Ranger Caitlin Strong, as Dylan took to the half-pipe again. Soaring in loose-fitting jeans and a baggy T-shirt.

Releasing his hold on the dashboard, Cort Wesley figured he'd take care of the past first, then go from there.

11

SAN ANTONIO, THE PRESENT

Peter was seated in a chair today in one of the downstairs treatment rooms, still wearing his bathrobe. He had wrapped his arms about himself and was shivering slightly as if frightened by what he registered. A breeze blown through an open window sent the blinds clacking against one another, the sound startling Peter enough to make him lurch from his chair. He glanced about, eyes brushing across the room's contents without seeming to really take anything in. Then he settled back with a pained grimace stretched across his expression, evidence of just how little tolerance his broken body had for movement of any kind. A combination of his current drug regimen and their desire to keep him reasonably coherent had kept the Survivor Center's physicians from prescribing painkillers stronger than Tylenol for now.

Watching him suffer was almost too much for Caitlin to bear, but that only strengthened her resolve to do something about it by reaching Peter when everyone else had failed. Toward that end, she held up a picture of the two of them together, one of the last taken before he left, tucking her emotions as far away as possible. Her former commander in the Texas Rangers, D. W. Tepper, had asked to meet her for coffee this afternoon and she contemplated that reunion to fight back the now familiar clog forming in her throat.

"Do these people look familiar to you?" she asked her husband.

"The woman's you."

"What about the man?"

"No," Peter said, shaking his head. "I don't know him."

"Anything else strike you about the picture?"

"They seem happy. Nice couple. Do you have any others?"

"Not with me."

"What about pictures with their kids?"

"They never had kids. They talked about it, but they never had any."

"Why?"

"Couldn't quite get things right. Complicated story. Do you have a story, Peter?"

"No. No story. Nothing at all."

Caitlin had read and studied enough about the victims of torture to know this kind of post-traumatic response, the very denial of self, was all about living in a fear indescribable to anyone who hasn't experienced such horror. The fear never really went away, every second of consciousness spent by the victims reliving the moments of the terrible pain inflicted upon them. The mind's only available responses were to forget in a kind of retrograde amnesia or to deny existence itself, in which case there can be no fear because there's no person to suffer from it.

Peter, suddenly fidgety with agitation, stuck a hand

into the pocket of his bathrobe and came out with a shiny quarter. Clutched it tightly in a clenched fist until the hand darkened with blood flow. But the rest of him seemed to ease.

"What are you doing?"

"They gave this to me somewhere else I was before I was here. Told me it was about value."

"Whose?"

"His."

Caitlin decided to take a chance. "Where were you before that?"

"Before what?"

"Before you got the quarter."

"Somewhere else."

"What about when you were worth more? Do you ever remember being worth more?"

Peter didn't answer, just held to his tight grasp around the quarter.

"Do you know where you are now?"

"With you."

"I mean do you know what state you're in now?"

"It doesn't matter because I don't exist."

"Texas. You're in Texas."

That seemed to register a little.

"You used to live here."

"I live here now."

"I meant in Texas. Then you left."

"Where'd I go?"

"Iraq."

"Ugly, bad place."

"You remember?"

"I guess I heard."

Caitlin rose and slid a laptop computer she'd placed on a portable stand over and positioned it in front of Peter. She'd already turned it on and logged in.

"You know what this is?" she asked him.

"A computer."

"Do you know how to use it?"

Peter didn't say anything, but he laid the quarter down on the stand and let his fingers stray noncommittally to the keys. Caitlin didn't press things, figuring this amounted to progress on several different fronts. She watched as he tapped out a few letters, seeming to be soothed by the tinny clacking sound. More fingers joined the first few.

"What am I supposed to do?"

"Just what you're doing."

Peter kept typing, faster now. Caitlin couldn't tell if there was any context to it and didn't want to distract him by positioning herself somewhere she could see. She watched as he studied what was appearing on the screen closer, intent and perhaps even enjoying himself. Then just as suddenly as he started, he stopped and gently eased the stand away from him. The wheels squeaked slightly against the tile.

"I want to go back to his room now."

"Whose room?"

"His."

"Can you tell me his name?"

Peter grew fidgety again, reaching into his pocket for his quarter and getting more agitated when he couldn't find it. Caitlin lifted it from the laptop stand and handed it back to him. Again he clutched it tightly in his fist.

"I want to go back to his room now," Peter said, rising tentatively on his weakened legs.

"I'll get your wheelchair," Caitlin followed, adding, "Peter."

Peter didn't respond or acknowledge her. Settling painfully into the wheelchair, while Caitlin stole a glance at the screen to see what he had typed.

12

San Antonio, the Present

Captain D. W. Tepper of the Texas Rangers rose from a booth in a coffee shop just down the street from the Survivor Center when he saw Caitlin enter.

"Now, ain't this a sight that'd make your daddy proud," he said, embracing her tightly. "You were still in my command, I could get written up for that hug."

"Guess we should thank God for small favors then," Caitlin told him, clearing her throat in the hope it might make her voice sound more normal around a man who was a part of her life now finished. Her glimpse at the computer screen had revealed only gibberish, Peter having typed nothing more than random letters with occasional words mixed in. Progress for sure, but not the magic clue she'd been hoping for.

"Amen to that, I say."

Tepper sat back down and Caitlin slid into the booth across from him. Tepper raised his cup of coffee to his lips as she settled herself, and she could see the arthritis that had nearly ended his career with the Rangers had worsened. He'd been tall and lanky for as long as Caitlin could remember and he looked just as lanky today, though a bit less tall. Tepper's close-cropped hair had exchanged more salt for pepper, but he wore his ever-present string tie, western shirt and cowboy boots that inevitably announced his approach with a distinctive clamor. His fingers, all stiff and puffy, made Caitlin think of her dad dying of heart disease before a similar condition had descended on him. She could smell the captain's aftershave as soon as she reached the booth, Aqua Velva she thought, same as Jim Strong.

"Yeah," Tepper said, as if reading her mind, "I miss him too. Jim Strong was a hell of a man."

"No better than you, Captain."

"Different, though. And you can call me D. W. now, Ranger."

Caitlin smiled, the irony of his statement not lost on her. "Rather keep calling you Captain, if you don't mind."

"Not at all."

Tepper commanded the San Antonio company of Rangers, one of six active in the state, each comprised of twenty-five or so men since the state legislature had increased the membership rolls from 120 to 134. One hundred and thirty-four men patrolling a state bigger than most countries was a tall order, but nothing new for the Rangers. It had been that way since the beginning, Caitlin knew, in both legend and fact.

"What I mind is being out of the country when your daddy died," Tepper continued, face twisted as if his coffee tasted bad. "Then I'm still over in that cesspool they call Iraq when you had your troubles, so I wasn't there to watch your back. Your dad always warned me not to keep re-upping in the Reserves. I listen to him, maybe things are different today."

"Hope you're not blaming yourself, Captain."

"I ain't good at much, Ranger, but I've seen enough trouble to know how to keep me and mine steered clear of it."

"There wasn't anything you could've done at the border that night for me and Charlie."

"Not talking about that night. Talking about after. That night ain't why you're not riding with the Rangers no more. After is."

A waitress came over and Caitlin ordered coffee before

responding to D. W. Tepper. "I did what I had to do, Captain."

"Yup, just like your dad and granddad would've done. Difference is they come from different eras, like me. Things weren't too complicated then. Matter of fact, long as you could handle a gun, they weren't complicated at all."

Caitlin recalled that Captain D. W. Tepper had taught himself to shoot with his left hand to stay in the Rangers after the arthritis turned his right one bad.

"You got back from Iraq four years ago, Captain. What is it you wanna talk to me about today?"

"You quit the Rangers, nobody makes a stink about what went down. Everything tied up in a neat little bow. I get back and there's nothing to be done about it."

"Too late, like you said."

Tepper watched the waitress set a mug down in front of Caitlin and refill his before leaning slightly across the table. "I need to get my hands around what happened in Mexico, Ranger. Need to know what it was made you throw everything away."

13

JUÁREZ, MEXICO, 2004

Caitlin had spent six weeks in the hospital and then eight more in rehab. Rehab was the toughest, getting her strength back from all the trauma and inactivity and trying to take pleasure in mastering simple tasks like climbing a set of stairs without having her breath desert her. Amazing all the things she'd taken for granted. When she started rehab, she couldn't even hoist a gun, never mind aim and shoot it. Caitlin started with one-pound weights, quickly progressing down the long row of chrome dumbbells in the physical therapy center. Eventually returning for long sessions by herself, after the scheduled ones were done, jacking up weights and punishing herself on the StairMaster machine. Because it wasn't enough for her to get back to "acceptable functionality," as they called it; she needed to get back to 100 percent; no, a 110 if she was to make good on the promise that had helped get her this far.

That promise went all the way back to that night in the desert, listening to a truck tear away through the sand and grit while she and Charlie Weeks lay in a sinkhole bleeding all over each other. She memorized the sound of that truck, imagining the surviving gunmen, one of them an American, hauling ass back into Mexico. She knew she'd clipped at least two of them to go with the three she and Charlie killed. But their escape clawed at her until she couldn't sleep no matter how many drugs they shot her up with. She couldn't sleep again until she resolved to finish what she and Charlie had started in the Chihuahuan that night.

That meant tracking down the drug mules who'd gotten away.

She was still officially on medical leave when she packed up her dad's old truck and headed south, flashing her silver Ranger badge cut from a Mexican cinco peso for ID at the border. The guards looked at her face, didn't ask for her name or make any further notation. Just waved her through and through she went into Juárez, Mexico.

The fact that she had entered the home base of an infamous band of killers and drug runners known as the Juárez Boys didn't matter much at that point. She was armed only with her SIG strapped around her ankle. Before climbing out of her truck at the General Hospital on Paseo Triunfo de la República, though, Caitlin clipped the holster to her belt.

Mexican hospital personnel were loath to provide information to American authorities even with documentation, never mind without it. But Caitlin had something going for her, two things actually: she spoke fluent Spanish and the Texas Rangers remained a name that still struck fear into the hearts of many Mexicans. That tendency dated all the way back to the Mexican War of the mid-nineteenth century just after Texas had secured its independence and been granted statehood. She remembered many of the bloody tales her grandfather had told her of Rangers riding in the company of army regulars, many of their encounters both north and south of the border having forged the fearsome reputation that Rangers carried to this day, especially in Mexico where they were referred to as *Los Rinches*.

Inside the hospital, it took two clerks and a supervisor to finally come up with the names of two Mexican natives who had shown up at the hospital just about the same time Charlie Weeks was pronounced dead. Both were suffering from gunshot wounds considered nonlife-threatening. The men had given false names that were corrected when an astute physician's assistant handed wallets containing their actual identities over to the charge nurse.

Their names were Rodrigo and Jesus Saez, brothers apparently who shared the same address in a downtown apartment building on Avenue Vincente Guerrero. They weren't home at the time but their talkative mother, an obese woman who used tequila to treat her diabetes, was more than happy to tell Caitlin where to find them on the promise that she made them pay her back the 1,000 pesos they owed her.

Caitlin found the brothers running a basement cockfight six blocks away. She waited until the basement emptied out, leaving her alone with them late into the night. One of the brothers was cleaning up the blood and chicken shit while the other counted out the night's haul.

Rodrigo and Jesus . . . she had no idea which was which and didn't care. They didn't see her until it was too late. Caitlin had her SIG out and fired two shots before either brother could even cry out, one bullet for each in the leg just over the knee. Huge tissue damage which meant lots and lots of pain. She bound their arms and gagged them, while they writhed on the ground crying tears of agony. Only time in her life she'd done harm to someone who wasn't trying to do likewise to her. Even then the feeling of shooting two unarmed men left a taste in her mouth like the burn of sour bile. But she'd gone too far to go back.

"Remember me?" she asked in Spanish, standing over them.

Rodrigo and Jesus Saez looked at her fearfully and shook their heads. In the light spilling from the naked bulbs strung overhead, the sweat beads on their faces shined like pearls.

"Don't expect you would," Caitlin continued, "it being so dark and all that night in the West Texas desert, so let me refresh your memory. Be about five months ago now. You ambushed me and my partner who had the bad fortune to die—bad for him and bad for you, since I lived." Caitlin fished some photos from her wallet and began tossing them at the Saez brothers. "Some pictures of the family you ruined, Charlie Weeks's family. Three daughters, eleven grandchildren who'll never see their granddad again thanks to you. So you boys want to have grandkids of your own, you best tell me what you were up to that night and who was behind it. Okay?"

Neither brother nodded. Caitlin shot the brother on her right in his other leg and then crouched over the one on the left. The bad taste in her mouth didn't return. "You Jesus?"

The man shook his head, gesturing with his eyes toward his brother who was now bleeding from both legs, thrashing about with eyes bulging over his gag.

"So he's Jesus. That makes you Rodrigo."

A nod.

"Good. Now that we're getting somewhere, let's have a talk, you and me." She yanked the gag from his mouth and watched his eyes widen, weighing the options he was about to be given. "Who were you boys working for that night?"

Rodrigo said nothing, panting with fear.

Caitlin pressed the still hot barrel of the SIG flush against the leg she hadn't shot yet.

"Please, señorita, if I tell you I will be killed!"

"And if you don't, you'll be crippled. Not much of a choice, I know, but it's the best you're gonna get tonight and it ain't gonna get that good again by a long stretch. Now, who were you working for that night?"

Caitlin made sure Rodrigo could see her finger tighten ever so slightly on the SIG's trigger, watched his eyes swim with fear. Then she let him see *her* eyes, let him see she would do it.

"Emiliato Valdez Garza!" Rodrigo almost shouted, naming the reputed head of the Mexican Mafia that ran drugs across the Texas border bound for all over the country. Most in the Rangers and the Department of Public Safety Narcotics Division were convinced Garza was no more than a made-up Robin Hood–like legend to deflect attention away from the true leaders of the Mexican Mafia and to win the hearts of the Mexican people in the process.

"He's not real," Caitlin said.

"He is, señorita, you must believe me!"

"You've seen him, met him?"

"No one meets or sees him, but he's real."

"And you know this because . . . ?"

"The friends of mine he has killed because they failed him."

"Like you."

"No, señorita, our work was complete when—" Rodrigo stopped abruptly, realizing he had said more than he should have.

"Keep talking."

"Please, señorita, your gun, it's hurting my leg."

"It'll do a hell of a lot more than that if you don't finish what you started to tell me."

"We had already made our delivery."

"You were on your way back," Caitlin said less surely, realizing she and Charlie must've had it wrong the whole time.

"Back home, sí."

"Where'd you drop off your drugs?"

"Not drugs."

"The hell you say."

"*Not* drugs!"

"What then?"

"Don't know. Crates, boxes. Something inside them that wasn't drugs."

Caitlin pushed the barrel of the SIG down harder. "You telling me my partner died for counterfeit sneakers or T-shirts?"

"I don't know. I only know it wasn't drugs."

Caitlin jerked her pistol away from Rodrigo and aimed straight for Jesus's head. "Tell me what it was or I'll shoot your brother in the face. Look me in the eye and see if I'm serious. Look me in the eye and tell me I won't do it."

"I can't tell you what I don't know, but . . ."

"Talk!"

"There was another man with us, an American! He was in charge. He dropped us at the border, to die."

Rodrigo's mention of an American confirmed everything she thought she'd heard that night. "Not all bad, I guess," Caitlin said to him.

"He was very scary."

"Did he shoot you in the leg?"

"No, señorita."

"Then I guess he wasn't scarier than me, was he?"

Rodrigo swallowed hard.

"What was this American's name?"

"I don't know. We drive the truck to Houston and unload it there."

"Houston?"

"*Sí.*"

"That was your only stop, you unloaded everything there?"

Rodrigo nodded. "The American was in charge. Afterwards, he comes with us back to Juárez to pay Garza."

"You poor dumb shit."

Rodrigo's eyes narrowed.

"He was going to kill you. Only reason you're alive today is 'cause my partner and I happened to be staking out the area."

"We won't be alive tomorrow now."

"Not my problem."

"Garza will find us!"

"Give him my regards. Tell him I shot you and I'm gonna shoot him."

Caitlin rose, brushing off her jeans even though they were clean. But the action made her feel no less dirty because the real dirt was in a place no amount of brushing could rid.

"How many boxes?" she asked Rodrigo.

"Three dozen, maybe four."

"How big?"

Rodrigo spread his hands to show her.

"You're full of shit."

"No."

"You were running drugs and nothing else."

"No!" Rodrigo rasped, throwing up his hands in front of his face as if to ward off an expected bullet.

"I'm not gonna shoot you. You're right, you and your brother don't get yourselves gone, you'll be dead anyway."

Caitlin reached down and counted a thousand pesos from the cash that littered the dirt floor.

"But don't worry," she told Rodrigo, "I'll pay your mother back the money you owe her."

14

SAN ANTONIO, THE PRESENT

"And did you?" D. W. Tepper asked her.

"What do you think?"

"Yeah, stupid question."

"You don't look surprised."

"That's pretty much the way I always thought it went down. Ever figure out if Garza caught up to the Saez brothers?"

"Nope. It didn't seem to matter much at that point. And there's no such person as Garza."

"I'm sure that's just what he wants you to think."

"You ever seen Garza, Captain?"

"Nope."

"A picture even?"

Tepper shook his head, stifled a raspy cough born of years nesting with Marlboro Reds. "Nope. Pray to God every Sunday but never seen him neither."

"See, Captain, that's the point. Mexican Mafia likes nothing better than watching us chase our tails in search of a spook story."

"There's plenty who'd disagree with you there, some of them Rangers."

"Nobody's perfect, even Rangers."

Tepper's drawn, tired eyes scolded her from across the table. "So, what, you working at this torture center's about some stab at forgiveness?"

"For what?"

"You just told me for what."

"I did what I had to in Juárez that night, Captain."

"Doesn't make it any more right or less drag on the conscience. It ain't the Ranger way, girl, ain't part of our code or any decent man's."

"Felt different at the time," Caitlin managed, stung by his comment.

"That supposed to justify what you did?"

"It's what kept me going through all the rehab."

"And look where that got you." Tepper stopped to steady his breathing, stifling a cough. "Only thing I can figure is working with these torture victims is gonna somehow make you feel better about what you did to the Saez brothers."

"Lots of things I'm trying to change in my life right now."

"Well, I knew something had changed you before you finally met up with Cort Wesley Masters; I just didn't know what."

Caitlin ran it through her head again, the events that followed her return from Juárez. "I filed a report based on anonymous sourcing and the Department of Public Safety dispatched a forensics team to the site. Took as many blood samples as they could find. One of them came back a match for Masters."

"The American you remember being there, giving the orders."

"Yup. And what went down from there, you pretty much know."

D. W. Tepper leaned across the table again, the cracks in his leathery face deepening into crevices. "Something you gotta hear now."

Caitlin looked at Tepper for a long time after he had finished telling her about Cort Wesley Masters being released from Huntsville.

"You're telling me this new kind of DNA test proved it wasn't his blood in the desert, when another test proved it was."

"DNA don't lie."

"It did the first time, apparently."

Tepper refitted the standard-issue Ranger Stetson hat over his head. Caitlin found herself studying the sweat stains burned into the brim.

"Been struggling with this ever since I found out myself the other day. I don't tell you, you can't be on your guard. I do tell you, what you did chews you up inside."

Caitlin's hands tightened into fists and she rapped one down on the table hard enough to rattle their coffee mugs. "That son of a bitch was there the night Charlie Weeks was killed, sure as I'm looking at you right now."

"No, Caitlin, he wasn't. And now you got a certifiable psychopath who may be out to end your life in a hurry."

"Cort Wesley Masters isn't a psychopath."

"What is he then?"

"I heard he took over his father's loan sharking business when he was only sixteen. I heard he came back from the first Gulf War with the ears and scalps of his Iraqi victims for souvenirs."

"You believe all that?"

"Question is where does the legend end and truth begin, Captain."

Tepper started to slide out of the booth, every joint creaking and cracking from sitting for such a long stretch. He coughed up some mucus, then swallowed it back down, his eyes growing curious.

"What do you think, Ranger?"

"That I should've killed him when I had the chance."

Tepper looked as if he were ready to offer a rebuke to her until another coughing spasm overcame him. His eyes fought back their watering and grew stern. "Think that's the way Jim Strong would've handled things?"

"Jim Strong never met Cort Wesley Masters, Captain."

15

HOUSTON, THE PRESENT

"Pleasant trip, I trust, Mr. Hanratty," Harmon Delladonne said to the man seated in front of his desk.

"Not really."

"I'd suspect so, considering you flew coach. If you wanted to sign the deal memo in person, I could have sent a jet for you," Delladonne said, extending a Montblanc pen across his desk.

Hanratty didn't take it. "I'm not here to sign your deal memo. I'm here to tell you to shove it."

Instead of responding, Delladonne rose and moved around to the front of his desk where a pair of brandy snifters had been set next to a decanter. Its crystal form glistened in a band of sunlight stretching from one of the windows on the far wall.

Delladonne watched Hanratty recoil at his approach, jostling his chair. Hanratty was a big man with unnaturally broad shoulders and thick white hair. A Korean War vet who'd earned a Purple Heart and Medal of Valor when he single-handedly stormed a machine-gun nest armed only with a knife. He breathed noisily through his mouth and smelled of talcum powder.

"You look tense, Mr. Hanratty. Let me pour you a drink," Delladonne said, removing the heavy top from the decanter. "This is Henri IV Dudognon, the most expensive cognac in the world," he continued, as he poured matching levels into the two snifters. "Something you'll now be able to enjoy with all the money I'm paying you. Come on, let's toast to our mutual success."

Delladonne extended one of the snifters toward Hanratty who refused to take that too. "I don't drink."

"A good time to make an exception, I'd say. So we can toast our futures."

"Our futures have nothing in common. I thought I'd made that abundantly clear."

Delladonne ignored him, rolling the liquid around in his glass. "This is as close to perfection as it gets, Mr. Hanratty. Aged for twenty years in the same distillery where it's been made for three centuries. When you sip Henri IV Dudognon, you're tasting history. You're tasting all the things that have come to pass, some you could control and others you couldn't. That's why I wanted you to toast with me, so we could celebrate the things we still can."

Delladonne studied the man against the backdrop of the sprawling office that made Hanratty look tiny and ineffectual. The motif of the office, which included a loft accessible via a steel spiral staircase, was never the same. The latest was Japanese, the office laid out with shoji screens, bamboo flooring and seat cushions on the floor as well as standard furniture. Japanese art, including portraits, landscapes and elegantly etched figures of calligraphy, hung from the walls in minimalist fashion in keeping with the reverence that Japanese culture has for open spaces. The forty-six-story steel-and-glass structure of MacArthur-Rain's corporate headquarters was a gleaming showpiece as well, dominating the Houston skyline from all angles.

"You understand why I'm telling you this, of course."

"No, I don't."

"Because men like us understand opportunity, know how to take hold of it when it's presented to us."

"There is no us. There's you and there's me, and that's the way it's going to stay."

"You didn't get where you are by turning away from the kind of opportunity I'm offering you, the kind of opportunity that will give you the liberty to appreciate things like Henri IV Dudognon and the money to buy them."

With that Delladonne tucked the Montblanc pen into Hanratty's shirt pocket.

Hanratty dropped it to the floor. "You can take your pen and your cognac and go to hell."

Delladonne laid his glass back on the desk. "If my offer wasn't generous enough, Mr. Hanratty—"

"I never read it."

"Then you can't know, can you?"

"I don't need to. Some of us are happy with what we've got and don't need million-dollar bottles of cognac to make us think we're better than we really are."

Delladonne's dark eyes brightened. "So you have heard of it."

"What?"

"Henri IV Dudognon. I never told you what it cost, but you knew."

"What's your goddamn point, Mr. Delladonne?" Hanratty posed, shifting anxiously in the chair.

"Simply that we're more alike than you think, just like I said. And if you'd read my offer, you'd understand how much I respect that. If you'd read my prospectus, you'd understand how vital your factories are to the security interests of this country."

"My jewelry factories," Hanratty repeated, realizing the sweat was making his shirt stick to the leather chair.

"That's right."

"But you can't tell me why."

"Classified, I'm afraid."

Hanratty nodded to himself. "You need my factories to build weapons. That's what this is about, isn't it?"

"I can't answer that question."

Hanratty's features flared anew. "You don't own this country, Delladonne. You may think you do, but it's a crock. You want to buy up every defense contractor in the country, go ahead. But leave my factories alone."

"I'd like you to reconsider. I'd like you to join me for a glass of Henri IV Dudognon," Delladonne said, extending Hanratty's snifter toward him again.

"I'm sure you would," Hanratty shot back, chest puffed out so his old-fashioned tank-style T-shirt pushed up against his white dress shirt. "How's it feel to have someone stand up to you, Mr. Delladonne? How's it feel to have someone tell you to go to hell?"

Delladonne slid back behind his desk. "There's nothing I can say to make you change your mind?"

"Not a fucking word," Hanratty said, rising slowly. He leaned over and plucked the Montblanc pen off the floor. "Think I'll keep this as a souvenir."

"Be my guest. But what a pity," Delladonne continued, shaking his head. "A truly sad day for all you've spent a lifetime building."

Hanratty started for the door along a thin stretch of sunlit flooring that made him feel as if he were clinging to the lone path through a wilderness. He stopped halfway there and swung round, something about Delladonne's tone gnawing at him. "What did you mean by that?"

"Check your BlackBerry. E-mail inbox."

Hanratty did, having trouble maneuvering his thick fingers about the tiny keyboard. Finally he found what he was looking for, turned rigid, broad shoulders shrinking.

"What, what the hell is *this?*"

"E-mails from your suppliers, coming in right on time."

"They're canceling our posted orders."

"Can you blame them? After all, your company's being investigated for violations of the Patriot Act. Rather serious charges."

"What in God's name have you done?"

"Nothing; you did it all yourself. But you'll have nothing to worry about, once the investigation clears you. Of course, in the meantime all your suppliers will be subpoenaed as well to see if they might be complicit in your activities. And your clients in the private sector will be informed of your status as a matter of course."

Hanratty stood there, trapped between thoughts. Outside, clouds swept over the sun, stealing his path to the door from him. He felt lost.

"I'm reducing my offer by one-third," Delladonne told him. "If the papers aren't signed in the next twenty minutes, I'm reducing it by another third. I want to make sure you understand that."

Hanratty remained motionless, silent.

Delladonne pulled the glass he'd poured for him away from the edge of the desk. "See, you should have joined me for a Henri IV Dudognon. There was never a doubt about how this was going to finish, only what side you were going to end up on." Delladonne held his stare at the man's hunched frame. Funny how he didn't look so big and broad anymore. "And you chose the wrong one."

Hanratty started to speak but got caught between breaths and ended up gagging. Then, choosing his steps carefully, he continued on to the ornate double doors that opened automatically at his approach.

"Don't forget to sign all four copies, Mr. Hanratty. You can keep the pen."

The doors closed after Hanratty had disappeared through them.

"Impressive," Clayton told Harm Delladonne, emerging from the darkest of the room's shadows behind an ornate pillar.

"The man's a true patriot. He just didn't know it. Now tell me about Goodwin."

"He's in some kind of rehabilitation center in San Antonio. Was found wandering the streets in Bahrain, just as we suspected. But the police took him to the British Embassy instead of ours. That was nine months ago, just before we last met."

"Nine months and you're only finding out about this now?"

"Took the British some time to realize his brain really is alphabet soup. Then more time passed while they put through the paperwork to get him out of the country, a predicament further complicated by the fact that it didn't take them long to realize he was an American citizen."

"So why not just transfer him to our embassy?" Delladonne asked.

"Because he wouldn't *say* he was American. Diplomatic protocols, you see. It's complicated."

"Wouldn't say," Delladonne repeated.

"Didn't say much at all, in fact, practically nothing. Other than to insist he didn't exist. Apparently it's an actual condition brought on by post-traumatic stress disorder. So he ends up in England and only then are arrangements made to transfer him back to an appropriate facility stateside."

"To Texas."

"A psychiatric hospital in New York first where they determined the cause of his PTSD. Then a facility in Florida, *then* San Antonio."

Delladonne inhaled deeply. "You're telling me your suspicions have been confirmed."

"We won't be getting anything more out of his head, if that's what you mean, sir."

Delladonne's dark eyes fixed on Clayton, not blinking. "You understand what you're saying here? You understand how vital the contents of his brain are to the future of this company and this country?"

"That's why I'm telling you personally, sir."

Delladonne sucked in another deep breath and let it out slowly. "But that same brain holds the seeds of our potential undoing, doesn't it?"

"It could, yes."

"Clearly an unacceptable risk. You understand?"

"I do, sir."

"Inform me when it's done, then."

"I will."

Delladonne started to turn away from him, then swung back. "And, Clayton?"

"Sir?"

"Erase his entire presence. As if he never existed."

"Who, sir?"

Delladonne smiled thinly.

16

East San Antonio, the Present

"Bad news, amigo," Pablo Asuna told Cort Wesley over the throwaway cell phone Masters had bought in Walgreens. "There's a price on your head."

"Juárez Boys or Mexican Mafia?"

"Take your pick. People are busing in to punch your ticket. Word is gun stores from here to El Paso are selling out of bullets."

"Guess I got my work cut out for me."

Cort Wesley's response to learning a bounty had been put out on him was to park Asuna's old Ford in the middle of East San Antonio's gang haven and look for a bar. When he'd grown up, this was a nice place to live. Hispanics mostly, many of them illegals having crossed over from Mexico, carving out their own modest slice of the American dream. When he'd gone inside five years ago, half the houses had grates on the doors and bars on the windows. Now all of them did.

Cort Wesley imagined living in fear, no one to call to report a drug deal going down or local boy being shot out of fear they'd be deported themselves. The gangs worked and lived here with impunity. Even the cops had programmed the streets out of their dash-mounted navigation devices.

Cort Wesley knew the thing about responding to a threat was not to show fear. The enemy thinks he's got you based on sheer numbers. Trick was to show the world the numbers didn't matter.

He found a bar on the east side in Windsor Oaks, home

to endless rows of dilapidated townhouses where the
gangs ran smack and recruited new bangers out of the
hopelessness. The bar was furnished with a pool table and
a half dozen customers who kept their eyes tipped downward over their warming brews or empty shot glasses.
The scent of stale beer rose from the rotting floorboards,
reminding him of how his clothes had smelled after the
beer can exploded in his grasp in Pablo Asuna's garage.

Cort Wesley fed eight quarters into the pool table's
slot, slammed it back in, and listened to the freed balls
rolling into position. He racked them, chose a cue and
sent the balls scattering across the table with a neat
break. One ball plunked into a side pocket and a second
rattled home in the corner.

He played both roles, stripes and solids, alternately;
even changing cues to better simulate actual competition.
He knew it was only a matter of time before word reached
the right people he was here, people who didn't keep to
themselves. Cort Wesley hoped it wouldn't take too long
because he really didn't like pool, and the waiting was
the worst.

Turned out it didn't take very long at all.

The door to the bar rattled open and five bangers came
in at once, fanning out through the smoke wafting in the
air. Weapons not out yet. Tough guys enjoying the process of making their point. Sneering and grinning and
letting him know their purpose. Probably waiting for him
to go for his gun, make the first move.

Cort Wesley listened to the clack of their footsteps, the
sounds as good as sights in the bar's murky lighting. He
reached down into the ball return to rerack for a fresh
game.

His hand came out with the Smith & Wesson 9 millimeter, firing at spots and shapes. He hit the first two
bangers in his sights with relative ease, then dove to the

floor and rolled to avoid the wild spray of bullets fired by the others.

Conscious of his dwindling bullets, he lowered his aim, felling another with shots to the leg and gut while a fourth ran for the door and the fifth dove behind the bar. Cort Wesley knew the fourth had made it out when a narrow plume of sunlight poured into the room, and turned his attention to the fifth.

He approached the bar with gun leading the way, ready in case the final banger popped up firing with the pistols he had glimpsed in both the kid's hands. Cort Wesley put two bullets into the murky mirror forming the bar's back wall. A sea of shattered glass sprayed downward, giving him the opening he needed to lunge over the bar and aim his Smith at a terrified kid who'd already shed his pistols. Gazing up at Cort Wesley in terror, pleading with his eyes.

"You tell your friends what happened, you hear?"

The kid nodded rapidly, still showing his hands.

"You tell 'em there's a lot more where that came from if they wanna come looking for me."

Cort Wesley backed away from the bar, eyes cheating for the door in case the final banger was lying in wait for him. He doubted it, but you could never be too careful. He was breathing hard, conscious of the stench of sulphur mixing with stale beer, wood rot and cigarette smoke.

Just as word had reached the streets about the price on his head, so it would now spread about what had happened to the first group come to claim it. In the life Cort Wesley Masters had chosen for himself, there was no running, no hiding, no negotiating. You were better than your enemies or you weren't. And if you weren't, you died.

Cort Wesley continued on, stepping over the first two

he'd shot. He slid through the door sideways; gun raised in case one of those perched at the bar had been a scout. But their eyes remained uniformly fixed away from him.

He stepped into the hot sun, grateful for the once-over it gave the cold clamminess that had settled over his skin. He thought about Caitlin Strong, standing in a similar bar in El Paso, ready to draw on him. Nothing like that today, the final banger nowhere to be seen and long gone by now.

His throwaway cell phone rang. Cort Wesley snatched it to his ear and recognized one of Pablo Asuna's numbers from the caller ID.

"Yeah," he greeted.

"Busy?"

"Not anymore."

"That's good, amigo. 'Cause I found your Texas Ranger for you."

17

SURVIVOR CENTER, THE PRESENT

Clayton sat in the second seat of the Expedition, checking off the names on the list before him. Seven patients inside, in addition to Peter Goodwin. A night janitor and a charge nurse. No other center personnel would be present this late, the building buttoned up for the night.

A six-man team accompanying him might have seemed like overkill, but Clayton preferred it for the precision and speed it allowed. In and out in under five minutes. Nobody left alive inside when they were done.

Just a simple night's work.

Caitlin sat by her husband's bedside, chair pressed close enough to the rails for her to reach right through them and touch him. She'd been moving herself closer with each session. But the closer she got, the more it hurt, bringing back memories of the distance that had grown between them before Peter had left for Iraq.

Peter's sleep cycles were a random mess, when he slept at all. His torturers had clearly used sleep deprivation among just about every other terrible technique, and the result was to throw his body clock permanently off-kilter. Peter existed, he didn't live, and the treatment aimed at bringing him back into the world was about changing that by restoring first his understanding, and then his quality of life.

But Caitlin hadn't returned to the center at midnight to continue that process. She'd come back late because the cloud of shock had cleared enough to make her think like a Texas Ranger again. Disable the camera in his room, and no one would ever know what she raised with Peter tonight. She could work unencumbered by fear that Rita Navarro or someone else might eavesdrop on their session and question why her words sounded more like interrogation than treatment.

She'd reviewed all the documents that had accompanied Peter to the center a dozen times now. He'd been found in Bahrain, where Caitlin assumed the torture that had so damaged his mind and body had occurred. So he goes to Iraq to build a cable television grid and ends up killed in an IED explosion. No remains to be sent back, very sorry for your loss.

So what was the army, or whoever else, covering up? Why not just tell Caitlin the truth, that he had disappeared and was feared kidnapped? Perhaps they were expecting a ransom demand that never came.

That, though, begged the question: what did Peter know worth torturing him over?

Cort Wesley passed the Survivor Center for the sixth time on foot. His mind locked on the first glimpse he'd gotten of Caitlin Strong. Turning around from a table in an El Paso bar to the sight of patrons scattering and a woman wearing the badge and Stetson of the Texas Rangers standing twenty feet before him, jacket hitched back to reveal the butt of a squat SIG Sauer pistol in its unsnapped holster. Her fingers danced in the air over it, form-fitting jeans hanging low over her boots. Cort Wesley was a good shot, but had never been in a position to have an outcome determined by the quickness of his draw. Even then, that's not what stopped him from answering her challenge. No.

What stopped him was the woman's eyes wanting him to do it, *begging* him to do it. Cort Wesley looked into those eyes and knew if he obliged her, she'd shoot him down, emptying her gun in the time it took him to find his trigger.

His mind kept flashing back to the long moment that passed while he decided whether to go for his gun or not. Caitlin Strong looked at him like she knew that, knew what lurked in the deepest depths of his soul just as she knew there was no way he could draw and fire before she put a bullet between his eyes.

In that instant of hesitation, Cort Wesley realized she had beaten him in a way no one had ever beaten him before and stole five years of his life in the process. He needed to take something just as precious from her in order to go on. Otherwise, the anger would keep festering until it chewed his insides into shoe leather.

The tail Pablo Asuna had put on Caitlin Strong had

followed her here, called Pablo to report once she'd entered the building. Cort Wesley didn't bother asking himself what the hell she was doing at a place like this because he didn't care. Whatever it might have been was going to end real soon anyway.

The woman had framed him. Putting a bullet in her head was just payback for five years stolen away, memories whittled from his making until there was nothing left to hold onto anymore. The new memories would start tonight with the past vanquished. Might not be much of a future, but Cort Wesley couldn't worry about that until Caitlin Strong fell just like the three he'd left in the bar.

Except he'd never killed a woman before, not even once. He tried to tell himself it didn't matter, that payback was payback. No reason to look at things any deeper than that. No reason to feel all stiff and knotted up over something that should have been much simpler than he was suddenly making it.

Cort Wesley was about to head inside the building when the doors to a black Expedition opened, forcing him to continue on down the street.

18

SURVIVOR CENTER, THE PRESENT

"It's time," Clayton said, dropping his notepad to the carpeted floor before him.

His men moved in eerie rhythm, the simplest moves, like opening the Expedition's doors, seeming synchronized. They'd been over the building's schematics and each knew his part. Clayton never rehearsed his missions.

Rehearsing got men dependent on everything being where they expected it to be. He preferred to choose the right men and let the circumstances dictate the precise order of their actions.

The simplicity of this operation defied the brutality it called for. But he had to cover his tracks and covering his tracks meant making this look like a gang strike. Something senseless and territorial instead of the carefully executed plan it actually was.

Appearances *were* everything, Clayton thought, as he climbed out of the Expedition with his men.

"Do you remember them hurting you?" Caitlin asked Peter, her hands squeezing the bed rails to still their trembling.

"No."

"Do you remember talking to me yesterday? We talked about the people who hurt you somewhere far away from here."

"Where?"

"A hot place where the sun burned your skin as soon as it touched it."

"I don't remember the sun."

"It burned your face. It must have come through a window when they wanted it to and burned your face."

"I don't remember it burning me."

"That's all right."

"I remember the cold. I remember it wouldn't go away no matter how much I wanted it to."

"Good, Peter."

Caitlin had been addressing him by name more frequently, an attempt to get him to accept his own identity. Just a small thing, but success in treating disorders like Cotard's was about stringing lots of small things together.

During the grueling months spent completing a two-year master's program in sixteen months, she had never once come across Cotard's syndrome specifically. In principle, though, it was similar in symptom and treatment to any number of disassociative personality disorders. Caitlin had done her thesis on schizotypical behavior in war veterans, and some of them had presented with symptoms similar to Peter's. The key, she had learned from the case studies, was to poke and prod such patients. Forcing them to confront too much at once risked making them withdraw even further from reality.

"Why'd you call me that?" Peter asked suddenly.

"It's your name," Caitlin managed.

"I don't have a name. You have to be alive to have a name."

"Were you ever alive?"

"Everyone was alive once."

"Can we talk about what that felt like?"

"Why?"

"I thought you might want to."

"I don't," Peter said, agitation beginning to flare slightly on his features.

"What about someone you remember?"

"I remember you."

"From yesterday."

"And the day before."

"Go back further, to when you were cold."

Caitlin decided to take a chance, even more glad she'd deactivated the camera in Peter's room for this session. She reached over and touched his shoulder, thumb pressed lightly into one of his two torn rotator cuffs.

Peter flinched, jerked away from her.

"Tell me about the cold."

"You weren't there. The ones who were didn't have faces."

"They wore masks?"

"They didn't have faces. I remember their voices."

"What did they sound like?"

"You."

"They were women?"

"They didn't have faces."

"But they sounded like me."

"Yes."

"They spoke English well?"

"Like you."

"Did they have accents, like Arabs?"

"Arabs?" Peter asked with an utterly blank stare, as if that word wasn't present in his revised vocabulary.

"Their accents."

"No, no accents. Like you."

"Like me."

Peter nodded. "Americans."

The black Expedition was still parked in front of the Survivor Center when Cort Wesley circled back up the block. He angled for the building entrance, his steps feeling slow and labored. It didn't seem to be getting any closer as he moved, like the sidewalk had turned into a treadmill, an endless concrete ribbon with no beginning or end.

A stoplight turned green in an intersection up ahead and a small pack of cars slid forward, forcing him to turn away from the spill of their headlights. When they were past him, Cort Wesley palmed his Smith & Wesson and started across the street.

19

SURVIVOR CENTER, THE PRESENT

Clayton's team had moved straight to the building's main entrance. Black specters that looked like fissures in the night instead of motion through it.

The six of them with Clayton leading the way had the lock popped and door resealed in less than five seconds from leaving the Expedition. They headed down the short entry hall purposefully, approaching the charge nurse seated behind a reception desk.

"Can I help—"

Clayton fired a silenced pistol shot into her forehead before she could finish. Impact forced her and her chair backward against the now blood-splattered wall. She bounced off it and flopped forward, coming to rest face-down on her desk blotter and exposing the gaping hole in the back of her skull.

Clayton heard a mechanical buzzing sound, a floor polisher probably, and pointed to the right down a hallway. Two of his men slid down it, hugging the wall, stopping at an open door. Clayton heard "Hey!" before one of them let loose with a burst from his submachine gun, sound suppressor affixed to its barrel.

In his mind, Clayton checked off the charge nurse and night janitor, the only two people in the center other than the eight patients on the second floor, including their prime target. The man he'd designated previously remained down here to secure the floor, while Clayton led the others for the stairs.

. . .

"Americans," Caitlin repeated. "Do you remember any of their names?"

Peter's eyes pulled off her, as if trying to escape whatever the fleeting memory had conjured up.

"Peter, please, try to help me. Do you remember any of their names?"

He fixed his eyes on the blinds drawn over the window, growing more distant. Caitlin walked around to the other side of the bed, back in his line of vision.

"Names, Peter. Try to remember the names."

"What names?" he posed fearfully, as if just awaking from another nightmare.

"Of the Americans."

"Americans . . ."

"Where it was cold."

Peter shivered and looked away from her again, giving Caitlin time to leave him in peace and process what she had learned.

She had assumed the obvious: that Peter's capture by radical Islamic terrorists had been covered up by his employers, since a death had less broad ramifications than a kidnapping. But the facts, the means of his torture, had never really supported that conclusion and now she understood why.

Because it was *Americans* who had tortured Peter.

Cort Wesley opted against using the main entrance. The building's rear opened into a shallow side street used only by service vehicles. He'd never been good at picking locks but a single thrust of his elbow cracked a window through its weathered wood frame. Cort Wesley cleared the shards away, unlocked the door from the inside, and eased it open.

Pistol in hand again, he stepped inside and moved

down the center's darkened back hall, a familiar scent reaching him. Relatively thin in the air but present all the same:

Gun smoke. He'd grown up with that smell, knew it better than he knew his own sweat.

Cort Wesley bypassed the elevator for the stairwell, saw a man in black standing vigilantly before it. On post. A military man wielding a military-style submachine gun with a silencer.

What the fuck?

Cort Wesley figured he should turn tail and retrace his steps out of the building. Whatever was happening was none of his affair, and the last thing he needed was a run-in with the kind of guys who wore their body armor to bed. But the man on post before him wasn't wearing any now; that much was obvious through his shooter's vest with pockets and tabs for extra ammo.

Cort Wesley started to back up, pistol still palmed, when the man in black turned his way.

20

SURVIVOR CENTER, THE PRESENT

Clayton waved his men past him down the second-floor hallway, the four of them fanning out toward the six rooms on either side, eight of which were currently occupied. His intelligence did not include the precise room where Peter Goodwin could be found, because it didn't matter. This wasn't supposed to look professional. Kill one person and the questions start flying. Kill everyone and people tend to dwell less on the answers beyond somebody with a cause or a political point to make.

Clayton watched as his men peeled off into the first four doorways in the last instant before the shooting began.

Pffffft . . . pffffft . . . pffffft . . .

The sound broke Caitlin's trance and for just a moment she thought she might have dragged it with her from her mind and memory.

Pffffft . . . pffffft . . . pffffft . . .

She recognized that sound, just as she knew such recognition was impossible. Had to be a television blaring suddenly, one of the torture victims on the hall switching on a movie after awaking suddenly or being unable to sleep. She chose to believe that because the alternative was unthinkable.

Pffffft . . . pffffft . . . pffffft . . .

Maybe not so unthinkable after all, Caitlin thought, hand dipping for her ankle holster.

The next instant found the SIG in her hand and the instant after she was at the door, back pressed against the near wall. She heard footsteps now, light and professional. The footsteps were closing, leaving her little time.

Pffffft . . . pffffft . . . pffffft . . .

Caitlin glanced out into the hallway and spotted the security mirror perched on the wall at the far end, giving up a view of three dark shapes twisting out of doorways with silenced smoking submachine guns in hand.

Her dad Jim Strong had always said he could teach her how to shoot with anyone, but neither he nor anyone could teach her instinct. The part of you that takes over your actions and determines their course without the intervention of rational thought.

So Caitlin was never actually conscious of lurching into the hallway with SIG rising. Her last conscious thought was of the positions of the three men as suggested by the mirror.

The first man turned out to be nearly upon her and she fired into his throat, showering the hallway with blood as he slammed up against the wall. The SIG's roar came in sharp contrast to the silenced submachine guns, but she had the element of surprise on her side long enough to drop the other two men with a blistering series of six shots, missing with only one, which ricocheted off a red exit sign.

A fourth figure whirled out from the far end of the hall, a black blur amid the darkness. He was sighting in on her when Caitlin emptied the last of her clip into him, even as a fifth figure dove out from a room fifteen feet down.

Caitlin spun back into Peter's room, feeling chips of the door frame chewed free by bullets shower her while more bullets thudded into the wall. The fact that they hit a stud was probably the only thing that saved her, her consciousness just now accepting the reality of what was happening.

She slammed Peter's door shut and dove headlong for the chair upon which her handbag, with a spare magazine inside, rested. The door had a single view plate window at eye level but no lock on the inside.

Caitlin snapped the fresh magazine home and was about to say some words of comfort to Peter. But he had lain back in bed, staring at the ceiling without fear or even awareness of what was going on around him. What was there to fear from killers, after all, if you already believed you were dead?

．　．　．

Cort Wesley didn't fire first, thinking he could still get out of this without gunplay. But a burst from the posted guard's silenced submachine gun chased him into a doorway. He twisted the knob and, finding it locked, spun back out with Smith blazing.

The guard, of course, could never have expected such a maneuver, could never have expected him to be armed in the first place. Cort Wesley caught him dead to rights, putting round after round into the guard until he finally doubled over backward in a heap.

His own shots mixed with the echoing din of a fresh barrage coming from the floor above him. That more than anything spurred him on toward the stairs instead of back out through the door. Attracted to the sounds of gunshots and battle like a drunk to a shot and a beer.

Maybe God Himself had delivered this opportunity to him, providing justice in an unjust world. It was like getting a free shot, a bonus round.

Cort Wesley mounted the stairs softly, but quickly, jamming a fresh magazine home into his Smith, almost wishing it wasn't going to be so easy.

21

SURVIVOR CENTER, THE PRESENT

The loud cracks of pistol fire from downstairs told Clayton his whole operation had gone to shit. Gunmen on both floors appearing out of nowhere. Phantoms dropping out of the sky.

The primary target was still perched behind a closed door thirty feet away, and Clayton signaled the lone survivor of his team to hold until he drew even. They'd take Goodwin's room together, firing at anything and everything that moved. Spray sixty shots in a neat arc and take their chances from there.

Clayton backpedaled, keeping his gaze peeled back down the hall in anticipation of the first-floor phantom's approach. The whole mess felt random, not orchestrated. He hadn't walked into a trap so much as badly miscalculated factors he could not possibly have considered. The mission remained all that mattered; success and escape different sides of the same coin.

Clayton reached his surviving team member and together they slid across the wall toward the closed door of Peter Goodwin's room.

Caitlin had pulled Peter down off the bed and pushed him beneath it. He didn't question or protest, just looked confused and then terrified, flashback memories of pain inflicted in another room far away triggered.

"It's okay," Caitlin told him, gaze holding on the door. "I'm here this time."

Peter stirred under the bed. She heard him whimpering.

The sound filled her with fresh anger and resolve. Caitlin had no doubt that whatever was happening now was connected to the terrible suffering he had endured. Add that to the awful reality that the men she was killing had slain the other innocent torture victims on the hallway, and it wasn't too hard for her to find the same steely place inside her that had surfaced in Juárez and El Paso nearly five years before.

Caitlin saw a shadow cross the door's view plate,

counted out a long breath and opened up with her SIG. Four shots, blowing out the window just as the shape she'd spotted would have crossed it. She thought she might have heard a gasp, but wasn't sure.

Then a fusillade of fire blew into the room, muzzle flashes lighting up the darkness through the shattered view plate. Caitlin rolled under the bed to join Peter, as flecks of tile and plaster smacked her face and arms.

Clayton watched his final man go down, clutching his head. Just a graze to the top of his skull, a lucky shot landed when he hadn't ducked enough to get all the way beneath the view plate.

Clayton knew it wasn't life threatening, just as he knew the man was now useless to him and couldn't be moved. Hesitating not at all, he put a single round into the back of his skull, watched him jerk once and still. Then Clayton snapped a fresh magazine home into his submachine gun and burst through the door firing.

Caitlin heard the soft clacks of the suppressed gunfire and felt the rattle of the bullets chewing up wall and window. Lying prone on the floor, she had her SIG aimed straight for the doorway now occupied by the gunman's legs.

Caitlin fired and kept firing, rolling outward to steady her kill shot even as her target hit the floor looking like his legs had been yanked out from under him and hit the wall hard. She stopped rolling free of the bed and steadied the pistol on a figure heaving for breath over two legs punched full of blood-soaked holes by her bullets. He was struggling to resteady his submachine gun when she fired.

Click.

It happened to the best of them, her dad had always said, losing track of how many bullets were left in a gun. Lousy luck for it to happen to Caitlin now for the first time.

The gunman looked at her sneering, angling his submachine gun on line under the bed to kill Peter first. Caitlin yanked her husband's terrified form out from beneath it, shielding him with her body, pushing both of them backward across the tile.

Clayton couldn't believe what he was looking at, the surprise almost enough to drown out the pain from his ruined legs. A ghost from the past come back to haunt him. Be nice to finish the job he should've finished years before. Just pull the trigger and watch the problems then and now disappear in dual blood plumes.

Simple as that.

Caitlin had just launched herself at the gunman, hoping maybe the gun would jam or he was out too, when the shot rang out. Anomalous since the unsuppressed roar was that of a clunky 9 millimeter, like a Beretta or Smith & Wesson.

Halfway to the gunman, she realized his face had slumped to his chest and the right side of his head was lost in a blood pool of gristle and gore. Then she looked up toward a shadow stretched across the doorway.

Cort Wesley couldn't say why he had done it exactly. It all happened so fast, the decision half made before he even steadied the gun from just beyond the doorway.

Did he know what he was doing, whom he was saving? Probably. Yes.

Did he understand why he'd come up to the second floor instead of fleeing himself in the first place? No.

So here he was, looking down on the Texas Ranger who had almost begged him to draw five years ago and then put him away on a frame. The Smith twitched in his hand, trying to think for itself.

Caitlin recognized Cort Wesley Masters from the floor, nothing she could do but freeze. Their eyes met and held, neither of them breathing. She glanced at his pistol, stopped somewhere between the floor and her.

Masters looked one last time at the man he had killed, then turned and walked off as the scream of sirens finally blared through the night.

22

Survivor Center, the Present

Caitlin was sitting on the curb outside the center when Captain D. W. Tepper of the Texas Rangers pulled up in a three-truck convoy that sliced through the police, rescue and media vehicles parked everywhere, choking the street. She watched a half-dozen Rangers climb out, wearing their Stetsons and long coats to ward off a light mist that was dragging a cold front behind it, and move across the sidewalk.

Her hair wet with the light rain and clothes still damp with sweat, Caitlin sat shivering as the Rangers, some toting their 12 gauges, fanned out along the building's front, looking like towering sentinels in the murky light spray from street lamps and headlights. Tepper entered the Survivor Center with three of the Rangers lugging evidence kits, only to emerge alone minutes later, boots kicking the mist aside as he made his way toward Caitlin.

He took a seat on the curb next to her, grimacing from the effort. "Governor wants us running point for a time," he reported, lighting up a Marlboro. The match threw an eerie glow across his face, exaggerating its suddenly ashen tone.

"I was at the scene after a nutcase named George Hennard crashed his pickup truck into Luby's Cafeteria in Killeen and then shot up twenty-two folks eating their lunch. I was one of the first inside of the Branch Davidian complex in Waco, ran point on the investigation. And I scouted the Davis Mountains on horseback in '97 when we went up against another whacko who proclaimed his land the Republic of Texas." Tepper looked up and Caitlin gazed at the gaunt, leathery face beneath his Stetson. "What I just saw inside was bad as any of those." He shook his head. "Two staff members, seven patients, and seven perps dead . . . looks like a goddamn slaughterhouse."

"They weren't whackos or nut jobs this time, Captain. And they were only after one of the patients."

"Which patient would that be?"

"Peter Goodwin. My husband, Captain."

Tepper looked at her and tossed his Marlboro into the gutter. "Man can't enjoy nothing these days. Folks who run the center know that?"

"Nope." Caitlin stopped and took a deep breath. "I suspect I wouldn't have been on the case if they had and Peter be dead now for sure."

"You gunned down all seven?"

"Just four."

"Math's off a bit."

"Leader took out one of his own and Cort Wesley Masters took out the man downstairs and the leader."

Tepper took off his Stetson and let the mist wash into his face. "Come again?"

"Shot the son of a bitch in the head as he was about to shoot me."

Tepper slapped the water from his hat and fitted it back on. "Fine mess indeed."

"Peter'll need protection. Whoever sent these men'll send more. That's for sure too."

"He'll be at the hospital by now. I'll post two men on twenty-four guard."

"Rangers?"

"Only kind I know." Tepper slid a bit closer. "We don't have to talk about this here, you don't want to."

"Best to sort it out while it's still fresh, Captain."

"That's quite a story," Tepper said, when she was finished.

"Wish it wasn't all true."

"So you got no idea who did this to him."

"Americans was all he said. But it's a safe bet whoever they are, they're the ones came for him tonight."

"With guns blazing." Tepper shook his head, hacked up some spittle he deposited in the gutter near his Marlboro. "Goddamn massacre in there's what it is. The men you gunned down were pros, Caitlin, army types by the look of things. Mercenaries at the very least."

"Kill the others to cover their tracks. I'm not there, nobody knows the difference."

"'Cept you were and now we do."

"Thanks to Cort Wesley Masters."

"You sure he wasn't with them, maybe had a change of heart?"

Caitlin weighed Tepper's question. "He had a change of heart all right, Captain. I'm guessing he came here gunning for me."

"Maybe he saves your life so he can take it himself later."

She shook her head. "I don't think so."

"Why?"

"Can't say exactly. Just a feeling I got."

"San Antonio local boys tell me they got a bar on the east side all shot up with two corpses and one shot-up gang-banger inside. They make Masters for it."

"Anybody talking?"

"Do they ever?"

Tepper cocked his gaze back toward the Survivor Center, the red wash of the police and rescue lights seeming to nest in the crevices lining his face. Cameras flashed and whirred, and reporters jockeyed for position on the sidewalk and street.

Tepper shook his head, looked as if he'd just swallowed something bad. He glanced back at Caitlin, then lifted something from his pocket and laid it down on the sidewalk between them.

Caitlin recognized it as her Ranger ID holder, Jim Strong's actually, she'd left on the desk of Tepper's temporary replacement when she quit. "What's this, Captain?"

"Your badge is inside, Ranger."

"Only God can make miracles."

"You made a deal to resign to spare the Rangers the embarrassment of an investigation. When I got back, I put it down as a leave of absence. I think it's time the leave ended. Provisionally, 'course, so I can't offer you a stipend, even money for gas or bullets."

Caitlin opened her dad's ID holder, caught the dull glimmer of her badge inside. "Why you doing this?"

"'Cause I know I can't stop you from doing what you're gonna do. That badge might open some doors that be closed otherwise, lend a little credence to your calling."

"Thank you, Captain," Caitlin said, and pushed herself up off the sidewalk.

Tepper tried to follow, failing until Caitlin lowered a hand to hoist him back to his feet.

"See," he said, "sometimes we all need a little help."

PART THREE

Texas' deadliest outlaw, John Wesley Hardin, a preacher's son reputed to have killed thirty-one men, was captured in Florida by Ranger John B. Armstrong. After Armstrong, his long-barreled Colt .45 in hand, boarded the train Hardin and four companions were on, the outlaw shouted "Texas by God!" and drew his own pistol. When it was over, one of Hardin's friends was dead, Hardin had been knocked out cold, and his three surviving friends were staring at Armstrong's pistol. A neat round hole pierced Armstrong's hat, but he was uninjured.

—Mike Cox, with updates from the Texas Ranger Hall of Fame and Museum, "A Brief History of the Texas Rangers"

23

HOUSTON, THE PRESENT

Harmon Delladonne had taken over his father's house, as well as his business. A 15,000-square-foot Georgian mansion located in the plush suburbs of River Oaks with ten bedrooms and twelve baths. He only used one of each, almost always alone, except on nights when mood and circumstance required company. And company meant an exclusive escort service with no questions asked.

Delladonne had time for sex; he had no time for love or romance. His father had introduced him to the world of prostitutes, just as he had introduced him to the world of business. Prostitutes on his twenty-first birthday, business, at least real business, shortly after that.

They were both in New York City in 1993 during the first attack on the World Trade Center. Father and son had rushed to the scene drawing as close as the police barricades allowed. The horror and fear were palpable in the air. Harm Delladonne could never remember seeing so many anxious, crying people.

But his father seemed to revel in it, his eyes gleaming in the glow of the constant swirl of revolving lights. He could barely keep down his smile.

"This is just the beginning," he said, as much to himself as to his son. "More attacks are coming, increasing in scale, until one day the world will change. That's what we have to be ready for. When the time comes, and this country needs what we have to offer, we're going to be there."

Harm stood by his father's side through dozens of acquisitions that brought MacArthur-Rain to the forefront of the then-nonexistent business of global security. He thought Franklin Delladonne had lost his mind, leveraging all the company's assets to buy up soft- and hardware companies, along with as many oil industry offshoots as he could get his hands on. He never listened to Harm's ideas or suggestions, even the discovery Harm was most proud of. First thing he'd commissioned on his own, and his father shot it down without so much as a demonstration.

"Just do what I tell you," his father told him. "Listen and learn."

Then 9/11 came and the listening and learning were over.

Almost overnight MacArthur-Rain was transformed into the government's ultimate go-to global conglomerate, having positioned itself with a virtual monopoly in areas of security and surveillance no one else had even considered. Franklin Delladonne's vision had made that all possible, but a stroke killed him prior to it being fully realized, leaving Harm to pick up where he left off.

And so he did, more ruthlessly and ambitiously than his father ever imagined. Never entrusted with any true responsibility by Franklin Delladonne while he was alive, Harm tried to prove his father wrong now that he was dead. By the time potential competitors reinvented themselves, MacArthur-Rain had gained an insurmountable advantage that rendered that competition nothing more than prime fodder for additional acquisitions. Every one of these was greeted with a like level of obsession by Harmon Delladonne, who knew even the smallest investment could lead to huge returns in the future. And under his stewardship, MacArthur-Rain positioned itself as the only company capable of so many things that the government seldom bothered to look elsewhere. It had been so long since they actually needed to submit a bid, that Harm to a great extent had forgotten how the process worked, thanks to the mutually dependent relationship he had forged with those who truly wielded power in Washington.

"MacArthur-Rain," his father had said suddenly to him, just days before his death. "Where does the name come from?"

"You never told me when I asked you."

"I wanted you to figure it out for yourself."

"What's the difference?"

His father had glared at him. "The difference is a vision that will not just usher our company into the future, it will also give us control *over* that future."

"Tell me, please."

"Figure it out for yourself."

To this day Harm Delladonne never had. He'd just dismissed his prostitute for the night, and was considering the origins of the company name for the first time in a while, when his phone rang. He snatched it from his bedside, expecting Clayton to be on the other end. Then he saw the ten zeroes projected in the caller ID and knew otherwise.

"What happened?" he greeted.

"Turn on your television."

Still lying naked in bed, Delladonne hit a button on his remote and a fifty-inch plasma rose from inside the entertainment center across the room. He switched to a local channel picturing a chaotic scene on a street not far from the Alamo. Delladonne recognized the building pictured as the Survivor Center Clayton had targeted, the reporter droning on and trying to get an interview with an older man who looked like a walking corpse wearing a Stetson.

"Clayton and his men are all dead," the voice on the other end of the line told him.

Delladonne wondered if he was dreaming. "This was supposed to be a simple operation."

"No such thing."

"What happened?"

"We're still trying to ascertain that."

"Then fucking ascertain it and call me back."

Delladonne's private line rang again ten minutes later.

"A Texas Ranger was inside at the time."

"You're telling me *one* Texas Ranger took out seven men?"

"Not by herself."

"*Her*self?"

"Someone else was involved, to what degree we've been unable to determine. A man named Cort Wesley Masters."

"Is that supposed to mean something?"

"It does to me. We made good use of his skills ourselves during the Gulf War. He didn't know it, of course. If he still worked for us, he'd be the first person I'd call now that Clayton is out of the picture."

"Guess we'll have to look elsewhere then." Delladonne was breathing hard and sweating through his silk sheets. The room felt like a sauna to him, in spite of the air-conditioning.

"I'd recommend going out of country."

"I was just about to say the same thing to you."

"Clayton was good. I'm better. The man I'm talking about is the best. A Venezuelan, former colonel in Chavez's secret police."

"Then what are you waiting for?"

24

SAN ANTONIO, THE PRESENT

Caitlin came through the door to her condominium with gun drawn. "Get your hands in the air and stand up slowly."

"That the way you greet all the people who save your life?" Cort Wesley Masters asked her from an easy chair in the corner of the living room, staring into the barrel of her SIG.

"Do what I say and keep your hands where I can see them."

Cort Wesley rose slowly, hands stretching upward. Caitlin saw the pistol wedged into his belt and yanked it out, SIG steadied on him the whole time. Kept it that way as she backed off.

"Can I put my hands down now?"

"I haven't decided yet."

"Maybe you forgot about me putting a bullet in that guy's head a couple hours ago."

"Not exactly your intention when you came to the center, I'm guessing."

"You arresting me based on intentions?"

Caitlin laid Cort Wesley Masters's gun down on the kitchen island. The townhouse was simply and sparsely furnished, and she'd done nothing to change it since Peter's departure for Iraq.

"How about carrying an unregistered firearm."

"I'm not carrying it, you'd be dead."

"You can sit down now," Caitlin told him. She watched Masters retake his chair. Her gaze fell on the lamp he'd switched on alongside it. "Should have left the light off."

"Why? Then you wouldn't have known I was inside and I'd miss the fun of seeing you with your gun out again."

"I could have shot you."

"You didn't in El Paso."

"That was different."

"Sure was. You thought I was guilty back then. Now you know I'm innocent."

"The hell I do."

"DNA speaks, Ranger."

"Not to me."

Masters looked back at the pistol. "You wanna put that down?"

"Not particularly."

"Then keep my gun as a souvenir. I'm not carrying it, you'd be history now."

"That thought had crossed my mind."

Cort Wesley Masters stirred slightly in his chair. "Explains why you haven't shot me yet."

"You had a similar opportunity earlier tonight, as I recall."

"You seem determined to make me regret that choice."

"So here we are."

She flipped on the switch for the overhead ceiling fan-light combo, letting the two of them see each other clearly.

"You don't look much like a Ranger these days."

"That what you risked getting shot to tell me?"

"Nope, ask you something."

"What?"

"Why?"

"Why what?"

"Why you framed me."

"I didn't."

"Bullshit."

"Listen to me, Masters—"

"Call me Cort Wesley. I save a woman's life, it puts us on a first name basis."

"That what your friends call you?"

"Don't have any friends. Well, one maybe," Cort Wesley said, thinking of Pablo Asuna.

"First time anybody ever saved my life before."

"Lots of firsts happening lately."

"You kill those two men in the bar earlier today?"

"Could've killed all five, if I had a mind to."

"Sounds like that makes you proud."

"Nope. Did what I had to, like you tonight. Gunned down five by my count."

"Four and that was different."

"How?"

"They were trying to kill me."

"Likewise. And you still took out twice as many as me."

"Tell it to someone else, Masters—"

"Cort Wesley."

"—someone who doesn't know you set those poor assholes up like targets on a shooting range in that bar."

"Got a price on my head. What I did should make plenty more assholes think twice before gearing up. Might've saved more lives than I took."

"That's one way to look at it," Caitlin said, and holstered her weapon. She started for the liquor cabinet. "Gonna pour myself a drink. Can I offer you something?"

"Whatever you're having."

"Bourbon."

"Suits me just fine."

Caitlin poured a couple fingers of Jim Beam into two rocks glasses, added ice cubes, and brought Masters's glass over to him.

"Thanks, ma'am."

"You have a drink in that bar earlier today?"

"What do you think?"

"Nope." She dragged a chair across the wood closer to him; not too close, though. "Also think you came to the center to kill me tonight. Right or wrong?"

"Lucky for you I did, in the end."

"That doesn't answer my question."

"Maybe finish what we started in El Paso."

"I seem to recollect I started *and* finished things then."

"Caught me on a bad day."

"I wasn't having a great one either."

Cort Wesley sipped some Beam, stopped and sipped some more. "Wasn't me in the Chihuahuan that night, Ranger."

"Blood evidence said otherwise."

"Past tense."

"Depends who you ask."

Cort Wesley swirled the brown liquid around in his glass, liking its pleasant heat burning his throat on the way down. First drink he'd had since entering The Walls. "You expect me to believe you didn't frame me?"

"No more than you expect me to believe you weren't there the night Charlie Weeks got killed."

Cort Wesley half toasted her. "Think about it."

Caitlin slid her chair a bit closer, hitching her jacket back to make sure he could see her gun. "Oh, I have."

"I'm talking about me and a bunch of drug mules out of Juárez. This at the same time I was working toward eviscerating the Juárez Boys, Mexican mob and anybody else who moved on my bosses' territory."

"Eviscerating," Caitlin repeated. "Nice word."

"Learned it in the prison library."

"In between shankings, no doubt."

"Read my file or ask the bulls, Ranger. I was a model prisoner."

"A changed man."

"Wouldn't go that far."

"Don't know. Otherwise I'd be dead."

"Guess you could say the same thing for me," Cort Wesley said and downed the rest of his Beam.

Caitlin matched him with a single gulp.

"Shot for shot, Ranger?"

"It beats bullet for bullet."

"Booze instead of blood."

"Wise choice."

Caitlin thought about refilling their glasses, but didn't.

"So how many men you killed, Ranger?"

"One more if you'd drawn on me in El Paso, Masters."

Cort Wesley rolled the rocks glass around in his big powerful hands. Caitlin thought he looked ready to crush it. Their eyes met and Cort Wesley felt a flutter in his gut. He couldn't remember ever seeing a more beautiful woman in the ways that mattered most to him, Caitlin Strong making him ache in places he thought were long dead.

"Don't know how many I've killed," he told her. "There was the army and then there was after."

"And now?"

"There was always somebody pushing the buttons before. Now there's nobody."

"So I guess what happened in the bar today was an accident. Dropped your 9 millimeter and it happened to go off six times."

"Smiths been known to do that."

"Maybe you should ask for your money back. Then again, even in Texas convicted felons can't own pistols."

"Falsely convicted, I think you mean."

"You come here to catch up, Masters, I think we're caught up."

Masters rose, not quite as tall as he looked in Peter's doorway, but just as broad. "That's some pretty bad folks who're after you."

"Appreciate the concern, I really do."

Cort Wesley glanced at her Stetson, hanging atop a coat rack. "Think I would've made a good Ranger?"

"Hundred years ago maybe."

Her cell phone rang and Caitlin eased it to her ear after three rings, recognizing D. W. Tepper's number in the ID box.

"Home safe and sound, Captain," she said, staring up at Cort Wesley Masters.

"Got some news here for you, Caitlin."

"That's Ranger Strong to you."

"Then listen up, Ranger. Fingerprints on the corpse in your husband's room identify the man as Clayton, no first name and lots of soldiering in his background. Goddamn killing machine, near as I can tell."

"Seem to be a lot of them in my life lately, Captain," she said, as much to Masters as to Tepper.

"It gets better. We ran his blood and came up with a second interesting match."

"From?"

"The Chihuahuan desert the night Charlie Weeks got killed, Ranger. Clayton, no first name, was there."

25

LA VEGA, VENEZUELA, THE PRESENT

Only one of the church's double doors was open, and Guillermo Paz turned sideways so it could more easily accommodate his bulk as he entered. His long, thick hair had draped over his face, and he brushed it back with his hands to make himself more presentable. Then he rubbed his palms on his army fatigues to wipe off the grease, turning the fabric dark in splotchy patches across the thighs. Sometimes he wore a bandana to collect the oil that slid from his scalp like a leaky faucet to make his forehead look bright and shiny. But he had stowed the bandana in his pocket for this visit, wanting to present as formal an appearance as possible for a man wearing generic army olive drab pants and shirt he seldom washed, since obtaining spares to suit his massive size was all but impossible.

The church lay at the base of the hillside containing one of Caracas' hundreds of slums, the slum where Paz had spent the first thirteen years of his life until he killed his first man. The latter of those years were dotted by memories of lugging buckets of water or propane tanks from the foot halfway up the steep hill to what passed for a home in order that his sisters and brother could bathe, eat and use the toilet. His mother seemed pregnant more often than not, but Paz barely knew his father, a small-time thief who used the profits of his thefts to guzzle down warm beer in any bodega or bar that would have him.

It had been his father who brought Guillermo Paz into the Venezuelan underworld by introducing him to the local crime boss known only as Carnicero, Spanish for "butcher," thanks to what happened to those who crossed him. Paz started out as a pickpocket but quickly mastered robbing tourists at knifepoint. All the proceeds, of course, were handed over to Carnicero, nothing ever held back on penalty of losing a finger or worse.

Today, as he strode up the old church's center aisle, those memories seemed so distant as to belong to another man entirely. The church, on the other hand, was exactly as he remembered. A ramshackle, rectangular building with a cracked cross above the door and patchwork wood and shingles atop the roof where a steeple had once stood. The interior remained surprisingly clean and well kept, the pews bracketed into the floor so they couldn't be stolen for wood with which to burn or build. In slums like La Vega, men had died for far less. The inside of the church even smelled the same—of must, mold, old sweat and rotting planks from the uneven floor. Paz had never visited the confessional as a boy, so he followed his instincts to a small alcove on the right, the same route he followed when he'd killed another priest just a few days before in another church.

The door to the confessional was warped and a darker shade than the frame around it. Paz smelled sawdust and wood rot and thought back to the boyhood nights spent in his slum house listening to rain pinging against the tin roof and feeling sheets of it misting through gaps in the wood slats hammered over the cardboard walls.

Paz ducked under the frame and squeezed into the cramped cubicle.

"You there, Father?" he asked.

A shape shifted in the dark, matching cubicle next to his.

"Yes, my son."

"I grew up here, you know, in the slum up the hillside. There was another priest here back then. A gang shot him down in the street because he wouldn't give them the proceeds from the week's collection plate."

"Were you a member of that gang, my son?"

"No, I hadn't started my killing yet. I would have stopped it if I could. That priest was the one who taught me how to read. He was starting to teach me how to speak and read English when he was killed, so I had to finish that on my own."

Paz began peeling away the top layer of wood from the confessional's armrest with a fingernail. The old wood came off easily, revealing an unstained layer below. He remembered being dragged here by his mother as a young boy and passing the time by carving his name into the back of the pew before him. Before he was done forming that thought, he realized he had started digging a *P* into the surface.

"As a boy, when I wasn't reading I robbed tourists shopping in the outdoor markets," Paz told him. "Never brought a dollar home, though. I had to turn the money over to the local boss Carnicero, who gave me a few dollars now and then, said he was keeping the rest for me like a bank account. One day I went to get some money from him in the bar he used as an office because my mother was pregnant and needed a doctor. He just smiled, said no, and offered me a beer. So I reached into his pocket for the bills and he bent my finger back until it snapped. I took my knife out in my other hand and stabbed him. He died right there, bleeding all over me. But I took the money he owed me from his pocket before I left." Paz tried to flex his right hand. "The finger still hurts."

"I'm very sorry, my son."

"I ran away after bringing my mother the money and didn't come back to La Vega for a long time. She's dead now too. But that's not why I'm here today."

"Why are you here?"

"I was thinking about confessing something before I do it instead of after. Can you do that?"

"Only if you seek God's blessing."

"More like His understanding. Got an idea if I'm already going to hell, then what have I got to lose?"

"It is never too late to make amends, my son."

Paz finished the *P* and went to work on the *A*, staying with capital letters since they were easier to carve with his nails. "Here's the thing, Father: when is it permissible to do something bad, something ordinarily wrong?"

The priest hesitated. "In the defense of one's self or others, I suppose."

"What about in service to a nation?"

"You mean, as in war?"

"Say I do."

"History would say yes, it is permissible," the priest said with great effort, sounding honestly pained. "Are you a soldier, then?"

"In the sense that I serve Venezuela, yes, but I don't wear the uniform officially anymore."

"Venezuela is not at war, my son."

"I leave the definition of such things to other people. See, I recently killed a man who got me to thinking. He was a priest like you. Was stirring up people to make trouble for the government. Poor bastards didn't know any better. That's why they weren't part of my contract."

On the other side of the confessional, the priest's breathing picked up. Guillermo Paz could hear him shifting about, began to smell the perspiration rising off him.

"So you seek, what, penance, absolution, *forgiveness?*"

"More like permission. Killing that priest got me thinking about the things I do and why I do them, and I thought I had an obligation to at least try."

"Try what?"

"To see if God understands."

"God understands all. That does not mean He accepts."

"I have to burn a village," Paz said suddenly. "Destroy a lot of people's worlds, all they've ever known. Another pain-in-the-ass bleeding heart is making trouble. Spreading lies about the government and buying these people's loyalty by building them new homes and schools. I'm told an example must be made of him. I'm told I have to do it this way."

"And that troubles you?"

Paz added a straight line to complete the *A* and started in on the *Z*, his favorite as a boy since the letter looked like a lightning bolt. "What I'm thinking is that my village wasn't much different. I look up the very hillside outside this church and all of a sudden I'm thinking about being a kid again, what that must have felt like. But then I remember it didn't feel any different than it does now. So I'm worried if I follow my orders, the village's children will stand a pretty good chance of ending up like me."

"Children are sacred souls in the eyes of God, my son."

"See, that's my point. There was nothing sacred about my soul. Maybe if Carnicero had killed me instead, he would've been doing me a favor. Stopping me from doing all the things I've done afterwards. You see?"

"No."

"I burn this village, how many others am I sentencing to death? I'd be better off just killing them all. I don't care about being forgiven, absolved, saved or whatever else you wanna call it; I want to be understood."

"God's understanding makes it no less of a sin, my son."

"That's my other problem, Padre. Killing's not even one of the seven deadly sins. You'd think if it was so important, it would at least be listed."

"Thou shalt not kill is one of His commandments."

"So that makes one out of two. Definitely room for interpretation there. I never thought of these things until recently, and now I'm wondering when I'm finished with this village maybe I come back to La Vega and plant enough dynamite on the hill to bring the whole mess down. So I'm here to warn you to clear out so you don't get swallowed by a river of mud, blood and shit."

Silence followed, during which Paz inspected the letters of his name scrawled in the wood. Funny how they looked no different than the ones he used to carve into the pews as a young boy. He figured if he checked carefully enough, he might find those still there.

"Padre?"

"We're finished, my son."

"Yes, true enough."

"You must go."

"Right, same for you, Padre," Guillermo Paz said, starting to squeeze himself from the confessional. "Remember what I told you."

26

SOUTHWEST GENERAL HOSPITAL, THE PRESENT

Peter had been taken to Southwest General Hospital where a call from D. W. Tepper had arranged for a private, corner room to simplify the Rangers' task of keeping him safe. Caitlin knew neither of the men guarding Peter, but they seemed to recognize her and rose from chairs placed on either side of the open door at her approach. She flashed her ID and badge at the Rangers anyway, waited for them to inspect both before entering the room and closing the door behind her.

Peter was sitting up, the bed angled to support his back. He had a pillow behind his head and shoulders and was staring at a fuzzy television picture with the sound muted. He didn't regard Caitlin as she approached. When she reached his bedside, he looked at her suddenly and began to cower, melting away into the sheets.

"No, no, no!" he stammered, eyes filled with the same

hopeless fear she recalled from the Survivor Center the night before.

"It's all right," she said soothingly. "You're safe."

She stretched out her hand, but he recoiled against her touch, his skin clammy and electric as if charged with some kind of desperate energy.

Caitlin backed off slightly from the bed and waited until Peter's breathing and gaze had calmed. "I brought something for you," she said.

She lifted the laptop case from her shoulder, unzipped it, and removed her Dell.

"Do you know what this is?"

Peter eyes changed from fearful to quizzical, continuing to follow her actions with the bedcovers still drawn up past his chin.

"You used to work with these. You were an expert."

Peter eased the bedcovers down, exposing a chest scarred by the impressions of electrodes across his flesh. "Dell sucks. I work on a Mac."

"You remember?"

"Dell sucks. I work on a Mac."

Caitlin placed the laptop atop the wheeled assembly with rotating arm and switched it on. As Peter watched intently, she eased the laptop into position before him.

"I want you to look at me."

He kept his eyes on the computer.

"I want you to look at me, Peter."

He looked Caitlin's way.

"What do you remember about last night?" she asked him.

He began to cower again, yanking up the bedcovers anew.

"Look at me, Peter, look at me. You're safe. They're gone. The men who wanted to hurt you are gone. I'm here. I'm going to keep you safe."

He relented at last, relinquishing his tight grasp on the folded-over top sheet.

"Now tell me what you remember about last night. But don't close your eyes. Keep your eyes on me as you speak, so I can keep you safe."

"Loud," he said finally. "Scared."

"I brought you something else," Caitlin said and fished a shiny silver dollar from her pocket. "Do you still have your quarter, to remind you you're worth something?"

"No," Peter answered, without checking his pockets.

She placed the silver dollar on the stand and slid it alongside the laptop. "Good, because you're worth more than a quarter. That's why I brought you this silver dollar, to remind you of that."

Peter picked the silver dollar up, clung to it briefly, then stuffed it in the pocket of the robe he was wearing.

"You're actually worth a lot more than that silver dollar to me. I don't like it when someone worth a lot to me is hurt. It makes me mad. Does it make you mad?"

"Mad," Peter acknowledged, although it was unclear whether he was answering or just parroting her.

"It makes me mad and makes me want to hurt the ones who hurt the someone I care about."

Peter was studying the keyboard screen, tapping keys as if to test it out.

"I want you to help me hurt them. I want you to look into your mind and tell me what you see."

Peter's fingers worked the keyboard, stopped.

Caitlin repositioned herself to see the screen, now alive with a single word: AMERICANS.

"You told me that last night. How many?"

LOTS DIFFERENT

"Did they all wear masks?"

SCARY

Peter typed with his eyes on the fuzzy television

screen, finding a place in his mind where things somewhat worked.

"Do you remember anything else, something that might help me find them?"

Peter seemed to be considering her question, while still not regarding the Dell's screen. He typed the letter *N* for no followed by, BEFORE I DIED.

"Did they ask you questions before you died?"

DEAD PEOPLE CAN'T REMEMBER

"What do you remember about being alive?"

PAIN

"They hurt you."

HURT ME

"Because you wouldn't tell them what they wanted to know. The Americans."

HURT PETER SO HE WENT AWAY

"I thought he died."

NOT RIGHT AWAY HE WENT AWAY FIRST

"Where'd he go?"

SOMEPLACE THEY COULDN'T FIND HIM

"So Peter wouldn't have to answer their questions."

HE WENT AWAY

"Did he ever come back?"

NOT WHILE THEY WERE THERE WHEN THEY WERE GONE BEFORE HE DIED AND WENT AWAY

"Do you remember the questions they asked Peter?"

TELL US

"Tell them . . ."

TELL US

"What?" Caitlin asked, fighting to keep her voice calm. "Tell us what?"

HOW TO MAKE IT WORK HOW TO MAKE IT WORK HOW TO MAKE IT WORK HOW TO MAKE IT WORK HOW TO MAKE IT—

Caitlin reached across Peter and stilled his fingers.

They rested motionless on the keyboard, his gaze never once breaking from the muted television. Back in his fugue state, no longer cognizant of her words.

"I'm sorry, Peter," she said softly anyway, not looking for a response or even recognition anymore. "Sorry about what happened to you, sorry that I chased you away. I didn't mean to, but I know I did. All I can do now is make it up to you. Do you know how I'm going to do that?"

Peter's eyelids flickered and for a moment, just a moment, Caitlin thought he was about to respond. But he didn't.

"I'm going to find the people who did this to you. I'm going to find the people who tried to have you killed last night."

Peter's gaze had gone distant again, as if he were listening to different voices nobody else could hear. Caitlin leaned over the bed rail and kissed him lightly on the forehead.

"I'm gonna make them pay. For both of us."

27

THE WALLS, THE PRESENT

Cort Wesley never thought he'd ever return to The Walls, not of his own volition anyway. But there was a rookie gun bull he'd got on quite well with inside who came to Huntsville straight from a stretch in Iraq and Afghanistan. Not much more than a kid who'd seen the worst of things and finally let them get to him. Got out with an honorable that could have helped secure him a better job than prison guard in general and The Walls in particular.

The young man's name was Frank Durgen but the cons called him Frankie Cakes because of his fondness for sweets, especially store-bought cupcakes, leaving him with jowls that looked like a birth defect atop his otherwise chiseled frame. Frankie Cakes had seen the very worst of this Iraq war, just as Cort Wesley had the last. Difference was his work had brought him into contact with the kind of private contractors, little more than paid assassins really, for which the original Gulf War had had no use.

"Ain't this weird?" Frankie Cakes greeted him in the Visitor's Center, not sure what to make of his return to The Walls.

"What can I say?" said Cort Wesley. "I missed the food."

"And the sanitary conditions, course."

"Right as rain, podner."

He hadn't been able to get Caitlin Strong out of his head. Went back to his room at the Alamo Motel from her apartment and couldn't sleep for what little remained of the night. Opened the blinds and shifted the bed so there'd be light in his eyes, but that didn't help either since every time he closed them all he saw was her. Started thinking about him having had his boys with Caitlin Strong instead of Maura Torres, the thoughts spewing their own crazy visions that made him think he was coming down with a fever.

Cort Wesley couldn't remember the last time he'd had drinks with a woman and what they'd done last night certainly passed for that, even though neither had drank all that much Beam. Truth was, except in Maura's case, he'd never shared much beyond a bed with any woman, the difference with Maura being he'd given her kids and that was it. Last night had eclipsed anything he'd ever shared with a woman before, gunning down two to her four. Saving the life of a woman once determined to take his. Seeing her on the floor shielding the man she said was her husband, desperate and helpless. Her looking so vulnerable was as much reason why he'd walked off as any, almost like he'd strolled in on her naked.

Nope, Caitlin Strong wasn't leaving his head anytime soon.

Frankie Cakes leaned forward, crossing his arms over the table. "You looking for a job, Cort Wesley?"

"Just some info."

"Can't talk about nothing inside. You know that."

"The info's about outside. Way outside. Talking military here."

"We do have that in common."

"You hear about that center got hit in San Antone last night?"

"Survivors of torture, something like that, yeah."

"I was there."

Frankie Cakes stiffened a bit, even his bulbous jowls seeming to tighten. "You here to claim your old bunk back, that it?"

"Nope. I was on the right side of things this time."

"Now that seems a whole bit peculiar."

"Don't it ever, podner. But it's the truth all the same. You want the details?"

"You always been straight up with me, Cort Wesley. No need."

"Some you need to hear. Like how a bunch of hacksaw military types gunned down seven torture victims in their beds. Real act of bravery, I'll tell ya."

"What's this got to do with me?"

"Where would you find men like that if you needed them?"

Frankie puckered his lips. "Not sure I'm comfortable answering that question."

Cort Wesley leaned across the table, close enough to Frankie Cakes to make him flinch, stealing his space from him. "Remember who you're talking to here, Frankie."

"Lots of places." Frankie Cakes pulled back as much as he could and looked around the room. "Some not much different than right here. Men ain't much different neither, 'least the ones I had occasion to work with."

"You still got friends in, right?"

"You talking about the military, I wouldn't exactly call 'em friends."

"People you can call, people maybe owe you a favor or two, just like you owe me." Cort Wesley stopped, his eyes saying the rest.

"Help you any way I can, Cort Wesley," said Frankie Cakes, clearly displeased with the prospects.

Cort Wesley sat back again. "Good. Got a name for you: Clayton."

"That it?"

"All you need to know right now. I want you to ask around, see what you can find." Cort Wesley extended his hand across the table and shook Frankie Cakes's. "I know you won't disappoint me, podner."

"Do the best I can."

The two of them standing up now, eye-to-eye with each other.

"Just make sure it's enough, Frankie."

Cort Wesley was barely outside The Walls when he dialed a number on his throwaway cell phone.

"Who is this?" came Caitlin Strong's greeting.

"Guess."

"Masters?"

"Didn't even need three tries."

"I'm hanging up."

"Then you won't find out what I got to tell you. About your friend Clayton." He listened to Caitlin Strong breathing on the other end. "Come on, Ranger, meet me for coffee. I'm buying. Make us square for the drinks last night."

"Not necessary."

"Okay. You can buy."

"You got something I really want to hear?"

"Cost you a coffee to find out."

"I've lived to regret less, Masters."

"Good. Then you won't be disappointed."

28

VENEZUELA, THE PRESENT

Guillermo Paz stood before the crumbling frame of the village's new schoolhouse as the flames crackled and hissed. Around him, the seven men who had accompanied Paz on this operation poked and prodded the villagers to keep them in a tight pack. The villagers could do nothing but watch in shock and dismay as the new buildings erected on their behalf slowly burned to the ground.

His orders were to burn *everything*: their ramshackle shanties, storage huts and meeting places too. But Paz couldn't find the sense in that. After all, those structures had been in place long before the bleeding hearts arrived spreading their false message of hope with lumber and construction plans, along with the promise of electricity and satellite dishes in the future. So he'd only burned what was new and thus the reason for his coming.

You're an ungrateful lot, he wanted to shout at the desperate mass of humanity consumed by their own weakness. *Don't you see what I have done for you? I could just as easily have left you with nothing but the mountains for refuge, even had you all shot as you stand. But I didn't. Instead I disobeyed my orders. For the first time ever, I disobeyed my orders and you thank me with tears and pleas for mercy. You have no idea what I have sacrificed for you, what I will leave behind me when I'm gone from this village. . . .*

The thoughts continued to churn through Paz's mind, but he pushed them aside. More of the schoolhouse's timbers and beams crumpled inward, coughing charred embers into the afternoon sky. Paz looked up at the dark clouds that had rolled over the sun. A storm was coming, something else for the villagers to be thankful for since it would save them the trouble of extinguishing the flames consuming this and the other buildings.

His men kept cocking their gazes back toward Paz for instructions, wanting to be gone from this place as much as he. He'd chosen them because they always followed orders implicitly and, like him, honestly enjoyed their work. He addressed them neither by name, because that would have been too respectful, nor rank, because that would no longer have been accurate. Instead, he'd christened these men the Seven Dwarfs since, compared to him in size, they essentially were. The point was lost on the majority of them, who'd never seen or heard of the American movie. They had been culled from Andes villages set back from civilization, like Paz pure-blooded Venezuelan Indian for whom electricity and running water were still luxuries and whose warrior tradition dated back centuries.

Paz mostly agreed with President Chavez that technology and education were good things only to the extent they could be controlled. Once the bleeding-heart foundations and international relief groups sank their teeth into things, the inevitable upshot was the fermenting of discontent among the masses. The reason why there were no rebels in Venezuela was that President Chavez knew when to make an example of those efforts attempting to provide an alternative.

Matters normally handled, on a freelance basis, by Guillermo Paz and his seven dwarfs. But not anymore, not after today once word reached Caracas that Paz had disobeyed. Worse, he had interfered in official state policy.

Don't you see what I have done for you?

His satellite phone rang and Paz stepped aside to answer it, angling himself away from the sun in order to read the caller ID. The ten zeroes made him smile.

"Been a long time," Paz greeted in English.

"Your services are required."

"Where?"

"The United States. Texas. And you'll need to get a team together."

Paz looked at his seven dwarfs, still poking and prodding at the villagers.

"I could use a change of scenery," Paz told the man on the other end of the line.

29

SAN ANTONIO, THE PRESENT

"Here you go," Caitlin said, handing Cort Wesley Masters his cup complete with cardboard sleeve he seemed fascinated by.

She took her seat again at a table on the patio outside

Starbucks on the Riverwalk on West Crockett Street, arranging her chair to be in the shade while Cort Wesley drank up the sun. A breeze seemed to be lifting off the nearby waterway, alive with tour boats and pedestrians along its edge. Just an illusion, of course, since the man-made channel's churning waters were more decorative showpiece. Caitlin remembered the first time her father had taken her here as a little girl. Not nearly as many tourists or stores back then, but they'd taken a boat ride during which her popcorn had spilled over the side.

"Says HEAR MUSIC COFFEEHOUSE over the entrance," Cort Wesley noted. "I thought we were just meeting for coffee."

"We are. Others like to get themselves some music at the same time. Something new, I guess."

"Well, I prefer the old."

"So what is it you've got to tell me?" Caitlin asked him.

Cort Wesley took a sip from his cup and nearly spit it out. "Shit, what is this?"

"A latte."

"Latte what?"

"You told me to get you whatever I was having."

"I thought it'd be coffee."

"It is of a kind."

"I'm talking the black normal tasting kind."

"You've heard of lattes, of course."

"Heard of 'em, yeah. Just never thought I'd be drinking one." Cort Wesley took another sip, trying to get used to the taste.

"They're everywhere now," said Caitlin.

"Yeah, a lot can change in five years," Cort Wesley followed, waiting to see her reaction. "Made a trip to The Walls this morning," he resumed, when she just kept sipping her latte.

"Hopefully not 'cause you missed it."

"Not hardly. I wanted to check some things with a military friend who works inside, got the kind of connections we can use."

"We?"

"I asked my friend to check out who was holding this boy Clayton's leash. Now that we know it was him in the desert that night your partner got killed and not me." Cort Wesley sat back and sipped his latte, pretending to like it.

"That what you came here to tell me?"

"My military friend said he'll check things out. Promised to get back to me soon."

"You should have waited 'til then to call me."

"Thought about it. Then I figured you deserved this opportunity."

"To what?"

"Apologize for jailing me for something I had no part in. I don't remember you saying how sorry you were for getting things wrong. Lady, there was a time . . ."

Caitlin leaned forward, meeting his gaze with the back legs of her chair pitched in the air. "A time what?"

Cort Wesley held her stare. "You really don't want me to answer that."

"Wouldn't have asked the question if I didn't."

He slid his chair back, ever so slightly, just enough to ease his hand closer to the pistol tucked into his belt beneath his shirt. "You wanna finish what we started in El Paso, just say the word."

"And me thinking we were past that."

"Some things are tougher to get past than others, Ranger."

"Like seeing your husband helpless as an infant after some genuine sadists had their way with him for God knows how long."

"He'd be plenty worse off than that right now, if it

weren't for me." Cort Wesley looked away long enough for Caitlin's glare to soften. "You too."

"Why didn't you just kill me instead?" she asked him.

"I wanted to."

"Something stopped you."

"And when I figure out what it was, I'll let you know."

Caitlin settled back in her chair. "Good thing, since I wasn't the one who framed you, Masters."

"Just like I wasn't the one who shot up your partner. Someone else put my blood in the desert to set me up. Thought you might be able to help me figure out who. I figure after last night you owe me that much."

Caitlin just looked at him.

"What are you doing?"

"Drinking my coffee."

"You mean latte."

Caitlin took another sip and uncrossed her legs, watched Masters fighting his eyes off the sight. "Thing I'm wondering is how they came by the blood that ended up in the desert. Don't suppose you left a deposit at the Red Cross."

"I used to spill blood, not give it, Ranger."

"Thing is I did some checking too 'bout how something like this could happen." Caitlin studied Masters briefly before continuing. "And what I found has to do with degradation of the blood sample. Difference between a sample taken from a blood bank or something and something fresher. They could tell now that what they found in the desert had been refrigerated. That's what got you exonerated."

"Means somebody had to have stolen my blood."

"Whoever's pulling the strings here put some serious thought into things."

"Sure, they chose me, easy target, knew you'd come gunning."

"And get myself killed in the process."

"That being the likely result almost sure to have figured into their thinking."

"Guess we fooled them, didn't we?"

Cort Wesley fumbled the coffee cup, realization flashing in his eyes. "Shit . . ."

"What?"

"I got kids."

"As in children?"

"That's right, Caitlin Strong. Two boys. But don't worry. They don't know I exist. They're safe, sound and oblivious to me on a cul-de-sac in Shavano Park. Anyways, right around that time I get contacted by their mother through my friend Pablo Asuna. One of the boys might be sick, she says, may need the kind of transplant with blood or something. I figure she's hitting me up for money but turns out she needs to find out if my blood's a match. So I go get a sample taken and sent over to some lab." Cort Wesley passed the coffee cup from one hand to the other. "Since it turned out the boy was fine all the time, it must've been a setup."

"There you go."

"Apology accepted," Cort Wesley told her. "Close as you can come, I imagine."

"You were set up, all right."

"Just not by you, Ranger."

Caitlin's gaze grew even more stoic and grim. "You got bigger problems now, Masters."

"How you figure?"

"'Cause whoever set you up knew you had kids."

Cort Wesley stopped drinking, laid his latte cup on the steel table before them. Caitlin looked at him, studying the way the sun hit his face. Until their first meeting in El Paso, she had known his looks only from mug shots. An angular and chiseled face with gray eyes and steel-black hair. Hard and unforgiving, but somehow forced, as if he were putting on a show for the camera. Up close the face was just as chiseled, but some gray hair had been sprinkled in with the black, softening his features somewhat. And his eyes were more like charcoal than plain gray.

"We got the same enemies here, that's what you're saying."

Caitlin hardened her stare. "Stay out of this, Masters."

"Too late for that."

She eased her chair back ever so slightly. "I'm warning you."

"Whoever was pushing drugs through the Chihuahuan took five years of my life away, Ranger."

Caitlin laid her hands on the wrought-iron table. "It wasn't drugs; something else, packed in crates."

"I don't really care what it was. I care who was behind it, one name coming to mind immediately."

"Garza?"

Cort Wesley spun the coffee cup around in his hands. "Never seen him personally." Caitlin watched him sip some more of his latte and wrinkle his nose from the taste. "I'm thinking I'll take a trip across the border, maybe change that."

"Forget it."

Cort Wesley puckered his lips and laid his coffee cup atop the table, pushing it aside as he rose. "Free country last time I checked, Ranger. I wanna go to Mexico, I'm going to Mexico."

Caitlin felt her shoulders stiffen, tightening against the muscles in her neck. "This isn't your fight, Masters."

"'Til last night, you mean."

PART FOUR

The often cited "One Riot, One Ranger" appears to be based on several statements attributed to Captain Mc-Donald by Albert Bigelow Paine in his classic book, Captain Bill McDonald: Texas Ranger. *When sent to Dallas to prevent a scheduled prizefight, McDonald supposedly was greeted at the train station by the city's anxious mayor, who asked: "Where are the others?"*

To that, McDonald is said to have replied, "Hell! Ain't I enough? There's only one prizefight!"

—Mike Cox, with updates from the Texas Ranger Hall of Fame and Museum, "A Brief History of the Texas Rangers"

30

SAN ANTONIO, THE PRESENT

First thing the next morning, Caitlin drove out to the offices of RevCom, the cutting-edge software company where Peter had worked. He had gone to Iraq on their behalf, meaning that's where the trail started.

The problem was RevCom was gone; its former location in the Center City Industrial Park on the outskirts of San Antonio's downtown business district now occupied by a company called DynaTech.

Realizing the task before her had just become substantially more complicated, Caitlin decided to check the place out anyway. Before opening the door, she fastened her Stetson over her hair, tied up in a bun. It felt good to be wearing it again, even better to feel the reassuring weight of the badge pinned to the lapel of her crisply ironed blue cotton shirt. She'd opted for trousers instead of jeans and they felt a bit tight in the waist and seat, reminding her just how many years had passed since she'd last donned them. She wore the same boots she'd worn the day she faced off against Cort Wesley Masters in an El Paso bar. Nice to have her SIG holstered back on her hip, as well, as opposed to strapped on her ankle.

Caitlin stepped through the same door she remembered from the entrance of RevCom and approached a reception counter, a lone woman seated at a desk behind it. A door with an electronic keypad stood just to her right, the secret world beyond closed off to all but a select few.

She reached the counter and removed her hat politely as the receptionist rose from her chair and approached. Not something she was used to doing, DynaTech hardly the kind of place that received many unsolicited visitors.

"How may I help you, Ranger?" the woman asked, forcing a smile.

"Well, that's a good question and, truth be told, I'm not sure you can. See, I'm looking for a company called RevCom. Think I might have the wrong place."

"You do and you don't. It's the right address but RevCom's gone."

"Ma'am?"

"Out of business. Kaput, as they say. Finito."

Something was wrong about the woman's tone. Caitlin couldn't say what precisely, or how she could even tell. Her dad had always told her to trust her instincts. A feeling was as plain as a smell, once you learned to distinguish one from another.

"Don't suppose you'd have a forwarding address, maybe contact info for 'em?" Caitlin asked, readying her cell phone for the anticipated information.

The woman shook her head. "I'm sorry, Ranger."

Caitlin subtly placed her cell phone down on the counter alongside a penholder. "Now ain't that a shame. See, there's new information just come our way about an employee of theirs thought to have been killed in Iraq some five years back. Man named Peter Goodwin."

"Thought to have been?" the woman asked, stirring that same feeling in Caitlin again.

"'Fraid I can't say any more on the subject, except to someone who worked for RevCom at the time. Wouldn't happen to be anybody here fits that description?"

"I told you they went out of business."

" 'Course you did. I just figured a few of their former employees might have stayed on."

"I wouldn't know for sure, but I can tell you there aren't any here now."

"Damn shame's what it is with this news breaking and all. You didn't know Peter Goodwin, did you, ma'am?"

"No. How could I?"

"When I mentioned his name, I thought you recognized it. That's all."

"Maybe I did. He was killed in Iraq, right?"

"Actually, ma'am, I'm not at liberty to say."

"But you already did say."

Caitlin smiled at her and redonned her hat. "Nothing more I can accomplish here. I best be going, ma'am. You have yourself a good day."

The woman looked as if she wanted to say something but stopped short, as Caitlin continued toward the door. She tipped the brim of her Stetson before exiting, cell phone left on the counter with its video camera lens angled for the woman's desk.

31

HUNTSVILLE, TEXAS, THE PRESENT

Cort Wesley met up with his young prison-guard friend Frankie Cakes again at the Cafe Texan restaurant on Sam Houston Avenue in Huntsville before heading south into Mexico. They sat in the smoking room so Frankie could continue fanning the habit he'd picked up in Iraq. Cort Wesley was glad for the choice since it was small, homey and many said served the best hamburgers in Texas. He'd spent five years within a mile of the place but, of course, had never been in a position to know if that were true or not. But he generally liked places that served breakfast all day and especially liked the ones that still had smoking sections because he was normally more comfortable around the kind of people who smoked.

They both ordered hamburgers and iced teas. Frankie Cakes came in his uniform that was wet with sweat in the underarms and over his flat stomach.

"Sorry, Cort Wesley. I got nothing for you, 'cause there's nothing to get."

"Really?"

"Looked under all the rocks I could find for your friend Clayton. Nothing there."

"Ain't that a shame."

"So," Frankie said, after draining almost all his iced tea in a single gulp, "you're not even out a week and some mess you got yourself into."

"Anything like that mess I got you out of with the Latinos?"

Frankie swiped his tongue across his upper lip. "You got no call to bring that up."

"You were right not to run drugs in for them, podner. I admire a man who sticks by his principles."

Frankie Cakes's brow grew shiny with a layer of sweat.

"So tell me," Cort Wesley continued, "is my next stop Warden Jardine's office?"

"You'd rat me out for something I'm finished doing?"

"Not if you stop lying to me."

"Huh?"

"You're a bad liar, podner. Saw it in your eyes as soon as I sat down. You sitting there making up what you were gonna say."

Frankie jammed his forearms down on the table hard

enough to rattle the shakers and sugar packets. "Look, I can't afford this coming back on me."

"Can't afford to have your drug dealing come back on you neither. Ever hear what happens to an ex-bull on the inside?"

Frankie Cakes looked around the room to see if anyone was looking their way. Then he shoved his chair farther under the table and lowered his voice.

"How exactly you know this guy Clayton?"

"I killed him a couple nights back, podner. Shot him in the head."

"You didn't think of mentioning that to me?"

"Didn't think it was relevant."

Frankie lifted his iced tea to his mouth in a suddenly unsteady hand and drained the last of it, letting the ice cubes smack up against his lips. "Oh, it's relevant, all right. It's pretty goddamn relevant."

"Take it easy there, podner."

"Take it easy? I shook some trees on your account, and what fell out could end up chasing me long after you and me are done."

Cort Wesley slid his iced tea across the table to replace Frankie Cakes's spent one. "I protect you from the Latinos?"

Frankie nodded.

"Well, I'll protect you from this too."

Frankie Cakes looked as if he wanted to laugh, but couldn't. "Yeah? You really think so? Lemme tell you something. The shit you stepped in here don't come off your shoes so easy."

"What are you talking about, podner?"

"I'm talking about Clayton. He ain't military no more. He is, was, with a private contractor for military-supported groups."

"What the hell is a military-supported group?"

"Private companies that offer military services for big bucks. You ever hear of Custer Battles, Blackwater or Professional Protective Services?"

"No to all. Didn't get to read the papers or watch the news much these past five years."

"Well, Clayton seems to have hired himself out to all, but PPS mostly."

"PPS?"

"Professional Protective Services," Frankie Cakes continued. "Clayton and a bunch of hard-edged Special Ops types been selectively signing up for PPS but there ain't a single mission-specific operation anybody I know inside Special Ops can find hide or hair of." Frankie paused to drink down a hefty gulp of Cort Wesley's iced tea. "So I keep checking on the down low, see about the postings of Clayton, no first name, and friends. Up comes a list heavy in Middle Eastern friendly locations like Abu Dhabi, Qatar, Saudi Arabia, Jordan, Egypt."

"Bahrain?"

"Yeah. How'd you know?"

"Never mind. Just tell me where this is leading."

"To what those countries all have in common."

"And what's that, podner?"

"Torture, Cort Wesley. Those are the countries where we've been sending prisoners to get coaxed a bit. Cattle prods rammed up their asses, you know the drill. And people behind shit like that don't like the trees they're hiding in getting poked to see what drops. Already had my phone disconnected. Next week I'm moving." Frankie gulped down the last of Cort Wesley's iced tea. His hands were visibly shaking when he laid it back down. "How the hell you get mixed up with medieval bastards like this?"

"Just lucky I guess."

32

SAN ANTONIO, THE PRESENT

Caitlin spent the next few minutes inside her SUV thinking back to the first time she'd met Peter in a bar and grill where she'd joined up with some of her former fellow Rangers nearly a year after she'd crossed the border into Juárez, Mexico. The occasion was her late father's birthday and, among hard-core Rangers anyway, it was tradition to celebrate the birthdays of those who had passed. All the whiskey shots and barbecue later, the Rangers still in attendance were finally done swapping Jim Strong stories. And up walks Peter, getting to the table just as it went quiet.

"I just wanna say I appreciate everything you do," he said to them all, though his eyes stayed mostly on Caitlin.

The Rangers, Caitlin included, raised what was left of their beers to him in a toast. He smiled graciously, paid his bill with a credit card and left the restaurant.

Though much more drunk than she'd had any intention of getting, Caitlin rose and said she'd be right back, making a beeline to the waitress who'd walked off with the credit card receipt to get the man's name. There were four Peter Goodwins listed as residents of San Antonio in the law enforcement database she logged into upon returning home to the house she'd inherited from her father, but only one Peter *F.* Goodwin. He was as surprised to hear from her, as she was to have made the call.

Truth was Caitlin had never dated very much, not even in high school. Back then she'd never been able to deal very well with young men's attitudes that left women little more than something to possess and screw to cement their place in the high school food chain. Add to that the fact that most were as intimidated by her as she was unimpressed by them. They always seemed too weak, too easily subservient. Caitlin had grown up around strength and been fashioned in that very mold, always figured the man in her life would be one who could outride and outshoot her. If not that, at least be someone who knew how to stand up for himself without his ego getting in the way.

One man took her to a roadhouse for dinner on their first date, only to have a greasy-haired drunk with his belly hanging outside his shirt come up to the table and ask her to dance.

"Excuse me, the lady's with me," her date said, "if you don't mind."

"But I do mind," the drunk said. "I mind you coming into my home and not treating me with the proper respect. Instead of your woman, think I'll have my way with you."

Caitlin saw the buck knife sheathed to his belt, no idea in the moment whether he intended to use it but not about to wait and find out. Before her date could move, she grabbed her beer bottle by the neck and smashed it into the drunk's groin. When he doubled over, she slammed his face into the table hard enough to splinter the wood. Local cops took the drunk away, not bothering to ask Caitlin for a statement. The man she'd come to the roadhouse with never called to ask for a second date.

Nothing comparable befell the early weeks of her relationship with Peter. He was smart, fun, engaging and it felt good to be around him. His company had helped distract her from the transitional period after leaving the Rangers that had left her feeling lost, and she often found herself thinking of him into the cold hours of the morning after he dropped her off. They began staying over at each other's places only after the first few months had solidified their friendship. They liked the same movies and music and, truth be told, Caitlin was happier around Peter than when she was alone.

So when he suggested they get married, she had said yes happily, though not excitedly. Suddenly there was a new future ahead of her and Caitlin looked forward to that as a way of finally breaking the past's hold, going so far as to sell her father's house and move into Peter's town house condo in Slate Creek at Westover Hills.

As it turned out, though, the past proved reluctant to let go.

"There it is," Caitlin said with a smile, retrieving her cell phone from the DynaTech counter five minutes after leaving it there. "It's a good thing my head's tucked inside my hat, or I might have forgotten that too."

Back outside, she drove halfway around the parking lot before finding a shaded space to watch whatever the recorded video had to show her. The picture and sound quality were pretty good under the circumstances, and the angle on which she'd perched the phone allowed for a clear view of the receptionist pressing out the number of whomever she'd called as soon as Caitlin was outside. She'd have to enhance the shot on a computer to read the numbers, left for now with a one-way conversation that was more than enough to stoke her curiosity.

The small cell phone screen pictured the receptionist still hunched over her desk with the exchange entered.

"Mr. Hollis, please."

A pause, while the woman fiddled with a pen, scratching designs into a notepad.

"Mr. Hollis, it's Grace Devallos over at DynaTech in

San Antonio. . . . Yes, sir, I know, but my instructions were to call if anyone came around asking about— RevCom, that's right, sir. . . . A Texas Ranger. . . ."

The woman listened for a time, stopped doodling and laid down her pen.

"No, her questions seemed innocent enough. She just asked about RevCom. . . . Yes, it was a woman. . . . Hold on, I wrote it down."

The woman looked toward the notepad again.

"Strong, Caitlin Strong. . . . Yes, I checked her ID. . . . She was dressed like Rangers always dress. . . . No, sir, she only asked about RevCom, if they'd left a forwarding address or something. . . . Yes, of course, sir."

Caitlin felt herself roasting inside the SUV, so she closed the windows and switched on the air-conditioning. Played the video a third time and was just starting a fourth when the phone rang.

"Caitlin Strong," she greeted.

"This is Ranger Berry over at the hospital, ma'am. Something going on here I think you should see."

33

JUÁREZ, MEXICO, THE PRESENT

The heat built up the closer Cort Wesley got to the Mexican border and by Juárez the humidity was beating back the air-conditioning in Pablo Asuna's old Ford. He probably should have asked Asuna for a better vehicle but liked the Ford's innocuousness and, after five years of not driving, was used to its ride now. He kept his eye on the temperature gauge the whole way, dialing back the air-conditioning in favor of the windows every time the needle flirted with the red.

Heat like this had always hardened his edge even more, welcomed today in view of the fact that he needed to get information out of people likely unwilling to provide it.

"Are you carrying any weapons with you?" a border agent asked him at the checkpoint.

"Wouldn't even think about it, sir." Cort Wesley smiled and was waved through into Mexico with his Smith & Wesson wedged under the driver's seat.

He could find no trace of the Saez brothers anywhere in Juárez. All a half-day's labor had earned him was the fact that their mother had died six months after Caitlin Strong had paid her a visit. And, no, the building landlord had no idea where Jesus and Rodrigo could be found. They were dead too, for all he cared.

The cockfighting arena where Caitlin Strong had met up with them was a boarded-up shell of a building now, and all of the neighboring businesses professed to have neither heard of nor met either of the brothers. Then he remembered Caitlin Strong mentioning a warehouse where the shipment they had trucked into the United States had been stored. Turned out the cockfighting arena had been a warehouse called El Candida, according to the dilapidated sign still hanging over what had been the entrance. When the Mexican phone book was no help in providing further information, he walked into a local real estate office to inquire about such space and left with a list of two more El Candida warehouses located on the outskirts of Juárez.

In this case outskirts meant a considerable drive, and Cort Wesley spent it sweating with the windows down and a hot breeze blowing through the car, thinking about Caitlin Strong. That night with the Saez brothers had changed her in ways she could only begin to imagine, brought her to a dark, unfamiliar place. A state of mind more than place, actually, that was difficult for any man, or woman, to rid themselves of. Cort Wesley had never done drugs but he'd known enough who had. Smack, crack, methamphetamines; whatever poison a junkie picked, they told the identical story when it came to getting hooked.

Cort Wesley figured it was the same for Caitlin Strong that night in Juárez. She'd crossed a line with the Saez brothers that left her a different person and no amount of volunteer work in a torture recovery center could change that. She'd figure that out for herself soon enough; far be it from him to tell her.

He parked outside the first El Candida warehouse outside Juárez and sat for a time in Asuna's Ford just studying things. The trucks were dissimilar in design and color and several were missing plates. Not hard to figure from that alone that these warehouses were still being used for the same purpose they'd been five years back, almost surely operated by the Mexican Mafia to smuggle marijuana and whatever else across the border.

Cort Wesley smoothed on some underarm deodorant and changed from a soaked shirt to a clean, steaming fresh one before making his way across the gravel parking lot into the front office.

"I'd like to see the manager," he said in Spanish to a girl behind the desk who looked all of sixteen. She was pretty with long dark hair and a full smile. A piece of jewelry— thin, black and maybe a half-inch square—dangled from a nylon cord looped over her neck.

"He's busy."

"Tell him I got business to transact. And I come with references."

"He's still busy."

"PPS."

"Excuse me?"

"Just tell him Personal Protective Services. He'll know what it means. Tell him Clayton sent me."

Cort Wesley was rolling the dice here, figuring it either got him an in or nowhere at all, which was no worse than where he was now.

"He'll be out in a minute," the girl said, after passing his message over an old-fashioned phone with lit buttons along the bottom of the faceplate.

"What kind of stone is that?" Cort Wesley asked, gazing at the small black object hanging over her shirt.

"This?" she said, holding it up. "I dunno. I just found it here one day. It was getting thrown out. I like trinkets, stuff nobody else has."

Cort Wesley was about to respond when a man emerged from the back of the warehouse. He was short and squat, five and a half feet tall and just as wide it seemed. A human fireplug or maybe a beer keg. He had no neck and it was impossible to tell where his waist ended and legs began. He emerged with two other men riding his rear with equally bad teeth and loose shirts worn outside their work pants to hide the pistols wedged up in their belts.

"Talk fast," the manager said.

Cort Wesley realized there was no air-conditioning going. Just commercial-strength blowers suspended from the ceiling over a concrete floor that must have once been part of the warehouse itself. The blowers did little more than move the heat around, leaving the air thick, stale and laced with the fetid stench of mold. Besides the girl's desk and pair of offices partitioned with unfinished plywood, there was the concrete floor, slab walls and nothing else.

"You store and ship shit or not?"

"Depends what the shit is, doesn't it?"

Cort Wesley took out an envelope and flapped it in the air for Fireplug to see. "I don't know, does it?"

"You want to do business, we can talk. But we're discreet here. References required."

"Discreet, yeah. How 'bout Clayton?"

"So we're starting with him, her, whoever."

"Him. And he's the one recommended you to me. Said you could move anything. In or out, doesn't matter."

"It doesn't, depending on what, where and how much."

"Same stuff as Clayton, maybe five years ago. Through El Paso using a couple of mules named Rodrigo and Jesus Saez."

"Never heard of them."

"You heard of Clayton."

"Why don't I take a look at what you got inside that envelope and then we can talk serious?"

Cort Wesley puckered the envelope open and flashed it, grinning.

"It's empty," said Fireplug.

"That it is. What I'm offering you here is your life. Figure that's worth more than enough to make talking to me worth your while."

Fireplug twisted toward the two men behind him. In the next instant, two beefy hands darted under twin baggy shirts.

Cort Wesley drew his Smith first, firing a single shot at each that blew both men back into the resealed heavy doors with holes bored through their foreheads. Before Fireplug could react further, Cort Wesley turned his gun on the young girl behind the desk.

"I'm guessing this is your daughter."

Fireplug remained silent, caught between thoughts and intentions. His milky eyes swam wildly.

Cort Wesley held his gaze on the girl. "That your father?"

She nodded fearfully, tears starting to stream down her cheeks.

"Relax, honey, you got nothing to worry about long as your daddy cooperates. If he doesn't, I'm going to shoot you in the face." Cort Wesley held the girl's terrified stare long enough to cast her a wink accompanied by a quick smile. He waited until she wiped her tears aside with no fresh ones to follow, before turning back toward Fireplug. "So, you ready to cooperate?"

"You're a fool for doing this," Fireplug told him. "You know who I work for?"

"Let me take a guess: Mexican Mafia."

"That's a what. Not a who."

"Garza."

Fireplug looked unsettled by the mere mention of the name.

"Heard he's not real."

"Oh, he's real all right, and you just killed two of his men."

"I thought they were your men."

"Same thing."

Cort Wesley glanced at the corpses. "Too late anyway. Question on the table now is do you and your daughter join them or not?"

"You would kill a child?"

"Only if you make me."

"What is it you want?"

"Five years ago an American named Clayton set up a shipment. Hired men from the Mexican Mafia to drive a truck they picked up here across the border. You remember what I'm talking about?"

"I remember," Fireplug told him. "But I only know Clayton as the voice on the other end of the phone."

"See how easy this can be? Now, you want me on my merry way, all you have to do is tell me what was inside the truck and where it was headed."

"The Mexicans were supposed to be killed. That was the plan."

"Figured that much out for myself."

"I don't know what was in the crates. Only the American, Clayton, knew where they were going."

"Let me ask you something again: names Jesus and Rodrigo Saez mean anything to you now?"

Fireplug's expression changed just enough.

"Thought so," said Cort Wesley. "Two of your men who were supposed to get killed that night. 'Cept they didn't. Came back here to tell you one hell of a story about a gunfight in the desert with the Texas Rangers, then went back to staging cockfights in another of Garza's warehouses."

"I don't know what you're talking about."

Cort Wesley resteadied his Smith on Fireplug's daughter. "Yes, you do."

"Houston!" Fireplug blared suddenly. "They delivered the crates to Houston! Paid me extra on account I was never gonna get my truck back."

"Crates . . . ?"

Fireplug nodded.

"But you don't know what was inside."

He shook his head.

"Where in Houston?"

"A skyscraper downtown with an underground loading area. The delivery was timed for after-hours. Easy in, easy out. They didn't know the address when they left."

"Downtown Houston."

"They said there was a park almost right across the street from it; no, not a park. Signs advertising the park was coming there." Fireplug's gaze was darting fearfully between his daughter and Cort Wesley. "It's all I know. I'm telling you the truth."

Cort Wesley lowered his pistol. "I do believe you are."

The color washed back into Fireplug's cheeks. His breathing steadied. "Would you really have done it, would you have shot my daughter?"

Cort Wesley cast the girl another wink and started backing up for the door. "Why don't you ask her?"

34

HOUSTON, THE PRESENT

Harm Delladonne watched the big man strolling about his office, studying the various paintings hung from the walls with an admiring glance.

"You got good taste," said Guillermo Paz. "No bowls of fruit, flowers, stuff like that. I like paintings with people in them. I like looking at their faces, imagining what they're thinking."

Delladonne tightened his gaze on Paz. "Why don't you tell me what I'm thinking, Colonel?"

"That maybe you got the wrong guy, some fruitcake who likes art instead of someone who can fix your problems."

"Are you the wrong guy?"

"Depends on the problems, I guess." Paz swept his eyes about the sprawling office, letting them linger briefly on the loft above, connected to the main floor by a steel spiral staircase. "Hard for me to figure a man like you having the kind that require a man like me."

"Is that a requirement for you taking the job?"

"Not with the money I'm getting paid for this one."

Delladonne met his stare, refused to break it in spite of the focused fury held in the big man's. "You love your country, Colonel?"

"I used to."

"Because I could buy it. That's right. I could buy up the oil futures, close up your wells and put your nation out of business. I just want to make sure we understand each other."

Paz nodded and broke off the stare, seeming to relent. "You know your name sounds like the poison. Belladonna."

"Take a seat," Delladonne said, offering him the Oriental armchair set before his lacquered ebony desk.

Paz didn't move.

"Take a seat, Colonel."

Paz approached and sat down, the chair creaking from the strain of his bulk that spilled off the seat. A stench rising off him assaulted Delladonne like driving past a garbage truck on a hot summer day.

"You were able to assemble a team?"

"What were my orders?"

"Where are your men?"

"Raping schoolchildren somewhere." Paz waited for Delladonne's reaction. "I'm kidding. That was a joke."

Delladonne slid a flash drive across the table. "This contains everything you need on your targets, all the information we've been able to collate."

Paz picked the flash drive up between two massive fingers. "Where can I look at this?"

"I'll secure an office for you downstairs."

Paz glanced around the office again. "You mind if I use yours? I kind of like the surroundings. Makes me feel, I don't know, thoughtful."

"Then, by all means, Colonel, be my guest."

"You believe in God, Belladonna?"

"I believe in His power."

"What if I were to tell you that I knew He was real?"

"I'd say I hope He's on your side."

"Guess we'll see about that, won't we?"

35

SAN ANTONIO, THE PRESENT

Peter was sitting up on his bed, surrounded by parts of the broken cable box he'd disassembled using some combination of coins scattered across the bedcovers. He now seemed to be in the process of reassembling the box, showing a focus and intensity much more in keeping with the man who'd left for Iraq two years ago. The precision with which he worked, fitting the chips, diodes and transistors back into their respective slots was striking and totally out of character with the man she'd been trying to reach.

Caitlin left the door open and rejoined Ranger Tim Berry in the hallway.

"Don't know how to explain it," Berry said, exchanging a glance with the other posted Ranger, a big man named Rollins. "One minute we look in he's lying on the bed staring at the busted television, and the next he's sitting up with the cable box in front of him taking off the back. Figured it was best not to rile him any, so we let him have at it and called you."

"Thirty minutes ago."

"Just about."

"He took the whole thing apart in thirty minutes."

"And also did some fiddling with the chip things," Ranger Rollins told her. "Don't think I ever saw him blink. Man gave a whole new meaning to the word focused."

"I'll say," Berry chimed in.

"But we made sure it was unplugged," Rollins added as an afterthought, "so he didn't hurt himself none."

"Is this what he did for work?" Berry asked her.

"Good question."

36

SAN ANTONIO, THE PRESENT

Caitlin stepped back into the hospital room and closed the door behind her this time. Peter didn't acknowledge her, too busy fitting the last pieces of the cable box back together and then using the quarter he'd been given at the Tampa Survivor Center to screw the top back on.

Still apparently oblivious to her presence, he climbed down off his bed and hobbled over to the wall-mounted television in his bare feet. Caitlin watched him reaffix the cable leads appropriately, tuck the cable box back into the slot tailored for it, and switch on the television.

Instantly a crisp picture and clear sound replaced the snow and static from the other day.

"That's better," Peter said, looking satisfied, vital, alive.

Then he climbed gingerly back into the bed, wincing as he lay backward against the stacked pillows, the familiar blank stare overtaking his visage again. Whether or not he was actually watching the television, Caitlin couldn't tell.

"That was good work," she said, not wanting to lose him.

Peter glanced her way, acknowledging her presence in the room for the first time. "Simple."

"You're very good at it."

"It's what I do."

His statement flushed Caitlin with a fresh rush of anger. How does an expert in cable television software integration end up being tortured in Bahrain? What if they had gotten the wrong man? What if this whole thing was about mistaken identity? It didn't seem possible, but then none of this would have seemed possible just a week ago.

"What else do you do?" Caitlin asked him.

Peter continued to look her way but didn't respond, starting to slip into his fuguelike state again. She thought of visiting the location of RevCom, his old company, of the phone call the woman behind the counter had made as soon as she had left.

Caitlin yanked her cell phone from her pocket. "Can I show you something?"

Peter's eyes flashed to life at the sight of the phone being extended toward him. Able to relate to machines now more than people. That was the key, the trick, what she'd been missing up until this point.

Caitlin jogged her phone to the video mode and selected the play command. Instantly the video of the receptionist at DynaTech moving back behind her desk and picking up the phone began to play. Peter's eyes widened, transfixed by the images on the tiny screen. Whether or not he recognized the interior as that of his former office at RevCom, she couldn't tell.

"Can you get this to play on the television?" Caitlin asked, pointing toward the wall-mounted set.

"Need tools," Peter said.

"Like what?"

"Tools. Cables. Leads. Ties. USB adapters. Gotta splice and rewire." Each item spoken as a separate sentence, a separate thought, his mind rewiring itself around the obstacles his torturers had left behind.

"I'll get them for you," Caitlin promised.

She approached Ranger Berry in the hallway, Ranger Rollins standing by the window overlooking the parking lot.

"Hospital must have an I.T. division."

"I.T.?" Berry questioned.

"Technology department for the phones, cable, that sort of thing. I want you to get a tool kit up here and give it to Peter Goodwin."

Berry frowned, looking critical. "Long as there's nothing sharp."

"Just keep an eye on him while he works."

"Works?"

"Ranger Strong," Rollins called from the window, "you should have a look at this."

Caitlin joined him by the window.

"See that car down there, black Mercury with the dented door?"

Caitlin found it quickly in her line of sight, parked in the steaming sunshine, all windows down. "What about it?"

"Pulled into the parking lot just behind you and been waiting ever since," Rollins reported. "One man inside, near as I can tell." He turned from the window to face her. "You want me to check it out?"

"No," Caitlin told him, "think I'll handle that myself."

37

Cort Wesley drove off in Pablo Asuna's Ford, only to park it in the shady section of a wreck-strewn lot a half block away and settled back to wait.

He didn't have to wait long.

It wasn't more than thirty minutes later that a pair of massive black SUVs tore up to the entrance of Fireplug's warehouse. Four men jumped out of the lead vehicle and three from the trailing one, all with weapons drawn. None of them Garza obviously, but likely to be his underlings, here to sort out the mess Cort Wesley had just made inside.

The gunmen emerged through the front door minutes later, carrying the bodies now wrapped tightly in garbage bags and duct tape. They hoisted the covered corpses through the lead SUV's tailgate. The one who looked to be in charge stood off to the side, smoking a cigarette. Fireplug was next to him, pleading his case. The leader seemed to be shrugging him off, ignoring his claims and explanations. Just stamped his cigarette out with his shoe and climbed back into the rear of the trailing SUV, as if Fireplug weren't even there. Then the vehicles tore out of the parking lot, heading back for the highway.

Cort Wesley pulled out after them in the thin traffic, keeping his distance. If they made him, things were gonna get ugly in a hurry, and he didn't like the odds. So he stayed back farther than he probably should have, playing it safe and drifting back even more when the SUVs turned onto Highway 45, heading south toward

Chihuahua. He left the windows open, avoiding use of the air-conditioning to preserve power and fuel, figured he had enough to get to the city, at which point he'd have to fill up.

The SUVs continued on, passing through the outskirts of village after village mired in abject poverty, then through a stretch of desert spawned by volcanic ash en route to the city. Cort Wesley felt anxious upon entering Chihuahua itself, since the snarl of traffic made spotting him all the easier. Pablo Asuna's Ford proved a blessing here, since it blended in perfectly with the other ancient wrecks with temperature needles battling the red.

From here the SUVs headed for the foothills of the Sierra Madres, a breathtaking expanse of mountains that dotted the landscape for as far as the eye could see. With his fuel gauge flirting with E, Cort Wesley was just about to abandon the pursuit when he saw the SUVs bank hard to the left toward a road that sliced through the lower reaches of the mountain range. The brush flora here was rich, lush green at the core but browning closer to the tips. Brown through and through meant it was dead, soon to be cracked and scattered by the wind with the remnants overtaken by the outgrowth of neighboring brush. If memory and knowledge served him right, Cort Wesley knew there were ribbons of streams cutting through the landscape. Last he knew, this area was still undeveloped. Judging from the Mexican *federales* guarding the entrance to what looked like a private road, that was no longer the case.

The SUVs passed by the uniformed *federales* without having to stop. Cort Wesley drove on, holding his breath hoping that they hadn't spotted him. Last thing he needed was to go up against corrupt cops who'd buried many a body in the desert he'd just driven through. So he parked along the road a good ways up and circled back down on foot until he was overlooking a series of land-rich estates, all enclosed by either walls or fences. His vantage point allowed him a glimpse of a few massive villas within, one with a horse paddock and another featuring individual basketball and tennis courts. He thought he might have heard the light *wop* of balls being hit, but couldn't see anyone playing.

Since he didn't know which estate the SUVs had pulled into, he figured he'd watch for a time, see which one they eventually pulled out of. Cort Wesley tightened his gaze downward, trying to narrow down the field a bit, hoping to spot an armed guard on patrol, all the indication he needed.

Whoever framed him, whoever stole five years of his life, might well be residing in one of the estates below. Cort Wesley took out his Smith & Wesson, passed it agilely from one hand to the other, weighing the odds.

Find the right house, wait until nightfall, and get his revenge while the getting was good. He still had four full magazines, sixty more shots, with him. Plenty.

Cort Wesley settled back to watch.

38

EAST SAN ANTONIO, THE PRESENT

Pablo Asuna heard the overhead bay door descending, the breeze he'd been relying on to keep the garage cool gone in an instant.

"Hey," he called, lifting his head up from under the hood of a supercharged Dodge pickup with an engine he had custom installed, "who did that? Who the fuck's there?"

Then he saw the big man; no, not big—huge. Five

average-sized men flanked him in the half-light. Different shapes and haircuts, not smiling. They looked like dwarfs compared to the big man.

"I like your truck," Paz said over the still-roaring engine, its idle fast but smooth.

"It's not mine. I'm just working on it."

"Stolen?"

"What's it to you?"

"Nothing. Just making conversation."

Could have been any number of things brought a man like this here, none of them good. Asuna started thinking about weapons, how close he was to something he could make quick use of: against this man, nothing came to mind.

"Ease into things, you know?" the giant continued.

"No, I don't."

The big man's face wrinkled in displeasure. "Everyone talks tough in this town."

"There's a good reason for that."

"I hear Cort Wesley Masters is the toughest of all. That true?"

"Far as I know, it is."

"And how far is that?"

"He's in jail."

"He was released."

"Oh."

"You've seen him. He's been here. Old friends catching up, maybe sharing a beer."

"You want me to get you one?"

The big man came closer, angling himself to keep Asuna pinned behind the Dodge's hood. The spread of a work light dangling overhead caught his wild black hair and sun-darkened skin. His eyes glimmered in the dim light. Cat's eyes, Asuna thought. Reveling in this, the enjoyment bleeding from his pores.

Asuna ran his gaze across the big man and the others, standing before him in no particular hurry to get anything done. That scared him the most, how casual they were, men who'd clearly done this kind of thing before. The big man came right up to the front fender of the truck now, close enough for Pablo Asuna to smell the oil from his hair. Another smell hung over him too, one that reminded Asuna of hunting trips with his father in Mexico; the stench of dead birds carried in a sack through the blistering sun.

Asuna considered his options, weaponless with the T-shirt bulging over his fat belly squeezed up against the big truck's hood. "I'm not telling you a goddamn fucking thing, poncho," was the best he could come up with.

He thought of the first time he'd met Cort Wesley Masters. The goddamn gangs moving in everywhere, wanting him to strip stolen cars for them. Told Asuna they'd punch holes with their dicks in all the women in his life unless he followed their orders. Asuna told them to fuck off. They were choking him with a belt hose when Cort Wesley walked in looking for an oil change. He shot the two gang-bangers dead, then insisted on Asuna's $19.95 special before they dumped the bodies in the nearest landfill.

The big man let out a deep sigh that sounded more like a growl. "I killed a priest in Venezuela and things haven't been the same since. But life goes on, you gotta agree with me there. But I just don't have the patience for this *carajo* anymore." Asuna watched the big man slide a bit closer to him. "So I have a question for you. About our friend."

"Masters ain't my friend, poncho."

The big man ignored him. "You don't have to tell me where he is—"

"That's good, 'cause I don't know."

"—you have to tell me where I can find his children."

39

SAN ANTONIO, THE PRESENT

"Step out of the car real slow now," Caitlin Strong ordered, pistol angled straight through the driver's window. "You wanna keep your hands where I can see 'em while you do it."

The man in the black Mercury remained rigid, risking a single glance her way when Caitlin thrust his door open. He started to climb out, having trouble angling himself properly with his hands raised in the air. He wore an ill-fitting shirt tucked into the waistband of polyester trousers that had gone wet in the seat and crotch from sitting too long.

"This isn't what it looks like," he insisted.

She shoved the man up against the rear door and frame, patted him down. "What is it exactly?"

"I worked with your husband. I worked with Peter."

Caitlin spun him around, no weapon to be found on his person.

"At RevCom," the man completed, facing her now. Both he and his car reeked of stale perspiration. Fast food, wrappers and crumpled bags were strewn about the interior. "I saw you there today."

"You recognized me?"

"We met once—well, twice actually. The second time was Peter's funeral."

"You were there?"

"Briefly."

"Should've stayed for lunch." Caitlin holstered her pistol. "You can put your hands down now."

The man lowered them to his sides. "I was afraid I'd end up just like him if I did."

"How's that?"

"Dead, and he's not the only one either. There are others. Three to be exact. All part of Peter's project team."

Caitlin glanced past him toward his car. "Get in."

"Where we going?"

"Nowhere."

"What's your name?" Caitlin asked when the Mercury's doors were closed. The sun moved enough to shield the car from its sizzling rays that had left the black interior scorching. Spared the heat for the next few minutes anyway, Caitlin watched the way the splintered sunlight framed the man's pale, milky complexion.

"Albert Johannson. From Wisconsin, if you're wondering why I talk this way."

"Tell me about RevCom."

"There is no RevCom."

"I'm talking about my husband and these other three men you just mentioned who were part of his team."

"Two men," Johannson corrected. "The fourth was a woman."

"They worked with Peter."

Johannson nodded, his skin turning a pinkish shade that was the first sign of a burn. "On the same project."

"You too?"

"Then I'd be dead *too*, wouldn't I?"

"Lose the sarcasm, Mr. Johannson."

"It's called being scared out of my mind."

"Even though you weren't working on the same project."

"All of RevCom was poisoned, Mrs. Goodwin," Johannson said, not noticing Caitlin tense at being called that. "They shut the place down as soon as Peter and the others disappeared. One day it was open and the next day the doors were locked and the place had been emptied out. . . ."

"Eighteen months ago now. So what are you still doing here?"

"Let me finish. My bank accounts had been emptied and closed, my credit was nonexistent. Even my cell phone was deactivated. They didn't steal my identity, they erased it."

"Who's 'they,' Mr. Johannson?"

"That's why I'm still here. Trying to find that out. Watching, waiting around for someone to show up I recognize from RevCom. DynaTech's a sham. Part of the same damn oufit. I'm sure of it."

"Watching and waiting around for eighteen months," Caitlin noted.

"Off and on, yes. Not as much since I've started to build my life back up. Starting from scratch again. You have any idea what that's like?"

"Some."

"I'm . . . sorry."

"So am I. For you."

The sun returned from its brief respite, burning through the windshield and adding more heat to the already flushed feeling that filled Caitlin. "You're telling me RevCom was responsible for all that happened, Peter and these three others."

"Not RevCom. RevCom was a sham, a cover, a front. Someone much bigger was pulling the strings. And when something went wrong, they yanked the whole floor out."

"But you're still alive."

"I was just software. Peter and the others were behind the I.T. Information Technologies," Johannson added, as if Caitlin needed the translation. "The project was theirs all the way."

She tried to fit the pieces together, her mind fighting the effort. Peter gets sent to Iraq, ends up being tortured in Bahrain around the same time RevCom gets shuttered. Something unexpected obviously to blame, something gone very, very wrong.

"All these suspicions and you don't tell anybody 'til I happen to walk in the door?" Caitlin snapped at Johannson.

"I told you it doesn't stop at RevCom. Who was I supposed to trust?"

"Rangers, for starters."

Johannson frowned, the fear pushing through even that gesture. "I'm from Wisconsin, Mrs. Goodwin. The legends of the erstwhile Texas Rangers don't carry much weight up there. And as for the local cops, state government, even the feds, whoever's behind the deaths could have a pipeline into them as well."

"What is it Peter was working on?" Caitlin asked him. "What is it got all these people killed?"

"Fire Arrow."

40

SAN ANTONIO, THE PRESENT

Caitlin knew the phrase all too well, from a story she'd told Peter not long after they'd first met, trying to interest him in the lore of the Rangers.

In 1871, a small wagon train of pioneers moving across the frontier had the misfortune of ending up in Indian country during one of the many uprisings that riddled Texas during that time. The pioneers managed to repel the initial attack and form the semblance of a defense, quickly pierced by a hundred Comanche firing flaming arrows through the air. Their targets, after all, might be able to stay shielded from the arrows alone, but not from the fires they set. Poor bastards would have to emerge from their cover to fight the flames back, exposing themselves to a fresh barrage.

It happened that a Ranger detachment of five men scouring the foothills in search of the renegade tribes' lairs came upon the onslaught after half the pioneers had perished. Half, though, were still alive and that was more than enough to spur the Rangers to ride abreast of one another straight for the Indian's high-ground position of cover, firing their Winchesters and Colts to chase them back as flaming arrows streaked overhead.

A painting of that famed ride hung for years in the Texas statehouse and was currently on display in the Ranger Hall of Fame and Museum in Waco. The painting lacked a signature but was blessed with a simple title: *Fire Arrow.*

Peter had named his project after the first Ranger tale Caitlin had shared with him.

"What was Fire Arrow?" she asked Johannson.

"I don't know."

"You worked for the damned company, didn't you?"

"But not on Fire Arrow, not directly anyway. I was just software."

"And Peter was just cable television bandwidth expansion."

Something flashed in Johannson's eyes. "That's what he told you?"

"It's not true?"

"I can only tell you this, Ranger. Whatever Fire Arrow was, it had nothing to do with cable television."

PART FIVE

[In 1916,] Rangers were given orders and wide powers to keep the hostilities in Mexico from washing across the river into Texas. Governor O. B. Colquitt wrote Ranger Captain John R. Hughes: "I instruct you and your men to keep them [Mexican raiders] off of Texas territory if possible, and if they invade the State let them understand they do so at the risk of their lives."

—Mike Cox, with updates from the Texas Ranger Hall of Fame and Museum Staff, "A Brief History of the Texas Rangers"

41

Cort Wesley had been watching the estates lining the Sierra Madre mountain road for hours now, nobody coming or going and no end in sight. A late-afternoon breeze had come up, cooling the day at last but doing little to make him feel more comfortable. He'd wedged the Smith & Wesson back into his pants, no longer seeing the sense in holding it at the ready. Be a lot more comfortable if the magazines were empty now and he was hightailing it back to the border, leaving blood in his wake.

He was a man of action, not thought, and times like these left him too much time to think. The last few minutes those thoughts had turned to Leroy Epps, an old black man he'd gotten to know inside The Walls. Epps was a lifer whose eyes were going thanks to diabetes and who barely left his cell anymore. Their cells were near each other when Cort Wesley first checked in and on days the old man was up to it, he would help him to the cafeteria and sit with him for lunch. Normally the last to arrive were lucky to get scraps, but he'd arranged for Epps's meal anyway to be put aside. They usually had a table, or half of one, to themselves, also prearranged. Just like dining in the finest restaurant, Epps mused once.

Another day his fading eyes stared across the table, studying Cort Wesley.

"Tell me 'bout your ilk, bubba?"

"My what?"

"Your ilk, the core of you. What makes you what you are?"

"Don't rightly know if I can explain that, champ." Cort Wesley called him that because Epps had held a share of the light heavyweight title for all of a single night before the boxing commission stripped him on a technicality and the lack of the right connections.

"Folks inside say you've killed a lot of men."

"I have at that."

"Any one of them not deserve it?"

"Guess that depends on who you ask."

"What about the first one, bubba? How old were you?"

"Sixteen. Just got my driver's license and was on a date. We're walking back to my truck from the movies and these Spanish kids step out in front of us, flashing knives."

"They want your money?"

"Never did say. First one comes at me, knife out, I don't give him the opportunity. I just turned it around on him and stuck it in his gut. He died right there on the sidewalk before the cops showed up. My date's father came and picked her up."

"You figured he was gonna kill you."

"That's what I thought, yeah, champ."

"But it didn't bother you, one way or another."

"Did what I had to. Why should it?"

"That's your ilk," Leroy Epps said, spooning up some half-frozen peas. "What makes you who you are. You're steel to the core. Not cold, not hot, just steel. Nobody gets through. You see what I'm saying?"

"Eat your lunch, champ."

"You let anybody through, it all comes apart. A man with your ilk can't have questions. Line's gotta be straight, bubba. No zigging or zagging, bobbing or weaving."

Cort Wesley had never understood what Epps meant until now, until Caitlin Strong came into his life. He wasn't talking about a physical line, so much as a mental one. No distractions, hesitations or doubts. Woman like Caitlin Strong gets into your head and nothing feels the same anymore. It wasn't so much the doubts, as the thoughts and questions after the fact. Wondering if she'd look at things the same way he did, maybe see him differently if she didn't. The three men he'd gunned down in that bar, for example. Cort Wesley was sure she'd disapproved of his actions and that made him rethink the whole incident in his head.

Line's gotta be straight, bubba. No zigging or zagging, bobbing or weaving.

Leroy Epps had died just before Cort Wesley's release. Too bad, since there wasn't a person in the world he wanted to talk to more. Ask the old man about his ilk now, how a woman like Caitlin Strong might affect it. Everything was fine until The Walls, when his thoughts kept turning to the sons he'd never met. First thing out what's he do but go and spy on them. Since then his mind has been all about them and Caitlin Strong, everything else having to push past one or both to get considered. Cort Wesley figured maybe that was what brought him to Chihuahua: if Garza was inside one of those estates hidden behind walls and nests of cypress trees, he'd have something fresh to think about.

His throwaway cell phone beeped, signaling he had a voice message. Cort Wesley checked the screen. He had eight missed calls and four messages, all from Caitlin Strong.

Something grabbed him tight upside the chest as he pressed the key to play his messages, anxiety already mounting when the single signal bar disappeared before he could hear them. Instantly his attention broke from the phantom Garza back to Caitlin Strong. He wanted to think about her smile, the neat lines of her legs and butt inside her jeans and the way the bottoms of them curled perfectly over her boots.

But all Cort Wesley could think of was what she had called him eight times about, as he hustled back to Pablo Asuna's Ford.

42

East San Antonio, the Present

Caitlin pulled up to the auto repair shop amid a sea of revolving lights. Seemed like everyone was pitching their hat into this ring, including San Antonio police, sheriff's department, and the Rangers. Ranger Berry had told her Captain D. W. Tepper needed her at a crime scene on the east side of town without going into detail about the horrific nature of whatever that crime was.

She saw Tepper waiting for her outside a service door on the near side of the closed garage bay with a row of six windows across its top. He was chomping grimly on a matchstick wedged into the corner of his mouth.

"Got you down here because the victim's a known associate of your friend Cort Wesley Masters," Tepper explained when she reached him. "Man's name is, was, Pablo Asuna. Small-time operator mostly, 'cept for his association with Masters. You need to see what was done to him."

Tepper lifted the crime-scene tape for both of them to pass under and through the door. The smell assaulted Caitlin instantly, a terrible mix of oil, blood and death. A body covered by a plastic forensic sheet lay on the floor alongside a souped-up truck.

"Never seen anything like this in my life before," Tepper was saying, "and I lived a long time."

They crouched over the body and Tepper pulled the sheet back.

"Oh my fucking God," said Caitlin.

"Was my first thought too. Looks like somebody peeled the skin off both his hands with that truck's fan belt. Enjoyed themselves so much they decided to do it to his face too. Truck was still running when the first responders arrived after somebody called 911 claiming they heard screams."

Caitlin turned away. Tepper covered the body up again.

"What I'd like you to tell me," he said, "is that it wasn't Cort Wesley Masters that did this."

Caitlin watched a forensics team lifting a massive footprint from a patch of oil halfway between Pablo Asuna's body and the door. She shook her head. "Asuna was his friend, like you said."

"I said associate, Ranger. You said friend."

"What size are those shoes?" Caitlin asked, moving toward the massive impressions left in the oil stains.

"Sixteen."

"Then it wasn't Masters."

"Could be he brought the giant with him."

"Masters works alone and it couldn't have been him anyway."

"What I'd like you to tell me next is how exactly you can be so sure of that?"

"Because he's in Mexico."

"Interesting fact to come by."

"You want to know how, just ask."

Tepper's expression stiffened. "When you're under my

command again, I expect to be told things without having to ask, Ranger."

"Yes, sir."

"Rather you didn't do nothing to be sorry about. A few nights back, Masters saves your life, vanishes, and now you happen to be aware he's in Mexico. What am I supposed to think about that?"

"Someone framed Cort Wesley in the desert that night five years ago. He wants to know who, Captain. So would I, because whoever it was got Charlie Weeks killed and was behind the attack on the Survivor Center sure as I'm standing here."

They stepped back outside and retreated into the shade.

"Past is done, Ranger," said Tepper. "You don't let it go, it'll eat you alive."

"This isn't about the past, Captain."

"Don't make me regret letting you work your husband's case."

"I won't, sir."

"Because this is blowing up fast. First a bunch of military types take down a torture center and now God know's who, or what, skins a man with a fan belt."

"Shit," Caitlin said, going cold.

"What?"

Caitlin started off, trailed by Tepper's gaze as he mouthed a Marlboro in place of his matchstick. "Ranger?"

"Something I gotta check out, Captain," she said, jogging back to her truck with a spare cell phone coming out of her pocket, "something I gotta check out now."

43

Guillermo Paz sat in the driver's seat of the van parked diagonally across the street from the home of Cort Wesley Masters's former girlfriend, Maura Torres. He wasn't particularly nervous about being spotted, since the van was standard cable television issue, stolen just a few hours earlier from the depot after Pablo Asuna provided the address in Shavano Park.

Man held out until Paz went to work on his face, wedging it down against the fan belt and watching flecks of skin and blood fly off like sawdust spilled from a circular saw. Asuna screamed himself hoarse before gasping out the answers to Paz's questions.

He was waiting for two of his dwarfs to show up now to snatch the kids. He didn't particularly care what they did with the woman, Maura Torres. She meant nothing to Paz because she meant nothing to Masters.

When he'd arrived in the van, a dozen kids maybe had been taking turns on the half-pipe. Paz tried to identify Masters's sons based on resemblance to the pictures he'd seen and realized he'd gotten both right when they went inside the stucco-style house. Nice house, nice yard. Not the kind of work he was used to for sure.

Paz checked his watch, figuring it would be just a few minutes more before the two dwarfs he was awaiting arrived.

.   .   .

Caitlin tossed her cell phone onto the SUV's passenger seat, watched it bounce once and settle. Cort Wesley Masters wasn't picking up, and the only person who could tell her where she could find his boys was lying on a repair shop floor with his face peeled off by a fan belt.

By a man with size sixteen feet.

She should have asked Captain Tepper for a shotgun. Going up against a giant with a small army behind him, based on the other footprints found at Asuna's garage, with just her SIG might not prove all that wise.

Of course, that assumed she'd be able to find the house where Masters's two sons lived in the first place. All he'd mentioned was Shavano Park, something about a cul-de-sac and a skateboard half-pipe. Lots of cul-de-sacs in Shavano Park but not too many half-pipes, and the kind of neighborhood Masters would've wanted his boys growing up in was likely in the town's northwest corner where the best schools were.

Listen to me judging this guy.

But she'd detected the pride and reverence Cort Wesley Masters harbored for his sons in his voice. He had let his guard down around her and Caitlin was still trying to discern what that meant.

Caitlin continued cruising the streets, recalling the grid from her days with the highway patrol. Pictured a human giant striding with two men on either side of him toward two boys riding a half-pipe on their skateboards.

Yup, should have brought a shotgun.

She saw a couple of teenage boys riding bicycles just ahead and slowed to wave them down. Made sure they could see her Ranger badge over the sill of the window.

"You boys wouldn't know anybody around here with a half-pipe would you?"

They didn't but a few blocks later, two girls sitting in the last of the late-afternoon sun pointed west.

"Three streets over," one said.

"Two boys, right?"

"The older one's hot," the other told her.

Caitlin jammed the truck's accelerator down.

"Masters, it's Caitlin Strong. Something bad's going down up here. Your friend Pablo Asuna is dead. I'm heading to the crime scene now. Call you again as soon as I can."

Cort Wesley played the message as soon as he got a bar on his signal indicator that disappeared before he could call Caitlin Strong back.

"Fuck!"

He almost smashed his throwaway cell phone against the old Ford's dashboard he'd already shredded, but then he'd be helpless to reach the Ranger no matter how strong the signal got. He knew whoever had killed Asuna did it to to get to him and could only hope it was someone making a point instead of pumping Pablo for information. Having arranged for money to be provided to Maura Torres and his boys, he was the only man on God's green earth who knew the address.

Cort Wesley got cold just thinking about that. Buckets of sweat were pouring off him, soaking the car's cracked upholstery, his blood feeling as if it were boiling off in-side him. He wasn't used to anybody doing anything for him, much less needing someone's help. He could drive a hundred miles an hour and still never get there in time, leaving Caitlin Strong as the only chance his boys had to stay alive.

44

Paz saw the car with San Antonio police markings heading down the street in his sideview mirror. As the car drew closer to the house across the street with the half-pipe in the front yard, he recognized two of his dwarfs in the front seat, each wearing khaki SAPD uniforms. Again, Paz didn't know whether they were authentic or not.

Unless they had exited through the back, Dylan and Luke Torres were still inside, had been ever since their mother had poked her head through the door and yelled out at them. Something about homework. The other kids who'd been riding the half-pipe dashed away on their bicycles.

Paz had never ridden a bicycle, that seeming strange to him for some reason now. Then he turned his attention back on the police car coming to a halt directly in front of Maura Torres's house.

Caitlin saw the two SAPD officers heading up the walk, breathing a sigh of relief. They had just passed the half-pipe and were climbing the front steps when she ground her SUV to a halt behind their cruiser. She leaped out and jogged toward them, noticing they were wearing work boots under their khaki trousers, just as the front door opened and Maura Torres leaned out toward them.

Work boots . . .

Caitlin remembered screaming *No!*, remembered

drawing her SIG in the same instant one of the cops was drawing his sidearm.

He fired.

She fired.

Maura Torres was blown back inside the house.

The cop's head rocked sideways, smacking him into the other one who was drawing his gun too.

The second cop shed the body of the first and twisted. Caitlin sighted in on him and fired. Four shots.

Boom, boom, boom, boom . . .

Like thunderclaps forewarning an early evening storm.

The bodies of both cops crumbling then, front door to the house still open, Cort Wesley Masters's older boy Dylan lurching into it from inside. Caitlin saw the confusion on his face, the shock claiming his features, his childhood ended then and there.

Thud, thud, thud . . .

Caitlin swung toward the sound of footsteps pounding pavement and saw the giant charging across the street, a submachine gun steadying in each of his hands.

45

SHAVANO PARK, TEXAS, THE PRESENT

Madre de Dios!

Paz cursed himself for stowing the submachine guns under his seat instead of alongside it. If he'd done that this would've all been over by now, the precious seconds lost never to be regained.

He couldn't believe the sight of the tall woman, made even taller by the white Texas Ranger Stetson, loping across the front yard, pistol out and firing. *Clack, clack, clack.*

One of his dwarfs shot and then the other.

He was out of the car by then, but too late by a hair again, because the woman had spotted him, her pistol coming round just as his submachine guns were coming up.

Caitlin fired as she ran, her aim thrown off at the last by the dive that took her sprawling into Dylan. Both of them went down even with Maura Torres's body as automatic fire stitched the air above them.

Firing her last two shots at the giant, she dragged Dylan all the way inside and kicked the door closed behind them. Snapped a fresh magazine home even as twin fusillades tore up the wood and sent bullets bouncing in all directions.

A mirror cracked. A vase exploded. Something fell off the wall.

A boy screamed.

Caitlin saw Luke, Cort Wesley's younger son, standing there over his mother in plain view of the window and left Dylan long enough to take him down at the legs. She heard the sizzling hiss of bullets overhead, the wall in line with where Luke's head had been punched with holes.

Caitlin realized she had dropped Luke directly atop his mother's body, the sight too horrible to consider while her mind flashed back to Charlie Weeks dying slowly in her arms as bullets flew everywhere that night in the West Texas desert too. But this wasn't the Chihuahuan and help would be coming soon enough if she could hold out that long.

Caitlin rose into a crouch and grabbed both boys by

the shoulders, dragging them toward the first wall break toward the kitchen. She'd just rounded the corner when a massive booted foot kicked in the shot-up front door. It cracked at the frame and Caitlin caught her second glimpse of the giant who had thought nothing of feeding a man's face to a truck engine, their eyes catching for the briefest of moments.

Wild, shiny hair. Burnt-brown skin. She thought she could smell a stink rising off him like fish oil and dried mud.

A swinging door led into the kitchen. Caitlin pushed the boys through it, then slotted the bolt, hitting the floor with the sons of Cort Wesley Masters pressed beneath her.

Paz fired twin bursts through the swinging door that suddenly wasn't swinging anymore. A single thrust of his shoulder would tear it free of its hinges and open the way for him. But he stopped his motion as quickly as he started it.

The woman Ranger was behind the door, waiting, begging for him to do just that. She'd be hunkered down low, below his expected fire burst with Cort Wesley Masters's kids protected by her frame.

Paz crouched low, steadied both his submachine guns even with the wood seam of the flimsy door six inches off the floor. He screamed as he burst through it, wood shattering all around him as he sprayed his fire toward the Ranger to finish the job.

Except she wasn't there, wasn't anywhere; Paz was left frozen by an indecision he could never quite recall feeling before.

. . .

Caitlin fired through the glass of the French doors leading onto a stamped concrete patio and then to the backyard beyond. Impact threw her trajectory off, not much but enough to make the rounds miss the huge target who'd come crashing through the door into the kitchen. He stayed low, beneath her sight line, and she backpedaled toward the storage shed she'd ordered Dylan and Luke to hide behind, firing off more rounds through the glass.

Her SIG's slide locked open just as she reached the boys, slamming her final magazine home and waiting for the fresh thump of the giant's steps thrashing across the soft backyard turf. Cort Wesley's sons were seated with their backs pressed against the shed, trapped between sobs and heavy rasps. Luke, the younger one, had his arms curled round his knees, rocking slightly. Dylan, the older one, was staring straight ahead, sniffling, eyes filled with hate and an intensity that reminded her too much of his father.

Caitlin looked at them and saw Cort Wesley, his spirit and soul tucked into smaller packages soon to seethe with the same violence that had so dominated his life. She wished she could take the boys in her arms and shield them from the horror that had now come irrevocably into their lives. Men like the giant who'd killed their mother and Masters himself were more like forces of nature whose deeds and actions polluted the lives of those around them no matter how much others tried to dictate otherwise. To his credit, Cort Wesley had tried to protect his sons from the kind of violence that had been visited on them today. In the end, though, his futile efforts had made them as much prisoners of his very being as he was.

The younger boy, Luke, pushed up against her and Caitlin drew him closer with her free arm.

"I wanna go see my mother," Dylan started, looking at the gun held in her other hand. "See maybe if . . ."

His voice drifted off along with his hope. Caitlin let him have the silence, listening to the sirens screaming in the distance with pistol clutched tightly and ready in case the giant was still out there.

46

SHAVANO PARK, TEXAS, THE PRESENT

Caitlin wouldn't let go of Dylan and Luke until D. W. Tepper arrived on the scene. She'd kept them away from ceaseless badgering by the local cops and kept them out of sight from the crime-scene technicians starting work on the body of their mother.

Captain Tepper finally climbed out of his truck with an unlit Marlboro dangling from the side of his mouth and a wan expression deepening the furrows in his leathery skin. He stopped briefly to consult with the local detectives and forensics techs, then continued on again. Night had fallen, but the blaze of headlights, portable lamps and television camera Day-Glo bulbs made it feel like day. Caitlin and the boys clung to what passed for darkness, watching Tepper emerge from the brightness. He gestured for her to join him and Caitlin left the boys huddled together against the side of the house, never taking her eyes off them.

"You wanna tell me 'bout them?"

Tepper followed the line of Caitlin's gaze to Dylan and Luke.

"Those are Cort Wesley Masters's sons," she said, just before her phone rang.

. . .

"Rangers are gonna send a chopper there to pick you up," Caitlin said, after telling Cort Wesley where to drive.

"Texas Rangers sending *me* a chopper. That's one for the ages."

She backed off a bit more to make sure his sons couldn't hear her. "Your boys need you, Cort Wesley."

"They don't even know me."

"Right now, that'll have to pass."

"Man who did this, you ever seen him before?"

Caitlin thought of the look in the giant's eyes, the smell that rose off him. "I'm not even sure it was a man."

"Come again?"

"Never mind. Just thinking to myself. I shot two of his men. Their bodies might tell us something once we get 'em IDed."

"Sounds like a paramilitary team. Clayton and company's replacements."

"They knew you had kids, Masters, and they knew Asuna would know where to find them. Your normal gang enemies aren't nearly that resourceful."

Caitlin listened to his breathing on the other end of the line.

"They see their mother get shot?" he asked finally.

"Leave it 'til you get up here."

"Just answer my question."

Caitlin didn't.

"That's what I thought," she heard Masters say before his phone clicked off.

47

Three hours later into the night, a Ranger SUV pulled up and Cort Wesley Masters climbed out. His sons were still munching on their leftover McDonald's and Caitlin left them to finish, while she met Cort Wesley off to the side of the yard where they couldn't see him. He was breathing fast and sweating through his shirt, his face red with so much rage Caitlin thought the veins in his temples might be ready to burst.

"I want to see Maura."

"You can't."

He glared at her. "You wanna be the one to stop me?"

"Medical examiner already took the body away."

"What'd they do to Asuna?" he asked, after sweeping his eyes about as if to take in the scene.

"You don't want to know right now."

Cort Wesley's skin was shiny with a thin layer of sweat. His breaths seemed to be growing faster and harder, like a bomb ticking down to triple zeroes. "Two people know me best in the world and look what happens."

"You still got your sons."

Masters looked at Caitlin as if just noticing she was there. "Guess I got you to thank for that."

"Just like I got you to thank for the Survivor Center the other night."

Their eyes held, neither sure what to make of the other's gazes.

"You need to talk to your boys," Caitlin said finally.

"Got something to tell you first."

"You're putting this off."

"I found the warehouse where those crates came from five years ago. Man inside remembered the shipment, couldn't say what was inside."

"You believe him?"

"Let's say I gave him ample stimulus to tell the truth." Cort Wesley shook his head and took a deep breath in through his nose. "Don't know what I would've done if one of my sons had been shot."

"They weren't."

"Thanks to you."

"I got lucky."

"That what you call it?"

"When a man's firing two machine guns at you, yeah, that's what I call it."

"I call it surviving, something you and I seem pretty good at." Cort Wesley blew his breath out in a steady stream. "What happens now to my boys?"

"I don't know much about the procedure. Any relatives?"

"'Sides me, you mean? Not unless they join the rest of Maura's family in Mexico."

"Guess they end up in the system."

"Foster care, some shit like that?"

"'Less you got a better idea, Masters." Caitlin waited as long as she could to see if he posed one. "Course their lives being in danger, them being material witnesses and all, I suppose Captain Tepper can round up some protection for them, for a time anyway."

"I'd appreciate that."

They stood off to the side of the half-pipe, while the police activity continued to flare around them. More media vehicles had now shown up to join the sea of others, eager to report on a Wild West-style shoot-out in the suburbs. Rumors of a Texas Ranger right in the middle of things. Wait until they got hold of the fact that these kill-ings were linked to the death of Pablo Asuna earlier the same day in East San Antonio, Caitlin thought.

Cort Wesley stuck a cigarette in his mouth but stopped short of lighting it and tossed it aside, only to be retrieved by Caitlin.

"This is still a crime scene," she reminded him.

"Right, musta slipped my mind."

"You get out of prison," Caitlin said thoughtfully, "off you go to watch Dylan and Luke skateboard."

"Wanted to see how they'd grown up. Hope you don't blame me."

"Only for talking to me right now instead of them."

"I'm close as I can get to that at this point."

Caitlin focused her stare on Cort Wesley's rough-hewn looks, a sharp edge to every part of him, as if he used a file on his skin and bone. "Not close enough," she said, starting to walk away.

"Hold up," he said, drawing even with her.

"You're not telling me the truth, Masters."

"Come again?"

"You park your car outside the house, who was it you really wanted to see?"

"I told you."

"You lied."

His stare hardened, forearms flexing to bands of knobby muscle. "Don't like being called something I'm not."

Caitlin shook her head, started on again.

"Where you headed?" Cort Wesley asked, keeping pace with her.

"Back to the hospital, see my husband. You wanna tag along?"

He stuck another cigarette in his mouth, again stopped short of lighting it. "If you don't mind."

Caitlin looked him square in the eye. "Not at all. Think

I'll have your boys ride with us so we can keep an eye on them up close 'til Captain Tepper gets them settled." She plucked the cigarette from his mouth. "Those things'll kill ya, you know."

"Something's gotta."

48

SAN ANTONIO, THE PRESENT

Dylan and Luke rode with them to the hospital in the backseat of Caitlin's SUV, the bags they'd packed stowed in the hatch. Luke was holding a handheld video game, playing it or not she couldn't tell. Dylan was staring straight ahead, his breaths making a slight wheezing sound. No one spoke.

Captain D. W. Tepper and a second Ranger bracketed them front and rear. Tepper's patchwork face had crinkled further at the sight of Cort Wesley coming along but to his credit he said nothing. It made Caitlin think of another of the Ranger tales of lore told to her by her grandfather.

"Texas Rangers got a long history of straddling the law," she said out loud, as much to break the silence in the SUV as anything. "I'm not talking about them necessarily committing illegal acts, much as forging alliances with bad men to go after ones who were worse."

She could see in the rearview mirror that both boys were looking at her now.

"My granddad liked to tell a tale 'bout the Rangers taking on Mexicans who were making war on the border around, oh, 1920, after World War I. These Rangers were outnumbered at times ten to one and, 'cause they were still traveling on horseback in those days, they tended to pack light: rifle and sidearm, that was it. Now 'round the same time what would later be referred to as organized crime was running moonshine whiskey across the state in trucks guarded by men wielding the original tommy guns. So the Rangers recruited them to help in their efforts at the border. Those moonshine runners had more to lose than anybody under the circumstances, so they signed on. As my granddad told it, a few of them were formally deputized. Years later, one was found dead in a Chicago alley still wearing the badge."

Another check of the rearview mirror found both boys studying her, Luke looking up from his video game and Dylan looking alive again.

"You ever shoot anybody before today?" he asked her.

"Yup."

"Kill anybody?"

"Yup. Not that I'm proud of it."

"You proud of what you did today?"

"Nope."

"Figured." Dylan sighed, leaning back with arms crossed. "Why?"

"'Cause I was too late to save your mom."

"What's it feel like to shoot somebody?" Dylan asked, after the SUV had lapsed back into silence.

His question was aimed at Caitlin, but it was Cort Wesley who answered. "Feels good, if it stopped them from doing the same to you."

"How many men you killed?"

"None that didn't deserve it and wouldn't have done the same to me, given the chance."

"A lot then, right?"

Caitlin watched Cort Wesley twist slightly in the

passenger seat to face Dylan, who flinched at the sudden motion, still jumpy from all that had happened. "Whether you've killed one or a hundred, it's the same thing. You look in the mirror and see somebody different staring back, you got call to worry."

Dylan nodded, though it was clear he didn't get Cort Wesley's point. Caitlin wasn't sure she did either. But she figured that was as close as he could come to breaking ground with his sons. Talk about something he knew best of all.

"That was a mighty good story, Caitlin Strong," Cort Wesley told her. "I think I heard almost the very same one from my great-uncle."

She glanced briefly his way. "You never told me your uncle was a Ranger."

"'Cause he wasn't. He was a moonshiner."

49

SAN ANTONIO, THE PRESENT

Peter's hospital bed was littered with precision tools, diodes, wires and chips. Caitlin couldn't tell which had come from what. He perked up at her appearance, shoulders lifting and eyes brimming briefly with recognition, before his expression flattened as if he'd forgotten why. Cort Wesley stood in the doorway directly across from Captain Tepper, watching his boys in the protective company of the night shift who'd taken over for Rangers Berry and Rollins.

Caitlin approached Peter alone, not wanting to risk startling him with the presence of strangers.

"I finished," he said, looking alive again as he had when she'd left.

He used the bedside remote control to turn on the television, then struggled out of bed and dragged his bare feet across the cold tile floor. Caitlin noticed they were bent inward, the toes gnarled and twisted. The screen coming to life stole her gaze from them, and Caitlin saw her cell phone had been wired to it via a thin connecting wire in place of the cable box. She identified at least one adapter and could tell he had been busy splicing any number of wires together in search of compatibility.

Peter jogged the phone's menu to video and activated the PLAY command. Captain Tepper edged into the room to better see when the screen brightened to life. Cort Wesley remained in the doorway.

The screen sharpened to reveal a much larger version of what Caitlin had watched on the tiny screen. She turned the volume up on the television and watched the receptionist retake her seat behind the desk and start doodling on a notepad before reaching for the phone.

"Mr. Hollis, it's Grace Devallos over at DynaTech in San Antonio. . . . Yes, sir, I know, but my instructions were to call if anyone came around asking about—RevCom, that's right, sir. . . . A Texas Ranger. . . ."

The woman quiet now, pen laid down.

"No, her questions seemed innocent enough. She just asked about RevCom. . . . Yes, it was a woman. . . . Hold on, I wrote it down."

Eyes back on the notepad.

"Strong, Caitlin Strong. . . . Yes, I checked her ID. . . . She was dressed like Rangers always dress. . . . No, sir, she only asked about RevCom, if they'd left a forwarding address or something. . . . Yes, of course, sir."

"Can you play it again?" she asked and took out her

notepad. "Peter?" she prodded, when he didn't respond, his expression remaining blank. Caitlin moved directly into his line of vision. "Can you play it again, please?"

This time Peter obliged robotically, working her cell phone once more. When the screen lit back to life, Caitlin focused on the woman's fingers on the telephone keypad, jotting down the numbers she was hitting.

Nine first for an outside line, then one for long distance. Area code 713. Houston.

Caitlin watched that part of the recording three more times to make sure she had the number right. Then tore off the sheet from her notepad and handed it to Tepper.

"You get me the address that goes with this, Captain?"

He folded the piece of paper in half and tucked it into his pocket. "When I started with the Rangers, a canteen that kept the water from boiling off was considered high tech."

"You still got your man."

"More often than not, anyway."

"Houston," Cort Wesley Masters echoed.

"Seems to have struck some chord in you," Caitlin noted.

"Those crates from the warehouse in Juárez, that's where they were headed."

She watched Masters move to the bed where Peter had scattered the tools and various unused parts. He lifted a small black square, shiny with green lines running through it, from the covers.

"What's this?"

Peter paid no attention. Cort Wesley looked to Caitlin for help. She took the black square from him and held it in front of her husband.

"Do you know what this is?"

"Computer chip. Cheap. Piece of shit."

"What's it do?"

"Nothing now."

Caitlin turned back to Cort Wesley. "Why the interest?"

He took the chip back from her. "Because in Juárez the warehouse guy's daughter was wearing something like this around her neck."

PART SIX

In February 1934, Lee Simmons, superintendent of the Texas prison system, asked [former Ranger Frank Hamer] if he would track down the notorious criminal couple Clyde Barrow and Bonnie Parker. . . . Hamer trailed Bonnie and Clyde for one hundred and two days. Finally, Hamer and other officers, including former Ranger B. M. Gault, caught up with the dangerous duo in Louisiana's Bienville Parish. The officers had hoped to take the outlaws alive, but when the pair reached for their weapons, Hamer and the others opened fire. The career of Bonnie and Clyde was over.

—Mike Cox, with updates from the Texas Ranger Hall of Fame and Museum Staff, "A Brief History of the Texas Rangers"

50

HOUSTON, THE PRESENT

The katana hissed through the air of Harm Delladonne's private dojo up in his office loft, slicing imaginary enemies. The sword was one of twenty in his collection, all antiques dating back as much as five centuries. Several had been smuggled out of Japan. Others had been refurbished to their original condition at considerable expense and time, five years or more.

Delladonne didn't care. He was a patient man for the most part, keenly aware that the things that were most important could not be rushed. Quality never sacrificed for speed.

The same held true for his vision for the country, his desire to see it safe and protected. For years money had been his prime motivation. Now, with literally billions in hand, he had turned the vast resources he had accumulated toward the far more daunting obsession to insulate the United States from its enemies now and forever. A crowning achievement that would leave the current administration and every other beholden to MacArthur-Rain.

Just as his father had envisioned but failed to accomplish.

Now, so soon after that goal had been tantalizingly within his reach, Delladonne felt it slipping from his grasp. And, worse, he had begun to fear he could not insulate MacArthur-Rain from the fallout over the latest attempt to cut the company's cord to its own failed efforts.

Fire Arrow . . .

The ultimate weapon, the weapon that could help Delladonne realize all his goals at once. If only Peter Goodwin had simply agreed to cooperate, that weapon would be operational now. The most dire enemies of this nation, the men his father had failed to stop, would be reduced to no more than minor inconveniences and distractions. Struck down when his will imposed it.

If only . . .

Then by now Harm Delladonne would have become more powerful than any president or politician. Not a king, not even a kingmaker. But the man pulling all the strings behind the curtain, just as his father had foreseen that day in 1993.

Delladonne considered himself a master at judging people, at how to get what he wanted from them by pushing just hard enough. But he had badly misjudged Peter Goodwin's resolve, and that failure now threatened the very fabric of his being. He'd retreated to his private dojo in the hope that slicing up imaginary enemies would compensate for having lost the opportunity to eliminate real ones.

Guillermo Paz had not reported in, and Delladonne imagined himself also cutting the big man in half for his stunning failure. The baggy sides of his kimonolike training hakama flopped in an invisible breeze as he repeated the simple moves of the kata again and again. There was such beauty in simplicity. And the simplicity of sword training held the greatest secrets of success in all things.

But everything else had turned absurdly complex. Delladonne had already heard from Washington. The powers controlling the purse strings of his multibillion-dollar government contracts wanted a meeting, the prospects of which held a grim portent for the once promising future.

Delladonne's private phone rang, the one line he'd had rigged in his dojo. He sheathed the katana and lifted the receiver, noticing the ten zeroes in the caller ID.

"I'm on my way down there now," the voice said.

"You damn well better clean up this mess your man made. You assured me he was good—the best, you said."

"He is."

"Doesn't say a lot for your judgment, does it? Have you at least heard from the Venezuelan?"

"I reached him this morning."

"And?"

"That's why I'm on my way down. Handle things up close and personal."

"I want him gone."

"That's the problem. He won't leave."

"Won't leave?"

"Says he has an obligation to a higher power to make good here. Honor his commitment."

"Higher power?"

"That's what he said."

"You're telling me he's still in San Antonio."

"Yes. To finish the job, he says."

"The Ranger knows what he looks like. They'll be looking for him all over the city. That makes him a liability. I want him pulled. Pay him off and send him home."

"My intentions exactly."

"You've worked with a lot of men like this."

"Never a man exactly like this, no, sir." A pause followed, the air heavy over the line. "How's your security?"

"You think he'd come after *me?*"

"I don't know what he'll do. Just be extracautious until I arrive."

Delladonne glanced from his sheathed katana to the rest of his swords mounted on the wall, each of which had spilled blood and taken lives. He was respectful of that reality each and every time he bowed in reverence before and after drawing one of them.

"Don't worry," he told the voice on the other end of the line.

51

HOUSTON, THE PRESENT

"I'm hoping you can help me, Mr. Hollis," Caitlin said to Charles Hollis. His title listed him as director of Internal Security for MacArthur-Rain Industries. The number dialed yesterday by DynaTech's receptionist had been to his exchange here at the company's headquarters in Houston. Caitlin had driven to the airport and flown here, as soon as Captain D. W. Tepper had reached her with the news.

"I'll do my best, Ranger," Hollis promised, not seeming anxious or on his guard. He had strawlike hair colored the chalk yellow of a bad dye job, cropped close enough to make him look military. But his blue eyes were weak and shifty, having trouble staying focused on anything for more than an instant. Kind of guy, Caitlin thought, who buys a uniform at an Army-Navy store and wears it to the shooting range, or to play paintball on a corporate outing. "Does this have something to do with one of our employees? Because that's the primary focus of my office."

"Corporate espionage, sabotage, that sort of thing?"

"It's more common than most realize."

"I'm sure it is, but that's not why I'm here, Mr. Hollis. I'm here about a company in San Antonio called Dyna-Tech. Used to be known as RevCom."

Caitlin studied Hollis's reaction, saw nothing of note.

"And why does that bring you to me?"

"Because someone from DynaTech called you yesterday."

Still no response, other than a slight flicker of his eyebrows.

"You must be mistaken, Ranger."

"Would've been late morning, early afternoon maybe."

"I was in a meeting at the time."

"Which time?"

"Both of them."

Caitlin studied him briefly. The man wasn't much of a liar. Of course, he couldn't have known that she had a videotape of the receptionist addressing him by name. "And it doesn't strike you as strange that someone from DynaTech would have called you?"

"Or someone in my department? Not really."

"Why's that?"

"Because MacArthur-Rain owns DynaTech. We purchased RevCom and managed the transition. I recall running background checks on all our new employees."

"Since you dumped all the old ones. Why'd you do that, by the way?"

"What?"

"Background checks."

"A requirement in the post-9/11 age, especially in view of this company's considerable international business dealings."

Caitlin eased her chair a bit closer to Hollis's desk. "When exactly did you swallow up RevCom?"

Hollis's expression remained etched in stone. "I don't

recall. MacArthur-Rain has any number of subsidiaries and off-sites, hundreds in fact. I deal with background checks and security issues for all of them, far too many to remember the precise details of each."

"What's an off-site?"

"Business we contract with to perform specialized services for us."

"Before you swallow them up, that is, like you did with RevCom?"

Hollis's face finally cracked. "I'm confused, Ranger. What exactly brought you here again?"

"Accusation made by a former employee of RevCom."

"And who's that?"

"Can't say."

"Can you tell me the gist of the accusation?"

"Nope. Not at this time."

"What can you tell me?"

Caitlin pulled from her pocket the black computer chip Cort Wesley Masters had lifted off Peter's bedcovers the previous night, recognizing it from a facsimile in Mexico. "Know what this is?"

"I'm afraid I don't."

"Ever seen one before?"

"Definitely not."

"Because we're thinking something like them, lots of something like them, were smuggled out of Mexico five years ago and delivered right here to this building," Caitlin said. "It's a simple chip, bit outdated now, I'm told. Who here would know something about that?"

"You'd have to talk to someone in our technologies division."

"Where's that?"

"Well, that all depends."

"On what?"

"Which technology you're speaking of. We have over a

hundred offices in more than sixty countries pursuing over a thousand projects at any one given time. Hospitals, schools, oil fields, reconstruction efforts—the list is too long to reel off now."

"What about military?"

Hollis didn't hesitate. "Of course."

"So you see what I'm getting at here."

"Not really."

"Maybe someone at MacArthur-Rain was buying cut-rate chips out of Mexico. Maybe some of those chips malfunctioned, caused a whole lot of people a whole lot of heartache. Maybe you can point me in the direction of the person I should be talking to on the subject."

"That could take some time."

"How much?"

Hollis was starting to get riled, impatience showing in the reddening of his neck just over his shirt collar. "It's doubtful the information you're seeking is even housed here. I'll need to track down where that division's located."

"What if it was related to the work you're doing in Iraq?"

"I'm not allowed to discuss the specifics of our government contracts."

"Even to tell me if you got people over there or not. Hell, I can get that from the newspaper."

"Then I suggest you keep reading," Hollis said, holding Caitlin's stare.

"You're not being much help here, Mr. Hollis."

"You haven't given me much call to be, Ranger."

"How 'bout to aid in the investigation into one of your government contracts?"

"We have our own internal division to handle such things."

"Very objective, I'm sure."

If that particular remark bothered Hollis, he didn't show it. Caitlin extended her hand across his desk, eyeing the computer chip lying before him.

"You don't mind, I'll have that back."

Hollis handed it to her, seeming to have forgotten it was there. "MacArthur-Rain does wish to cooperate with you, Ranger."

Caitlin rose and stood over his desk. "You're a lousy liar, Mr. Hollis."

He started to come out of his chair but stopped and sat back down. "Excuse me?"

"I spoke to a woman named Grace Devallos yesterday at DynaTech, so she called you. She told you all about me, who I was. But when I met you a few minutes ago, you pretended you never heard of me before, even though you were probably pulling my file off some database yesterday. You wanna tell me I'm lying?"

"No, Ranger, you're just wrong."

Caitlin looked down at his phone. "How 'bout you make a call to your boss? The two of us can go see him together, set all this straight."

"My boss?"

"Owner of the company. CEO, CFO, COO, B-O for all I care." She picked up the receiver and stuck it out toward him. "Come on, make the call."

When he didn't, Caitlin simply nodded and spun the phone toward her.

"Okay, just give me the extension and *I'll* call him."

Hollis tried to look intimidating. "You're out of your jurisdiction, Ranger."

"You're not from Texas, are you, Mr. Hollis?"

"No, I'm not."

"Then let me enlighten you: know what a Ranger's jurisdiction is?"

"I'm afraid I don't."

"As far as his or her horse can ride. Of course, it's cars now, so I guess that means we make our own jurisdiction when we get there." Caitlin slid back from his desk. "I'm here now. I don't get to have a heart-to-heart with your boss today, I'll just wait a bit." She fastened her Stetson back in place. "Tell him I stopped by, if you don't mind. And that I look forward to catching up with him real soon."

52

HOUSTON, THE PRESENT

Albert Johannson was in the midst of giving his statement to the Rangers when Caitlin's call caused a temporary delay.

"All that time you didn't know you were working for MacArthur-Rain," she said from a bench in Discovery Green overlooking a man-made pond. She thought she saw some fish cruising about the surface, but wasn't sure. The park was like an oasis in the midst of a desert of the steel and glass that formed downtown Houston.

"How could I? There was nothing about it in the employment contract or anything else I had to sign or read. No corporate gatherings or off-site meetings. Nothing like that. But it makes sense, that's for sure."

"Why?"

"Because MacArthur-Rain's the Antichrist of modern conglomerates. The master of the no-bid contracts. Know why?"

"Tell me."

"Because they don't have any competition: they've bought it all up."

Caitlin let Johannson's comment settle a bit. "All right, let's try something else. Tell me where most of Peter's work for RevCom was focused."

"Signal integration."

"What's that mean?"

"Obtaining Internet, phone and television all from a single provider. These providers have been offering to bundle these services for years. By 2009, 2010 maybe, they'll have a virtual monopoly on sales and service, not to mention wireless routing, so everything is channeled through the home PC."

"I think something about his work attracted the attention of MacArthur-Rain. I think that's what gave birth to Fire Arrow, Mr. Johannson. Some big government contract took Peter and his team to Iraq, and it was MacArthur-Rain all along."

"You still don't get it, do you?"

"Why don't you tell me, Mr. Johannson?"

"When it comes to that kind of work, MacArthur-Rain *is* the government."

Cort Wesley Masters sat down on the bench next to Caitlin as soon as she'd repocketed her cell phone.

"You followed me all the way to Houston," she said to him, in what had started out as a question.

"Protecting you, I prefer to call it."

"How's that?"

"By making sure no one else was following you."

"And?"

"I'm it."

"That's reassuring."

"How was your morning?"

"Not sure yet."

"Stir the pot a bit?"

"We'll see." She hardened her stare on him. "Seems to me you got better places to be right now, Masters."

"Damned if I can think of any, Caitlin Strong."

"How 'bout with your boys?"

"Rangers got that handled," he said, looking away from her in that moment. Caitlin wondered what it was in his eyes he didn't want her to see. "Nothing I can do they can't right now and I'm deeply appreciative for the help."

"Your boys are gonna need other kinds of help. Counseling, something like that."

"We'll get there in time."

"You don't seem to be in any particular rush."

"You handle your business and leave mine to me."

"You plan on hanging around them this time?"

"Was no other time, Ranger."

"And me thinking birth qualifies."

"I had an arrangement with their mother. Things are different now obviously."

"Different today than yesterday, tomorrow too."

"What's that supposed to mean exactly?"

"You're not telling them the truth yet, Masters. Allows you the freedom to turn your back and walk away. Straight out of their lives as quickly as you wandered in."

"You being the expert here is based on what? 'Less you got kids of your own stashed somewhere I don't know about."

"I'm not a parent, but I had one, just one, after my mom died. And the loneliest I ever felt in my life was the day my father died. Got through my mother passing 'cause we had each other. When he died, it was just me. I still remember that feeling plain as day and I don't really think I ever got over it."

"Now you know what I'm doing here, Ranger: making sure the same thing doesn't happen to my sons, at least not yet. You think that giant's gonna just fly back to whatever shit-smelling country he came from? You think a company like MacArthur-Rain's just gonna give up and admit they been beat? Nope, they ain't going away and you know it, know it so well you decided to pay them a visit up close and personal today. Let them see your face, face of the person who gunned down two of the ones they sent yesterday." Cort Wesley grinned knowingly. "No different at all, Ranger."

"From what?"

"From yours truly. Me walking into that bar the other day in East San Antonio was the same thing."

"Except I didn't shoot up the place."

"No, you just shot your mouth off. Same thing in a lot of ways, sticking your intentions right in their face."

Caitlin yanked the right leg of her jeans down over her boot to even it with the left. "Still doesn't make me like you."

"Except we're still both doing things the way they were done before, not now. You and me, we play by our own rules and when they don't work we make new ones up."

"If you can't see the difference, Masters, I can't begin to explain it."

"I can prove I'm right."

"How?"

"The look in your eyes when I sat down next to you: you were glad to see me and don't bother trying to deny it."

Caitlin didn't.

"My kids, your husband. I'm the only one knows what you're feeling, willing to do whatever it takes to make this right."

"I'm not conceding your point."

"You telling me the lawmen who made the Texas Rangers legends weren't as much outlaws as the men they gunned down?"

"You asking me if they skirted the law sometimes, the answer is yes."

Cort Wesley let her see he was staring at her. "Sounds like breaking the law to me."

"You should know, Masters."

53

SAN ANTONIO, THE PRESENT

Guillermo Paz stood outside the San Fernando Cathedral on West Main Plaza in San Antonio. A plaque outside said it was the oldest cathedral sanctuary in the United States. Paz didn't know what that meant exactly and didn't care. He would've preferred a church in east San Antonio but too many of them had locked doors and bars across their stained-glass windows.

Paz walked up the stone steps and entered the chapel where the famous Alamo hero Jim Bowie was married before dying at the hands of Santa Anna, who used the building as an observation post. Bowie was buried in the church's graveyard, along with Davy Crockett and Colonel William Travis.

He didn't know where Santa Anna was buried, even though the great general had been a childhood hero of his until Paz realized how he'd squandered all his vast power on a foolish crusade, just like Hugo Chavez was doing in Venezuela now. Maybe this was an opportune time to have made the move circumstances had forced upon him. There were plenty of Chavezes in the world. And the best thing about them was that they'd always need men like Paz.

But now another set of circumstances had forced him to seek counsel from a priest yet again. Of course, San Antonio was nothing like La Vega, the slum in which he had grown up, and the San Fernando Cathedral was nothing like the crumbling church structure at the foot of the hillside. Even the crucifix that hung atop the weathered door was cracked in two.

Inside the cathedral, he squeezed into a confessional only slightly larger than the one in La Vega. Instantly the door slid back, revealing a face cloaked in shadows on the other side of the screen.

"Bless me, Father, for I have sinned. It has been four days since my last confession."

"How can I help you, my son?"

"I need to talk to you about something that happened yesterday."

"Did you commit a sin, my son?"

"I tried to kill some people. I failed. I'm not sure which is the greater sin."

"Excuse me?"

"Two children and a woman. This is turning into some week. First, back home I disobeyed orders for the first time by not burning a village, and then I come up here and fail."

The priest considered his words. "Perhaps you made yourself fail."

"Padre?"

"Perhaps you could not let yourself kill these children you mentioned."

Paz hesitated. "Hadn't thought of that to tell you the truth."

"But it's possible."

"Look, it's the woman I'm here about. Our eyes met, Father, and I knew the look in them because I know my own. It was like I was looking at myself, and I don't know if I can finish the job now because I'm afraid of what might happen."

"Killing is a sin even God cannot forgive without cause, my son."

"You ever read philosophy, Padre?"

"A little."

"I do a lot, thanks to a priest like you who taught me how to read. Kierkegaard's my favorite, because I've always been able to relate what he says to my life. Take ethics, for example. Kierkegaard believed that ethical development begins when an individual forms a total commitment to something. He thought that was the road to self-understanding. Whether that road gets you anywhere or not depends on how well you live out your beliefs in an honest and devoted way."

"And does that describe you, my son?"

Paz felt thoughts rattling around in his head he couldn't quite get a handle on. "It did. Now I'm not so sure. Here's the thing, Padre. Kierkegaard left the judgment stuff to others, mostly yourself, which is why I've always liked him."

"So you're saying this woman has made you see and judge yourself differently."

"I think that's it, yeah. I've gone my whole life and never run into anyone like this woman before. I'm not even sure she was real now. There was something about her. . . . Could she be an angel, Father, one of the badass ones who fought the devil and all?"

"God has His reasons for whom He places on this earth, my son."

"Amen to that. I knew it had to be true or how else could I be the way I am? Live with all the things I've done. No way unless I was supposed to be doing them, right?"

"God may supply our nature, but what we do with that nature is up to us. The concept of free will."

"I never thought I had that before, thought I was just a piece of someone else's grand scheme. Yesterday I looked into this woman's eyes and saw the other part of me too."

"You are free to decide not to kill, my son. I believe that's what happened to you yesterday."

"I never fail, Father, never."

"Perhaps your definitions of success and failure are confused. Did you ever consider that?"

"Not really, no. You know the story of David and Goliath?"

"Of course."

"I always figured David killed him because inside he was just as much a monster. He just didn't know it yet. So this woman, she's just like me. But she doesn't know it yet either."

"What are you afraid of, my son?" the priest asked Paz, his own voice cracking with fear.

"Nothing until yesterday. Now I'm not so sure. This woman scared me, Father. More than anything else, I think that's what I came here to confess."

"There is no shame in fear."

"What about failure?"

"There is no shame in that either, only the failure to try to become a better man."

"You think I can do that, really?"

"All men can. Look into your heart and soul and you'll find the strength you need."

"Face my fear . . ."

"Yes, my son."

"Overcome it."

"Before it overcomes you and turns you weak."

"I think I get it." Paz took a deep breath, his chest free for the first time since before he'd met the eyes of Caitlin Strong. "I feel a lot better."

"In fear and weakness there is shame. Acting out of

shame is the devil's due. Acting out of virtue makes you a soldier in the army of the Lord."

"I like the way you talk, Father."

"Have I helped you, my son? Will you steer a path clear of sin now?"

Paz started to ease his massive bulk from the cramped confessional, the wood creaking from the strain. "I can't promise that, Father, but I'll come back and let you know either way."

54

SAN ANTONIO, THE PRESENT

"Turns out Mr. Albert Johannson's story checks out," D. W. Tepper told Caitlin from behind his scuffed pine desk. "Other three members of this Fire Arrow team are dead for sure, one from a brain aneurysm and two from accidents."

"What kind of accidents?"

"Car and a fall down the stairs."

"You read the autopsy reports?"

"Not even sure there were any."

"Can you check?"

"Why?"

"Just a feeling."

Tepper's office was situated on the second floor in the darkest part of the San Antonio Ranger Company D headquarters to help him avoid use of the air-conditioning as much as possible since he said it played hell with his sinuses. He had also trained himself to work with the lights off during the day, helping to keep the room even cooler while leaving it perpetually gray. Caitlin remembered he was also keen on opening the windows in the morning to let in the cool breeze, and then closing them well before noon, leaving his office as stuffy as it was bleak. Old Wanted posters, some stretching back a generation or more, adorned the walls. The office smelled of a mix of stale cigarette smoke and musty newspapers.

The building was located on South New Braunfels, halfway between downtown and the Riverwalk. An innocuous two-story slab set off by itself with no tree shade and not much growth to speak of lifting out of the pale dirt.

"Along with this Johannson fella," Tepper continued, "RevCom had nine full-time employees in 2007 when your husband disappeared. Of those, three are dead, three have disappeared, and the others we're still looking for."

"Hollis lied to me about having any contact with DynaTech or any knowledge of RevCom. I'm sure of it."

"Why you figure he'd do something like that?"

"Under orders, I'm guessing. Didn't impress me as the kind of guy you call to handle the heavy lifting."

"Which brings us to MacArthur-Rain."

"Run a check, Captain, and you'll find both RevCom and DynaTech are subsidiaries of theirs."

"So they shut down RevCom around the same time Peter supposedly dies in Iraq."

"This all started years before that."

Tepper's expression tightened. In the room's murky light, the furrows in his face looked like black divots. "The night Charlie Weeks got killed in the West Texas desert."

"MacArthur-Rain put the bullets in those mules' guns, Captain. Clayton worked for one of their subsidiaries, something called Professional Protective Services. That company's dirty as dirty gets."

"Don't get to be as powerful as they are without having their waters muddied, I'm afraid."

"Clayton, no first name, running things that night in the Chihuahuan for them instead of Cort Wesley Masters like we thought originally."

Tepper puckered his lips the way he would if he was still packing chew in there like he used to. "Discussion always seems to come back to him lately."

"He's in the middle of things now, like it or not."

"You like it or not?"

The question might have seemed simple enough but the portent in Tepper's sagging eyes told Caitlin otherwise. "He's been helpful so far."

"And?"

"He saved my life."

"And?"

"The one decent clue we've got is these computer chips he's latched onto."

"And?"

When Caitlin remained silent this time, Tepper decided to answer for her.

"When I gave you back your star, Ranger, did I have to remind you that association with known criminal elements wasn't in the handbook?"

"He's no criminal element anymore, Captain."

"How many men you figure he's killed?"

"I have no idea."

"Take a guess."

"I don't know."

Tepper frowned. "That's my point: *nobody* knows. I talked to someone in the gang unit at SAPD. He told me some tallies put it over a hundred. FBI's thinking about naming a whole new category after him."

"Juárez Boys, Mexican Mafia and a whole host of wannabes accounting for all of them."

"You know that for a fact?"

"Course not."

Tepper seemed to weigh his next words. "Anything I can say to discourage you from spending any further time in his company?"

"Not if he has information that could be vital to this case."

"And what exactly would that entail?"

"I don't know yet, not for sure."

"Got his kids stashed at a safe house confiscated from a Mexican family that was running dope from a youngest boy in middle school to a grandmother who sold to her senior center friends who couldn't afford health insurance." Tepper leaned forward, then back again. "Something I wanna make clear: I'm doing this 'cause he saved your life. That reason alone."

"His prison guard friend also linked Clayton and others from this MacArthur-Rain subsidiary to the same countries where men like Peter were taken to be tortured."

Tepper's eyebrows flickered. "You didn't call him your husband."

"He doesn't know I'm his wife."

"Makes for a complex situation."

"Still makes Peter the only RevCom employee who can tell us what Fire Arrow was all about."

"Think you can get it out of him?"

Caitlin shrugged, picturing Peter hovering over a hospital bed strewn with tools, wires and pieces of the cable TV box. "I'm making some progress."

Tepper looked visibly disgusted, his face squeezed tight to the point where the shadows seemed ready to swallow the rest of it. "Americans torturing Americans . . ."

"Seems to be the size of it, yeah."

"Go get 'em, Ranger."

55

Larrito walked softly up the stairs toward his room on the third floor, holding the brown shopping bag tightly so the bottles inside wouldn't clack against each other. He'd been holed up in this roach-infested motel that stank of piss and stale sweat for three days now and had changed rooms to start each one. He'd shuttered his warehouse and sent his daughter to Tijuana to stay with his sister until things settled down.

Larrito couldn't say when that would be under the circumstances. Pedro and Luis had been with him for two years, surviving any number of unpleasant encounters only to be gunned down in a single breath by the big American who'd come calling. But it wasn't the big American Larrito was hiding from now. No. He worked for a man who did not like mess and this was surely one better to run from than try to explain.

He worked the lock of his withered wood door open and turned the knob with the key held in his mouth, tasting the rust. Pushed the door open and entered, holding fast to his shopping bag as he flipped the wall switch.

Nothing happened.

And then he saw the two figures in the corner of the room on the far side of the bed, flanking a man seated in the room's lone chair.

Larrito dropped his shopping bag to the floor, listening to the crackle of bottles breaking, as the smell of beer and tequila wafted up toward him.

The room's thin, tattered curtains let in the spill of lights from the marquees along the opposite side of the street, some of the letters projected backward across the cracked paint of the walls. A red flashing hue tinted the seated man's face, making him visible only in alternating seconds; enough for Larrito to see he had a white fedora hat tipped low over his forehead that obscured everything above his nose. He was immaculately dressed in a cream-colored suit, matching shirt and tie.

"You know who I am?"

"*Sí, jefe.* You are Garza."

"Some think I'm the devil, others God. Still more believe I'm nothing at all. *No longer,* eh?"

Larrito remained silent.

"I have some questions for you, Señor Larrito," Garza said, speaking just loud enough for Larrito to hear. "Since you've been a loyal employee of mine for several years, I assume you don't have a problem answering them. Is that correct?"

"*Sí, jefe.*"

"My men told you not to leave the warehouse unattended, that they would be returning with more questions, did they not?"

Larrito nodded.

"Answer me."

"They did."

"You disobeyed them. You ran."

"I was afraid, *jefe.*"

"That this American would come back."

"Yes."

"He scared you."

"Yes."

"As much as me?"

"No."

Garza shifted slightly, enough for the red glow to catch

his eyes. Larrito thought the sockets looked empty. Or maybe the eyes were all black, with no whites at all.

"You're a weak man, Señor Larrito."

Larrito didn't bother arguing.

"A disgrace to your people, *my* people," Garza continued. "Men like you have forgotten we were once a warrior nation with a proud heritage. I've spent my life trying to live up to that heritage and working to restore the legacy of our grandfathers. The drug business gives me the money and power I need to accomplish this, but it also allows me to punish the Americans who see us as peasants fit only to wash their clothes and mow their lawns. They see us this way, while their children buy our drugs. They see us this way, while my people take over their cities with guns, cash and the kind of violence that sends them fleeing to their gated communities in SUVs the size of buses. Someday when they try to take those cities back, they will know us for the warriors we are and they will understand how badly they have misjudged us. How are we to accomplish this, while depending on the likes of you?"

"I am sorry, *jefe*."

"Tell me about the American, Señor Larrito."

"He knew things from years ago. About the shipment to Houston."

"You told my men that."

"Yes."

"Did you tell him the shipment went to Houston? I strongly advise you not to lie to me."

Larrito tried to swallow, his mouth too dry to manage the effort. "I told him. After he shot Pedro and Luis."

"You should have let him shoot you too." The man flashed something in his hand. In the naked glow sifting through the flimsy curtains, Larrito could see it was a husk of black dangling from the black cord through which it was looped. "You know what this is, Señor Larrito?"

Larrito's bowels had already turned to ice. He tried to speak and for a moment found he had no breath.

"It belongs to my daughter," he rasped finally.

"Actually, it's mine. Part of the shipment trucked to Houston five years ago. What I need to know now is whether the American saw your daughter wearing it."

Larrito tried to re-create the picture in his head, couldn't quite fit all the pieces together. "Maybe."

"That's what your daughter said too." Garza frowned. "I was hoping you could be more specific."

56

SAN ANTONIO, THE PRESENT

"You tell your captain I was out here?" Cort Wesley Masters asked, after Caitlin had closed the door to her SUV behind her.

"Didn't think he'd take kindly to the news."

"Here I am, all the same," he said, shifting his thick shoulders about in search of comfort. Caitlin noticed he hadn't unsnapped his shoulder harness.

"You said you had someone you wanted me to see."

"Need you to do something for me first."

"After."

"This a negotiation, Caitlin Strong?"

"You tell me."

"After's fine."

"What is it you need done?"

"You to tell my boys the truth."

"No."

"No?" Masters asked like a man not used to hearing the word.

"That's gotta come from you."

"How 'bout we do it this way: I tell the older boy while you tell the younger."

"Now who's doing the negotiating?"

"I'm just trying to do the right thing, podner."

"We're not partners."

"Lot we got in common right now from where I'm sitting, Ranger."

"Doesn't make us any more than we already are."

"Which is?"

"Still trying to figure that out," Caitlin told him.

"So how's a woman get to be a Texas Ranger?" Cort Wesley asked her as they drove through Terrell Hills, an upscale suburb of San Antonio where Volvos and BMWs dotted the driveways and children's bicycles littered the well-trimmed lawns.

"Runs in the family. How's a man get to be Cort Wesley Masters?"

"Runs in the family."

"I'm not talking about your dad being a loan shark and you taking over the business," Caitlin told him. "I'm talking about after."

"Blame the army."

"Why?"

"They showed me the only thing I was good at and taught me how to do it better. That was a war that didn't last long for most people, but I was there a bunch of times before and after, handling the stuff nobody read about in the papers. Iraq was only the first stop on the merry-go-round. Trouble is it came to a halt after a few years and I didn't have a lick to show for it. Only one thing I was good at and the Branca family was more than happy to pay me to keep doing it."

"Killing."

Cort Westley smirked at her. "Know what I think? I think in high school you used to like guys like me."

"Bad boys?"

"Yeah."

"No."

"You're lying to me, Caitlin Strong," Cort Wesley said.

"Guess that makes us even for last night."

The breath whistled through his lips. "Some things I just choose not to tell people."

"Like how you really felt about Maura Torres."

"Not gonna leave that alone, are you?"

"Saw it in your eyes last night. She didn't ask you for the kids, did she?"

"First one kinda just happened. Second one was different."

"Your idea, not hers."

"You figure that out all by yourself?"

"Heard it in your voice when you talked about staying away to keep them safe."

Cort Wesley could only shake his head. "All Texas Rangers as good as you?"

"Plenty are better."

"Was a time I wanted to be a Ranger."

"Really?"

Cort Wesley nodded. "It's the truth, all right; every boy in Texas does. Then I found out they gotta follow the rules these days like everybody else."

Caitlin looked him in the eye. "I'm a fifth-generation Texas Ranger, Masters. The first rode after the very Mexicans who massacred three hundred and fifty of Sam Houston's men at Goliad. He understood better than you and me what it's like to take on somebody whose level of conviction allows them to go as far as they need to get whatever it is they want."

Cort Wesley's features tightened. "These sons of bitches come after my kids again, they're gonna find out what conviction really is, Caitlin Strong."

57

TERRELL HILLS, THE PRESENT

They pulled up in front of a two-story hacienda design home in a plot that looked no more than five years old, judging by the lack of tree growth, which left the homes to boil in the unbroken sunlight.

"You ready to tell me who lives here exactly?" Caitlin asked him, easing her SUV into park.

"Former associate of mine."

"Branca family?"

"Not the muscle side. Nothing to be afraid of."

Caitlin pushed open her door. "I'm not afraid."

"Identity theft," Cort Wesley said, joining her outside the SUV.

"What about it?"

"Big business for people like the Brancas these days. Man who lives in this house started out with his wife and two kids in a studio apartment. Built his own computers and wrote his own software. When the Brancas decided to move into identify theft, he was their man. Knows his way around those machines like Colt knows pistols. Name's Jimmy Farro, though he used to be called Jamie Formosina."

"Latino."

"Genius doesn't discriminate, Ranger."

The man who answered the front door was thin and wiry with patchy skin and bumps stitching his jawline. He gazed out at first with the kind of perfunctory smile he probably used to greet Girl Scouts and the paperboy. The smile disappeared when he saw Cort Wesley, his expression slipping further into dismay when he noticed the woman wearing a Texas Ranger badge standing next to him.

"Been a long time, Jimbo," Cort Wesley greeted.

Farro's eyes remained riveted on Caitlin. "Heard you were ins-s-s-side."

"Get your old stuttering habit back, Jimbo?"

"Only when I'm ner-ner-nervous."

"No reason to be nervous around me, podner."

"I'm out of the g-g-g-game now, with the Brancas leaving town."

"What I just tell you?"

"That I got no reason to be nervous around y-y-y-you."

Cort Wesley just looked at him. "You mind if we come in?"

Reluctantly, Farro held the door open for them, his gaze back on Cort Wesley, the mix of trepidation and anxiety in his eyes stopping just short of fear.

"Interesting company you're keeping these days, Cort Wesley."

"Well, I'm a changed man now." Just as he finished three kids, two boys and a girl, none over the age of five, ran past for the foyer and charged up a nearby staircase. "Looks like the same can be said for you."

"Told you I was d-d-d-done," Farro insisted, stiffening slightly again.

"No worries from me there, 'specially with me being responsible for all this. I don't push you on the Brancas, you're still hacking high school computers to change kids' grades for meal money."

Farro didn't bother disagreeing.

"So the thing is, podner, I need you to identify a certain computer chip for me."

"You try Radio Shack?"

Caitlin watched Masters harden his stare just a little—enough.

"They don't owe me, Jimbo. You do."

58

TERRELL HILLS, THE PRESENT

Farro led them down into the basement, overhead lighting snapping on courtesy of sensors to reveal an array of computers and servers lining an entire wall. The machines were set atop a white platform that seemed an extension of the wall itself. Another smaller wall featured a variety of printers, fax machines and transmission relays, evidence of high-volume cold-calling. Caitlin didn't bother considering what a man with the skills of Jimmy Farro was doing with all those phone numbers.

"Show it to him," Cort Wesley told her, wasting no time.

Caitlin produced the chip salvaged from the hospital cable box and handed it to him.

"What do you wanna know?" Farro asked, not impressed by what he was looking at.

"Recognize it?"

He started to hand the chip back to her. "Open up old cable boxes, you'll find one of these inside. A dinosaur by today's standards. Ten, twelve years old maybe. A relic. This what you came here to ask me?"

"Not quite," said Cort Wesley. "Want you to picture a chip about half, more like a third of the size. Same design, only lots thinner with green lines running through it forming some kind of maze."

Something changed in Farro's expression, as if all the air had been sucked out of his cheeks. "Green lines . . ."

"That's what I said."

"You're bullshitting me, right? This s-s-s-some kind of joke?"

"You're stuttering again, Jimbo."

"Just answer my question."

"You ever known me to be a comedian?"

"Not until today, no."

"What exactly did I just say?" Cort Wesley said, eyeing Caitlin now.

"You have one of these chips, either of y-y-y-you?"

"Nope. Saw one, though. Down at a warehouse in Juárez that shipped a whole mess of them across the border and into Houston maybe five years ago."

"How many?"

"Don't know exactly. Four dozen crates maybe. You do the math."

Farro moved to a drawer, slid it open, and removed a chip that looked identical in all ways to the one Cort Wesley had seen dangling from the girl's neck at the warehouse. "Like this?"

"Looks to be, yeah. I'd say almost definitely."

Farro held the chip before him, treating it like a gemstone. "Take a closer look."

"Green lines look a little off. Other than that . . ."

"Other than that, exactly." He redeposited the chip in the drawer and slammed it shut, turning his focus on Caitlin. "This a setup or something?"

"No, sir."

Back on Cort Wesley now. "That how you got sprung from jail, telling the Rangers you'd cooperate with them?"

"Yeah, that describes me to a T, Jimbo."

"You have any idea, either of you, what the chip you're describing is exactly?"

"As I recall," said Caitlin, "that's what we came here to find out."

"Cerberus. Sound familiar?"

"Big three-headed dog that guarded the gates of hell," Caitlin answered when Cort Wesley remained silent.

"Gates of hell being the operative phrase here and Cerberus being the name of the project, and the ch-ch-ch-chip, you're referring to."

Cort Wesley ran his eyes over Jimmy Farro's collection of custom-made computers. "You on the straight and narrow these days, podner?"

"Less than most, I suppose."

"Making a buck on other people's social security numbers—you must have that down to a science by now, especially with no Brancas to have to include in the split."

"What's your p-p-p-point, Cort Wesley?"

"Wouldn't want anything to happen to your bread and butter, now would you?" he asked, running a hand along the sleek black frame of one of the computers.

"I do something to piss you off?"

"You're getting close, podner. You got something to say, just say it." Cort Wesley smiled, ever so slightly. "I mean, you're among friends here. What's Cerberus?"

"Nothing before 9/11. The b-b-b-beginning of a new age after. You know everything you hear about warrantless wiretapping, shit like that?"

"Yes," Caitlin answered.

"It doesn't mean a thing, all smoke and mirrors to keep

the country's attention away from where the shit is really going down."

"Cerberus," repeated Cort Wesley.

"Different kind of guardian, equally hellish. I know since I've written similar types of code myself."

"And what kind of code is that, podner?"

"The Cerberus chip, once installed into a computer, becomes a kind of data relay system," Farro told them, in his element now, his chain of words unbroken. "Every e-mail, every word processing document, everything purchased on the Web, and every site visited on the Internet gets stored in the chip to be transmitted to a central server system—essentially a massive storehouse that captures everything a person does while they're on their computer."

"Even if they're not online?" Caitlin probed.

"Doesn't matter a hoot, Ranger. Because the next time they log on, everything they've done since the last time gets transferred. The central server then catalogues the information and searches on a constant basis for red flags in terms of terminology, locations noted, products purchased, sites visited or searches run. Forget Big Brother, my friend, this is Big Daddy. The ultimate in data mining."

"You're telling me the government actually *did* this?"

"I don't know. Nobody outside of a select few do really. It's always been an urban legend. They produced the experimental chips, like the one I just showed you, which worked just fine. But whether they actually went operational has been anybody's guess." Farro paused and sucked in some breath. "Until now, since you actually located one of these chips."

Cort Wesley shook his head, not buying it. "Five years inside The Walls I think I went online ten times maybe, so I'm no expert here. Seems to me, though, that lots of people would've seen these chips when they made repairs or upgrades."

" 'Cept the chip you saw and the chip I just showed you hadn't been cased yet."

"What's that mean?"

"Computer companies outsource their work to independent manufacturers. Identical chips get made for all of them but are cased to fit each company's design and specifications. Once they're snapped home, nobody knows the difference or has reason to look."

"Say this was 2004," Caitlin suggested.

Farro considered the date. "Sounds about right. Three years after 9/11. It'd take that long to go from design to production to distribution."

"Where could chips like this be manufactured?" Cort Wesley asked him.

"Lots of places."

"Mexico?"

"Back then? I doubt it. Chip manufacture requires skilled workers in a sterile environment. We're not talking about sewing seams on blue jeans here."

"But it's possible, right?"

"Plenty of it going on down there today, in fact, but those plants are all relatively new. So, sure, they could have manufactured Cerberus down there, but not . . ."

"Not what?" Caitlin asked.

"Answer her, podner," Cort Wesley instructed when Farro remained silent.

"It's like this," Farro said finally. "Cerberus wasn't the only thing the government stuffed up its sleeve after 9/11. I heard rumors, stories, about something even more invasive maybe not right away, but not too far down the road."

His words left her stomach rumbling. "Like what?"

"I don't kn-kn-kn-know, Ranger," Jimmy Farro told her. "And I don't want to know."

59

Caitlin found Rita Navarro, director of the Survivor Center for Victims of Torture, seated behind her desk staring blankly out the grime-pasted window. Still officially closed, the center was no longer considered a crime scene, allowing staff and volunteers to return to sort through the pieces of their ruined work and sort out what to do next.

Caitlin stood in the doorway, waiting for Navarro to acknowledge her. Navarro's long straight hair was tied back in a ponytail, pulled away from her face to reveal the ridged depressions beneath her pitched cheekbones, like cavities, that made her look sad and older as well as lost, the strain of the past few days showing in her dull eyes and chewed fingernails.

"I'm sorry," Caitlin said when Navarro finally looked her way.

"What happened wasn't your fault. You were almost killed yourself."

"That's not what I was apologizing for, ma'am. I was apologizing for the fact that I lied to you."

Navarro's eyes narrowed slightly.

"John Doe is my husband." Caitlin waited for Navarro's eyes to change, her point sinking in. "Peter Goodwin."

Navarro remained silent for several long moments before responding suddenly. "Your dead husband, you mean."

"A shock to me too, that much is the truth," Caitlin told her and proceeded to lay out all she had pieced together from RevCom to Fire Arrow to Peter's trip to Iraq that had left him ultimately in Bahrain. Navarro listened attentively, showing no emotion whatsoever, as if there was nothing left of her to feel. "I can't tell you why I didn't say something from the start," Caitlin finished. "Guess it's 'cause I knew you wouldn't let me stay on the job if I told you the truth. And I had to try, I had to help him. When I saw him sitting there in that room, I knew I had no choice.

"Yes, you did," Navarro said simply.

Caitlin nodded in concession. "You deserved the truth. You treated me square and I'm sorry for not returning the favor."

Navarro's expression remained flat and unchanged. "I don't know if I can reopen. I don't know if I can face it all again." Her gaze sharpened, looking professorial. Caitlin didn't think she'd been wearing makeup the first time they'd met, but she needed it now. "I see you're wearing a badge again."

"Seemed like a good idea under the circumstances," Caitlin offered.

"You killed men the other night. You've killed men before."

Caitlin nodded, a single time. "Not that I'm proud of it."

"Is it hard?"

"Not particularly, ma'am, not when they're trying to do likewise to you. For me, for lots of Rangers, that's the way it's always been."

"Part of the creed."

"If we want to keep at it, yeah."

Navarro's eyes went distant again. "They brought me upstairs to identify the bodies. I haven't slept since, not really slept. All I keep thinking of is how much they suffered, all they endured, just for it to end like it did. I'm having trouble living with that. That's why I don't know if I can do this anymore."

"That would be a shame, 'cause you're damn good at what you do. You just never come face-to-face before with the type of evil that does the kind of things you've seen come through these doors."

"Never told you how I got into this, did I?"

"No."

"Bunch of years ago, I was doing volunteer work for Doctors Without Borders in Sierre Leone. Happened to be there when the civil war there really heated up. I saw things I still spend every day of my life wishing I hadn't. Spent two weeks on the run myself from both the rebel forces and the army. Hard to tell which was worse or who beat out the other in terms of depravity. I came to Sierre Leone a committed idealist and left more disillusioned than I'd ever been in my life. Watching a machete's work will do that to you."

"You saw human nature up close and personal."

"And I resolved to do something about it. That's how I was finally able to sleep again. Now the nightmares have returned and I feel like I'm back where I started."

"I know the feeling," Caitlin told her.

60

SAN ANTONIO, 2006

Caitlin couldn't say exactly where things began to go bad for her and Peter; more likely, they had never really been good to begin with. Not that the blame lay with him. Thinking back on those years, Caitlin couldn't find fault with a single thing Peter had done but plenty that she had. It was as if she was committed to sabotaging whatever chance their marriage had to succeed. Peter had proven patient, considerate—even overly so.

She remembered a time at a county fair where she'd grown frustrated with him for no reason other than he couldn't learn to shoot straight at a penny-ante midway gallery attraction. He had laughed; she had sulked. Her birthday was coming up a week later and he bought twin water pistols, insisting she try teaching him again.

They seldom spoke of Peter's work and not at all of her longing for the world of law enforcement she'd left behind. Peter kept the focus forward, on helping her find something else to throw her passion behind. Her success as a Ranger volunteer in schools led them to consider teaching, until the realities of pursuing that as a profession hit home. Peter had a substantial amount of money stashed away from profit-sharing arrangements with two software companies he'd been part of and offered to buy a business for her, any business. Caitlin recalled her father saying he wanted to buy a motel when he retired, but other than careers in various offshoots of law enforcement that was the only thing that moderately appealed to her.

One day Peter took an afternoon off from work, insisting he had a surprise for her. He drove onto the campus of San Antonio College and pulled up in front of the main complex of buildings.

Caitlin looked about, shaking her head. "I'm not interested in teaching what I don't do anymore," she told Peter, aware San Antonio College had a very well-regarded law enforcement training academy.

"Not what I was going to suggest," he said.

"What then?"

"The social services department. You like helping people so much, why not turn it into a profession?"

"You mean like counseling?"

"I mean whatever you want it to be."

"Lemme think on it."

"Too late."

"Huh?"

"I already enrolled you," Peter said, reaching into the backseat and returning with a textbook in his grasp. "Your first class starts in twenty minutes. In that building over there, on the right."

61

SAN ANTONIO, THE PRESENT

Rita Navarro sat still for a time when Caitlin had finished. "You got your husband to blame for being here."

"Ironic, isn't it? 'Specially when you consider he's here because of me."

"I don't think I . . ."

"Another part of the story," Caitlin told her, leaving it at that.

Navarro shifted in her chair. The desk lamp before her flickered then went out. "I'm thinking about buying a gun."

"Don't recommend that at all, if you're asking me."

"Think I'd feel bad about killing the kind of men I saw in Sierra Leone, the kind of men who came here the other night?"

"No, ma'am, I don't. That's the problem and it's a road you don't wanna go down. Trust me."

"It worked for you."

"Sometimes nightmares are better than nothing at all."

Their stares held for what seemed like a very long time. Then Rita Navarro let out the breath she'd been holding.

"Thank you, Ranger."

"For what."

"Just thank you. But you didn't come back here to counsel me, did you?"

Caitlin finally came all the way into the room. "I've been calling you 'ma'am' but the truth is I should be calling you 'doctor.'"

"I'm a psychologist."

"That's why I came back. Wanted to ask you some questions about my husband, his treatment."

"How is he?"

"I'd say better, 'cept I'm not sure what that entails exactly."

"Cotard's is tricky. Very difficult to treat. Wherever he's been taken, they're sticking with the medication protocol, right?"

"Yes, ma'am. I mean, Doctor."

"Rita'll do."

"Peter's doing some things the way he used to, mechanical things. I'm not really sure he realizes it's him doing them, though, if that makes any sense."

"It makes perfect sense." Navarro smiled sadly. "I'm actually starting to believe you're pretty damn good at this."

"Tell me how to do it better."

"Well, there's no book on Cotard's. But this case, your husband's, was brought on by PTSD, post-traumatic stress disorder. And treating cases that lead to a similar psychotic break is often achieved by utilizing trigger points."

"Trigger points?"

"The where, when and what. You gradually reintroduce the patient to the source of their pain. Before they can remember and reenter the world as we know it, they have to accept what's happened to them. Running away from it is what put them in their states in the first place, remember."

"Confront the past."

"In so many words," Navarro nodded.

"And how does this reintroduction happen?"

"Different ways. I've seen amazing results with pictures, videotapes, recorded voices. I've even heard of personal visitation having a profound effect."

"As in going back to where it all happened."

Navarro nodded very slowly, then resumed, "But any of those direct evidence strategies are fraught with risk. Just as they can lead to a breakthrough, sometimes a sudden and dramatic breakthrough, they've also been known to lead to a setback or even total withdrawal. Confronting patients with the source of their pain could make them feel it all over again, you see."

"Wish I didn't."

"It's an all-or-nothing approach generally frowned upon by the psychiatric community."

"Like to ask you a question now, if I may," Caitlin said.

"Of course."

"First time we met, during our interview, you asked about my relatives in the Mexican War. When you asked me that, something in your face changed."

"That's not a question."

"Was I right, Rita?"

"The year would've been 1875."

"My great-granddad, then. Fought lots of battles on the frontier and border with cattle thieves."

"Rancho Las Cuevas," Navarro intoned slowly. "Ever heard of it? Ranger?" she prodded when Caitlin remained silent.

"I have heard of it, ma'am, but I'm not proud of what happened there."

"Rangers came over the border to catch cattle thieves who'd crossed from Rancho Las Cuevas," Navarro related. "It was night and thick fog had washed in. The Rangers got to the ranch and started shooting, kept shooting for quite some time."

"I know the story."

"Anyway, as many as twenty men were killed by Rangers that night. Problem was the fog confused them and they hit the wrong ranch. Las Cuevas was another mile down the road."

"We've made our share of mistakes and been responsible for more than our share of senseless deaths maybe. But a person has to live in the times to understand them fully."

"I understand that," Navarro told her. "But there's something I'd like you to understand."

Their stares locked and held.

"The family that owned that ranch, the family that lost five of their own that night, was named Navarro."

Caitlin swallowed hard. "I'm sorry" was all she could think of saying.

"No need. You weren't there and we don't know if your great-grandfather was either. I'm telling you this because you asked, because you're right, it still does bother me. And I wanted you to know you're not the only one chasing the past."

"I appreciate your concern, Rita, I really do."

"There's one more thing I need to tell you about Peter, based on what you just told me."

"What's that?"

"I've worked with a lot of veterans of the Iraq War suffering from PTSD. Every single one of their chart workups I've seen included plenty about certain physical maladies like rashes and other skin conditions brought on by a combination of the climate, the spiders and the various bugs native to that region. I'm not exactly sure what this means, but, well . . ."

"Keep going," Caitlin urged.

"What's bothering me here is that none of the exams done on Peter Goodwin from the time he was found in Bahrain mention any of those symptoms. So if you ask me, Ranger," Rita Navarro finished, "he was never even in Iraq."

PART SEVEN

[In the 1940s,] former Ranger Manuel T. "Lone Wolf" Gonzaullas headed the Department's Bureau of Intelligence, which gave Rangers the benefit of chemical, ballistic and microscopic testing in their criminal investigations. In their early years as part of the DPS, Rangers were paid automobile mileage and furnished a Colt .45 and a lever-action Winchester .30 caliber rifle by the state. Rangers still had to provide their own car, horse and saddle, though the DPS issued horse trailers.

—Mike Cox, with updates from the Texas Ranger
Hall of Fame and Museum, "A Brief History of
the Texas Rangers"

62

Houston, the Present

The limousine cruised down the private drive lined with
stately old oak trees draped with Spanish moss. Harmon
Delladonne looked at them and thought of the things they
had paid witness to through the years. The amount of
power that had passed through the gates of the River
Oaks Country Club, after all, was staggering. The path to
the presidency even could have and had been laid on the
tips of cigars smoked and brandy sipped in the library
bar upstairs in the palatial clubhouse. A private retreat
within a private retreat. The other members knew, understood. There were ample other places for them to discuss
the day's play or evening's plans without encroaching
on the discussions of those with much greater ends in
mind. There was even a private rear entrance to the library bar up a staircase accessible beyond a sign that read
NO VEHICLES PAST THIS POINT.

Upstairs the senator was already halfway into his
brandy and sucking on a Cohiba when Delladonne approached. He did not rise when he saw Delladonne or
offer him the matching leather chair set across from his
own with a mahogany cocktail table eased closer to
his side. The man establishing his territory, setting the
agenda.

"We haven't spoken since your return from Washington," the senator said, greeting him. "I was told the

recording equipment malfunctioned, but there are no plans for the committee to recall you."

"A wise decision on their part," Delladonne mused, settling into the chair that was waiting for him.

"Maybe not." The senator sucked on the cigar, the smoke wafting upward before it reached Delladonne. "MacArthur-Rain's very important to this country, Harm."

"The reverse is true as well, Senator."

"But, just for argument's sake, what's this latest contract worth to the company?"

"Ten billion dollars conservatively," Delladonne said, without hesitation. "More reasonable estimates put it at closer to twenty-five."

"Then it's in our mutual interest to consider the prospects of our futures under the auspices of the new administration."

"Ours or the country's?"

"Same thing, like it or not." The senator maneuvered his chair, so Delladonne could see over his shoulder a wall lined with wood-framed photographs of those members of this exclusive club who had passed away. "I'd offer you a cigar but I know you don't smoke. A brandy but I know you almost never drink. What do you do, Harm?"

"I make your life easier, Senator. Just don't expect someone who couches his ambitions in qualifiers or takes every step as if they're afraid of falling through ice."

"No, you prefer walking on water. Not lately, though, right, Harm? That's why I needed to see you." The senator leaned ever so slightly forward. "People in Washington got short memories and your actions are making them want to forget MacArthur-Rain ever existed."

"Sounds like the way the members of the Oversight Committee felt until the recording equipment malfunctioned."

"Enemies are one thing, allies something else again." The senator jabbed at the air with his cigar, leaving smoke holes dangling between him and Delladonne. "They read the newspapers, watch the news. San Antonio's turned into a war zone, Harm, and even the best friends you've got in the Capitol are afraid of getting caught in the cross-fire."

"Does that include you, Senator?" When the man seated across from him remained silent, Delladonne continued. "You, all of you, need me to do your job, because you've forgotten how to do it."

"That the way you see it?"

Delladonne shifted his chair so the wall of death was no longer in view. "Because that's the way it is. You people have abdicated your responsibility, can't get one single thing accomplished successfully. Then a new administration comes in and what do you do? Turn up the screws on the only ones doing the work you're supposed to do, the work that's needed. You want to criticize me, Senator, go ahead. But just tell me who'd do your dirty work if people like me, and companies like mine, weren't around?"

The senator left his cigar in his mouth and clapped his hands. "You're good, Harm, I'll give you that. Your daddy was a BB gun compared to the howitzer you've turned into. Your daddy had enemies too, but he always knew when to back off so they'd never outnumber his friends. Smart as you are, that's a trick you never learned."

"I don't do tricks, Senator. Instead, I take stock of the future. The next phase of Fire Arrow means we can get to our enemies anyplace anytime. Halfway around the world or just down the street. No culpability, no recriminations, no comebacks."

"Guess you haven't been following the news reports

about murdered torture survivors and shoot-outs in the suburbs."

"I'm willing to do what it takes, Senator. That's what separates us. If Washington won't, I will."

"No, Harm, you won't. I called this meeting to tell you I'm pulling the plug."

"On what?"

"On you, MacArthur-Rain, on everything. No hearing, no subcommittee, no microphones to malfunction. Figured you deserved hearing that in person."

Delladonne squeezed the chair arms, digging his nails into the wood. "You speaking for yourself here?"

"And others."

"Who?"

"Some things are better left unsaid, Harm." The senator went back to his cigar, savoring the taste. "Your dad built your company from the ground up. He'd be proud of the heights you've taken it to. If he were here, he'd advise you to lay low for a while, wait for your time to come again."

Delladonne let the words settle. "Man like you should always be aware of the space left on the wall over there," he said, tilting his gaze toward the wood-framed photographs.

The senator grinned, ignoring the comment and not missing a beat on his cigar. "Something I get asked a lot, but don't know the answer myself: where'd your father come up with the name MacArthur-Rain?"

Harm Delladonne rose and looked the man square in the eye. "Some things are better left unsaid."

The senator sat behind his computer in the study of his thirty-second-floor condominium in uptown Houston's Turnberry Tower. The incomparable view of the city he loved, from every window, pleased him to no end. He used that view, and that love, to motivate him to write the e-mail he'd composed in his head on the drive back from his meeting with Harm Delladonne.

That e-mail, encrypted and sent via secure server, would be before the eyes of the people who needed to see it in mere minutes. He had chosen his words carefully with Delladonne, but had no call to be similarly coy about his intentions now. Once the e-mail was sent, MacArthur-Rain's efficacy would be reduced to a level from which it could never recover, no matter the amount of lobbying and payoffs expended toward that end.

The senator logged on, sipping his brandy as the e-mail box awaited his words. He laid his fingers over the keys, began reconstructing his thoughts.

The senator had just finished the obligatory greeting when something like a shock hit him in the forehead. He felt a warm trickle running from his right ear and stretched a hand up toward it, two fingers coming away wet with blood. They went numb in the next instant, followed by his hand, then his entire arm. The senator tried to reach for the phone but nothing moved. Felt his face, actually *felt* it, falling toward the keyboard that clacked when it struck.

The last thing the senator registered was the smoke rising from the computer's housing, accompanied by the stench of fried wires. Across the screen, meanwhile, an endless series of meaningless letters dissolved into blackness an instant before it descended upon him as well.

Harm Delladonne sat behind his computer for a long time in the wood-panelled private study that had been his father's after it was over. Actually working the system himself this time left him feeling fulfilled and vindicated.

Realizing in that instant more than ever the awesome potential of Fire Arrow, the senator having proven his very point for him.

If only they could get it right. . . . If only Peter Goodwin had cooperated. . . .

But it wasn't too late. Thing about the future, Delladonne thought, was it would begin again tomorrow.

63

SAN ANTONIO, THE PRESENT

"Bahrain," D. W. Tepper repeated from behind his desk.

"On my nickel," Caitlin told him. "I'd just like to go there in an official capacity."

"Little out of the jurisdiction of the Texas Rangers, ain't it?"

"In a manner of speaking. But that's where I'll find the answers I need to find."

"Gotta know the right questions to ask and who to ask them to first."

"I got some ideas, Captain."

Tepper ran a finger along the furrows on his face, the tip seeming to disappear into the deepest of them. "Won't be able to carry a gun over there, Ranger."

"Don't expect I'll need one."

"I'm not so sure of that," said Tepper, as he started to suddenly sort through the clutter of his desk. "We got those autopsy reports on the other members of your husband's tech team you asked about here somewhere, one of them anyway. . . ."

"What'd it say?"

Tepper gave up searching for the pages he was looking for. "Turns out the victim who fell down the flight of stairs suffered an aneurysm first. That's what really killed him."

"Two out of three now."

"Third dying in that car accident. That be the woman."

"Single car?"

Tepper found one of the pages he was looking for and pushed it away from his eyes to better read it. "Went off the road and hit a tree, according to this. Car caught fire, so there wasn't much left to autopsy."

"Could be three for three then, couldn't it?"

"I suppose." Tepper's eyes narrowed with concern. "Be careful wherever this takes you, Ranger."

"Too late for that now, Captain."

64

ALAMO HEIGHTS, THE PRESENT

"Barn looks empty," Cort Wesley Masters noted as Caitlin drove down the long driveway. "Guess you can't have everything."

The confiscated residence in which the Rangers were watching over Dylan and Luke Torres was an 8,000-square-foot red-stone mansion that sat on four and a half lush acres. The property, paid for with drug money, was on the market for $2.5 million and featured a pool, tennis court, tree house and a two-stall covered horse barn Cort Wesley had glimpsed on the property's perimeter.

His remark had been meant to elicit a laugh from Caitlin but it hadn't come out that way.

"You got call to be nervous," she told him.

"I got call to be a lot of things and not one of them's a father."

"If it means anything—"

"It don't."

"If it means anything, I think you're doing a brave thing. Owning up. Trying to pull something out of this."

"Maybe make my boys' lives even worse."

"I don't see that happening."

"You don't know me well enough yet. You remember our deal, right?" Cort Wesley asked her, sounding like an anxious kid himself.

"I'll sit down with the younger boy, while you talk to the older."

Cort Wesley's eyes drifted back to the horse barn, as they pulled up to a Ranger posted in the shade of an elm tree not far from the entrance. Caitlin braked her SUV and threw it into park. She and Masters climbed out and headed along the thick Bermuda grass for the covered entrance, just a single step to mount in order to reach it. A second Ranger opened the door before Caitlin had a chance to knock. Over his shoulder, Caitlin could hear the tinny *thwack* of a video game blaring loudly in a spacious family room immediately off the foyer on the right. One of Cort Wesley's sons blasting away at bad guys, just as she had to save their lives a few nights back.

Moving toward the family room, Caitlin saw it was the younger boy, Luke, behind the controls while Dylan busily waxed a skateboard that was nicked up but already shiny with decals. It looked to her as if the older boy was going over the same spot over and over again.

Even from the brief glimpses she'd gleaned in Shavano Park, she could tell Luke most resembled his mother while Dylan was the spitting image of his father, from the wide brow to his angular jawline. Their noses were the same and so, even more strikingly, were their piercing charcoal-colored eyes.

She could feel heat emanating from Cort Wesley, his powerful frame seeming like molten steel overflowing from a mold. "You mind if I talk to you?" he asked his older son, clearing his throat in the middle of the question.

Dylan shrugged, joined Cort Wesley on his feet.

"Let's go outside."

"Can I bring my skateboard?"

"Not a bad idea."

65

ALAMO HEIGHTS, THE PRESENT

Dylan balanced himself on his skateboard, scooting back and forth across the driveway. They had stopped out of earshot from the posted Ranger but still far enough from the street for Cort Wesley to consider them safe.

"I watched you skating the other day," he told Dylan.

The boy brushed the black hair from his face. "Huh?"

"I was parked across from your house," Cort Wesley said. "Down the street a ways."

"Orange Ford."

"Yeah. Surprised you remember."

"Ugly-ass color like that's tough to forget."

"I borrowed it."

Dylan looked at him more curiously. "So, what, you skate or something?"

Cort Wesley smiled slightly. "Never, nohow. I prefer other things to skating."

"Like what?"

"Guns."

"What kind?"

"Any kind. I knew your mom," Cort Wesley added, pushing back the heaviness that had formed in his throat. "We kind of dated a long time ago."

"You trying to tell me you're my dad?"

Cort Wesley could only look at him.

"My mom told me he was the toughest man she'd ever seen, both inside and out."

"Guess she had things right," Cort Wesley heard himself say.

Dylan held his gaze downward, rolling his wheels over the ridges in the pavement. He stepped off his skateboard and kicked it up into his grasp. "Those men dressed as cops who killed my mother, was it 'cause of you?"

"Yup."

"Would they have killed Luke and me?"

"I don't think so. Think they wanted to use you against me, something like that."

The boy stared into a pair of deep-set dark eyes that were identical in all ways to his own. "What'd you do to them?"

"You know that woman who shot the fake cops?"

Dylan nodded.

"I shot a man was about to do the same to her."

"Shit," the boy said.

"Yeah."

"You wanna play?" Cort Wesley's younger son asked her.

Caitlin watched Luke blowing away monsters with skulls for heads, leaving bloody, dismembered corpses behind. Blasting one and moving on to the next, simple as that. Closer to real life in some cases than he realized.

"I'm not much good at these kinds of things."

Luke's character missed a shot on screen and got hit as a result. The screen lit up with ONE LIFE LEFT, making Caitlin think, If only.

"Your mom ever tell you anything 'bout your dad?" she asked the boy.

"That he was trouble."

"True enough, I suppose."

Luke finally turned from the game toward her. "You know my dad?"

"Yes, I do."

"Who is he?"

"Well, he's outside with your brother right now."

Luke held her gaze and lost his last life in the video game, the screen flashing GAME OVER in bloodred letters set inside a grinning skull.

"What's the game called?" Caitlin asked him.

"Night Raiders. It's not mine. It was already in the console when I got here. Found some others, if you wanna check around, see if there's one you might be good at."

Caitlin shook her head. "I don't think there's any such thing."

"But you're good with a real gun. I saw you. At least I think I did. I'm not sure if I really remember."

"You were in shock."

"I was trying to get to my mother."

"Brave move."

"The man you say is my dad looks brave. Tough too. Is he tough?"

"Very."

Luke moved his gaze down to her badge. "What's it like to be a Ranger?"

"Well, it's a real proud thing. Lots of years and tradition behind it that make you feel like you're worth something."

"They got a game here called Texas Ranger. You want me to look for it?"

"Sure."

Luke stated sorting through the pile of video games strewn over the hardwood floor. "Gotta promise me something, though."

"What?"

"You can't let me win."

"I don't think that'll be much of a problem."

66

ALAMO HEIGHTS, THE PRESENT

"I always wanted to learn how to shoot," Dylan was saying, skateboard clutched tightly against his side. "Mom wouldn't let me."

"Be glad to teach you. Here, lemme see your hand."

Dylan held his free one up for Cort Wesley to study.

"Gotta find you the right weapon that feels good in your grasp."

"What do you use?"

"Anything I can get my hands on. A Smith & Wesson 9 millimeter right now, but that's not in the same league as a Glock. Best damn gun on the market."

"The Ranger lady carries a SIG."

"You recognized it?"

"From my gun magazines and, 'sides, everybody knows SIGS are standard issue for Rangers and plenty more cop types too." Dylan pursed his lips and blew the hair from his forehead. "You gonna get the men who killed my mom?"

"Every last one of them."

"Promise?"

"Yup. I take my responsibilities seriously too. I didn't always, but I do now. You and your brother, you're my responsibilities. Whole different kind of ilk entirely."

"What's ilk?"

"Measure of a man," Cort Wesley said, repeating old Leroy Epps's words from inside The Walls. "Where he comes from, where he's going."

"What's my ilk?"

Cort Wesley let Dylan see his eyes before he answered. "You're looking at it."

"I don't wanna hear anymore, not now."

"Whatever you say, podner."

"I'm not saying I don't ever, just not now."

"I understand."

"But you'll be around."

"Ain't going anywhere."

Luke popped the Texas Ranger game into the console and sat back as the screen brightened back to life.

"Here," he said, handing Caitlin a controller.

"What do I do?"

"Kill as many bad guys as you can. You aim with the toggle wheel and fire with either of the red buttons. My score's on the left, yours is on the right."

The Texas Ranger character appeared on her side of the screen. Big man with a big chest, narrow waist and pair of guns strapped to his hips. Looked a lot more like Cort Wesley Masters than her. A virtual spitting image, in fact.

"Level one," Luke said, working the controller. "My mom never said much about my dad. I'd ask her sometimes but it was pretty clear she didn't wanna talk about him. I thought he was probably dead or something."

"He paid for your house, been making sure you lived good."

"Well," Luke corrected, "lived well. Hey, you gotta start shooting or you'll get yourself killed."

Caitlin did, trying to get the hang of things while Luke effortlessly blasted away at outlaws and desperadoes. No Indians or Mexicans, she noticed, to be politically, though not historically, correct.

"That gun you're shooting, it's called a Colt Peacemaker. Became standard Ranger issue around 1875." Caitlin was finding a rhythm to the game, syncing with her words. "First handgun the Rangers carried was the original Patterson five-shooter which turned into the first ever six-shooter named after none other than Ranger Captain Samuel Walker who helped Colt develop it for shooting on horseback."

Luke kept blasting away, expending hundreds of shots instead of just six, reloading with bonus points.

"Key was replacing the old paper cartridges ignited by a percussion cap to rim-fire metallic cartridges in the 1860s," Caitlin continued, "and then the more powerful center-fire variety that accompanied the debut of the Peacemaker you seem to have quite a touch with there."

Luke glanced from the game toward her without missing a single shot. "What happens to us now? You think we'll be able to live with my dad?"

"That'd be my guess."

Luke leaned in against her as he knocked off a fresh slew of bad guys. Caitlin resisted the temptation to draw the boy in closer to continue working her console, feeling her throat go heavy.

"That big guy gonna be back?"

"No, he won't."

"You can't know that, even if you are a Texas Ranger. I've been dreaming about him. Wakes me up every time."

"We're gonna take care of him."

"Who?"

"Your dad and I."

"You sure?"

"Absolutely."

Just as her game figure got caught in a vicious cross fire and was blown away.

"Guess you're gonna have to do better than that," Luke told her.

67

HOUSTON, THE PRESENT

Harmon Delladonne was seated behind his desk in the darkness of his office when his private line rang, the caller ID lighting up with the ten zeroes he'd come to recognize.

"It's about time," he said.

"Time for what, Belladonna?" greeted the thick, nasally voice of Guillermo Paz.

Delladonne checked the caller ID again. "What are you doing, calling me from this line?"

"Man it belongs to doesn't have need for it anymore. Where he is, they don't use phones."

Delladonne suddenly felt chilled. "He was supposed to give you a message."

"He did; then I gave him one of my own."

"Maybe you're forgetting who you work for here, Colonel."

"Not at all. That's the problem. Wind's picking up. There's a storm brewing. My mother was a good woman and strong. Only saw her cry once when I told her I'd killed Carnicero, the local crime boss, 'cause she knew it meant I'd have to go away. She had visions, saw things before they happened enough so the neighbors stayed clear because they thought she was a *bruja*. I came home after killing Carnicero with money for her, she was already crying, like she saw it in advance. Something like that can take its toll."

"What does this have to do with anything?"

"I think I may have some of that *bruja* shit in me too. Hits me like electricity. Makes the hair on my arms stand up. I got that feeling now. You never told me if you believed in God, Belladonna."

"I want you out of the country, Colonel."

"You didn't answer my question. About God. I figure if He gives you certain powers, abilities, you're supposed to use them, not let them go to waste. God made me who I am for a reason. Makes me figure I'm working for Him more than for you."

"Your services are no longer required. Go home, Colonel."

Paz didn't bother telling him that was now impossible. "Those my new instructions?"

"They are."

Delladonne heard Paz breathing heavily, thought he could smell his thick, oily scent of something spoiled over the line. Reminded him of the smell wafting up from a corpse laid out on a mortician's table.

"Job's not finished yet" was all Paz said.

"You'll be paid in full. I'll see to that. And we'll do something extra for the families of your two dead men."

"They don't have families."

"More for the rest of you to split then."

"You think it's only about the money, Belladonna?"

"Yes, Colonel, I do."

"I'm gonna have to think about this."

"Listen to me, Colonel—"

But it was too late. The line was already dead.

Delladonne looked up, realized his office blinds had been open the whole time, but the day had darkened to a near nighttime shade. Outside wind lashed against the windows and thick black clouds continued to roll in from seemingly all directions at once.

A storm was coming all right.

68

HOUSTON, THE PRESENT

Caitlin sat in the terminal, waiting for her flight to be called. The first of several that would ultimately bring her to Bahrain. She had maxed out a credit card to handle the expense, then packed lightly in a single carry-on piece of luggage since she didn't expect to be in Bahrain too long. The extra time she had given herself to check in left her looking at her fellow passengers, as if in search of something she had in common with them.

She wore her badge but not her gun. International law prohibited her bringing one with her and, once in Bahrain, handguns were strictly forbidden. As visiting law enforcement personnel, traveling without formal portfolio, she lacked the efficacy to flaunt the law or seek an exception. The lack of a weapon left her anxious and tight. She felt the same way she did in the kind of dream where you realize you're naked, so unlike her fellow passengers whose most overt displays of anxiety lay in the frequent checks of their watches.

Caitlin didn't have to fly to Houston first, but a call placed on a whim to the CEO of MacArthur-Rain determined her itinerary.

"Mr. Delladonne's office."

"This is the assistant manager calling to confirm Mr. Delladonne's luncheon reservation for this afternoon."

"Seventeen Restaurant at the Alden-Houston Hotel," the female voice droned. "One P.M. The reservation is for three."

"We'll look forward to seeing Mr. Delladonne then."

Caitlin had made her travel arrangements accordingly and was standing inside the stylish lobby of the Alden-Houston Hotel, appointed in muted tones and black leather seating with white throw pillows, when a pair of bodyguards escorted Harmon Delladonne through the entrance. She recognized his tanned face from the picture on the company's Web site. He looked younger at first glance, tall and thin enough to wear a narrow cut European suit—Italian probably, Caitlin figured. She pictured the frame the suit contained as sinewy and lithe, evidence of a man who spent lots of time on the stationary bike or treadmill and watched what he ate.

She didn't know who Delladonne was meeting at *17, the hotel's upscale restaurant, and didn't care. Just waited fifteen minutes to give them time to get settled and ordered before she entered the restaurant, passing the hostess's station and making fast for Delladonne's table set slightly apart from the others against the red papered wall.

"Sorry for intruding, Mr. Delladonne," Caitlin greeted, ignoring the other two men at the table, "but I was wondering if I could have a word with you?"

Delladonne's eyes locked on the badge pinned to her shirt. "What does this pertain to, Ranger?"

"Be better if we discussed that in private, sir."

His gaze darted to the lounge area, to summon his two bodyguards no doubt. Delladonne's lunch guests aimed their eyes downward.

"As you can see, I'm in a meeting. Why don't you call my office and schedule an appointment? You can tell my secretary what it's about."

Caitlin felt her cheeks flush with blood, imagined her face taking on the same color as the bright red wall at her side. "Sir," she said, over the thumping of her own heart, "I'm afraid that won't do at all. I told your man Mr. Hollis that, and now I'm telling you."

And then Delladonne's bodyguards were at her side. Each several inches taller than she, both of them with pistol bulges beneath their suit jackets.

Delladonne dabbed at the corners of his mouth with a linen napkin and grinned at his guests as if to reassure them. "I'm afraid it's going to have to do, Ranger. As you can see I'm busy here."

"You know my husband," Caitlin blurted out before she could stop herself. Her heart was hammering her chest, feeling as if it were about to cave through the ribs.

"Pardon me?"

"Peter Goodwin. Maybe you don't know him personally, but he worked for one of your subsidiaries, company called RevCom."

Delladonne laid his napkin back on the table, looked at her smugly.

"You had your thugs torture him in Bahrain. He told me he was going to Iraq to make cable television available, solve all that country's problems with a hundred channels per household. That's what he told me 'cause that's what he believed. But he never really went because you never had any intention of sending him there. You sent him to Bahrain instead and had him tortured enough to turn a fine and decent man into a broken mess."

Delladonne's expression tightened, his next glance signaling his bodyguards. They reached out for Caitlin's arms, only one of them getting there. She hammered that man in the face with an elbow, feeling the cartilage of his nose compress on impact. He doubled over, hands going to his face, as Caitlin smashed a fist into the groin of the second. She snatched his gun from its holster first, then ripped the other man's free amid the flood of blood pouring from his nose.

Caitlin stood back up and dropped the pistols on Delladonne's serving plate, after ejecting the magazines. His luncheon guests jerked their chairs away from the table, as if afraid they were next.

But Caitlin ignored them, focusing on Delladonne. "I assume your men have licenses to carry those things."

Delladonne looked up at her, staring. "You said I know your husband."

"I did."

"Truth is I've never met the man, but I know you," Delladonne said, seeming to gloat. "Think you would have made Ranger if you didn't have family tradition on your side?"

"That's not what I'm here to talk about today, sir."

"With good reason, I suppose, given the reputations of your father and grandfather."

"Sir?"

"They were both corrupt, on the take from Mexican drug dealers pushing black tar heroin across the border." Delladonne's expression flashed with overly dramatic surprise. "Don't tell me you didn't know. I just assumed you picked up where the two of them left off."

Caitlin took a step closer to the table, not fully registering his comments. She felt cold sweat running straight down the center of her spine. "I know you were behind what happened to my husband and I'm gonna nail you for it."

"You are sadly mistaken, miss."

"Sir, I know you are dirty. I know you're dirty and I know you're behind the murders of seven innocent people who had survived the wrath of their own governments only to face yours for no good reason at all. I know you're behind the murder of a woman named Maura Torres and another man named Pablo Asuna, and the attempted murders of two young boys."

Caitlin started to slide away from the table, trembling inside her jacket and conscious of the stares upon her from all over the restaurant.

"I'll go call your secretary for that appointment. Have a nice lunch now."

69

HOUSTON, THE PRESENT

Caitlin waited for her flight to be called at Houston's Hobby Airport, unable to get the accusation lodged against her father and grandfather by Harmon Delladonne out of her head. As sinister and deceitful as he might have been, Delladonne did not strike her as someone who would make something like that up. Concoct the circumstances and scenario, perhaps, but his tone indicated to Caitlin that the source for his outlandish claim had its origins somewhere else.

Not that both Jim and Earl Ray Strong were without fault either. They, and hundreds more like them, had grown out of a Texas Ranger tradition born of Indian fighting and border clashes where the level of brutality had often made it hard to distinguish one moral code from another. In retrospect those Rangers, reared on a frontier ethos and sensibility, faced criticism for taking their mandates too far.

Official recognition was long in coming to the Texas Rangers and even that came at the expense of the militia mentality that had made them what they were. Many clung to the old ways until, as in the case of Jim Strong, it ate them up alive, or, like Caitlin, brushed them aside. She'd left something terribly unfinished that day in El Paso when she'd thrown her career away to challenge Cort Wesley Masters to draw.

She'd grown up with all the Ranger legends about hard men living off the land. In those days the Rangers weren't even an officially recognized body, more like minutemen, as they were called upon their inception in 1835 to repel Indian attacks on the frontier. With not only Indians to contend with in the north, but also Mexican incursions to deal with in the south, the mandate of the original Rangers quickly expanded.

The founding of the legendary Jack Hayes's company took place in San Antonio. Not coincidentally, the Strong family had resided there ever since, generation after generation attaching themselves to that city's company of Rangers all the way to her. Her granddad's Colt Peacemaker, dating back to 1873, was one of the first weapons Caitlin ever fired as a little girl. Recalling that day and so many others, it was impossible for her to picture her father and grandfather as anything but the last of the true heroes. Their taking money from drug runners to look the other way from shipments of black tar heroin being smuggled into the country made no sense any way she ran it through her mind.

Up against powerful forces she could not fathom or identify, Caitlin wished they were here alongside her right now to accompany her to Bahrain. Sitting in the departure area, she let her thoughts turn back to Cort Wesley's sons, the feeling of warmth that filled her when the younger Luke rested his head against her shoulder. She wished she had someone to share the pangs of emotion even the memories stoked in her, for some reason wanted to believe that the boy's stoic defensiveness, a shield more than anything, described his father as well. She wanted to believe that because it would help her explain Cort Wesley Masters in her own mind as well as help her justify not only the alliance they had formed but also the feelings she was beginning to harbor.

She enjoyed his company, looked forward to it even. Her granddad had told her tales of sometime allegiances forged between Rangers and outlaws in old Texas to beat back the common enemies of Indians and Mexicans. So was their relationship different or would the end of the battle they were waging now leave them foes again?

Caitlin admitted to herself that she much preferred the former. Rising from the floor after Luke had trounced her at the Texas Ranger video game, she had spotted Dylan standing atop his skateboard, the extra inches leaving him almost eye-to-eye with his father. Cort Wesley had reached out and laid a hand on the boy's shoulder. Caitlin considered how many men had perished from that hand and contrasted that against the warmth of the gesture. She couldn't see Cort Wesley's face but she knew it had been hard for him to do, just as entering his sons' lives had been. It made her see him in an entirely different light, held in an esteem she reserved, frankly, for very few. Watching the man overcome himself and his own nature. It left her to wonder if this was even the

"You've got Captain Tepper to thank for that."

"Wasn't him told my younger one the truth."

"I think he already knew mostly."

"Yeah, the older one too. I'll tell ya, Caitlin Strong, I live a hundred years I'll never do nothing tougher than that."

"I was thinking about that, made me want to ask you a question."

"Shoot."

"'Fore you went inside The Walls, you never got it in your mind to do what you did soon as you got out? Watching them from your car, I mean. Maybe someday knocking on the door and reintroducing yourself to Maura Torres."

"I came out a different man than I went in. Too much time to think, you know what I mean."

"Anything in particular?"

"Visitors. Watching these hard-pipe gang members and guys who'd shank you for a stick a gum or do a contract kill for a cigarette going all misty-eyed with their kid sitting in their lap on Sundays. I'm in five years, the only man who came to see me was Pablo Asuna and not too regular neither. If I didn't have anyone outside, I guess it wouldn't have bothered me. But the fact is I did and that made me resolve to do something about it if I ever got out."

"Think you ever would've gotten out of that car, if things had stayed status quo?"

"Can't really answer that now. Thing is I know who and what I am. What scares me a little is I think my boys like me more for that."

"'Cause you make them feel safe, Masters. They know you can beat down the monsters that came into their lives."

"I don't want the fear from this to last."

"I've spent a lot of time with victims," Caitlin told him, "and I can tell you the process takes its own time. Never the same twice."

Cort Wesley felt his breath quicken. "The men we're after were the ones put me away, killed Maura and would've done God knows what to my boys if you hadn't been there."

"All true enough."

"Same men who killed a bunch of people who'd been through plenty already to get to your husband."

She didn't respond this time.

"God'll forgive anything we gotta do to make this right, Caitlin Strong."

"You really care whether He does or not?"

"Just nice to have Him on my side for a change."

Cort Wesley could hear her flight being called in the background and was glad to say his good-byes. Glad because he was starting to feel uncomfortable having told Caitlin Strong things he had no one else to tell. He had come from a line of loners who chose to be around people only when it suited them or their needs. He could not recall, for example, a single time his father had hugged him, nor did he feel slighted by the lack of such a memory. The question of when his father had even last touched him crossed his mind in the moment he laid his hand on Dylan's shoulder and left it there instead of pulling it quickly away.

Cort Wesley found himself wanting to take both his boys shooting and hunting, the things he felt capable of making them better at. But none of that could happen with powerful enemies determined to waylay his plans and intentions. So he didn't seek to modify or refine his nature, because that very nature was the only thing that stood between his sons and the terrible fate others would bring upon them. Him alone. Well, not quite, he thought.

Because there was also Caitlin Strong. First person he'd ever known, man or woman, that good with a gun and not hesitant to use it. Truth be told, the people she'd killed in her time weren't that dissimilar from the ones he had. He guessed that was why she didn't waste time judging him anymore. They were the same, and both of them knew it.

The very same enemy had brought them together for the express purpose of vanquishing that enemy from their lives. And there was no way to accomplish this if they weren't willing to hit back as hard as they'd been hit. Cort Wesley knew he had the stomach for it and was pretty certain Caitlin Strong did as well.

What worried him was how that would leave her in the end, if it left her standing at all. Cort Wesley wasn't used to worrying about anybody and in the space of a mere week, he'd found himself with three lives wedged permanently into the core of his consciousness. When this was over, Caitlin Strong might find a deep dark place in herself she loathed and blame him for showing her the way to it. When this was over, without need of the protection he offered, his boys might tire quickly of his tense spectral presence in their lives. And, current feelings aside, he was scared of what the shape of his life would look like after this was done.

Being tough wasn't about not feeling fear, it was about knowing how to make that fear work to your advantage. Cort Wesley could do that when threatened by adversaries or when walking into odds regular men would have run away from. But this was a different kind of fear because there were no particular weapons or skills he could bring to beat it back.

Life in The Walls had taught him a lot about life, both good and bad. The things he needed to do to make it better without trying to effect the kind of change that would never happen. Because people never changed, not really, at least not at the core of their natures. Behavior, though, was something else again. It was a matter of changing focus and priorities, to make choices based on those changes.

His boys, for starters. And Caitlin Strong.

Caitlin Strong.

He liked saying her name in his head. Inside The Walls, lots of cons got by staring at pictures of their women taped to the concrete slab walls. Some of the pictures were dog-eared and faded, shots of wives and girlfriends long gone, only their memories and now crinkled faces left to cling to. Cort Wesley remembered any number of conversations with sad men who wanted nothing more than to discuss the people they'd loved and left on the outside. The sadness kept them going, clinging to the hope that some day it would be over.

Cort Wesley had never understood what they'd been getting at until now.

71

San Antonio, the Present

Guillermo Paz sucked in his breath before once again climbing the stone steps into San Fernando Cathedral on West Main Plaza in San Antonio. The double doors rattled closed behind him and he heard his footsteps echoing on the tile floor as he angled toward the confessional.

The interior of the church looked entirely different than it had just a few days earlier. And it smelled cleaner, less musty, as if the world were changing before him, things happening beyond his control.

Paz squeezed into the same confessional he'd used the last time and felt the wood creak as he sat down on the bench, door left open a crack to give his legs room to breathe.

"I'm back, Father."

"Oh, Lord," a familiar voice muttered. Through the screen, Paz could see the priest cross himself, seeming to cringe.

"Bless me, Father, for I have sinned. Not a lot lately, though. I've been conflicted, trying to figure a lot of things out. Do you believe in fate, Father?"

"Some would say it's another word for God's will, my son."

"You agree?"

The priest seemed reluctant to commit himself. "I believe a man's fate is his to do with what he pleases."

"See, that's exactly what I was hoping you'd say."

"My son, have you heeded my advice from our last visit?"

"I haven't killed a single person since."

"I'm pleased for you then, making inroads to escape the handicaps of your nature and rearing. Those are difficult challenges to overcome, my son."

"I feel like I'm changing, Padre, like that change is being forced upon me."

"How so?" the priest asked, clearly more relaxed.

"The people who called me here want me to go home. Before my job is finished."

"And this bothers you?"

"Like I told you last time, I feel I've failed."

"Them or yourself, my son?"

"Boy, Padre, you're really hitting the nail on the head today."

"Have you searched for the reason behind that failure?"

"I don't think you want to hear about that."

"I'm talking about searching your soul, my son. Failure, like anything else, happens for a reason. And, like everything else, it's God's will. The challenge for us who serve Him, you and I, is to discern what that reason is."

"Give me an example."

"You told me about a woman."

"The Texas Ranger."

"There must be a reason why she came into your life now."

"Lesson to be learned or something like that, right?"

"Or something deeper and more permanent. You said she made you feel strange because she was different. I'm wondering if the reason you noticed is because you're the one who's different."

"That's deep," Paz said, shifting his bulk in a futile search for comfort in the cramped confines of the confessional. "I think it comes down to sides. I always knew which one I was on before. Now I'm not so sure. That makes me feel even stranger."

"You came to me seeking to change, my son. But the fact is you've already changed and what you've really come to me for is to help you understand what you're going through."

"But I'm *not* proud of anything, Padre. Difference is I find myself wanting to be. Kierkegaard also said that meaning comes from desiring that which is beyond reason. I never understood that line, and now I see it's because I never experienced it. I should just get on a plane with my men and find another country to call home. Bank my money and forget this ever happened. But I can't, not until I finish what I've got to finish with this woman. See what I'm getting at here?"

"You've found meaning in the belief that your fates may be intertwined."

"Does that happen?"

"All the time. We're seldom fortunate to realize it, though."

"They'll just bring in someone else to finish the job I couldn't. Probably have the whole thing in the works already. So me leaving changes nothing in the great big scheme of things."

"You must consider yourself and your own needs first," the priest said.

"That's exactly what I'm doing, Padre. The problem is what that means for the woman as well as me, our souls being entwined and all like you said, if I'm gonna find that meaning Kierkegaard talks about I've been missing up to this point. Can you tell me what I should do?"

"That is for you to decide, my son."

"How 'bout a hint?"

The priest thought for a moment. "When you leave this country, do you wish it to be as the same man you were when you arrived?"

"No," Paz told him definitively.

"Then you have your answer."

"I do?"

"Your work is not yet done here."

Paz started to shimmy himself from the booth. "You know something, Father? I think you're right."

72

CHIHUAHUA, THE PRESENT

Emiliato Valdez Garza sat behind the desk overlooking his spacious grounds, being patrolled at the time by men armed with assault rifles and holding leashed pit bull terriers. He had spread a number of pictures before him, all of the same man, his subordinates standing at the foot of his desk, knowing enough to leave him in silence.

"What was his name again?" Garza asked, smoothing his hair back.

"Cort Wesley Masters," one of his subordinates answered.

"And these things you've told me about him, you're certain they're true?"

"Most of them, if not all. He has killed a lot of our men."

"Scum for the most part who probably deserved it. This man, he is not scum at all."

The subordinates remained quiet.

"He looks Mexican to me. You think he might have Mexican blood?"

The men standing before Garza's desk looked at one another, shrugging.

"There was a time when men like this dominated Mexico. True warriors. If this man were standing before me now, we wouldn't be facing the issues we're facing. This is a man much can be expected from, little of it good from our point of view. Are we certain he was the one watching from the hills?"

"He matches the description provided by both the

federales and Larrito from the warehouse. Our associates in America tried to deal with him. They failed."

"Perhaps they tried to be subtle."

"No," the man standing before the desk said. "They hired someone known for quite the opposite."

"Who?"

"Colonel Guillermo Paz of the Venezuelan secret police."

"Dirección de los Servicios de Inteligencia y Prevención. Paz has done much work for us as well, impressively and thoroughly. Another true warrior descended from the same Indians as our ancestors. You're telling me he was unable to kill this man Masters?"

"A Texas Ranger intervened."

"A Texas Ranger? After all these years . . . I lost many relatives to their guns over the years in the border wars. The beginning of Mexico's end as a proud nation. Perhaps changing all that begins here, eh?" Garza nodded slowly, to himself. "I think I will call our American associates, offer our services to handle this matter from this point on, so they can go about the things they are better suited for."

Garza reached for his phone and worked a number programmed into his speed dial.

"Buenos días, Señor Delladonne. . . ."

PART EIGHT

Rangers continued to add to their legend during the 1950s. When inmates in the Rusk State Hospital for the Criminally Insane rioted and took hostages, Ranger Captain R. A. "Bob" Crowder and the leader of the mob had a conversation and the inmates surrendered.

—Mike Cox, with updates from the Texas Ranger Hall of Fame and Museum Staff, "A Brief History of the Texas Rangers"

73

BAHRAIN, THE PRESENT

"So what business exactly do the Texas Rangers have in Bahrain, Ms. Strong?"

"Well, Mr. Smith," Caitlin started. "I'm sorry, was it Jones?"

"No, it's Smith," said the man behind the desk on the American Consulate's second floor. "It was Jones yesterday."

The man smirked. He was tall and broad with a close-cropped military haircut and carried himself with a confidence bred from the kind of combat experience that stripped all fear. He reminded Caitlin of a milder version of Cort Wesley Masters without the edge or careless certainty. He wore a suit that was tight in his shoulders and chest but swam loosely closer to his narrow waist.

"You knew I was coming."

"Your office notified the ambassador as a matter of protocol. He thought the reason for your visit might be more in my neck of the woods."

"*He* thought?"

"It was a mutual decision."

"So you ask me about my business, but you already know why I'm here."

"I like to hear things firsthand. That way I can smile politely and send you on your way."

Caitlin had landed at Bahrain International Airport on

the island of Al Muharraq barely an hour before. Stepping outside the terminal, she was assaulted by the heat. Every bit as oppressive as the Texas summer, the sun seeming to ride the tops of the office buildings forming the Manama skyline across the water beyond. The long flight had left her stiff and stuck to her clothes. A shower was what she really longed for, but there were more pressing concerns to take care of first.

Caitlin had taken a taxi across the causeway into Manama, reaching the city's diplomatic section minutes later. The pale, limestone American Consulate was nestled among similar buildings on the block, each enclosed by a gated fence that looked more decorative than protective. There were no Marine guards patrolling the meager grounds or standing their post at the entrance. Caitlin simply rang the buzzer alongside the front door, announced herself into a speaker, and heard a buzz followed by the door clicking open.

At the reception desk, she asked to see the ambassador but was taken to the office of Mr. Smith instead.

"You can understand my problem, I'm sure," he resumed.

"Actually, I can't."

"Bahrain's an ally, Ranger. We can't have accusations of torture being levied against the government."

"I never said it was the government."

Smith, Jones, or whoever, tightened his brow. "Am I missing something here?"

"An American, a resident of Texas, was tortured in this country. Just not, we believe, by any officials of Bahrain."

"Then I'm not really sure how I'm supposed to help you."

"You could show me around. If you're too busy, I'll just take the tour myself."

"And, what, look for buildings with signs reading Torture Is Us?"

Caitlin gazed about Smith's sparse office. "Wouldn't happen to have one lying around here now, would you?"

"That's not funny, Ranger."

"Do I look like I'm laughing?"

"Long way to come to tell a bad joke."

"The man who was tortured was my husband, Mr. Smith. How's that for a punch line?"

Smith settled back in his chair, going quiet. He gazed across the desk, sizing Caitlin up. "Hope you're not expecting to make an arrest here."

"Nope. I'm just looking for the place where it happened."

"Why?"

"Got my reasons."

Smith shifted his chair to face her head-on, making his shoulders look even broader. "You need to make them my reasons too, if you want my help."

"You speaking for the United States government, Mr. Smith?"

"The relevant part of it for your purposes anyway."

"CIA?"

Smith shrugged her comment off. "Put any three letters together, you're bound to get something relevant, Ranger."

"What am I supposed to call you?"

"Huh?"

"You called me Ranger. How am I supposed to address you? I'm thinking maybe 'Agent.'"

"Mister will do."

Caitlin cocked her head slightly to the side. "No first name?"

"Not today. We aren't gonna know each other long enough to dispense with the formality."

"Know what?" Caitlin asked, feigning disappointment as she rose. "I get the point. Think I'll just take my problem over to Bahrain's interior ministry, see what they can do for me."

Smith sneered. "Nobody official will talk to you without a consulate official present."

"Don't be so sure of that. I can be pretty persuasive."

"You don't even speak the language."

"Do you?"

"Enough to know how to lie."

"You lying now, Mr. Smith?"

"I'm speaking English."

Caitlin leaned forward and laid her hands on the edge of the desk. "Two choices—that's what you've got from where I'm standing. Either you help me out and I'm gone from your hair in less than a day. Or you don't help me and watch me make a mess of things for you with your friends in the local government."

If Smith was riled, he didn't show it. "Come on, a nice girl like you . . ."

Caitlin spun the stiff wooden chair set before his desk around and straddled the seat. "Let me tell you a story. My dad was a Ranger too. One night he walked into a Laredo bar in search of information about who beat up a woman pretty bad. Knocked four of her teeth out, broke a couple ribs and an arm. She got away before he could rape her, and my dad came calling to see what the regulars inside could tell him. You know much about Texas, Mr. Smith?"

"Not particularly, no."

"Well, suffice it to say Texans have a way of keeping to themselves and protecting their own. So my dad walks into this bar that's not much more than a beer joint with a tackle shop in the front to a chorus of stares that could melt ice. He tries to handle things in a polite and friendly manner—diplomatic to use a term you're more accustomed to." Caitlin tightened her gaze and her tone. "But when that didn't work he set the building on fire and got the information he needed from customers being treated for smoke inhalation. Perpetrator's truck was blocked in by a fire engine and my dad arrested him behind the wheel."

Smith's eyes narrowed on her. "You threatening to burn down the consulate, Ranger Strong?"

"Only metaphorically."

Smith's eyes blinked more rapidly, weighing his options it looked like. "Tell you what, I'll give you the rest of today. Whatever you find, or don't find, you're on a plane out of here first thing tomorrow."

"Sounds fair enough."

Smith pursed his lips, then curled his upper one over the lower. "Just empty your pockets first."

Caitlin rose and reached in with both hands. "I left my gun back in Texas."

"Not a gun I'm worried about," Smith told her, "so much as matches."

74

TERRELL HILLS, THE PRESENT

"I thought we were finished," Jimmy Farro said, after opening his front door to find Cort Wesley standing there.

"We will be soon, podner. Just give me a few minutes of your time."

"Do I have a choice?"

Cort Wesley's answer was to brush past him inside. "Got any iced tea?"

"In the fridge."

"I'll pour you a glass too. We can drink them downstairs in your office."

Farro followed him into the kitchen, nerves in a jumble. "I'm trying to stay out of this kind of st-st-st-stuff."

"There you go with the stuttering again, Jimbo."

"I haven't stuttered in five years."

"Leads me believe you don't make me for the changed man I've become," Cort Wesley said, pulling a pitcher of iced tea from the refrigerator. "Just wanna ask you a couple questions, podner. Be on my way again 'fore you know it."

"What k-k-k-kind of questions?"

Cort Wesley found the glasses and laid two of them on the counter. "Tell you downstairs. You take sugar with your tea, Jimbo?"

"I need to find manufacturing plants in Mexico," he told Jimmy Farro when they were amid his array of computers.

"You check the yellow pages?"

"Do they make computers down there these days?"

"Lenovo just opened a new plant. Take advantage of all that cheap labor."

"I'm not looking for Lenovo or anything else you can find in the yellow pages. I'm looking for places people would want to keep on the quiet."

"So what do you w-w-w-want from me?"

"Tell me how to find them, podner."

"I'm not psychic, Cort Wesley."

"No, but you're smart. Come on, you wanted to find a place that was manufacturing or assembling computer chips, what would you look for?"

"Air exchangers," Farro said with little hesitation.

"Huh?"

"Chips have to be produced in a clean environment, virtually sterile. You see videos, the workers are always wearing masks and latex gloves."

Cort Wesley looked as if he had never seen those videos.

"But the biggest problem is dust, so chip assembly lines require these massive exchangers that basically clean the air to two parts per million on a continuous basis."

"I find who bought these air exchangers, I find who's making chips."

"Maybe. Yeah. We d-d-d-done now?"

Cort Wesley switched on the computer he was standing next to. "We will be, soon as you tell me who purchased these damn things down there."

It took two hours for Farro to generate the list Cort Wesley had come for. Since there were only a few manufacturers cranking out the kind of air exchangers required for chip assembly, he explained it was a relatively simple matter to hack their internal billing records to see where those exchangers had been shipped.

"There's more than I thought here, Cort Wesley," Farro told him. "Any way we can narrow the search a bit?"

"Go back to 2003 or so."

"The Cerberus chip," Farro realized.

"On the money as always, Jimbo."

Farro's fingers glided effortlessly across the keyboard. "Got three addresses for you," he reported. "No way to tell whether they're legit or if the plants are st-st-st-still in operation."

"Just print them out for me, podner. Then I'll be out of your hair."

75

Bahrain, the Present

"This is the place where the local authorities found him," Caitlin told Smith, standing amid a sea of tourists at the Bab Al Bahrain marketplace.

She could hear the sizzling of food roasting over open flames, the scents of garlic and lemon heavy in the air. There were tables set both outside in the sun and beneath the shade of a canopied veranda where several diners stood as opposed to exposing themselves to the intense heat. Caitlin imagined Peter standing here, starving and emaciated, felt the familiar flush of anger that continued to fuel her.

"According to the report," she continued, snapping off shots of the place with her disposable camera, "he proceeded here from City Gardens."

"Heading east then," Smith surmised.

"Important since his dazed state likely means he traveled in a straight line."

"From the west," Smith said, looking back that way.

"Yes."

"Lots of places to the west."

"But the condition of Peter's feet and light sandals indicate he didn't walk that far, maybe a mile, mile and a half or so."

Smith followed her gaze. "So we're looking for a site generally within that distance from here."

"Pretty narrow grid. An office or apartment building."

"Not an office building," Smith told her. "Office buildings have cleaning staffs. With apartments people keep to themselves."

"You've thought this out pretty well."

"I've got a good imagination."

"What kind of man tortures another?"

"Why don't you tell me?"

The knowing, sententious look in Smith's eyes told Caitlin as much as his words. "Guess you've done your research."

"I read your file, the kind nobody knows exists."

"I'm not proud of lots of things I've done."

"We all do what we have to, Ranger. Difference here is you weren't under orders at the time."

"There a point to that?"

"You enjoy the process?"

"Not in the least."

"Tell yourself that long enough and maybe you'll start buying it."

"I never did it again."

"Maybe if you had, you wouldn't have needed a gun. So crass, Ranger. You should've given me a call, asked for a few pointers."

The casualness of his remark chilled her. "So those mules could've ended up with their brains scrambled like Peter."

"Instead they limp for the rest of their lives."

"You sound like you're judging me."

"You think finding the men who tortured your husband will absolve you of your own indiscretions."

"Analyzing me now," Caitlin said, shaking her head slowly.

"Lessons of experience, Ranger. Take it for what it's worth."

Caitlin clung to the shadows as best she could, the whole city like sitting inside a sauna, the heat building a throb in her head on top of the fact that Smith's attitude made her fear she might knock his pearly teeth out the next time he flashed his sardonic grin. Finally, she just pulled the disposable camera from her pocket again and fired off more shots of the *souq*.

"I saw pictures taken at the British Embassy where he was brought originally," she said, once she had emptied half the roll. "He had patches of sunburn on his face, like in a grid."

"Say they left him by the sun during the hottest times of the day."

"Something you've done, Smith?"

Smith's expression didn't even flicker. "Just say. Temperature variances are a staple of benign interrogation."

Caitlin eyed him with disgust. "That term, benign interrogation, you're kidding, right?"

"You're not the only one looking for a way to sleep at night, Ranger."

"I sleep just fine, thank you, Smith."

"Knowing you did what you had to."

"That's right."

"You think it's any different for people like me?"

"It should be."

"Not what I asked you."

"It's the question I'm answering all the same, Smith. Don't try equating what I did in Juárez with what you've done just about everywhere else."

"Intelligence gathering, Ranger. It's the same thing."

"No, it's not."

"What's the difference?"

"I don't do it for a living, Smith."

"Really? Could've fooled me."

Caitlin looked at him in silence.

"Clock's running, Ranger."

"I'd like us to check those buildings. Apartments, you said."

"Tell you what, we'll go back to the consulate and I'll set the computers to work on narrowing the list down a bit. See what we can see."

"So long as you find me that building, Smith."

"If nothing else, it'll give us a chance to get better acquainted."

"Swap stories about inflicting pain."

"There's a thought."

"I can't wait," Caitlin told him.

76

MEXICO, THE PRESENT

The three addresses Jimmy Farro had come up with were all located in the Mexican state of Coahuila de Zaragoza, the first location in the violent border town of Nuevo Laredo. Once again, Cort Wesley had driven, only this time Caitlin Strong had insisted he use her SUV. He was grateful since, unlike Pablo Asuna's now abandoned Ford, the air-conditioning worked and, even more important, the interior smelled of her. Not a sharp scent, just something soft like lilacs and some kind of talcum powder. It made the drive south from San Antonio that much more pleasurable.

But the drive also stoked memories of Pablo Asuna and Maura Torres, two people he was close to who'd been murdered because of their association with him. Caitlin Strong had been more right than she realized about his feelings for Maura. They'd been little more than kids at the time, and she wanted no part of him, keenly aware of where he was headed. He promised her he was ready to give up that life and move on to another, if they settled down. They did but, as it turned out, he couldn't and Maura threw him out halfway into her first pregnancy.

Cort Wesley was there when Dylan was born and came around regularly until a pair of bangers from the Mexican Mafia showed up looking for him. Maura stuck a shotgun in their faces and told them to get lost. She'd just learned she was pregnant with Luke at the time. First thing Cort Wesley did was take care of the bangers. Second thing was to move Maura up to Shavano Park and swear off seeing her again, even when Luke was born. And he'd stayed true to his word until the day after he got out of The Walls and found himself parked across the street from the house he'd bought for her with Branca crime family money.

Cort Wesley's status and reputation earned him a single bunk in The Walls. He awoke one morning a few months into his stay to find a note taped around a shank fashioned of a filed-down toothbrush with bedsheet strips wrapped around its handle. The note anonymously ordered him to murder an alleged prison informant on penalty of Leroy Epps being executed if he failed to comply. Cort Wesley had hoped keeping to himself would be enough to get the other inmates to steer clear of him. But he'd erred in striking up a friendship with the aging Epps, who seemed genuinely interested in what he called Cort Wesley's moral "rehabilitation." Cort Wesley had visited Epps in the prison infirmary when his diabetes got bad, distressed to see how the whites of his fading eyes were stained permanently red now from leaking blood.

In any event, the note quite correctly stated that Cort Wesley wouldn't be able to protect Epps twenty-four hours a day. The informant in question was Billy Traggar, a

scared shitless white pretty boy in The Walls for acciden-
tally killing an undercover cop in the commission of a
drug deal. Kid had a wiry frame, wore his hair in a ponytail and floated from group to group in search of one to
make his stretch inside as tolerable as possible. When
none of that worked, he began accumulating dirt on his
molesters and abusers to trade for a transfer to the protective custody wing.

Cort Wesley's response to the note ordering him to
shank Billy Traggar was to contact Warden T. Edward
Jardine to spill all the dirt the boy had intended to,
thereby eliminating any need for his death. Passing the
information on came with two additional caveats: that
Billy be transferred as agreed and that Leroy Epps be allowed to share Cort Wesley's cell. In the closed society of
prison, he had violated two sacrosanct rules in the con-
vict code of conduct: first by becoming a rat and then by
mixing with a man from another race, as cell mates no
less. But Cort Wesley cared nothing for any code that
would threaten the lives of both an old man and a poor
mess of a strung-out kid.

He had bucked the long-entrenched system and found
himself cast too often in later months as protector of the
weak and infirm to the point where no hit could be ordered inside The Walls without his approval. The inmates with hopes of release knew he was a soldier for the
powerful Brancas who could get to them once freed or
their families now with a simple phone call. So in trying
to lie low he had actually ended up becoming the de facto
head of the toughest criminals and lifers the state of
Texas had to offer.

Maybe it worked, maybe it changed him, because Cort
Wesley considered himself a lifer at that point too. The
rules that had worked for him outside didn't carry over to
the inside and, just as plainly, he needed to find new ones

to redefine what was going to pass for the rest of his life. When word came down that a DNA test had exonerated him for the murder of a Texas Ranger in the stretch of the Chihuahuan Desert that reached over into West Texas, he was already too far along in the process to go back to being the man he used to be. Maybe getting that Smith & Wesson 9 millimeter and heading over to the Survivor Center to find Caitlin Strong was about claiming it back. As things turned out, though, it became more about giving his old self up for good, his moral "rehabilitation," as Leroy Epps had called it, at last complete.

But the tests kept coming. First, Maura's death plopping his boys down into his life, then his feelings for Caitlin Strong and now this trek to Mexico to please her as much as to make amends to Maura Torres who had him figured from the beginning and ended up paying the ultimate price for daring to love him. He imagined what Leroy Epps might say about that now, imagined the old man sitting next to him in the passenger seat of Caitlin Strong's SUV, smelling the talcum powder he layered on himself to hide the sour scent of skin turned bad by diabetes.

"How you be, bubba?"

"You tell me, champ."

"Good, from where I'm sitting. How you see it?"

"Truth is I had a shot with Maura Torres. When I walked away from her, I never thought there'd be another."

"Something changed."

"This Texas Ranger. I look at her, I see a future, something I never really considered much before, 'specially when we were inside since there weren't any prospects for one."

"*Something to seize sounds like to me. Man, what I wouldn't give for a cee-gar right now. . . .*"

"*I don't want to fuck things up again, champ.*"

"*More than you be hurt by that this time, bubba. Got kids in the mix, something I never made time for myself.*"

"*And ain't that a hoot!*"

"*I had it to do again, that be the first thing I'd do different. Let that be a lesson to ya, bubba. Just 'cause Maura Torres wasn't the right one doesn't mean you turn aside from the possibility. This Ranger gal might be just the thing to round out that ilk of yours. You know it and I know it, so let's just leave things there.*"

Cort Wesley grinned just before the old man's image vanished from the passenger seat. But for a long stretch into the drive that followed, Cort Wesley continued to smell the sweet scent of talcum powder, making him wonder maybe, just maybe . . .

77

BAHRAIN, THE PRESENT

The list Smith had come up with took them to the neighborhood of Umm Al Hassam, a middle-class enclave on the capital Manama's southern coast lined with a mixture of old villas and the kind of newer apartment buildings that fit the profile of the site where Peter had been tortured. The problem was that it was three miles from Bab Al Bahrain where he had been found, farther than the condition of Peter's shoes and feet had indicated.

"There are four buildings that best fit our profile," Smith explained on the drive over. "They cater to lots of businessmen who may only use the apartments for a few days every month, if that. Kind of places people stay out of one another's way, don't mix much because they literally might not speak the same language. What other criteria can we use to narrow things down?"

"Peter was found wandering in the *souq* nearly nine months ago, probably because the site was shut down suddenly. New administration taking over and all."

"Right." Smith snickered.

"So we're looking for a place where the occupants vanished suddenly, probably leaving the furnishings behind."

"Might not be as strong a clue as you think."

"Why?"

"Because these kind of situations call for long-term leases, not month-to-month."

"How are those leases paid?"

"Up front normally to minimize the paper trail. Wire transfers into the leasing company's account. They get their money, they don't look any further."

"There you go then, Smith. Something else to go on."

"Experience in these matters does have its benefits," he told her, not drawing a rise this time.

"Ready to tell me your real name, Mr. Smith?"

He nodded slowly, seeming to relent. "Okay, it's Jones."

Their questioning of each of the four buildings' landlords focused on apartments with southern exposure to the bright Bahrain sky during the time of the day when the sun was strongest. In all there were six apartments contained in three of the buildings that fit the criteria perfectly. Access to each was accomplished by simply handing the superintendent an envelope. Multiple apartments meant multiple envelopes.

Of the first four, three were furnished as normal apartments and the fourth wasn't furnished at all. The fifth apartment proved to be something else entirely.

"This isn't the standard building lock," the superintendent said in excellent English. "My key will not open it."

"So the tenants broke the rules," Smith said.

"Indeed they did."

"What can you tell us about them?"

The superintendent consulted his clipboard. "It's leased to an investment banking firm in London."

"Name?"

"Phillotson Capital Partners."

Smith looked as if that was all he needed to hear, reaching into his pocket to emerge with yet another envelope. "Tenants are required to provide access in an emergency, correct?"

"Yes."

Smith handed him the envelope. "This is an emergency."

78

NUEVO LAREDO, THE PRESENT

Cort Wesley had the list of the three locations where high-output air exchangers had been shipped in 2002 through 2003 open on the passenger seat. He crossed the border with a short line of vehicles and opened the SUV's windows to warm the chill he'd begun to feel.

The first address on the list in Nuevo Laredo had been converted into a sugar refinery with the air exchangers shipped in 2003 nowhere in evidence.

"Computer manufacture?" the manager said to him. "Sure. This was a Gateway assembly plant until they were purchased by Acer a few years ago. We bought out their lease."

"What about their equipment?"

"They took pretty much everything with them. The building wasn't much more than a shell when we moved in."

"I'm talking about huge rectangular machines attached to what would have looked like blowers and fans with lots of piping and ductwork hanging about."

"Yes," the manager said, "I remember them being removed. I remember because they were so heavy and cumbersome, they had to be disassembled first."

"What'd you do with them?"

"Junkyard."

Cort Wesley's next stop was two hundred miles southwest in Monclova, actually the foothills on the outskirts of the town in a gated building under heavy guard. The umbrella of overgrowth hanging down from the surrounding trees and brush would have rendered the building virtually invisible from the air, and he also noticed the roof had been painted green to further disguise its presence.

Cort Wesley felt his neck hairs stand on end. If this wasn't the place where Garza, or somebody else, had manufactured the Cerberus chip for MacArthur-Rain, it was the site of something equally nefarious. Cort Wesley was in no position to storm the building alone, nor would that have been the most prudent strategy under any circumstances. He considered reporting a relative of his inexplicably disappearing from the site, or being under some kind of duress. If this were the kind of place he suspected, though, the Mexican *federales* and other authorities would have been paid to look the other way no matter what.

Cort Wesley considered creating a distraction, but the most effective here—fire or some kind of explosion— would be impossible to effect unless he got much closer. He figured there would be guards patrolling the perimeter outside the fence as well and, almost on cue, he noticed one dressed in a khaki uniform and cap standing at the edge of the heavy brush. Standing a post instead of patrolling, which suited Cort Wesley's needs equally well.

He took the man by surprise effortlessly and, under gunpoint, forced him to change into his clothes. Once dressed in the man's uniform, Cort Wesley slung his submachine gun over his shoulder and pressed his knife against the man's lower back. Very simple matter to drive it home, if the guard did not cooperate fully.

As expected, having a prisoner in hand gained Cort Wesley swift access through the main gate and an easy approach through the remainder of the outside security right up to the building. An uneasy moment followed where the guard at the entrance eyed the similarly uniformed Cort Wesley with as much suspicion as he eyed the apparent prisoner.

"Take him to the boss," he said finally, thrusting open the door and gesturing with his submachine gun for both of them to enter. "I'll get a hole dug."

With the door closed behind him, Cort Wesley found himself in a sprawling warehouse-style space filled with the pungent stench of alcohol, preservatives and other harsh chemicals he could not identify. Peasant workers garbed in surgical masks and pocketless smocks sifted through huge piles of white powder while others labored near complex machines that looked like modern versions of moonshine stills. A constant hum droned loudly, courtesy of the ceiling-mounted recirculators and floor-standing air exchangers.

Cort Wesley realized he had stumbled upon one of the mythical Garza's massive drug dens, nothing whatsoever to do with chip assembly. The guard wearing his clothes must have sensed his distraction because he chose that moment to break away.

"Help me! He's a—"

That was as far as the man got before the knife Cort Wesley threw lodged in his back. The attention of all turned his way, and Cort Wesley responded by whipping the dead guard's submachine round from his shoulder and letting loose with a spray. He angled his fire upward at first, shattering a portion of the fluorescent lighting overhead, which sent glass raining down on the workers.

He aimed his next spray for the largest congestion of chemicals, instantly coughing up hot, orange flamed fires and spilling any number of caustic chemicals over anyone unlucky enough to be near. Screams rang out, trumping both the air exchangers and the heavy thump of panicked footsteps rushing for the door against the determined efforts of the remaining guards to stem the surge.

Cort Wesley led the charge outside, crashing through the door with the dead guard's bandana pressed against his mouth to feign exposure to some awful loosed chemical. That sight was enough to make the outside guards back off, concern for their own safety turning them hesitant to respond by blocking the path of their fleeing fellow guards and peasant labor.

Cort Wesley slipped past them in an advertent stagger, heading straight for the main gate through which a number had already fled. He pretended to collapse in the nearby brush, only to quickly regain his footing and continue on to Caitlin Strong's SUV parked off the road up the hill with ample brush for cover.

He leaped inside and screeched away. Just one more address left ahead to go with the chaos he was leaving behind.

79

BAHRAIN, THE PRESENT

Caitlin and Smith entered the apartment after the building superintendent had used a selection of tools to remove the lock altogether. It wasn't easy and once open they could see the door had been replaced as well with one of the heavy, soundproof variety.

Even though the apartment was blisteringly hot from the lack of circulation and switched-off air-conditioning, Caitlin felt chilled to the bone. All the blinds were drawn, the only light coming courtesy of the thin shafts emanating from the hallway.

She had entered the agonized world her husband had known for months. And, one way or another, it was her fault.

"So," Peter asked her, "what do you think?"

"What do I think?"

"Repeating the question is just a way of delaying giving an answer. You can't tell me you haven't thought of it yourself."

"Having a baby? Actually, I haven't."

"It'll be a boy."

"How can you know that?"

"You told me you were the only Strong firstborn ever to be a woman. Odds are in our favor, Caity."

She forced a smile. "I get my first report card and you spring this on me. . . ."

Peter wrapped an arm around her shoulder. "Come on, I'll help you with your homework. I'm pretty smart, you know. Think about it. Kid with my brains, your toughness."

"You saying I'm not smart?" she quipped at him.

"Nope. That I'm not tough."

"You would like me to wait?" the building superintendent asked in English.

Neither Caitlin nor Smith replied. The apartment felt stuffy and smelled of disuse. But the pungent scents of powerful antiseptic cleaners hung in the air. Already starting to dissipate with the opening of the front door, the stench remained strong enough to turn Caitlin's stomach and make her even queasier. She had wrapped her arms about herself upon entering and now felt powerless to return them to her sides. She watched Smith move to a light switch and flip it on.

Ambient, recessed bulbs cast murky lighting downward, making enough of a dent in the front room to reveal a series of cots still covered in hastily draped bedcovers. Caitlin imagined them smelling of stale sweat shed by men posted here on a rotating basis, the thought of a shower in such confines never even entering their minds. And, true to that assumption, her inspection of the single bath revealed hand towels and soap but not a single bath towel.

There were two bedrooms, the first of which was totally empty, the only evidence left by the previous occupants here being scratches and weight impressions dug into the light-wood flooring. The former occupants had clearly fled in a hurry and had made little effort to disguise that fact.

"Locals would be my guess," Smith noted. "More watchdogs than anything. The pros must've left them in a lurch. So they abandoned the place, took whatever was in this room maybe to cover their own asses, maybe to sell. Like video equipment, televisions."

Caitlin looked around the room, not at him. "This ever happen to you?"

"I always finish what I start."

"Present tense, Smith."

"There's a reason why I'm posted in this part of the world, Ranger. And I believe in my country."

Caitlin finally turned his way. "So did my husband."

She backed out of the room first, moved to the second bedroom and reached out for the knob of the closed door. Her brain gave the command to turn it, but her hand wouldn't comply, as if she'd still find Peter on the floor, cowering in fear and pain, stinking in the indignity of his own body waste. She closed her eyes and that gave her the will she needed to complete the effort. She pushed the door inward, feeling its heaviness matching that of the one at the apartment entrance.

"I'm sorry," Caitlin told him.

Peter tried not to show how disappointed he was. "Hey, in vitro almost never works the first time. Odds again. We'll just try again."

"I'm worried it'll never work."

"Why?"

" 'Cause maybe I'm not supposed to have kids. Maybe there aren't supposed to be any more Strongs."

"No more Strongs becoming Texas Rangers, you mean."

"Would that bother you?"

"Not so long as it's his choice and not yours."

"Could be a 'her,' you know."

Peter kissed her lightly. Caitlin ran a hand through his sandy brown hair. It was thinning on top but he wore it long to disguise that fact. He still had big doe eyes the world hadn't shrunk yet and a grin that usually made her smile too in spite of herself.

"Not a chance," Peter said.

The room was beyond night black, it was pitch. Windows seemed to be nonexistent, which she knew was impossible, given Peter's sunburned skin, which meant heavy wood or even steel shutters had been installed, to be opened and closed based on the whims of evil men.

Caitlin felt the chill in her receding, overcome by the hot flash of anger that spread downward from her face. Instead of freezing, she was suddenly sweating profusely enough to smell the salt rising out of her body. Her mouth was so dry she could barely swallow. Her hand felt for the switch, flipped it on.

What barely passed as light shed dim radiance that struggled to descend from the ceiling. Either the fixture had been covered with some kind of colored tape or fabric, or an extremely low-wattage bulb had been installed. Another trick of Peter's torturers, she guessed, regulating the light to confuse day and night until they became indistinguishable from each other. Time lost along with the dignity of life itself.

Caitlin felt herself seething, picturing it all in her mind

as her eyes adjusted well enough to the dark blur. It wasn't a medieval torture chamber, full of terrible devices atop a blood-splattered floor. Quite the opposite. As far as she could tell, the sum total of the entire room was a single bare mattress set atop a steel cot built into the wall. There were chains and manacles affixed to the cot's iron posts, along with a simple steel table and two folding chairs coated with rust. Beyond that, nothing. Benign interrogation, as Smith had called it.

What she saw, though, was still enough to bring the chill back, battling the heat flush that continued to surge through her.

"You shouldn't feel guilty," Peter said, hugging her tight.

Caitlin tightened her arms around him. "I really wanted this. I wanted it so much. Not at first maybe, but for sure now."

"There's other things we can do, try."

"Waste of time, money."

He eased her away from him. "I was talking about adoption."

"No."

"We'll talk about it later."

"My answer'll be the same."

"Why?"

" 'Cause every time I look at him, I'll think about my own failing."

"How about a her?" Peter said, hoping for a smile.

The sad blankness remained fixed on her expression. "I can't do it, I just can't."

He got up off the couch, started away.

"Where you going?"

"You tell me, Caity. Where am I going? Where are we going?"

"We'll figure it out, Peter."

"I hope so, because I can't do this anymore. You wanna know the real reason I want a kid so bad?" he asked, staring at her harshly for the first time she could remember. "Because I'm tired of raising the one I married." He turned away and started to walk off. "I can't do this anymore." He stopped and looked back at her. "An opportunity's come up, something that'll take me away for a long while. Tell me not to take it, Caity. Tell me not to take it and I won't."

Caitlin didn't meet his gaze, didn't respond. She heard the front door open and close again.

"This is definitely the place," Smith said from the doorway.

"Why didn't they kill him?" Caitlin heard herself ask him.

"*They* weren't here. Pulled out would be my guess, leaving only the local babysitters, who didn't know shit, behind. When *they* didn't come back, the babysitters abandonded the place. Probably figured they were leaving your husband to die."

"Was this military?"

"Not at all. Military doesn't use babysitters."

"I meant private military."

"You want to pin this on somebody like MacArthur-Rain, don't expect any help from me."

"Why?"

"Because a few years from now I'll probably be working for them."

Caitlin took out her disposable camera and started taking pictures of the room with the heavy wood shutters open and the dark fabric peeled off the light fixture. Her mind framed each shot in the moment before the flash ignited and then held it in her mind like a memory card.

The chains looped round the steel bedposts, hanging off the side of the bed. . . .

More chains affixed to the bed's legs coiled like steel snakes across the scuffed floor. . . .

The bare white walls that were chilling in their cold starkness. . . .

The grated windows that accounted for Peter's checkerboard sunburn. . . .

The heavy shutters that could turn day to night. . . .

The flat table behind which Peter had likely sat across from his interrogators. . . .

A simple black hood used to cover his face to further disorient him lying beneath that table. . . .

What looked like a metal washbasin they had likely filled with frigid water and held his face in propped up in a corner. . . .

The camera in her hand took on the feeling of a pistol, Caitlin imagining she was firing bullets instead of snapping pictures, wiping out the men who had perpetrated this horror.

Caitlin backed up into the doorway, trying to get a few shots capturing the full but meager scope of the room. Smith approached her a few times, only to stop as if repelled by the electricity dancing off her skin.

What had they wanted from Peter? What secrets of Fire Arrow had they tried to pull from his decaying mind?

In spite of herself, Caitlin pictured the whole ugly process, the vision curtailed every time she tried to project the questioning process. Her imagination could only go so far, certainly not to the level of what all this had been about.

Not yet anyway.

The camera's shutter button locked, the roll empty. Smith chose that moment to finally address her.

"We should get going. Before anyone notices."

"Nobody noticed Peter."

"You need help booking a flight out?"

Caitlin turned toward him, camera held at her side like a pistol. "Trying to get rid of me, Smith?"

"You make me feel uncomfortable."

"Because you've been on the wrong sides of rooms like this?"

"Just never had to deal with the fallout before. And the people I visited in rooms like this weren't American-born computer geeks; they were foreign terrorists." Smith hesitated. "This would be a good time to get things straight in your own head."

"Meaning?"

"You want your husband back, Ranger?"

"None of your goddamn business."

He ignored her response. "Because that man's gone and he's not coming back. So if you're thinking about picking up your lives where they left off, or even starting over, you can forget about it."

"Thanks for the advice."

"I'm just getting started. I know something about guilt, Ranger, and you think that's going to be enough to hold the two of you together, think again. You're no more the same person than your husband is. You want some real advice: move on, for both your sakes."

Caitlin found herself thinking of Cort Wesley describing himself as a much different man coming out of prison than he'd been when he went in. But the mere consideration of him brought the guilt back and left her desperate to move her thoughts somewhere else.

"You're a walking cliché, Smith," she said, more to

change the subject than anything else. "Anybody ever tell you that?"

"I only used to be. Used to be an anachronism too. Then 9/11 happens and all of a sudden my phone's ringing off the hook. Old school's made a comeback because it's the only way we can win."

"The scary thing about people like you, Smith, is that you honestly believe your own bullshit."

"And in my country, like I said before."

"Sometimes," Caitlin told him, "it's the same thing."

80

SALTILLO, MEXICO, THE PRESENT

The final stop on Cort Wesley's list was an address in Saltillo. It made sense, he figured, the city being one of the few true highlights of the Mexican economy, with residents enjoying the highest income per capita in the country.

Saltillo's economic base was built on the construction of tile and manufacture of multicolored serapes for export. More recently a DaimlerChrysler truck assembly plant had moved in, along with General Motors and Delphi Auto Parts. The rich and broad-based factories that dominated the city of more than a half million people would make the perfect setting for a state-of-the-art chip assembly plant. The labor was relatively skilled and plentiful, and warehouse-style spaces could be found in abundance. Add to this the fact that the city was shielded on one side by the Zapalinamé Mountains and offered swift flight through the Chihuahuan Desert on another.

The problem was the address he pulled up to was no

more than a shuttered storefront in plain view of El Complejo Industrial Ramos Arizpe, the sprawling industrial complex that housed the massive General Motors plant. Cort Wesley parked his car farther up the street, so as not to disturb a group of boys kicking a soccer ball about. He approached the building and rapped on the door to no avail. The collection of dust blown in from the desert, built up on the windows inside and out, was enough to tell him the storefront had been abandoned for some time.

He noticed that the boys about Luke's age who'd been kicking the soccer ball had stopped, gathering to watch him. Cort Wesley wondered why they weren't in school, a new manner of thinking given the way the last week had unfolded.

"Buenos días," he said, moving lightly toward the boys.

"Buenos días," a few of them returned, suspicious of the big stranger whose Spanish betrayed his American roots.

"Anybody know anything about that building across the street?" he continued.

The boys exchanged silence and shrugs until Cort Wesley produced some dollar bills from his pocket and spread them about.

"Does anybody know anything now?"

"No." The oldest-looking boy grinned, stuffing the bill in his pocket.

"I know a little," another boy said.

The older boy punched him in the shoulder.

"What?" the younger boy snapped, emboldened. "I can tell him if I want." Then, to Cort Wesley, "For this many more." And he held up five fingers.

Cort Wesley flashed a five-dollar bill and handed it to him. The boy wedged it deep in his pocket, beaming with satisfaction.

"Sometimes men come out of that building, men who never went in."

"It's haunted!" an even younger boy chimed in.

The oldest boy bounced a soccer ball off his head. Once, twice . . . the third time, Cort Wesley caught the ball and held it against him.

"Casa del Diablo," the boy he'd paid said. "That's where they come from."

"House of the Devil," Cort Wesley said in English.

"It's not a house, it's a town," the oldest boy said, eyeing the soccer ball in Cort Wesley's grasp.

"It's not a town, it's a place like hell."

"You're stupid," the oldest boy said, twirling a finger at his temple. *"Loco."*

"It's real, I don't care what you say. It's where the men come from. Once someone went inside to see and they never came out."

Cort Wesley cocked his gaze toward the storefront, flipped the soccer ball back to the oldest boy, then started across the street.

"Where you going?" the boy who'd pocketed his five asked him.

"Inside."

81

BAHRAIN, THE PRESENT

Caitlin stood on the sidewalk, imagining Peter's trek from Umm Al Hassam all the way to the Bab Al Bahrain. He had been found by the authorities right around this time. Nine months ago that would have put the sun directly to the northeast in the *souq*'s direction.

Peter had walked toward the sun. It made perfect

sense. How he managed such a distance in his weakened condition was all that escaped her. A response to shock probably.

Caitlin's next and final stop was the British Embassy where officials proved gracious enough to let her use her second disposable camera to snap pictures of the room where Peter stayed while his unprecedented situation was being sorted out. The small room had been unoccupied since then and, even though it had clearly been cleaned, Caitlin thought she detected the same stale smell that had wafted off Peter in both the Survivor Center and, later, the hospital. As if the pain of his suffering had been indelibly burned into his being to become part of whatever fabric he touched.

Click, click, click . . .

The process here proved easier than back at the apartment, hope captured in the view window instead of pain. Smith and a British Embassy official hung back through the process, giving Caitlin her space. She tried to imagine how she might introduce all the pictures to Peter, how he might react to them, based on the cautionary words spoken by Rita Navarro.

"Can I give you some advice?" Smith asked her before they climbed back into his car.

"Coming from an expert in these matters, go right ahead."

"You need to forget what you've seen."

"A little late for that, I expect."

Smith looked at her grimly. "Then turn back the clock. When all this is over, get hypnotized, get drunk—whatever it takes."

"That your secret?"

"You live with it long enough, you get calluses where you need them. You don't have those, Ranger. You may think you do, but you don't."

"I appreciate you looking out for me, Smith."

"It's not just you, it's the men you'll wanna make pay for what they've done, what you've seen. That kind of thing pulls you in and doesn't let you out. And that's a place you absolutely don't want to be."

"Already been there," Caitlin told him, "and know the territory."

82

SALTILLO, MEXICO, THE PRESENT

The kids watched Cort Wesley use a stray brick to hammer the lock free of the hasp bolted into the door frame. Opening a secondary lock was as simple as smashing the glass portion of the door and reaching a hand through the jagged shards.

The city of Saltillo was built over a network of natural limestone tunnels, accessible beneath the Cathedral de Santiago and running all the way to the city's limits. The appearance of men exiting the store without entering could only mean that someone in the vast Mexican underworld, perhaps even Garza himself, had forged an access route to those tunnels beneath this storefront in order to negotiate the city freely, unencumbered by law enforcement. Or perhaps that access had been there all along, and the storefront had been chosen for that express purpose.

Either way, the link between Mexico's thriving criminal enterprise and the clandestine manufacture of computer chips might well be serviced by a dummy address from which the air exchangers could be routed anywhere without leaving a paper trail. Routed to a place called *Casa del Diablo.*

The House of the Devil.

Once inside the store, Cort Wesley used a stray board to tap the chipped tile floor in search of the tunnel entrance. When his search yielded nothing, he turned to the walls, finding not a hatch but a doorway opening onto a wooden ladder leading downward. Cort Wesley pictured Garza's drug dealers and enforcers claiming the tunnels as their own private traverse beneath Saltillo proper. Free access to Mexico's richest city—a criminal mastermind's dream.

Few without intimate knowledge of the United States' urban underbelly and prison system had little notion of how powerful the Mexican Mafia had become. Once little more than a disjointed series of street gangs, the group was now organized into a formidable and dangerous force in every major city across the country. Someone had linked the previously disparate gangs into a deadly unit dedicated to drug dealing and murder. Cort Wesley had witnessed the Mexican Mafia's work firsthand during his days with the Branca crime family in south Texas. But he had always passed Garza himself off as nothing more than a myth.

Until now.

There was too much coming together here to suggest anything but a single centralized figure behind it all. Drugs and murder was one thing, after all; manufacturing high-tech computer chips, like the one Jimmy Farro called Cerberus, something else again.

Cort Wesley didn't bother descending into the tunnel. He wouldn't find the air exchangers down there or a convenient route to wherever they had been taken, to a place that didn't exist on any map.

Casa del Diablo . . .

Home, no doubt, to Emiliato Valdez Garza.

PART NINE

Reporter: I understand, Sir, that you carry a .45. Why is that?
Ranger: 'Cause they don't make a .46.

83

SAN ANTONIO, THE PRESENT

"Me again, Padre," Guillermo Paz said when the confessional hatch slid open.

The priest didn't shrink away as he did the last time, instead he actually seemed to lean closer to the screen. "Welcome back, my son. What have you come for today?"

"I think I've crossed the line, Father."

"What line is that?"

Paz started scratching at the confessional ledge with his fingernail, just like he had back in La Vega. The wood resisted his attempt to peel back a layer, maybe carve his name here too, but he kept trying. "Still trying to figure that out exactly. But it's the kind you can't step back over."

"This sounds positive to me, my son. Like you have heeded His word."

"That's the thing. I think I finally understand what He wants me to do."

"And what's that?"

"Make a difference. Everything I've done before—let's face it, most of it bad—never amounted to much. Always thought it was a matter of who I was killing. Now I realize I was asking the wrong question."

"You should have been asking why."

"You're really good at this."

"Thank you."

"You sound like you've done some killing yourself—on the right side of things, of course."

The priest scratched at his nose, cleared his throat. "I've seen war, my son. As a chaplain."

"Held people's hands as they died and all that."

"Something I wished I never had to do."

"What'd you tell them?"

"That the Lord was with them."

"Implying He wasn't when they got shot, blown up or whatever. How'd you live with that?"

"I've been reading Kierkegaard myself lately."

"Really?"

"He argued that a divine command from God transcends all ethics. Such a distinction means that God does not create or impose morality."

"Leaving it up to us as individuals to create our own."

"Exactly. So God, according to Kierkegaard, cannot be blamed for the actions of man. And each man must choose his own course."

Paz managed to finish the *P* and left the carving there. "I'm glad to hear you say that. It's what I started realizing for myself."

"Then you'll be going home?" the priest asked, perhaps a bit hopefully.

"No, not ever. I closed that door when I refused to burn that village. Besides, my work here's not finished yet."

"I thought you said—"

"I did. This is different work, opening a new door. Kind of like starting over, from scratch."

"I cannot absolve you of the sin that comes with killing, my son, no matter the who or the why."

"Don't need you to, Padre. Already absolved myself."

"Then what can He do for you today?"

"More like what I can do for Him . . . and you. I just

wanted to let you know I'm sending you something. What's the biggest donation your church has ever received?"

"At the risk of sounding ungrateful, that is not for me to say."

"No problem. My donation's coming and it's substantial. A lot of money came my way for this latest job. Now it's yours. I just hope the source doesn't bother you."

"It would have after your first visit. Not now," the priest said and listened to the big man let out a long sigh.

"You asked what I came for today, Father. I think it was to hear you say that."

The priest took his time composing his response, had just started to speak when he realized the man in the confessional was gone. Only then did he realize what had struck him that was different, that he hadn't been able to identify until now. The salty, sodden smell that had hung over the big man previously had been replaced by something less acidic and bitter. Not pleasant, but not altogether revolting anymore either.

"May the Lord be with you, my son," the priest said to no one at all.

84

HOUSTON, THE PRESENT

Caitlin saw Cort Wesley Masters waiting for her at the foot of the escalator in the international arrivals terminal. A stoic, stationary figure amid the bustle unfolding around him. He seemed untouched by it, invisible, it seemed, to the masses.

At the bottom of the escalator, Caitlin draped her arms around his thick shoulders, embracing him. She hadn't planned to do it, didn't understand why she had. The long flights passed mostly stiff and without sleep in a coach seat, too many hours left to herself and her own thoughts after the difficult hours spent in Manama. Every time she managed to drift off to sleep on the flight home, she dreamed of Smith; always in different poses and postures, all of them equally menacing for their deception and undercurrent of violent explosion.

She felt Cort Wesley's arms tightening around her, hard-packed hands stroking her back. "Guess I don't have to ask how your trip went," he said, sliding her away from him.

Caitlin wanted to kiss him, again not sure why. He represented something to her she didn't yet comprehend, his powerful detachment transcending the upshot of the misery that had dominated her mind for the better part of two days now without respite. He was as strong as Peter was weak. He represented the "moving on" Smith had raised in Bahrain, letting go of a part of her life she clung to out of the false belief that her actions now could alter the past. Still, it took all her strength to pull away, to make her mind move elsewhere.

"How about yours?" Caitlin heard herself ask him.

"I think Garza is real."

"Why?"

"Can't say for sure. It's like a smell that keeps showing up at different places. Something's going on down there I can't quite put my finger on. Level of organization can't be explained any other way I can figure."

"What about the manufacturing plant?"

Cort Wesley shrugged. "It's there, all right. I just haven't found it yet."

"What did you find?"

"A town that don't exist. *Casa del Diablo*."

"The House of the Devil . . ."

"Interestingly enough."

She started crying in the parking garage when they reached her SUV, let it out for Peter and Jim Strong and her granddad, and for whatever cancerous monster was eating up D. W. Tepper's insides. There was no future she could see, only the past with nothing to be found there but pain.

Cort Wesley Masters took her in his arms and held her, Caitlin feeling like a little girl again in her father's grasp, smelling the Aqua Velva with her face pressed against his beard stubble. When she moved, she thought it was to ease herself away but then she was kissing him, stronger than she'd ever kissed any man before. She waited for Masters to break it off and, when he didn't, thought about ending it herself, but didn't either.

Still holding her, she felt him jerk open the door with his free hand, the two of them tumbling into the SUV's backseat. Caitlin ended up on top of him, reaching back to yank the door closed before kissing Masters again, harder and deeper. She felt his hands on her blouse, her belt, felt her own doing the same as if they belonged to someone else. Somewhere her mind gave the order to stop and pull back, but her body failed to oblige, responding to something she couldn't identify that was foreign and welcome at the same time.

In the end the act itself didn't match those moments leading up to it, though it left her fulfilled in a way she could not accurately describe. In the minutes they lay intertwined, their bodies twisted to conform to the backseat's confines, all the pain from both the past and the present didn't hurt anymore. Feeling him inside her pushed it to the edges of her mind. Once there its significance, for however brief a period, was reduced to the point where it at least seemed that all her wounds could be healed.

For a man with such a well-deserved reputation for brutality, Cort Wesley Masters was a surprisingly gentle and considerate lover. He didn't seem to care what she felt for him, even as his own passion overflowed, knowing her actions were rooted deep within her, a place she didn't comprehend and hadn't come to grips with yet. She felt his callused hands caressing her through the whole of it, lingering after they were done and Caitlin was content to lie atop him with her head resting on his chest.

She stayed like that until a parking garage security guard rapped on the steamed-up windows with his nightstick, making both of them feel like wayward teens as they scrambled for their clothes. Caitlin cut the conversation short when she flashed the guard her Ranger badge and he backed off subserviently.

She let Masters drive, both of them silent until they'd reached the interstate heading back toward San Antonio.

"I'm guessing your trip didn't go too well," he said finally.

"Found what I was looking for, if that's what you mean."

"Actually, Caitlin Strong, that's exactly what I mean."

She wiped her eyes with her sleeve. "I saw the room where they tortured Peter. Fucking bastards, I'm gonna shoot every last one of them."

"Come on, gotta leave a couple for me there, girl. I imagine there'll be plenty to go around."

"Taking on the whole Mexican Mafia and the biggest private contractor the government's got, I expect so."

"No shortage of bad guys."

"Nope, just good ones, Cort Wesley."

"Not entirely, Ranger."

Caitlin lapsed back into thought and Cort Wesley let her have her space, resisting the urge to reach over and take her hand in his.

"It's my fault," she said suddenly.

"What?"

"What happened to Peter. He left because our marriage wasn't working, because I couldn't have kids."

"Things ended between me and Maura Torres mostly 'cause we did."

"I wish it was that simple for me."

"Don't need to go where you're going, Caitlin Strong."

"I think I do." Caitlin's eyes, dim and distant, fixed on him. "'Cause I lied. Told Peter the in vitro never took. Truth is I never tried it and stayed on the pill the whole time. I looked him right in the eye and lied, pretending to be sad about it. Something I gotta live with every day now."

"Beats dying," said Cort Wesley.

85

SAN ANTONIO, THE PRESENT

Caitlin and Cort Wesley drank coffee while they waited for her pictures to be developed. Thirty minutes, the clerk at the drugstore's photo counter told her, forty at the most.

They sat across from each other in silence. Caitlin felt talked-out, thought-out and flat-exhausted. But she knew sleep wouldn't come if she tried for it and, even if it did, she was afraid of the nightmares sure to be formed by the residue of Bahrain.

"I don't know if I can do this," she said finally. She was halfway through her third cup and the caffeine buzz had started to take hold, leaving her hands jittery and her teeth clacking together.

"That a question or a statement?"

"Feel free to weigh in."

"Know why prison changed me, Caitlin Strong?"

"No."

"It changed me 'cause the man I was when I went in wouldn't have been able to last a month in there, never mind a lifetime. You find a way to deal but that's not really living, it's just getting by. So when I get out, all of a sudden the world feels like a whole different place. You figured me out really good before, knowing how I felt about Maura Torres. Took me a while to figure it out too. Keeping her and the boys outta my life was the hardest thing I ever done. Worst part of it all was thinking I was gonna be in prison forever and having the choice taken away from me."

"What's that have to do with Peter?"

"He's in prison too, Ranger, only the walls are different 'cause they're in his own head. When I was inside, I would've done anything to get out. I'm guessing he feels the same way. Whatever you can do to make that happen for him, you do."

"And if it makes things worse?"

"Can't be worse," Cort Wesley told her. "That's my point."

"Yes, it can."

"How's that?"

"It was my fault," said Caitlin.

86

Caitlin and Peter sat in the kitchen drinking coffee while he waited for the car that would be taking him to Houston to catch his flight to Iraq.

"What I want to know," he asked Caitlin, "is will you still be here when I get back?"

The frankness of his question had caught her by surprise. "I don't know."

"You're not happy."

"It's not your fault."

"That doesn't matter. Whoever's fault it is, you're still not happy and that's not right."

"I don't blame you," Caitlin told him.

"This isn't about dispensing blame."

"I blame myself."

"I'd rather you blamed me, Caity. I'd rather you blamed me because then whatever you're going through would be easier to get over."

"I thought going back to school would help."

"You miss the Rangers."

"It's in my blood," she conceded.

"And what you are, and you haven't been the same person since you walked away."

"Didn't want to give them a chance to throw me out."

"You don't know it would've gone down that way."

"Got a pretty good idea."

"So go back. Find out for sure."

Caitlin sipped her coffee. "That horse has left the barn."

Peter dumped the rest of his cup out in the sink, peering out the window for the approach of the livery car's headlights. "I come back, I don't want it to be to you like this. I want it to be to the Caitlin Strong I met in that bar celebrating her father's birthday."

"Then you better go invent a time machine, Professor."

"You want to be a Texas Ranger again," Peter continued, ignoring her, "and until you get back to being that person, nothing else in your life is going to work. And that includes us, me."

"What's that supposed to mean exactly?"

"It means as long as I'm here, you've got an excuse to keep going to school, taking classes, pursuing a degree, even though you don't enjoy any of those things. When was the last time you went to the range?"

"I don't know."

"Yes, you do, Caitlin. Yes, you do. I'll bet you know when the last time you shot a gun was down to the hour and minute. All this is about punishing yourself and as long as I'm here it'll keep being that. Me going away gives you the opportunity you need." Headlights blared at the apartment building's front and a horn honked lightly. "When I get back from Iraq, I want to hear that you took it."

Caitlin walked him to the door, but not outside. They hugged and kissed each other lightly. She was back looking out the window, when the black Lincoln limousine pulled away.

87

Caitlin's cell phone rang, D. W. Tepper's number flashing on the caller ID and driving her out of her trance.

"Start your yelling," she told him.

"I don't even know where to begin."

"How 'bout with Harm Delladonne?"

"He's talking about suing us for you putting his body-guards in the hospital."

"Men were twice as big as me, four times when you consider the two of them. I was putting this son of a bitch on notice, Captain. Making a statement."

"Making a mess is more like it. Stow your attitude at the door when you enter a public place on Ranger busi-ness from now on, miss. We got a goddamn travesty on our hands."

Caitlin was squeezing her cell phone so hard, her hand hurt. "I found the place where Delladonne had Peter tor-tured in Bahrain. Make a nice slide show at MacArthur-Rain's next board meeting."

"We got a problem on that end. The Rangers been pulled off the whole goddamn case."

"By who?"

"Governor. He called me this morning."

Caitlin's heart was beginning to hammer again. She could feel sweat forming on her brow, anger building up inside her like bile. "How'd you respond?"

"Told him to go fuck himself and get off MacArthur-Rain's payroll. My suspension starts tomorrow. We'll be able to hold things together for a while, least 'til the highway patrol gets settled in my office. Think I'll shit in a drawer, see how they like that."

"How long, Captain?"

"Couple days at most. After that, we're on our own."

"We?"

"Your daddy made me promise I'd always take care of you. Just standing by my word."

Caitlin bit her lip, hesitating. "Gotta ask you something on that note, D. W."

"Uh-oh."

"Delladonne said both Jim Strong and my granddad were corrupt, that they took money from Mexican drug runners to let black tar heroin pass over the border. I need to know if that's the truth."

"You don't need to know nothing, Caitlin. What you need is to forget you ever heard such a fool thing."

"Too late for that."

"This ain't a discussion to be had right now. . . ."

"It is for me, Captain."

"Let me finish. You want a simple answer and there ain't one."

"Did they take money or not?"

"Not for black tar heroin, no. The point was to keep that deadly shit out, but to do that we had to open up the way for the runners to bring the marijuana on through."

" 'We,' D. W.?"

"What we did back then cut a lot of ways. Sometimes to do the most good, you gotta do a little harm. Black and white had already vanished from the spectrum. Was a gray world then and it's even grayer now."

"Jesus Christ . . ."

"Did we let it go? Yes, we did. Did we ever take a dime for looking the other way? No, we did not, not a dime or a single penny, and that's the God's honest truth."

Caitlin held her eyes closed, and they were still closed

when she responded. "Don't know if I can live with that, Captain."

"You trust your dad and granddad, and me, you can. We did plenty worse in our service, believe you me, and some of that makes up the stories that have become full-out legends. Truth be told, we saved a lot of lives keeping that black tar shit out of the country and you'd be best advised to keep that in mind before you go passing judgment."

"Guess I'm no one to be judging anybody."

"What you did with Harmon Delladonne?"

"As good an example as any."

"You did what you thought you had to, Caitlin."

"It feeling right doesn't make it that way."

"No, but that's as close as we can be expected to come. And we're really up against it on this one now, Ranger. We don't break this case soon, we don't break it at all."

"Just buy me those two days. That's all I need."

"Your horoscope say that or something?"

Caitlin moved the cell phone to her other ear. "Peter's the key to this, Captain. Once he tells us what's really going on, we can break Harmon Delladonne, the governor and MacArthur-Rain over our knees."

"Something else I need to tell you. Remember your husband's coworker ran her car off the road?"

"Sure."

"I asked them to have another look at the coroner's report. Too much head trauma and burns to tell if she suffered an aneurysm or not, but there's strong indication she was dead *before* impact." Caitlin heard Tepper suck in a deep, labored breath. "What exactly we looking at here, Ranger?"

Caitlin thought of the pictures that would be ready any minute. "That's what I hope to be able to tell you soon, Captain."

88

Caitlin spent the next twenty-four hours by Peter's bedside, trying to prod his mind from its mire. At first the pictures gained her nothing but the pained stare she had come to know so well.

But then something began to change. Whether spurred by the pictures or not, Peter began focusing on the disassembled parts of the laptop she had left behind. Caitlin watched him work on the circuit board, connecting it to the cable box, jerry-rigged into the television, while paying her no heed whatsoever.

She'd had the best of the pictures she'd taken in Bahrain blown up to eight-by-ten, a kiosk-style machine at the drugstore spitting them out one after another. As Peter continued his dutiful work, Caitlin laid the pictures of the Bahrain apartment where the torture had taken place across the bed in places Peter could not help but see. He began to regard them slowly, even if just to uncover some of the precision tools atop which they lay. As night bled to day and then back to night, his scrutiny of the pictures began to intensify.

His expression began to change as soon as he summoned the will to reach out and touch them, neither the empty visage Caitlin had seen upon first meeting him in the Survivor Center nor the focused intensity of the former I.T. expert reconstructing the machines in the room toward some unknown end.

"Peter?" she said, but he didn't regard her.

Each time his attention returned to the pictures, his

looks grew more lingering and quizzical. Each time the interludes between his scrutinies of them grew shorter.

"Peter," she repeated, still with no results.

Finally his expression tightened. His breathing became more rapid, his face going through a myriad of emotions as if recovering all of them at once. His upper body spasmed once, then a second time. He began to tremble and shake horribly, his whole body trying to turn itself inside out. He gasped for breath, going red in the face. It was all Caitlin could do not to take him in her arms and comfort him, because she knew there was no comfort to be offered for what must be coursing through his mind that was fighting to free itself.

"Uh," he muttered, "uh."

Caitlin recalled Rita Navarro's words of warning and came to feel she'd made a terrible mistake. What right did she have, with a dime-store degree and all of one patient to her credit, to play with anyone's life? What had she been thinking?

"Peter."

He started to look at her.

"Peter!"

He finished turning his head, met her gaze.

"It's me, Peter. It's Caity."

Peter screamed, bit his lip, dribbled blood, screamed again. His eyelids flickered madly, as if rerecording his memories in fast-forward. Then he threw himself backward, pushing as far as the wall at the head of the bed would let him.

Caitlin moved and his eyes followed her. They bulged, looking ready to burst from their sockets, his gaze cast over her shoulder, no doubt seeing the vanquished ghosts from Bahrain.

"Everything's all right," she tried to soothe. "You're safe. Listen to me, Peter. You're safe."

His expression relaxed slightly, becoming more confused than terrified. He regarded Caitlin dispassionately, as if seeing her for the first time.

"I won't let anything happen to you, Peter. I promise."

"Who? What?"

Caitlin reached out and took his hands. "It's me. It's Caity."

"I, I, I . . ."

"Peter."

He continued to regard her, recognition flashing as he caught up to the present.

"Where, where," he started, lips forming the word before it emerged. "Where . . ."

Caitlin reached out and took his hand. "I'm here. I'm with you, Peter."

He yanked it from her, pushed himself away. Swung his gaze about the room in terror, as if momentarily believing he was back in Bahrain.

"You're home, Peter. You're in San Antonio."

"Where?" he asked her in a voice she at last recognized.

"Home. Do you remember what happened to you?"

Peter's eyes were alive again but wild, his mind still racing to catch up with his life. "Why am I in a hospital? What happened to me?"

"Do you remember what they did to you?"

"What *who* did to me?"

Caitlin tightened the spread of the pictures from the apartment in Bahrain so Peter could better see. He regarded them through narrowed eyes, his breathing rapidly picking up. He started to fidget, touching the photographs with a finger while making no effort to turn away from them. When he finally did, his eyes found hers, brimming with a spark of recognition.

"Caity . . ."

Caitlin made small talk with him for what felt like an hour, not sure really since she was afraid to look down at her watch for fear of losing him again once their stares broke. But his gaze sharpened more and more as he listened to her words. He asked for water, then food, acknowledging her presence in the room, while not necessarily her all the time. And the pain was always there, displayed in a wince or grimace, not far behind any single gesture, no matter how simple.

More time passed, during which Peter studied the pictures closer, arranging them in chronological order atop the bedcovers as if to reconstruct the missing parts of his life. He didn't shake this time, showed no signs of panic other than a slight rise in the level of his breathing.

When he finally looked up and let his gaze linger on hers, Caitlin swallowed hard and pushed the next words past the lump clogging up her throat. "What happened, Peter?"

89

HOUSTON, EIGHTEEN MONTHS BEFORE

The livery car with Peter Goodwin and the members of his Fire Arrow team inside took the downtown Houston exit off the Sam Houston Tollway, bypassing the airport.

"Excuse me," Peter said to the driver.

"Orders, sir," the man said to him and then lapsed into silence.

"Wait a minute, *whose* orders?"

"I'm not at liberty to say."

"What's going on? Can you say that?"

The man's response was to slide the partition back up, walling himself off from his four passengers. Minutes later, with the first of the morning light burning across the sky, he pulled the limousine into MacArthur-Rain's underground garage. Two plainclothes security guards were waiting there to escort Peter and his team of two men and one woman up in a private elevator that took them in rapid fashion to the very top floor of the building.

The elevator doors opened to reveal a man Peter recognized from both *Fortune* magazine and coverage of various congressional hearings at which the man had been summoned to testify.

"I'm Harmon Delladonne," he said greeting them. "I'm sure you're aware of that. What you aren't aware of is that you work for me. MacArthur-Rain owns your company. RevCom is one of our subsidiaries."

Delladonne's office was huge and sprawling, taking up a good measure of the floor with the ceiling stretching two stories in height. Peter noticed a loft area was under construction. Wrapped artworks rested against matte-finished light walls, the scent of fresh paint still heavy in the air. He noticed a Japanese shoji screen tucked in a corner and some Oriental tapestries laid out over an elegant seating area composed of laquered furniture and rattan.

"Would have been nice if somebody had told us," one of Peter's team members said.

"There's a reason why we didn't, I assure you, due mostly to matters of security." Delladonne had a monotone voice that sounded prerecorded, like the GPS machines offering turn-by-turn directions. "In the post-9/11 age, with all the work we do for the government, keeping our efforts decentralized is another word for discretion, safety too. It was all for your own good."

"So we're going to Iraq for *MacArthur-Rain*?" Peter asked him.

"Actually you're not going to Iraq at all. That was just a cover. Security reasons again. But the letters you write home, or e-mails you send, or phone calls you make, will appear to come from there. More discretion."

"For our own good," Peter added for him.

Delladonne forced a thin smile. "Indeed, especially your financial good. The work you're about to enter into on our behalf will make you all very wealthy."

"And what work is that?"

"Fire Arrow, of course."

Peter tensed. "And what does that have to do with the government exactly?"

"Don't be naïve, Dr. Goodwin. Everything involves the government these days."

Calmer now, Peter studied Harm Delladonne, but couldn't get a fix. He was more like a creature of animation than a real person, his features constantly shifting. Not a hair out of place and an even tan that looked sprayed on. A still photograph set to jumpy motion— that's what he made Peter think of. He knew Delladonne's father had been the founder of the company, but it was Harmon who had built it into the international industrial behemoth that it was today. When Eisenhower bemoaned the growing power of the military-industrial complex in his farewell speech, MacArthur-Rain had been exactly what he'd been referring to.

"We've been following your work on Fire Arrow very closely," Delladonne continued. "We want to commend you on developing technology that will help keep this country secure for decades to come. Technology we now control." Delladonne waited for Peter's response. When none came, he continued, "You should know that we also feel Fire Arrow has additional untapped potential. Different applications of the project that intrigue us."

"Which applications are those?"

"All in good time, my friend. That's why you and your team members are here, after all."

"I'm not your friend."

Delladonne's eyes took on the look of marbles wedged into his sockets. "Yes, you are, Dr. Goodwin, because otherwise you're my enemy. You see, you're either with us or against us."

"MacArthur-Rain or the country?"

Delladonne flashed his animated smile. "Same thing."

90

SAN ANTONIO, THE PRESENT

Caitlin sat there looking at Peter, his face pale and drawn, not sure what to make of what he said. "Did you lie to me?"

"No, I just didn't tell you all of the truth."

"About Fire Arrow."

"I couldn't, Caity. I had to sign papers, nondisclosure agreements thanks to all the national security issues involved." He gazed at his twisted, swollen fingers, as if to imagine completing such a simple task now.

"So the integration stuff, that was just a front."

"No. That's where Fire Arrow started, what must have attracted MacArthur-Rain's attention to RevCom in the first place."

"You really thought you were going to Iraq?"

"Right up until the moment Delladonne told me we weren't."

"What is Fire Arrow, Peter? If you can remember, if you can tell me, it'll help me help you."

"They've got to be stopped."

"They will be."

Peter stiffly brushed the pictures aside, worked the laptop's keyboard toward him and fumbled for the remote for the television. "It's what I've been working on here. Didn't even realize that while I was doing it. Felt like a dream, or like someone else was doing it and I was watching. I thought I was sleeping and in the dream I didn't exist. But I wasn't really dead either."

Peter shifted the laptop around so its screen was facing her. "See."

The laptop screen now featured a video feed of her and Peter. At first she thought the source was simply the computer's internal webcam; then she realized the angle was all wrong.

"The television," she realized, utterly dumbfounded. "It's coming from the television."

"Because that's what MacArthur-Rain wanted," Peter told her. "To turn every television in the country into a window into every home."

"How?"

"Long story. Begins in the wake of 9/11 when anything done in the name of national security was deemed acceptable, including spying on our own citizens."

"The Cerberus chip," Caitlin muttered.

Peter's once lifeless eyes widened. "How did you know—"

"Never mind that for now," she said, recalling the visit she and Cort Wesley had paid to Jimmy Farro. "What else did the government do, besides give a whole new meaning to the term spyware?"

"Televisions. Every set manufactured after 2002 was outfitted with a built-in camera."

"How? *Where?*"

"Simple really: Standard IrDA."

"What's that?"

"Stands for Infrared Data Association. For our purposes here, that refers to the infrared receiver already in place keyed to the television's remote control." Peter lifted his gaze toward the wall-mounted television again. "On that set the receiver's right there in the center, what looks like a small window. See?"

Caitlin followed his gaze and realized it was indeed the receiver's viewpoint currently projected on her laptop's screen.

"With government approval," Peter continued, "MacArthur-Rain had CCDs, Charge Coupled Detectors, installed on every digital television manufactured from 2003 on: essentially small, virtually undetectable silicon grids of photo sensitive capacitors that most of today's digital cameras, and cell phones, use to record imaging."

"But televisions can't transmit that kind of signal."

"No, but computers can."

"Fire Arrow . . ."

Peter nodded. "That's right. The Fire Arrow wireless integration software picks up the data stored in the CCDs in every television in the household, whether on or off. The detectors are motion sensitive, activated once sensors pick up the presence of someone in the room."

"Are you saying MacArthur-Rain can spy on everyone in the country at once?"

"No. Processing that much data in real time would be virtually impossible for any server. The plan was to go after more specific targets, similar to other more mundane surveillance programs. But if you're asking me how many—"

"I am."

"—then I'd say the system could handle several million households at once, more as time went on. Look at it as super high-capacity data mining."

"Cerberus wasn't the only thing the government stuffed up its sleeve after 9/11," Jimmy Farro had told her and Cort Wesley. *"I heard rumors, stories, about something even worse, something even more invasive maybe not right away, but not too far down the road."*

"Political enemies, anyone who disagreed with the causes the government, and MacArthur-Rain, supports," Caitlin said, rotating her gaze between her dual images and feeling a chill at the thought of potentially being processed in a nanosecond by a central server as well. She looked back at Peter suddenly. "And you gave them Fire Arrow to make it all work."

"I had no choice. RevCom owned Fire Arrow and MacArthur-Rain owned RevCom. No choice at all."

"But if you gave them what they wanted, why did they torture you?"

"Because," Peter told her, "they wanted something else."

91

HOUSTON, EIGHTEEN MONTHS BEFORE

Peter Goodwin sat fidgeting in the chair before Harmon Delladonne's ebony wood desk. In the few days since he'd been here, construction on Delladonne's loft area had been completed. The musty smell of lubricant from the newly erected spiral stairwell stretching up from floor level filled the sprawling room.

"Your specifications for the Fire Arrow chip have been

approved," Delladonne told him. "Once we have the final schematics in place, we'll be ready to move on to the manufacturing stage."

"Then my team members and I can go home. From Iraq, I mean," Peter added.

Delladonne looked at him. "Not quite yet. I appreciate your patriotism, Dr. Goodwin."

"Giving you the ability to spy on virtually every American doesn't make me a patriot."

"It does if it makes this country easier to defend from enemies committed to destroying us." Delladonne rose and walked out from behind his desk, taking the chair next to Peter's. "It's about avoiding another 9/11, Dr. Goodwin, potentially one that's far worse. I want you to picture those hijackers staying at hotels the night before. Hotels with Wi-Fi, hotels with computer access via the television in every room. If Fire Arrow was active then, we would've known, wouldn't we? Our software would have flagged those sons of bitches and 9/11 could've been prevented. Yes?"

"That's the point," Peter acknowledged.

"And what if those terrorists could have been eradicated on the spot as well?"

"I'm not following you."

"Eradicated—killed."

"I know what the word means, Mr. Delladonne. It's the context that confuses me."

Delladonne held up a small cylindrical object with dual, uneven prongs extending out from one side. "You know what this is, of course."

"Simple capacitor."

Delladonne flashed that same smile again. "Capacitor, yes. Simple, no."

"And what does this have to do with me?"

"We need you to tell us how to make it work."

92

SAN ANTONIO, THE PRESENT

"Work how?" Caitlin asked him.

Peter ran his hands over his face. "My head hurts, Caity, I hurt everywhere. I can't talk about this anymore."

"Please."

"Not now."

"You've got to, Peter, before it slips away."

"My head . . . I can't."

"Delladonne killed your three coworkers. They all died of brain aneurysms, but he killed them somehow, didn't he?"

Peter was trembling, hands still covering his face.

"It . . . hurts."

"I know."

"I can't."

"Please try. For your friends Delladonne killed. For what he did to you."

Peter's expression had gone utterly blank, looking more through Caitlin now than at her. "I refused. Told him I wouldn't do it."

"What did Delladonne do then?"

Peter's expression flashed back to life, eyes widening in fear again. "He made me watch."

"It's one-way glass," Delladonne explained, holding the capacitor in his hand, "your friend doesn't know we're watching him."

Peter looked at Darnell Stimson, one of the three

members of his team, working quietly behind a PC, alone in the room.

"He can't see or hear us," Delladonne continued, passing a silent signal to a technician on the other side of the room in which he and Peter were standing. "I'd like to show you something."

Seconds later, Stimson's hands and arms began quaking. A spasm rocked his body, his legs shooting up and out, kicking the worktable as he tumbled over backward. He hit the floor writhing horribly and then stilled, eyes locked open and sightless as a thin trail of blood seeped from his right ear.

Peter began banging on the glass, yelling Stimson's name futilely before swinging back toward Delladonne. "What'd you do to him? What the hell did you do?"

"What do you think I did?"

Peter noticed smoke was rising from the computer's housing. He imagined he could smell the stench of burnt metal and wires. "Shocked him. Electrocution."

"Try again, Dr. Goodwin."

Peter gazed at the capacitor Delladonne was still holding. "Some sort of wave or pulse traveling through the computer."

"That's better."

"Oh my God," Peter said, realizing what Delladonne meant. "A laser, fired through the computer's internal webcam."

"A pulse laser specifically, what we like to call a directed-energy weapon," Delladonne explained. "Enough energy stored in the capacitor to fire it once and once only. Superheats the brain enough to cause an aneurysm. Almost the perfect crime, but not quite. That's where you come in."

Peter was looking through the glass again at Stimson's body. "I'm not a murderer."

"*I invented the technology myself while at college,*" Delladonne said, ignoring him. "*Had the help of the entire computer-science department—they just didn't know it. I tried to get my father to buy into the concept but he wouldn't listen. So I demonstrated it to him— firsthand.*"

Peter couldn't believe what he was hearing.

"*That's how this company became mine, Dr. Goodwin; allowed to be shaped in accordance with my vision. My father may never have told me where the name MacArthur-Rain came from, but he told me the future was ours and he was right.*"

Peter looked back at Darnell Stimson through the glass. "*I'm going to have you arrested.*"

"*You haven't even asked me what the problem is, what I need you for.*"

"*And I don't intend to.*"

"*The problem is the high-power consumption of the pulse superheats the capacitor, burning it out, and fries the circuit board in the process. Leaves the kind of trail that would betray our intentions and capabilities, and we simply can't have that. I was able to replace my father's computer so no one was any the wiser, but clearly a more practical solution is warranted. My people here tell me it's a matter of regulating and containing the energy flow so only the minimum amount of energy required is utilized. And they also tell me that makes it a software problem. We've been at it for years now without any progress. Now that you're here, that's going to change.*"

"Fire Arrow," Caitlin muttered when Peter finished, struck by the irony. "But why you?"

"The Fire Arrow software technology was all about

regulating signal flow for integration purposes. Use the least energy possible to avoid overloading a system's storage capacity so nothing would freeze up. Delladonne's problem with his pulse weapon was overload but the principle was the same. He wanted me to moderate the flow of energy into the capacitor, make his weapon work without shorting out the entire circuit board. No burnt wires or fried capacitor left behind as evidence. Just a person suffering an aneurysm. It might take the victim longer to die, days even, eliminating any possible connection whatsoever. Even the computer would still work."

"So MacArthur-Rain wasn't just out to spy . . ."

"No, no, not at all."

". . . they wanted the ability to kill anyone they were spying on."

"Anyone meaning *everyone*. Ultimately. Inevitably. The capacitors rigged to work in conjunction with the new Fire Arrow chip in perfect harmony."

"But their victims would have to be online."

"At first."

"At *first*?"

"Integration, remember? Everything in the house running off the computer, including televisions that already have cameras inserted in their infrared remote receivers. You think it would be hard to build the capacitors into them too?" Peter was speaking rapidly now, ahead of his thoughts, his agitation increasing. "Not now, not yet. But a few years down the road—that's what Delladonne was looking toward. Securing the future, he kept saying, securing the future. Fire Arrow made it all possible. Fire Arrow."

Caitlin hesitated. "Could you have done it?"

"I don't know. I think so. The principles weren't all that difficult. But I never tried. Pretended I was cooperating. Then I crashed their system, whole damn mainframe along with every speck of work they'd done up until that point. Took them days to reboot and rebuild the program."

"Imagine that pissed off Delladonne some."

"He tested the system on another of my coworkers when the system was back up. Waverly, the woman."

"She was killed in a car crash according to the police report."

"Bates was the last, when I still wouldn't cooperate." Peter began sorting through the photos now strewn over the bed. "I can't remember any of this, not consciously anyway, not yet."

"Maybe it's better."

"Feels like it all happened to somebody else, somebody who's dead."

"Definitely better."

"I need to know, need to see it all, be able to put it together."

"Give it time."

"There's a lot still missing. I remember you being a Ranger, but not what kind of car you drive. I remember what our condominium looks like inside, but not the outside of the building. I remember things, but can't tell if it's me in the memories or somebody else."

"We'll get through this, Peter. That's a promise."

"You don't sound like you mean it."

"Want to hear me say it again?"

"It's not that. Something's . . . different. You've changed."

Caitlin thought of Cort Wesley. Her eyes met Peter's and in that instant she felt certain he knew what had happened in the back of her SUV. "We've both changed," she said lamely. "Thanks to Harm Delladonne. It's time to make him pay for that."

He shook his head slowly. "You don't know them, Caity. You don't know these people."

"You'd be surprised."

"They don't lose. They *can't* lose. They own the world, Caity. That's what you're up against." He managed to finish his deep breath. "I'm sorry I lied to you."

"I understand."

"I want you to understand I was doing it for us. I thought if I could make that kind of money . . . but our problems were never about money, were they? I remember that much too."

"They weren't our problems, they were my problems."

Peter's gaze drifted to her shirt. "You're wearing a badge, Caity."

"I'm back with the Rangers."

Peter flirted with a smile, looking as if he had almost forgotten how. "That's good, right?"

"Definitely."

"It feels like yesterday we talked about that, right before I left—for Iraq, I thought. Remember?"

"I do."

"How long ago was that?"

"A while."

"How long, Caity?"

"Eighteen months."

Peter's lips trembled. His eyes emptied, blinking rapidly, then he returned his gaze to the pictures from Bahrain.

"It's like there's a wall I can't get through, a wall with no door," he said, touching the pictures again as if that might make a difference.

Caitlin heard a knock, the door opening before she had a chance to acknowledge it to reveal Captain D. W. Tepper standing there, face puckered into a grim, wrinkled mask.

"We gotta go, Ranger."

"What happened?"

"Get a move on. Tell ya on the way."

Caitlin's legs felt like steel-weighted posts as she started toward the door. "Bad?"

"As it gets," Tepper told her.

93

HOUSTON, THE PRESENT

"It's done," Emiliato Valdez Garza told Harm Delladonne.

"Your efforts are appreciated," Delladonne replied.

"Appreciated? Is that really the best you can do, me bailing your gringo ass out of this and all?"

"I believe the continuance of our relationship is in the best interests of both of us."

"Best interests. I guess you can call them that. Right now that means getting my hands on this genius of yours."

"We went at him with everything we had."

"That's a vacation compared to what I'm going to do. You should have called me in the first place, kept things in the family. Could have avoided all these complications."

"It will all be worth it in the end," Delladonne told him.

"You're right. Know why?"

"I've got a feeling my answer won't be the same as yours."

"On account of us having different priorities, you mean, eh? Truth is the *contrabando* I move for you is no different than drugs or people to me. Just another form of merchandise. You trying so hard to make your country strong, you don't realize you're helping me do the same with mine."

"I have no idea what you're talking about, Garza."

"Then let me enlighten you, Mr. Del-la-donne. I'm shit to you, just like Mexico is shit to America. But all this money you're paying me is helping to build a Mexican Mafia army in every city your country's got. You spend all your efforts keeping America safe from her enemies outside, you don't realize what my people can do from the in."

"You telling me all this—what am I to make of that?"

"That it doesn't matter you know, because you can't stop it. The Mexico of my ancestors is coming back, Mr. Del-la-donne, and you're helping to make it happen. So, *muchos gracias.*"

"*No más disparates.*"

"You think this is nonsense, eh?"

"I think you're crazy."

"Crazy enough to work with you."

"We're both businessmen, Señor Garza."

"And you don't give a shit how I do my business, so long as I can clean up your mess for you. Don't realize I could be making a bigger one in the process."

"Are you threatening my country, Mr. Garza?"

"Just saying it's something you're gonna have to live with."

"I've lived with worse."

Garza almost laughed. "You really don't know who you're dealing with here, do you?"

"No," Delladonne told him. "Do you?"

94

ALAMO HEIGHTS, THE PRESENT

The entire street had been blocked off by the time the car with D. W. Tepper, Caitlin and Cort Wesley pulled up. Tepper's badge thankfully still got them passed through the barricade and they drove through to join the armada of rescue, local police, highway patrol, Ranger and unmarked vehicles that had turned the road into a parking lot.

"I still don't damn well know how this happened," Tepper said. "Kept this whole thing off the books. Didn't even use the walkies, just cells."

"But the house," said Caitlin, "it was listed as confiscated by the Rangers."

"At one point, sure."

"There you go," sneered Cort Wesley, still gnashing his teeth.

He leaped out of the SUV before Tepper got it all the way to a stop, Caitlin not far behind with the captain himself lumbering after them. They got as far as the local San Antonio cops who'd strung crime-scene tape haphazardly across the last of the curving front walk, affixed to a pair of tall orange cones.

"That's as far as you go," one of the locals said, sticking out his chest.

"Maybe you missed my badge," Caitlin told him.

"No Rangers allowed. Them's the orders."

"Two of our men are the ones who got shot in there."

"Hey, they're not my orders, ma'am. Talk to the highway patrol. This is their case now, on orders of the governor through the Department of Public Safety."

"It's Ranger," said Caitlin. "And you can kiss my ass."

She gave Cort Wesley a tug on his shirt to make him back off with her. His arm felt like banded steel. She got a shock from just touching him.

"Anything more about the boys?" he said to the cop, trembling from the effort of restraining himself.

"Who's asking?"

"Their father," Caitlin answered, "and I'd strongly recommend that you answer."

"Nothing. Whoever shot up the place must've taken them along," the cop replied matter-of-factly.

Shot up was an understatement, Caitlin thought. She counted eight bodies still lying atop the lawn and sidewalk, awaiting the arrival of a crime-scene unit. The front of the mansion itself looked like a war zone. Chips and divots marred the red-brick exterior and there wasn't a single window left whole. The door was the worst, the scariest of all, because it was gone. Missing altogether, along with most of the frame and vertical windows on either side. Caitlin imagined the two Rangers inside holding the fort against an onslaught of a dozen or more gunmen. Ultimately, based on the missing door and the tire tracks dug into the lawn, the attackers had driven a car or truck straight into the door and rammed it. Even then the shards of windshield glass littering the walk and nearby lawn showed the Rangers inside hadn't gone without a fight.

"Okay," Captain Tepper told Caitlin and Cort Wesley after they'd retreated to the shade of an elm tree, "this is what we got. Witnesses report either six or seven vehicles, none with license plates, tearing down the street to the house. Four or five bangers jump out of each and start shooting. One of the witnesses, a Vietnam vet, said it reminded him of the Tet Offensive. Rangers took four, five bullets each but not before taking down at least eight of them and wounding a half dozen more."

"Mexican Mafia?" Caitlin asked him.

"By the look of things, yeah."

"Garza," muttered Cort Wesley.

Tepper snorted and coughed up some mucus. "No sign of your boys anywhere we can see. But those Rangers would've kept them safe right up to the last."

Cort Wesley turned back toward the yellow crime-scene tape strung before the entrance, shoulders straightening as if he were ready to tear right through it. "I wanna see inside," he said, starting forward.

Both Caitlin and D. W. Tepper blocked his way.

"If I was still in charge here, you'd be inside already," Tepper told him. "But the governor's boys are calling the shots now." He shook his head in disgust, spit out another wad of mucus. "Fucking world's goin' to hell." He looked at Caitlin. "Back in the day, your dad and I'd just draw our guns and let 'em try to stop us."

She smiled at him and touched his shoulder. "Jim Strong's not here, but his daughter is. Say the word, Captain, and we go."

Tepper shook his head. "Nah, just blowing off steam, I guess. But I get the governor in a room anytime soon, we'll see how much of the old days I remember."

A cell phone rang, then another: Caitlin's and Cort Wesley's at the same time. They raised them to their ears and hit the answer buttons in eerily matching fashion.

"I assume you know who this is," a Spanish-accented voice greeted them.

"Garza," they said almost together.

"Let's make this fast. You know what I've got and you know what I want. The Ranger brings her husband, the outlaw gets his sons back."

"Bring my husband where?" Caitlin asked.

"Why don't you tell her, outlaw?"

"Casa del Diablo," said Cort Wesley. "The House of the Devil."

"Hey, outlaw, you got any Mexican blood in you?"

"Fuck you."

They both heard Garza chuckle. "I knew it, outlaw. Look forward to meeting you in person."

Part Ten

A Ranger was at a formal dress affair in his tuxedo. He was sitting next to a gentleman at the dining table with his tuxedo jacket open. His model 1911 .45 caliber was obvious to anyone looking.

The gentleman looked at the Ranger and said, "I see you are wearing your .45 . . . you must be expecting trouble."

The Ranger responds, "No, sir, if I were expecting trouble I would be carrying my 12-gauge shotgun."

95

SAN ANTONIO, THE PRESENT

D. W. Tepper looked at them, weighing what Caitlin had just told him in the shade off to the side of the yard. "You ever hear what Davy Crockett said when the Congress in Washington finally pissed him off? 'You can all go to hell. I'm going to Texas.'" He coughed up more mucus but swallowed it back down. "That's the way I feel right now. We're gonna play this our way, Caitlin, the way Jim Strong would've played it."

"What about the governor?"

"He can shit in his hat for all I care."

Tepper laid it out for them. A whole squadron of Rangers riding shotgun from a distance through the trip into Mexico. Make sure they had the means to match Garza's firepower with their own.

"Where's this town that don't exist at exactly?"

"We don't know," Caitlin answered. "He hasn't told us yet."

"Said he'd call us when the time was right, after we cross the border," Cort Wesley answered, tightening his hands into fists over and over again as if wishing for something to punch. "Means he'll likely be keeping tabs the whole way."

"Son of a bitch holds all the cards, don't he?"

. . .

They knew Garza could be watching them at any time and decided to make that work for them instead of against. First, D. W. Tepper used whatever influence he had left to arrange a private plane to take them as far as an airstrip just short of the border. At that point, Rangers would escort Peter Goodwin to the men's room. Another Ranger, dressed in identical clothes, would be waiting inside and would emerge in Peter's place, going on from that point in a vehicle that would be waiting.

The vehicle would be equipped with a homing beacon that would allow the Rangers to track them into Mexico and beyond. Tepper had arranged for sixty Rangers and fifteen vehicles drawn from companies across the state to accompany that vehicle into Mexico, keeping their distance all the way to Casa del Diablo. Once over the border, they'd have no authority and no calls would be made to the Mexican authorities to grant them any. The whole thing was off the books and all of the Rangers contacted were told they could opt out if they so chose. None did.

Just like the old days, as Captain Tepper had told Caitlin. Both Jim Strong and her granddad would have been proud.

Inside Ranger Company D headquarters, she listened to the chatter, the planning, never prouder to be counted among these men upon whom civilized times had forced methods and manners without sacrificing the ideals and frontier heritage on which they were founded. And yet she knew Tepper's plan was doomed to fail. Despite the intricate planning and precautions enacted, Garza would be prepared for exactly what the Rangers intended to do.

"My thoughts exactly," Cort Wesley agreed. "Question being, what does that leave us with?"

Caitlin's phone rang, both of them tensing as she stepped aside to answer it, Cort Wesley with too much on his mind to pay attention until she snapped the cell phone closed again a few moments later and walked back toward him.

"As I was saying, Ranger, what does that leave us with?"

"With one chance, crazy as it may sound."

Cort Wesley watched her slide her phone back into her pocket. "Something to do with that call?"

"We'll see."

He waited for her to say more, resuming himself when she didn't, the hopeful look in her eyes telling him enough. "Don't suppose we got much of a choice right now, do we?"

"This or nothing."

Cort Wesley nodded grimly. "Then let's go get my boys."

96

SAN ANTONIO, THE PRESENT

"You don't want to do this, I'll understand," Caitlin said to Peter in his hospital room. "After all you've been through, it's nobody's right to ask you to do any more."

"You want me to say no, Caity?" he asked her, grimacing through the pain that racked him every time he moved.

"A big part of me does, yeah."

"Which part is that? Not the Texas Ranger, I'm guessing."

"Let me answer your first question a different way: I don't want you to do this."

"What would you do if you were me?"

"I'm not you."

"Here's the thing," Peter said, smiling slightly. It wasn't much, but the simple gesture reminded Caitlin of the warm, gentle man she'd fallen in love with. "This may be my only chance to get back at the people who did this to me."

Caitlin remained silent.

"I know we talked last night, but I don't remember all the details. They're slipping away, no matter how hard I try to hold onto them. It's like trying to remember a dream."

"Not the way I'd put it exactly."

"I don't remember anything about Bahrain," he told her, the pictures she'd taken arranged neatly before him on the bed. "I look at the pictures, hoping for a spark, and sometimes I get a flash of something, but that's it."

"That's likely a good thing."

"If I can't remember, I can't deal with it. Then the rest of me will start slipping away again. You and I both know that."

"Doesn't mean you have to go along with our plan."

"You and this Masters, a killer?"

"I'd be dead now if it weren't for him," Caitlin said defensively.

"I feel bad for his kids."

"They're what all this is about now."

"I don't go along for the ride, those kids are dead."

Caitlin shrugged, nodded.

"I do and I end up back at MacArthur-Rain, doing their bidding."

"No, you won't. Not if I can help it."

"Can you, Caity?"

"Wish I could say I was sure, but I can't. There was a time I never doubted anything. Now that I look back, I figure maybe that made me reckless, left me feeling sorry for myself when I should've been moving on. I'm not gonna make that same mistake again. I'm not gonna lie to you or myself. We're up against it this time for sure. But these men gotta go down. If I didn't believe that in my heart, I wouldn't let you go now any more than I should have let you go eighteen months ago."

They lapsed into silence, Peter's gaze starting to waver until a fresh bolt of pain seared through his spine.

"The two of us, we never really had a chance, did we?" he asked her.

"Came into each other's lives at the wrong time. Wasn't either of our faults. We just didn't know enough to recognize it ourselves."

"You bring me some real clothes?"

"I did."

Peter started to climb out of bed, remembered his pain pills sitting by its side in a plastic cup and swallowed them down. He slid his legs around gingerly, feeling all the pain Bahrain had left him to suffer.

"Then let's get to it, Caity."

"Gonna be hell to pay once your captain gets wind of things," Cort Wesley said outside the king-cab truck he'd rented, after they got Peter settled in the spacious rear seat, no easy task considering the toll even the slightest exertion took on his battered frame. Watching him walk in a hobbled gait, thanks to the strain from the awkward positions he'd been forced to assume, almost brought tears to Caitlin's eyes and strengthened her resolve even more.

She looked from Cort Wesley to her cell phone. "Captain Tepper will be calling soon as we miss the rendezvous. He'll alert the border patrol once he's onto us."

"There's plenty of places we can cross neither him nor anybody else knows about."

"Let's hope so," said Caitlin.

97

The Mexican Border, the Present

"I shoulda known," D. W. Tepper said, when they finally pulled over so Caitlin could return his call from a gas station pay phone.

"You said it yourself, Captain."

"What'd I say?"

"That we'd do this the way Jim Strong would have. Well, that's what I'm doing."

"Am I missing something here?"

"You are, sir."

Silence and static filled the line. For a moment, Caitlin figured she'd lost the connection. Then D. W. Tepper's voice returned.

"I don't abide what you're doing, Caitlin, but I understand it. Problem being if you don't come back, I don't know how I can live with myself. Not that I got much living left in me, anyway. . . ."

Caitlin took a deep breath, steadying herself. "This is about more than me now, D. W."

"Two Rangers got killed over this yesterday, lest you forget."

"I haven't forgotten. They're in my thoughts too. You gotta trust me, D. W. I know what I'm doing."

She heard him take a deep chortling breath. "You have any idea how many times Jim Strong said that to me?"

"Was he ever wrong?"

"Not even once."

"There you go, then."

"Can you tell me what it is you got up your sleeve? Can you tell me that much anyway?"

"You wouldn't believe me if I did, Captain."

They took turns driving, night having fallen by the time they reached the border. Peter slept restlessly in the backseat, shifting and shaking, his dreams haunted by the men who had broken his body and mind. He needed a constant stream of painkillers just to take the edge off the agony, further marring his sleep with whimpers and moans, as if he were responding to nonexistent voices.

Cort Wesley was behind the wheel when night fell and the border came and went with nothing to advertise its presence. Just saw grass, chaparral and endless rolling hills growing out of the dust-soaked flatlands. They ran the air-conditioning on high but kept the windows cracked open to let the outside smells of sage and weak cinnamon inside the cab to keep the air from getting stale. More miles came and went, the road surface growing increasingly uneven before seeming to vanish altogether.

Then both their cell phones rang.

98

MEXICO, THE PRESENT

"I'm impressed," said Garza, "you coming alone."

Caitlin and Cort Wesley exchanged a wary glance. "You a man of your word, Garza?" she asked him.

"Guess you're going to find that out firsthand. Just

keep heading south. Make your destination between Torreón and Saltillo."

"That where we'll find Casa del Diablo?"

"You'll see."

"Man's eyeballing us at night in the middle of nowhere," Cort Wesley bemoaned, shaking his head.

"Welcome to the postmodern world," said Peter, stirring in the truck's rear seat.

"Mister, I just spent five years inside slab concrete walls where the television got two channels. Postmodern and me aren't exactly compatible."

"Get used to it. Traffic cameras, security cameras, ATM cameras, cameras at the bank, the supermarket, your picture taken every time you make a credit card transaction. Carry a cell phone and anyone can find you at any time. Turn on your computer and somebody's following what movies you're renting, what books you're buying and what sites you're visiting on the Internet. Privacy's done, finished."

"I'd like to tell you something," Cort Wesley said.

"Please." Peter beckoned to him.

"I wanted to thank you. It's a brave thing you're doing."

"I remembered something else," Peter told them both. "Wrote it down so I'd have something to hold onto. That last night in Houston after I quit the project, I went to sleep figuring I'd be back home the next morning. Then I wake up with a terrible headache in a small, steamy, hot room with bright lights in my eyes. First thing I remembered so far about Bahrain."

"Delladonne never got shit from you," Caitlin told him. "Threw animals more fit for the zoo into the mix and still couldn't get what he wanted. You beat him, Peter, you beat him with your brain and your will."

"Other three members of my team weren't so lucky."

"But who knows how many other lives you saved in the process?"

Peter held his gaze out the window into the empty darkness beyond. "I don't want to remember any more of what they did to me, Caity. I look at those pictures from Bahrain and I don't want to remember what happened in that room. I'd rather slip away again."

"You're not going anywhere."

Peter turned back, regarding both Caitlin and Cort Wesley. "Two of you got something planned. You wouldn't be walking into this otherwise."

"We'll see," said Caitlin.

Their cell phones rang again four hundred miles past the border, midnight having come and gone, the sky turning from black to gray, the moon starting to slip out from behind the clouds.

"You're getting close now," Garza told them. "There's going to be a gravel road up ahead two miles that runs along the Sierra Madre. Take that road and keep the mountains on your left. Casa del Diablo's not too far away at that point. Hey, *el Rinche*," he said, using the old Mexican slang for "Ranger," "you there?"

"I'm here," said Caitlin.

"There's going to be a whole new war starting soon. Not limited to Texas, though. Call it a full-scale invasion. You're going to need a million Rangers to win this time, *el Rinche*, you can bank on that."

"I wanna talk to my boys," Cort Wesley told Garza.

"I understand you've killed a number of my associates over the years, outlaw. You sure you've got no Mexican blood pumping through you, not even a little? Think hard now."

"Put my sons on, *boludo*."

Garza chuckled lightly on the other end of the line. "They'll be on speaker, you get any ideas."

A pause was followed by a crackly voice clearing its throat, then, "It's me. Dylan."

Next to Caitlin in the passenger seat, Cort Wesley's hands were trembling. "He treating you boys all right, son?"

"Not really, no. But he hasn't hurt us. We're okay mostly."

"Mostly?"

"We're scared."

"Got call to be, son, but not for much longer. On my way to get you right now and all this is gonna be a bad memory come the morning."

Silence.

"You still there, boy?"

"I'm here," Dylan said, choking back sobs.

"Tell your brother what I told you."

"He's here. He heard."

"Just a little longer now. We're almost there."

Click.

Caitlin watched Cort Wesley staring out the window into the moonlit night beyond, the air rich with the sweet scents of mesquite and sagebrush.

"This better work, Ranger."

99

Casa del Diablo, the Present·

They continued down the gravel road, keeping the hulking shape of the Sierra Madre on their left the whole time. The mountains shrank in the growing distance, as the road angled to the west deeper into the Mexican wasteland.

Casa del Diablo appeared first as a speck of light that gradually grew into a dim swatch carved out of the dark night. It was like looking at a half-developed picture, the town before them not fully formed. Emerging from shadow toward a low-wattage substance.

Drawing closer, they realized the road had curved subtly back to the southeast. Combined with the western bent of the Sierra Madre in these parts, the result was to make the mountains the border for Casa del Diablo's entire western flank and part of its southern. Any form of ground attack could be easily repelled and a strike from the air could succeed only in daylight and even then at its own peril, based on the defenses Caitlin expected Garza had set in place.

Caitlin hadn't seen an electrical line for a hundred miles, meaning power here was self-generated. The gravel road's approach spilled onto a single main avenue that bisected a series of buildings of varying sizes on both sides of it.

Caitlin slowed the truck to a crawl, the windows open now to let in the smell of sun-baked dust and char coming from a wood fire somewhere about. Up close, the town was much darker than from afar, as if Garza had

turned roof-mounted lanterns on to act as a beacon for
them. There was also a loud droning hum, like a giant
pack of buzzing mosquitoes in the air. Generators in all
likelihood, massive ones concentrated mostly in two large,
faded wood-frame buildings diagonally across from each
other on the lone street. Strangely, the moon that had
been prevalent mere minutes ago had disappeared from
the sky, even though she could see no cloud cover in evidence.

Maybe this really was the House of the Devil. . . .

The truck's headlights sprayed light on random multi-
story buildings that looked like flophouses or cheap hotels.

"Where Garza must house his workers," Cort Wesley
noted grimly, following Caitlin's gaze. "Peasant labor.
My guess being that the only way any of them leave here
is either in a box or with a promotion up the food chain."

"The former much more likely."

"Yeah."

Rival headlights blared at them suddenly from the far
end of the street. Caitlin brought the truck to a halt and
killed the engine. In the slots between the glare, she
could see a number of armed men flanking a white-suited
figure holding each of Cort Wesley's sons on either side
of him. A fedora was tipped low over his forehead, cloak-
ing the rest of his face in shadows.

"Garza," Cort Wesley said, half under his breath,
opening his door as Caitlin opened hers.

They emerged from the truck together and moved into
the spill of its headlights dueling with those of the vehicles parked farther down the road behind Garza and Cort
Wesley's sons. Heat mist rose from the engine block and
wafted forward, adding to the murkiness of the night.
Caitlin trailed it upward and caught sight of the gunmen
on the rooftops and in the windows. Dozens of rifles

aimed downward on them, reducing their margin of error to zero.

"That's close enough," Garza said in nearly perfect English. The spill of their headlights caught his white teeth wide with a smile. "Have the genius climb out now too."

Caitlin moved to help Peter from the cab's rear, watching him wince as he extended his feet and let them touch the ground. His muscles had cramped from the long ride and he needed her support just to draw even with Cort Wesley, still crimped up and listing to one side.

"I've heard a lot about you, outlaw," Garza continued, "about both of you. Are the two of you really as good as I hear?"

"Depends on your definition," Caitlin told him.

"I've never killed an *el Rinche* before."

"Do that tonight and you better find another planet to inhabit, you know what's good for you."

Garza took his hands from his pockets and showed them his empty palms. "This doesn't have to end that way. I'm a man of my word, Ranger. Which is more than I can say for the two of you."

Caitlin and Cort Wesley exchanged a quick, uneasy glance, wondering if their whole plan had gone to hell.

"You're both carrying pistols. Would you be so kind as to toss them well out before you?"

Caitlin and Cort Wesley complied, both breathing a sigh of relief. Their pistols lifted through the air like horseshoes, kicking up dust into the cool night air when they landed.

"That's better. Now we can do business. Send the genius forward and I'll send your sons forward."

"You're not gonna let us walk out of here," Caitlin charged, her voice echoing slightly through the town's emptiness.

"Yes and no, *el Rinche*. The outlaw and his sons will be free to walk out of Casa del Diablo. If they can survive the desert, they get to live." Garza curled his upper lip toward his nose in the semblance of a snarl. "You can live too if the genius decides to talk. If he doesn't, he's gonna watch my men slice you up one piece at a time. You can send him this way now."

Peter pushed himself forward between Caitlin and Cort Wesley. She reached out and grasped his shoulder, pleading with her eyes. But he shook his head slowly, shrugged her hand off and hobbled on into the five rows of headlights. Through the haze Caitlin could see Dylan and Luke start forward as well, the older boy with an arm tucked over the younger one's shoulder, helping him on.

In that moment Caitlin thought of lying on her back in the West Texas Chihuahuan Desert with Charlie Weeks, certain she was going to die. But this gave helplessness a whole new meaning. There was nothing she could do, absolutely nothing. She felt like a fool for betraying D. W. Tepper and hated herself for betraying the legacy of Jim Strong and all the others who'd come before him, a proud lineage done a terrible disservice by her in the Mexican wilderness. All because she had put her trust in someone she had no reason to trust at all.

That's when the roar of a powerful engine drew everyone's attention to the head of the street. A pair of high beams flashed on and a black SUV ground to a tire-squealing stop a hundred feet behind their truck.

Caitlin glimpsed Garza raise the low-hanging tip of his fedora and cup a hand over his eyes, squinting to better focus on a huge, long-coated figure who climbed out of the SUV, the springs recoiling in relief at his exit. From his size and anomalously agile gait, she recognized him as the giant she'd dueled with at Maura Torres's house.

"What are you doing here, Colonel Paz?" Garza yelled to him, his words echoing in the cool night air. "Did Delladonne send you?"

Guillermo Paz stopped well back of the pickup truck, sheathed in the spill of his SUV's headlights. "Come to finish what I started."

"That's no longer necessary."

"Yes, it is."

And that's when the first blast sounded.

100

CASA DEL DIABLO, THE PRESENT

About time, Caitlin thought.

She hit the ground hard as Cort Wesley rushed out toward the point where his sons and Peter were about to converge. Above her, high to the right, a raised portico on which a trio of gunmen had been perched had been blasted into smoky splinters, no trace of the gunmen anywhere to be seen.

Caitlin rolled onto her back, thinking of the weapons stowed on the truck's rear-seat floor, as the giant yanked back the sides of his long coat and whipped out a pair of shaved-down assault rifles with duct-taped banana clips. The clips gave him sixty shots from each instead of thirty, the shaved-down assault rifles looking like toys in his grasp. He opened fire on both sides of the street simultaneously, shredding windows as well as the men poised behind them. His aim was uncanny, making Caitlin think of young Luke Torres, son of Cort Wesley Masters, shooting every bad guy in sight in the Texas Ranger video game.

• • •

"Do you know who this is?" the Spanish-accented thick voice asked after she answered the call in Company D headquarters, as Cort Wesley looked on.

"No."

"Think back a few nights. Think about my eyes."

And then she remembered the giant rampaging through Maura Torres's home, impervious to the bullets she poured his way. Meeting his gaze in that one moment had stuck with her ever since, enough to have her dialing down the air-conditioning every time she thought of it. Listening to his quiet breaths on the other end of the line, Caitlin was sure she could smell that odor like spoiled meat again.

"I want to help you," he'd told her. "My way of squaring things."

"With who?"

"Not really sure about that yet."

"How 'bout why?"

"Haven't got that answer either."

"And I'm supposed to trust you?"

"Close your eyes and pretend you can see mine again."

In spite of herself, Caitlin complied.

"You believe me now?" he asked her.

"Shoot him!" Garza was yelling. "Shoot them all!"

In that instant, more RPG fire sizzled like Fourth of July firecrackers twisting for the sky. Massive chasms dug in the buildings coughed shards of glass and wood fragments into the air to shower back down on the street, filling the night with the smells of scorched lumber and flesh. Caitlin thought she might have heard screams but they were drowned out by the now constant cacophony of gunfire tracing both up and down from the center of the street.

More figures, much smaller, lurched out from positions of hiding to join the giant in raining fire on the forces of Emiliato Valdez Garza. Caitlin took advantage of the chaos to scrabble through the onslaught of bullets and gun smoke toward the arsenal stowed in the back of their truck.

Cort Wesley took Peter Goodwin down first, hitting him high and hard enough to spill him forward into Luke and Dylan. The four of them crumbled with Cort Wesley on top shielding the other three. Goodwin's bones felt brittle as bark, the jarring impact seeming close to breaking them free of his flesh.

"Ranger!" Cort Wesley yelled.

"Coming!" Caitlin Strong yelled back at him and he twisted from the clump to see her dashing forward with twin M-16s in hand through the rattle of bullets kicking flecks of dirt and rubble against her boots and jeans.

On the other end of the street, Cort Wesley was dimly aware of Garza's men encasing their boss in a protective bubble that withered with falling bodies as more fire raged from the giant and his men. They were tiny compared to the giant, darting and dashing through the smoke and mist.

One knelt and fired an RPG into the largest building on the eastern side of the street, the one from which the loudest hum of generator music had emanated. The upper part of a wall exploded on impact, a miss mostly but enough to reveal the bright lighting of what could only be Garza's chip manufacturing plant beyond. The small man was reloading his launcher when a barrage of fire from an adjacent roof cut him down from behind.

"Masters!" Caitlin Strong screamed, tossing him one of the M-16s.

He rolled off Peter Goodwin and his boys, angling to fire on the circle of men enclosing Garza. But the man in the white suit was gone, only his low-hanging hat rolling across the kicked-up gravel in his place.

In that moment, Guillermo Paz was still unsure exactly what he was doing. Even as expended shells danced from his twin assault rifles, even as the bodies tumbled from his bullets like pop-up figures in an arcade game, he was trying to make sense of it.

He had never considered himself a thoughtful man until recently when the blurred realities of good and evil began to tug at him. He had confessed as much to priests in two countries now but their words had brought him little solace. His solace, instead, was to be found in the bullets that had defined and determined his life. And in the spill of heat and deafening bursts, the mire of moral murkiness began to recede.

He finally grasped the meaning he had glimpsed in Caitlin Strong's eyes that had changed him. In protecting those boys she'd shown a side of herself that Paz realized he longed for. He needed to find the same singular meaning in himself, to see in his own eyes what he had glimpsed in hers. Kierkegaard himself had said as much, and finally Paz knew what he had to do to be true to the philosopher's words:

Destroy the woman's enemies, those who had stolen his mission and in so doing determined their own fates.

"I want to help you. My way of squaring things."

That was Paz's test, to get the woman to trust him. Do that and he'd be free to move to the next level, take the next step and see where it brought him.

The assault rifles clicked empty simultaneously. Paz stopped to reverse the magazines, feeling bullets smack up against his body armor like BBs against flesh. He resumed firing and reached the truck that had delivered the woman and the others here. Paz had planned everything with the five dwarfs he had left, the location of Casa del Diablo well known to him thanks to President Chavez's business dealings with Garza.

Paz saw his evolution crystallized before him, saw the steps he needed to take to fulfill it. He wanted to know the woman's strength, feel that strength, share that strength.

"And I'm supposed to trust you?"

"Close your eyes and pretend you can see mine again."

Paz felt a bullet take him low, just over the knee, and another sneak under his flak jacket and burn into his side. Still, he kept walking, killing as many men as he could see.

"You believe me now?"

101

CASA DEL DIABLO, THE PRESENT

Caitlin followed the circle of men enclosing Garza down a plank sidewalk fetid with mold and storm backwash. Workers spilled out of the assembly plant in a constant stream, fleeing in all directions and making it impossible for her to find a sight line to Garza with her M-16, a rifle she'd never once fired anywhere but the range. Finally she discarded it, slowing to snatch pistols from the belts of two of Garza's soldiers in its place.

She ran with both pistols clacking away in her hands, firing through the gaps in the sea of workers rushing from the plant. One of Garza's guards went down, then another, by which time Caitlin had stooped to replace her empty pistols with two more. When only three of his guards remained, the shrinking circle veered left through the doors of the factory, pushing past a stream of exiting workers garbed in surgical masks and latex gloves.

Caitlin pressed her shoulders against the wall alongside those now open doors. Part of the wall two stories up had been taken out by an RPG, smoke and flames continuing to belch out from inside. She could feel the heaviness of the structure in stark contrast to its ramshackle appearance. Casa del Diablo, headquarters of Garza's vast criminal empire, had been built to look weathered, old and thus innocuous. A ghost town. But that was just another sham to cloak the truth within.

His men, those who made and packaged his drugs, worked and lived here. But Casa del Diablo wasn't just about drugs; the hum of machinery and sudden wash of clean, cool air from inside the building in which Garza had taken refuge told Caitlin this was likely where the Cerberus chip had been manufactured and where the Fire-Arrow chip was being produced even now.

This place had killed Charlie Weeks and ruined Peter's life. In all the stories told by her granddad, of lying in wait your whole life to make the bad guys pay, she finally saw a just ending for herself.

She waited for the last of the plant's workers to emerge, shedding their sterile garb as they fled, and then twisted through the doorway firing, finding herself inside a massive multileveled floor brightly lit by the haze of white, glowing fluorescent bulbs. The air-conditioned chill cooled her steaming skin and she scanned the area in search of Garza and his men to no avail amid the long rows of bench seating where workers had been assembling the Fire Arrow chip Peter had designed. Her ears struggled against the blare of a high-pitched fire alarm activated by the numerous explosions that had pierced the now smoke-filled plant from the street.

A few more steps inside brought her to the heavy machinery that packaged and sealed the chips' shipping containers. Motion flashed to her right and Caitlin hit the floor hard, barely avoiding the salvo of bullets fired on her from everywhere at once it seemed, while just over her head conveyor belts rolled in a continuous arc, lugging boxes ready for shipment.

Caitlin crawled about the floor as more fire chimed overhead, clanging into the heavy machines and ricocheting off the reinforced walls. More men than she thought inside, obviously, having failed to account for the guards already on their posts.

But Garza was among them, and if the phantoms of her past were to be slain, and the ghosts vanquished, she had to finish this here and now.

Cort Wesley cared only for his sons. In those long, endless minutes they were all that mattered, and he kept them covered with his body while firing his M-16 defensively in an expanding arc at Garza's soldiers who spilled out of the buildings in what seemed like a constant stream.

"Keep down!" he yelled when Dylan raised his head, Cort Wesley smelling the fear rising off the boy.

The gunfire slammed his eardrums, his mind filling with a rage that shortened his breaths and left him screaming inside. He couldn't kill everyone behind the deaths of Pablo Asuna and Maura Torres, but he could kill plenty here in Casa del Diablo. He saw Maura with every sweep of the M-16's barrel, with every clack of expended rounds, realizing in those moments how much he had missed her in their years apart. He should have gone up and knocked on the door instead of remaining on the street in Asuna's old Ford. Had driven off promising himself to do it another day, which now would never come.

Missed opportunities. But not now, not again.

Cort Wesley yanked a spare magazine from beneath his jacket and slammed it home, missing nary a beat of bullets or fury pouring outward. He dragged Peter Goodwin in closer, aware that the big man and his much smaller troops had lost the element of surprise that had won them the first round. Around him, fires in the surrounding buildings crackled and hissed, throwing flickering light that occasionally flamed bright onto the chaos.

"Come on," he said suddenly, dragging his boys up to their knees. "The truck, we've got to make it to the truck!"

"I . . . can't," Goodwin managed.

"I'll carry you if I have to, just get ready to move!"

Cort Wesley wasn't thinking of the truck for escape now, so much as cover. Big heavy steel sides in the tailgate that would hold against small arms fire, the exterior doors too if he could get them inside the cab. He got his boys up first, shielding them as best he could while lifting Peter Goodwin bodily to his feet. He looped an arm around the hobbled man's shoulders to hoist him along, Dylan and Luke close against him while he rotated the M-16 in his free hand, clacking off quick bursts of bullets.

The giant and his men caught his advance down the street and offered covering fire. Two more RPGs whizzed overhead, blasting men literally into the air on impact. Cort Wesley continued on through a fissure in their fire, emptying the last of his bullets into a pair of Garza's onrushing soldiers and then swung the butt around one-handed, cracking it across the face of a third.

That cleared a path to the truck and he took his boys and Goodwin in tow for the final stretch, feet that might have been yards. Cort Wesley's ears were nearly deaf from all the gunfire and the stench of sulfur thickening in the smoke made him feel sick.

But he still managed to heave his boys over the truck's heavy steel rails into the bed and then reached down to hoist Goodwin after them. Goodwin's back arched with a sudden spasm, Cort Wesley left to fear he had broken the man's withered spine until Goodwin crimped himself into the fetus position once inside the bed.

Cort Wesley left the three of them there and ducked back to the cab, shouldering a 12 gauge shotgun and whipping round an AR-18 ArmaLite assault rifle, a semi instead of a full automatic, which suited him just fine.

He leaped up on the truck's hood, felt it buckle under his weight as he began sighting in on anything that moved.

The gloriousness of it all might have moved Paz to tears if he'd had occasion to celebrate the moment. The demons inside him that raised the questions he'd posed to the confessional priests were being slain at last. In the killing fields before him there was purpose and understanding, the men dropped by his bullets falling to a greater cause that at last defined him.

He reloaded for the third time, fresh magazines snapped home in place of expended ones left hot on the gravel floor. He felt the ping after ping of bullets against his body armor, was certain at least two more found him, making four in all. He'd worry about the severity of the wounds later, for now rejoicing in the electricity dancing in the air with the gunfire that recharged and refueled him.

The only thing missing was the woman. He wanted to meet her eyes again to see if they were as deep and clear as he recalled. The meaning he'd found in them had filled Paz with the one emotion he was utterly unfamiliar with: fear.

The Ranger had scared him with her virtuous intensity, her willingness to die for strangers while Paz had so often lived to kill them. Their essences merging, Paz seeing what he needed to become, understanding in that moment the crux of everything that had drawn him to Kierkegaard's ramblings on spiritual evolution.

So this, this was his *becoming,* his great moment of control over a cosmos he had misunderstood up until now. His own country, the only home he'd ever known, was gone for him now and Paz felt strangely liberated by that reality.

Above the clamor and crackle of fire and gunshots, Paz heard the bay of game birds soaring through the sky to announce the promise of a dawn that would leave him seeing the world in a new light. He was certain of that much, even as he racked back the slides on his guns and began firing anew.

102

CASA DEL DIABLO, THE PRESENT

Caitlin felt the bullets drumming overhead as she pushed herself along the floor on her stomach, tasting bitter dust on her tongue. The din of the machinery had the dual purpose of disguising the approach of Garza's men toward her, as well as hers toward them. She figured the first man she saw would be baiting a trap, so she ignored his head popping up and continued on, coming around enough to bring her on a path that should cut across that of the men lying in wait.

The man whose head had popped up looked puzzled, turned his gaze sideways and to the right.

Caitlin lurched upward and followed his eyes with her bullets. Four men caught in the line of her two pistols, two of them felled instantly by her fire.

Around her the conveyor continued to curl around, shedding boxes no one was there to neatly lift off. Bullets clanged into a machine just above. Caitlin rolled sideways and found a space between the machines up an aisle where a set of legs attached to boots stood. She opened up with both her pistols and the boots tipped sideways, accompanied by wails of pain that rose briefly over the shouts, orders and gunfire coming from outside in the square.

Caitlin thought of Peter, Cort Wesley and his boys, resolve hardened anew by why she was doing this. She heard the thunk of heavy footsteps and rolled onto her back, firing up at two figures who'd rushed her across the conveyor, scattering boxes as they went. They crumpled atop each other to be swept away atop the churning belt.

Her pistols clicked empty, two fresh ones to be found near the bodies curving away from her now. Caitlin lurched atop the conveyor and scrambled forward ahead of its pace. She leaped down from the belt near a body that had dropped near the shrink-wrap dispenser that coated the boxed chips in a final, protective seal; had just crouched to retrieve the dead man's pistol when Garza himself spun out a yard before her, gun angled down in line with her face.

Cort Wesley stopped firing, his ears filled with a ringing that drowned out all other sound. He felt as if someone had stuffed cotton in them and he couldn't pull it out. He had shells left in both his ArmaLite rifle and his 12 gauge, but there was no one left to fire them at. Garza's troops were now divided between the bodies strewn everywhere and survivors fleeing into the night with the workers from the assembly plant.

As he leaped down from the truck's hood, Cort Wesley nonetheless remained wary of gunmen still poised in windows or on rooftops. But none offered any fire as he swept around to the truck's rear, his heart thudding almost loud enough for him to hear.

"Dylan! Luke!" he called. His voice sounded like garbled static in his own ears. "Dylan, Luke!" he repeated, begging for a response as he leaned in over the truck bed's side.

Dylan eased Luke up first, then himself to follow. He was huffing for breath, his face twisted in relief and, for the first time in more than a day, the absence of fear. Luke's cheeks were tear-stained and he was sniffling. Cort Wesley reached out for him and his younger son collapsed in his arms, only one arm used to comfort the boy while the other clung fast to the 12 gauge.

"It's done, Goodwin," Cort Wesley said, but the Ranger's husband didn't stir. "Goodwin?" He slid Luke away and felt for a pulse. "Oh, shit."

While up the street a ways, the massive figure who had saved all their lives sank to his knees.

There was no one left to shoot, a fact greeted by Guillermo Paz with a strange emptiness and detachment. His hands had cramped up so badly he couldn't discard his assault rifles. He felt tired but relaxed, as if a soothing nap was about to take hold.

Paz scanned the street in all directions, resplendent in

this world surrounded by corpses of his making. In the new way he defined his life and existence, killing these men had actually *meant* something. Paz felt awash with true triumph, clean in a way he could not comprehend, even though the dank sweat rising through his clothes smelled like spoiled vinegar. He felt strangely content, having achieved the passion he'd seen in the Ranger's eyes. The sight had left an indelible mark on his mind and became the final impetus needed to ensure his transition from what he was to what he would be from this day on. Not that Paz totally understood exactly what that was yet; he only knew that he liked what he was feeling.

None of his dwarfs came forward, which he took to mean they'd all perished in the gunfight. Good men, yes, but easily replaceable. And replace them he would, although in that instant, Paz could not say exactly what kind of mission it would take now to demand his interest. He looked forward to visiting the first church he could find, of confessing the night's actions to the priest.

"Bless me, Father, for I have sinned. I killed many men tonight but the cause was just and I need to know if God understands such things. . . ."

But the blessing he truly needed was from the Ranger. Just wanted to meet her gaze again to see if he recognized what was there.

Garza's linen suit was filthy, his face dappled with sweat and grime. He seemed to have trouble catching his breath and the pistol looked uncomfortable in his hand.

"Mujer de mal genio," he snarled. "Now stand up."

Caitlin rose from her crouch slowly.

"I want you to keep looking at me, *el Rinche*. I want to see the life die in your eyes when I kill you."

His own eyes bled hatred, the gun an afterthought in

his mind, providing the opening Caitlin needed. She barreled into Garza and felt him trying to jerk his gun around into her. The pistol roared, and for an instant Caitlin thought she'd been shot until she saw the gun angled slightly away from her, the bullet missing her by no more than an inch.

She clamped a hand onto Garza's wrist to keep the barrel off her and crashed forward until he slammed into the housing of the shrink-wrap dispenser. His shoulders set off the sensor, the spout spitting shrink wrap over nonexistent boxes. Garza snapped his face forward, to head butt her, Caitlin thought, until his teeth sank into her cheek.

Caitlin screamed but held fast to Garza's gun hand, surprised by the strength summoned from his wiry frame. It was like trying to hold back a train and she knew she wouldn't be able to keep the gun off her much longer. All she could do was jerk her free hand out high and hard into his face, bending Garza downward and back.

Under the spout of the shrink-wrapping machine.

The plastic molded itself to his face, clinging to his skin to be sucked inside his mouth when he tried to breathe through now sealed lips. Caitlin held Garza there as the machine continued to *pfffft, pfffft, pfffft* over him. His face vanished in the haze that had swallowed it, Caitlin feeling the heat of his pinned pistol clacking off harmless shots. With it finally emptied, his eyes bulged from stolen breath and finally came to rest on Caitlin's. She held his gaze, until the life bled out of it and Garza's eyes locked open for good.

103

Casa del Diablo, the Present

It took all of her energy just to walk out of the smoky remnants of the assembly plant. She had never felt so spent, not even after lugging Charlie Weeks back to their vehicle in the desert with a bullet inside her.

She stepped off the wood plank sidewalk, heading toward the truck where Cort Wesley Masters was standing protectively over his sons, when she saw the massive figure from Maura Torres's house kneeling in the street.

Paz, he'd told her his name was when he called, Guillermo Paz.

Mine's Caitlin Strong, she had said back.

I know.

Their gazes met and held, for much longer than they had that night in Shavano Park.

Guillermo Paz smiled at her.

Caitlin turned away to seek out Cort Wesley again, something all wrong about the way he was staring at her. She knew before she reached the truck, before she looked into its bed to see Peter's still form.

She wanted so much to cry then, to just let it all out, but she was too beaten and exhausted to even let go. All she could do was sink into Cort Wesley's arms, the two of them standing over his two boys huddled low by their feet. A shaft of moonlight hit them, just as the wind picked up, brushing the stench of blood and smoke through the air over the fallen bodies.

"We gotta get moving, Ranger," Cort Wesley said finally.

Caitlin separated herself from him, turning her gaze up the street toward the giant again. But Guillermo Paz was gone.

Epilogue

*The Rangers are what they are because their enemies
have been what they were. The Rangers had to be superior to survive. Their enemies were pretty good . . .
[the Rangers] had to be better . . .*

—Walter Prescott Webb, *The Texas Rangers*

San Antonio, One Week Later

"I been officially reinstated," D. W. Tepper told Caitlin in
the rear of the limousine headed for Peter's funeral.

Caitlin wasn't surprised, given that Tepper had been
given credit for the daring operation undertaken by the
Rangers in cooperation with Mexican authorities to finally bring down the leader of the murderous Mexican
Mafia. As if emboldened by the news of Emiliato Valdez
Garza's demise, law enforcement agencies across the
country launched similar raids on Mexican-Mafia strong-
holds, decimating their numbers in unprecedented fashion over the course of the last seven days.

"I'm glad to hear that, Captain," she said, "I truly am."

"Well, I'm not gonna ask you what your plans are right
now. We still got plenty to sort through here, but when
the time comes . . ."

"What about Harm Delladonne, Captain?"

"That's one of the things we're working on."

"He's gonna skate, isn't he?"

"We're getting ahead of ourselves here, Ranger."

"This isn't over, Captain. Not so long as MacArthur-Rain's still out there gunning for us all."

Up in his loft, Delladonne selected a katana from his sword rack and began practicing his kata, making cut after cut. In spite of everything that had happened his motions felt freer, more relaxed. Garza, his secret town and chip assembly plant were all gone. Indictments would likely follow stateside, but it was nothing he couldn't handle; there were too many people occupying seats of the highest power imaginable who wouldn't want him talking. The first shipments of the Fire Arrow chip were safely stored right here at MacArthur-Rain's headquarters, and it wouldn't be hard to find another manufacturer to replace Garza. This would certainly placate his friends in Washington and give them call to help him silence the Ranger and her cohorts when the opportunity availed itself.

Delladonne lost track of time, the repetition of his practice cuts taking him to a different plane where he was free to dream of the secure future he was helping to make for the United States.

Then he heard the soft click of his security doors sealing closed, followed by the clack of steps across the bamboo floor below. Delladonne returned his sword to its *sia* and gazed over the railing.

"*Buenos días*," said Guillermo Paz.

Caitlin arrived at the cemetery to find Cort Wesley Masters standing well back of the grave site with a son on either side of him, an arm over each of their shoulders.

Caitlin had walked over and silently took his hand to lead all of them up to join her in the front.

They stood now over the open grave of Peter Goodwin with Cort Wesley's sons between them. His younger boy Luke clung to him while Dylan stood next to Caitlin.

Captain Tepper had taken his rightful place amid all twenty-seven Rangers attached to San Antonio Company D more toward the rear. The ceremony itself was carried out in the very way it would have been if one of their own had been the deceased.

For reasons she didn't understand, losing Peter this time was harder than the first. She'd missed him then, but hadn't missed being *with* him. She wondered if anything was worth all he'd endured and sacrificed, and that left her feeling lost, as if the meaning had been sucked from her life. With the slow loss of Casa del Diablo from memory and into legend, she wondered what she'd be left with.

Had she squandered her second chance with him?

Had she really wanted it?

Caitlin turned to Cort Wesley to find him already looking at her. She didn't know what his eyes were saying, but liked their message all the same.

Paz gazed down at Harm Delladonne, now duct taped to his desk chair placed in the middle of his bamboo floor. "You believe in God, Belladonna? I asked you that before and you never answered me."

Delladonne looked up at him, didn't speak.

"Anyway, what I've been realizing lately is that He really does have a plan. Trick is to figure out your place in it, and I think I've finally got a much better notion about mine. Still a work in progress, though. That's why I'm here."

As if on cue, the fire alarm began to screech.

"What's going on?" Delladonne demanded. "What have you done?"

"Bringing your life's work to end, Belladonna. Nothing but a hole left behind."

"Hole?"

Paz leaned over, grimacing, to fasten one more strip of tape across the man's mouth and then stepped back to inspect his handiwork.

"Front-row seat, Belladonna," he said over the blare of the alarm. "I imagine it'll feel something like an elevator ride, express to hell."

Paz turned for the door, started to limp away, then stopped and swung round again.

"Oh, something I was curious about. The name of your company, it comes from an article from a long time ago titled 'MacArthur's Rain,' doesn't it?"

Delladonne looked up at Paz, stupefied.

"I read the article in Spanish a few years back. Talked about how the great general wanted to rain nukes down on the Chinese in Korea, and if Truman had let him what a different place the world would be now. Everything different, the example set once and for all. Hey, look at the bright side, Belladonna."

Paz started limping for the door again.

"You're gonna get to experience the feeling of MacArthur's Rain firsthand now."

After Caitlin had tossed the first shovel full of dirt atop her husband's coffin, Dylan took her hand and held it tight, feeling just like Cort Wesley's only smaller.

The cool breeze carried the scents of fresh-cut flowers, carnations and lilies, she thought, as well as hibiscus trees. The leaves rustled pleasantly, drowning out the minister's quiet ruminations about a man he had never met and who had no real grasp of the suffering Peter had endured for what he believed in.

The ghosts of her present had left to join those of her past, none of them seeming to have the kind of hold on her they used to.

"What now?" Cort Wesley asked her when it was over and the crowd had begun to disperse.

"I was thinking about getting something to eat," Caitlin replied, pretty sure that wasn't the kind of answer he was looking for.

"I grill a pretty mean steak."

"Really?"

"Plenty about me you don't know yet."

She looked at Cort Wesley, then his sons. "I guess the same can be said for just about anyone."

Guillermo Paz was standing in Discovery Green, a safe distance from the MacArthur-Rain building, when a series of crackling rumbles shook the world. Paz knew that meant the truck packed with the deadly combination of fertilizer and ammonium nitrate had ignited right on schedule inside the building's underground garage. He'd mixed it in Pablo Asuna's repair shop, finding that strangely appropriate.

The rumbling took on the din of a giant bass drum pounding at the rear of the band, growing quickly into a quake Paz could feel at his very core. Then, as he watched, the entire shape of the MacArthur-Rain building collapsed, picking up speed as it crumpled and sending a mammoth gray cloud coursing outward in all directions.

"*Elogiar Dios.*" Paz smiled. "Praise God."

. . .

"I just need a minute."

Before joining Cort Wesley and his boys in the rear of the limousine, Caitlin stood alone and let her gaze wander up the cemetery's sloping tree line to a set of flowering cottonwoods that blew rhythmically in the breeze. Amid that grove, just for an instant, she thought she saw the shapes of her father and granddad standing casually alongside each other between two of the trees. Her granddad had his Samuel Colt pistol dangling from a holster on his hip while Jim Strong leaned against a tree with a matchstick wedged in his mouth and purpose plain in his eyes.

Then the breeze shifted and they were gone.

Turn the page for a preview of

STRONG
JUSTICE

✦

JON LAND

Available in June 2010
from Tom Doherty Associates

A FORGE HARDCOVER   ISBN 978-0-7653-2336-1

I

El Paso, Texas, the Present

Caitlin Strong approached the police command post set up behind the ring of squad cars bearing the markings of both the El Paso Sheriff's Department and Texas Highway Patrol. The cars formed a makeshift perimeter, essentially barricading the city's Thomason Hospital. Above, clouds raced across the sky, leaving the sun to come and go over the scene.

El Paso's sheriff Bo Reems and Captain Rafael Mercal of the highway patrol saw her coming at the same time, sharing a glance that dissolved into a sneer.

"Took your sweet time getting here," Mercal said between lips now pursed into a scowl.

"Rangers covering the area been sent to watch the border," Caitlin told him.

The blazing sun slid out from beneath the clouds again and she studied herself briefly in the reflection off Mercal's mirrored sunglasses. Free of her Stetson, her black, wavy hair tumbled past her shoulders, evidence of a broken promise to herself for weeks now to cut it. Her skin was naturally tan and unblemished, save for the scar left on her cheek a year before when a Mexican drug lord had bitten down in a fight that had left him dead. At first glance her dark-blue eyes seemed too big for her face. But Caitlin had learned from her grandfather how to hold them wide enough to see things people would never have thought she could, like the sheriff's deputies snickering and whispering just out of earshot.

"You boys wanna join us up here?" she asked them and, embarrassed, the deputies quickly turned away.

Caitlin felt a sudden breeze kick stray patches of her hair across her face. "Austin figured watching the border was more important under the circumstances," she said, brushing the hair aside, her back to the snickering deputies now.

"Austin," Sheriff Reems started, "didn't need to send nobody here at all."

"Procedure, Sheriff."

"More like bullshit, if you ask me."

"I didn't," Caitlin said and swept her gaze about the ring of officers watching the cordoned-off access road, wielding shotguns and M-16s as if they expected an attack any moment. "Looks like you're fixed to fight a full-scale war."

"These drug cartels out of Juárez want to get somebody, no border's gonna stop them," said Mercal. "No Ranger either."

Mercal had been an all-conference defensive end for the University of Texas. His record for tackles had stood for some time and he would have gone pro if not for tearing up his knee in the Cotton Bowl. Caitlin noticed him grimacing now, but not from the pain, she thought.

"Sandoval?" she asked, referring to Fernando Lozano Sandoval, a commander with the Chihuahua State Investigations Agency who'd survived an assassination attempt and was being treated inside.

"Mexican gangsters cut through six of his guards that were fronting the building and four more inside," Sheriff Reems answered. In stark contrast to Mercal, he looked as wide as he did tall. One of Reems's officers had once told Caitlin that the sheriff had never once left the state of Texas. He breathed noisily through his mouth and she could never recall a time when the underarms of his khaki uniform shirts weren't darkened by sweat, today being no exception.

"They killed a bunch of bad guys in the process," added Mercal, turning his gaze back on the building. "But the rest took Sandoval hostage in the intensive care wing."

"How many bad guys left?"

"We got no eyes inside the building to tell us. Best guess is three or four of the original dozen come to finish the job on Sandoval that started in an ambush on the other side of the border in Juárez. This being the only level-one trauma center for three hundred miles, he got brought here."

Caitlin joined Mercal's gaze on the hospital, holding her eyes on a third-floor bank of windows. "Snipers?"

"Four of them." Mercal nodded. "Best I've got. But the Mexicans left inside know enough to stay clear of the glass. SWAT team on site and ready to go."

"But no communication with anyone inside."

"Not a peep," said Sheriff Reems. He pulled a wad of tobacco from his cheek and tossed it to the ground. "We been calling every phone on the wing and used the bull-horn to tell them to call us." He shook his head, his bulbous jowls flapping like twin bowls of Jell-O. "Nothing."

Caitlin dug a finger into her hair. "You mind if I try something?"

"Matter of fact, I do," Mercal said, spine straightening to give him back the height that was mostly a memory. "Austin says we gotta have a resident Ranger, that's fine. They don't say we need to let you involve yourself in our affairs."

Caitlin returned her gaze to the windows. "People in that intensive care wing might feel otherwise. And you been at this too long already for it to end any way but bad."

Mercal exchanged another glance with Reems, whose cheeks puckered as if he were readying to spit the tobacco he'd already discarded.

"I'm offering you cover here, Captain," Caitlin resumed, paying deference to the man in charge while ignoring the sheriff. "Things end bad, it'll fall on the Rangers."

"What exactly is it you're fixing to do, Ranger?"

Caitlin pulled the SIG Sauer from her holster and handed it to him.

"You'll know soon enough, Captain."

Holster empty and Stetson back in place, Caitlin stretched her hands into the air and walked straight for the hospital's main entrance, feeling the gazes of the deputies and highway patrolmen following her the whole way. But it was something else she felt even stronger coming from the third floor: the eyes of other men upon her, likely perched behind some wall cover where a glimpse was all they could grab unless they decided to expose themselves to a shot.

Caitlin passed members of the SWAT team camouflaged by the bushes set in a small strip garden just before the glass doors, but didn't acknowledge them for fear of alerting the men watching from the third-floor windows to their presence. She walked slowly through the glass doors and then straight to the elevator, doing everything possible not to conceal her presence.

Inside the cab, she tightened her Stetson over her hair so it rode lower on her forehead and pressed 3, then stood right in front of the doors with hands raised again as the door slid open.

A pair of wide-eyed gunmen sweating in the air-conditioned hall greeted her, holding Heckler & Koch submachine guns—expensive hardware for simple drug gang members.

"Acuéstese en el piso!" said one with a deep scar that looked like an exclamation point down the right side of his face. "Down on the floor!"

Caitlin lay facedown on the tile just beyond the elevator.

"El Rinche," Scar spit out.

He checked to make sure the elevator cab was empty while the other gunman patted her down roughly through her jeans and denim shirt, paying special attention to her boots to make sure no pistol was holstered to her ankle.

"¡Levántate! Get up!"

Caitlin rose, hands back in the air.

"¿Qué te quieres?"

"I want to make your lives easier, that's what I'm doing here," Caitlin said in Spanish. Then, when her remark produced only a confused stare from Scar, "I'm gonna take the place of those kids over there." She gestured toward a pair of boys and a girl trembling so hard beneath their bedcovers their IV lines were jiggling. "Means you can let them go."

Caitlin could see eight other beds occupied, all set against the windows with only terrified faces visible above the bedcovers, one of which belonged to Fernando Lozano Sandoval. A third gunman stood against the wall nearest the windows while a fourth man, the youngest of the bunch, sat in a growing pool of blood with his shoulders propped by an empty bed, bleeding from both leg and shoulder wounds.

Caitlin's gaze met Sandoval's briefly before moving on to a pair of children a few beds down. Arms still raised, she started slowly forward, sliding between Scar and the other gunman.

"¡Para te! Stop!"

"You're in better shape than you think," she told him, her gait purposely deliberate. "Once we get the kids out, I'm gonna talk you through walking out of this as protected witnesses in the service of Mexico instead of perps. Right, Mr. Sandoval?"

The man from the Chihuahua State Investigations Agency nodded fearfully, looking like a disembodied head resting atop the pillows.

"I'll shoot you, *el Rinche*!" Scar threatened.

"Do that and I won't be able to help you and your wounded young friend down there. Two of you look alike. You brothers or something?"

She reached a young boy's bed and laid her Stetson down atop the bedcovers. "Let's get you ready to move," she said as reassuringly as she could manage to him.

Caitlin began to unhook the monitoring machines. She heard Scar yelling at her, glimpsed the third gunman lurch away from his perch against the wall.

"No!" Scar screamed at him too late.

The first sniper bullet caught him in the face, the second in his throat, resulting in twin plumes of blood splattering over Caitlin and the bedcovers. She felt the sting of splintered bone smack her cheeks, as she dug a hand into her Stetson and yanked out the .40 caliber pistol she'd taped under the dome.

She saw Scar twist his submachine gun on her, finger finding the trigger an instant after Caitlin jerked hers twice. She put two bullets into his chest, and he dropped like an oak tree, getting off a single wild spray that found nothing but wall.

Caitlin felt the hiss of a bullet surge past her ear and swung toward the final standing gunman, dropping into a crouch. She registered the pistol trembling in his hand as she shot him dead center in the forehead.

He fell at the feet of the wounded man, more of a boy

really, who was fumbling a pistol into his off hand. Caitlin could still feel the surge of adrenaline rushing through her, electricity dancing along the surface of her skin, turning her nerve endings raw. Instinct took over before thought could intervene. She'd shot the wounded kid three times before she even felt the pistol reheating in her grasp, muzzle flashes flaring like shooting stars she used to wish on as a little girl.

The blare of the gunshots deafened her to the screams and sobs of the hostages, all safe and alive, as Caitlin turned toward the window, raised her arms, and waved them to signal Captain Mercal and Sheriff Reems that it was over.

"You Rangers sure know how to make a mess," Mercal told her, huge beads of sweat still dappling his face.

He and Caitlin watched the body of the last gunman being carted away.

"Gotta make a mess sometimes to get things cleaned up," Caitlin said.

Mercal swiped a forearm across his brow, leaving a patchy wet streak upon his sleeve. "Well, you got the biggest set of balls I ever seen, woman or not."

"Stop, please," Fernando Lozano Sandoval told the orderlies wheeling his bed from the room when they reached Caitlin. "I know who you are, *señorita*."

"You can thank me later, sir."

Sandoval's expression wrinkled in displeasure. "I would rather thank you now. Many in Mexico know of you. They believe it would be better if you stayed out of our country."

"It's out of my jurisdiction anyway, Mr. Sandoval."

"I'm talking about your most recent investigation into missing Mexican girls."

Caitlin felt heat building behind her cheeks. "You mean the ones being sold as sex slaves?"

"These are dangerous men, Ranger."

"I thought we were talking about the girls."

"You saved my life. I'm trying to return the favor. You do not want these men as your enemies."

"If they're bringing kidnapped children across the border, they're already my enemies. Why don't you just tell me where to find them?"

"You want to die that much?"

"Funny how you didn't ask me that when I was gunning down your captors. I'm starting to think I've been looking in the wrong place, Mr. Sandoval. Instead of warning me off, just point me in the right direction. Do that, sir, and we'll call it even."

Sandoval looked around him, picturing a different outcome. "Nuevo Laredo," he said finally.

"That where I'm going to find what I'm looking for?"

"Only if you're *loco* enough to try." Sandoval's gaze recovered its focus as quickly as it slipped away. "The men you are looking for have much of Mexico in their pockets."

Caitlin backed away from Sandoval's bed, so the orderlies could slide him on again. "Then I guess it's a good thing I'm from Texas."